REMEMBER MY NAME
REBECCA RATHE

Cover Design by Caravaggia Arts

Edited by Book Witch Author Services

Proofreading by Feral Fiction Edits

LeST is
MooRE

CONTENT WARNINGS

REMEMBER MY NAME is a standalone contemporary MM romance with high spice and graphic sexual content. Please keep the following triggers in mind while deciding if this book is for you:

Content warnings may include spoilers.

Trigger warnings include but are not limited to: drug and alcohol use (including mention of underage drinking and marijuana use), mentions of drug and alcohol addiction and treatment, secretive relationship, forced/non-consensual "outing" by external sources, sexual intercourse without protection or discussion about safe sex first, homophobia, (consensual) rough/aggressive sex, and of course strong language and graphic sex acts.

Instances of sexist, transphobic, homophobic, and ableist language may be present throughout the book. This language does not reflect the author's beliefs or ideals, but are a realistic portrayal of lived experiences.

LeST is
MooRE

"It is not enough to be tolerated. Especially when that tolerance comes with the caveat of making yourself smaller. Tolerance is bullshit. You deserve and should demand acceptance.

You can't hide who you are to protect small minds."

-Shawna Landry-Ryan

LeST is
MooRE

If this book is extra slutty, it's because I followed the dopamine.

PROLOGUE

LUC

What am I doing here?

Bright flames flare from the towering bonfire when a couple of guys toss a heavy log onto the pile. Their carelessness shakes a burst of embers skyward, causing me and the others sitting peacefully to jolt back and cover ourselves. Over the arm I raise to shield my face, I watch sparks fly into the night sky.

Shooting a scowl towards the careless assholes and their piss-poor attempt at an apology, I adjust my seat away from the circle, further withdrawing into the shadows. I sit back, staring at the label of the beer I've been nursing for so long it's turned warm and flat. The smell of burning wood clings heavy in the air, threaded with cigarette smoke, citronella, and salt. The crash of the tide rolling in lulls me into a more relaxed state.

I guess the party isn't that bad. Aside from almost having my eyebrows burned off, the bonfire is nice. There aren't too many people, no one seems obnoxiously drunk, and it isn't loud. It's fine. Chill, like Shawna promised.

My best friend is somewhere in the crowd, laughing loud enough for me to hear her over the music and the waves. She begged me to join her at the beach house she rented for spring break, and I agreed to stay for one night. After all, this is my *last hurrah*, as she called it. The last weekend before my life changes completely. Before the draft. Before I become someone people watch on Sundays instead of regular, plain Luc Martín from Cane Ridge, Louisiana.

It's not really something I'm excited about. I'm not a fan of drawing attention to myself, and the idea of playing in the NFL comes with way too much of it. I'm not a first-round pick or anything, so there won't be too much fanfare outside of my small town. It'll be a *very* big deal there, and I'm sure that will present enough opportunities to embarrass myself publicly. Especially if I get drafted to a home-state team. The Shreveport Cyclones are my number one choice, mostly because it's close enough to home that I can still check in on my family and help them when needed.

No matter where I end up, I'll be grateful. Football is the only thing I've ever been good at, the one thing that makes sense. My coaches have been telling me since high school that I'm good enough to play professionally, but I wasn't sure the fame, fans, and celebrity were for me. Still, it's an opportunity I can't turn down.

All I have to do is make it through my first four-year contract, and I'll make more than enough to help my family. That's what matters. Not headlines, not jersey sales. Not millions of dollars in endorsement deals and all the excess that gets thrown at professional players.

I just want to make sure my folks don't lose their house. It's nothing fancy—a modest house built on a low hill, surrounded by acres of sugarcane fields. It's beautiful, but old. The foundation is failing badly because of the red clay beneath the house shifting and settling over decades of wet and dry seasons. The work that has to be done to fix it is far too expensive. Right now, the only chance they have of paying for the work to fix the foundation is to sell the property that's been in my family for three generations.

My dad is going to hate everything about this plan. He didn't want me to even entertain the draft until I finished my degree, but my chance is now. An opportunity like this might never come again. And I know my stubborn dad won't accept my help easily, but as proud as he is, even he can't turn down an opportunity to save our home.

So, yeah. My life is about to change in incredible and terrifying ways. A little downtime from studying, working out, and practicing won't kill me. If only I could train my brain to stop thinking about everything it thinks I should be doing instead of sitting on my ass staring into the flames.

And then I notice him.

I'm not sure where he came from. Maybe he was on the other side of the bonfire before we almost got blasted and everyone shifted their positions. It doesn't seem possible that I wouldn't have noticed him in the small crowd congregating around the fire. He's only a few feet from me now, sitting in the sand with his back resting against a log with a guitar in his lap. He's strumming it idly, not talking to anyone, not even the girls inching closer to him, hoping to catch his attention. My lips quirk with amusement at the way he's steadily ignoring them, or maybe he really doesn't notice them.

It's not surprising he's got their attention, though. He's good-looking, but it's more than that. There's something about him—an energy or aura, something different that makes him stand out. From the way he's ignoring everyone, he seems a little withdrawn, almost in a broody bad boy way. His frame is long and lean, although it's hard to gauge his build through his loose jeans and t-shirt. I'd venture to say he's probably over six feet, maybe a couple of inches shorter than me. His dark, shaggy hair flops over his eyes when he bends forward, and when he rakes it back, his fingernails are painted black and he has rings, or maybe those are tattoos, on his fingers. Long, almost delicate fingers that bring a lit joint up to his soft, pink lips.

He catches me looking before I even realize that I've been staring at him. He doesn't react or say anything to me, but without glancing up, he holds out the joint in my direction.

I'm so surprised by the gesture that it takes me too long to register that he's offering it to me. I shake my head. "Oh, um… no. Thanks, though," I tack on quickly, not wanting him to think I'm rude or judgmental about it.

That's when he looks at me. And smiles.

His direct attention hits like a sucker punch. His smile is small, barely a lopsided quirk of his lips, but there's amusement sparkling behind the most vivid green eyes I've ever seen. A ring on the left side of his lower lip catches the firelight and draws my attention. That's… *something*. Like he's noticed me looking, his smile widens. I feel it stick in my chest, warm and disarming, and suddenly I can't look away.

He bites his lip, and I clear my throat, which seems to make him chuckle. Heat rushes up my neck, and I drop my gaze fast, embarrassed to be caught gawking. I turn toward the waves instead, watching them slide in and out over the surf, silver under the moonlight. It's almost hypnotizing.

"It's beautiful, isn't it?" His voice drifts across the fire, shocking me back to awareness. "I love how small the ocean makes me feel. It puts everything into perspective. Life feels so big and important, but existence is nothing compared to the depth and endlessness of the ocean horizon."

The words alone would've been enough to pull me back to him, but it's the *sound* of his voice that does it. There's a gravelly rasp beneath the softness, a worn edge like his throat has been lived in, scraped raw and broken in just right. It makes every syllable drag through you, like it's meant to stay under your skin.

When his gaze flicks back to me, I almost gasp at the brilliant green of his eyes on me again, blazing with the reflection of the firelight. That voice and those eyes together feel like too much. A ripple shoots through me, a shiver rolling down my spine so sharp it makes me tense. It's sweltering out here with the bonfire heat baking into my skin, the sweat of an unseasonably warm spring dampening the back of my neck, yet goosebumps rise across my arms like I've just gotten out of an ice bath.

What the hell is wrong with me?

I don't get rattled like this. Not by people, ever. It's not even that he's a guy. I've never reacted to *anyone* like this.

He shifts the guitar in his lap and starts plucking at the strings, soft and careful, his focus drifting out towards the tide again. The sound weaves through the waves crashing on the shore and the crackle of the fire. It's a slow tune, simple at first, then carrying words, his voice finding the melody.

That rasp of his wraps around the lyrics and turns molten in my veins.

It takes a moment to register the words that fall from his lips, a familiar song bent into something entirely new. The edges of *I Hope You Dance* fray in all the right places, catching against his throat, turning every line into something that feels private. It's not polished or clean. It's raw in a way that makes my chest ache, like he's dragging the song out of a place I didn't even know existed.

The sound locks me in place. Every instinct I have, every habit I've built over the years about staying steady and unreadable, falls apart under the pull of his voice. It isn't even the song itself, though I know the words well enough. It's *him*. The rasp, the ache, the way he sounds like he's pouring pieces of himself into every line.

I'm not used to being moved. Not like this.

My life has always been about control. Of my body, my game face, of whatever storm is waiting for me at home. With just a few chords, a few fractured notes, this stranger is undoing me like it's the easiest thing in the world.

Heat licks at my skin from the fire, the sticky press of summer clinging to me. My beer sweats in my hand and my shirt sticks to my back. Still, I can't stop the goosebumps prickling over my arms, can't stop the way my breath keeps hitching like it's caught on something I can't quite swallow.

It's not logical. It doesn't make sense. He's just some guy at some party. He's not even singing to me. But my heart is beating wrong, and I can't look away. The only thought circling my head is that if I close my eyes or do something even as simple as breathe or swallow, I'll miss something I can't ever get back.

The whole world falls away until it's just him and that voice, curling through the firelight, spilling out towards the tide.

I can't breathe right. Can't move. I can't do anything but stare. His voice wraps around me, raspy and warm, and I swear it feels like it's inside me, like *he's* inside me, vibrating through my ribs, making my pulse stutter out of rhythm.

The guitar hums low and steady, until his voice thins out on the last word, fading into the crash of the waves. The fire pops, shooting sparks into the sky.

For a second, nobody moves. Not him. Not me. Not the people around us, who surely must have heard what he just did, but I can't look away long enough to give them any notice. It's just the ocean, the night, and the echo of his voice still working its way through my whole body.

Then he glances up, catches me staring again, and smirks like he knew I would be.

"What's with that look?" He asks playfully, his voice still carrying that same rasp that makes my skin prickle. "Don't like that song? I take requests."

The words hit like a splash of cold water, jolting me out of whatever spell I'd been under. I blink, fumbling for anything to say. "Just wasn't expecting *that*."

"What were you expecting?" His smile is playful and curious. He turns around to face me, the shiny varnish of his weathered black guitar reflecting the flickering flames.

"I don't know." I shrug, heat climbing the back of my neck. I gesture to his faded *Rage Against The Machine* t-shirt. "Don't suppose I could expect *Bulls On Parade* with an acoustic guitar," I laugh.

His grin widens, sharp with mischief, and a second later the first chords ring out across the fire.

I laugh under my breath, shaking my head as he leans into it just enough to make a point. "Seriously?"

"You got me started now," he says, that rasp still curling around every word. Then, cocking an eyebrow, he switches to an impressive version of *Killing In The Name Of,* using the strings all the way up the fretboard to pluck out the opening riff. I had no idea an acoustic guitar could do so much.

He laughs at my facial expression. "Still not a fan?"

I smile but hesitate, scratching at the label on my beer. "Honestly? I don't know much about music, but I know enough to recognize that you're really, really talented."

He chuckles, soft but cutting, like I've confirmed something he already knew. "Careful, I'll think you're flirting with me."

The words shouldn't make me laugh, but they do. A short, surprised sound that catches in my throat. He grins at me over the fire, lip ring flashing, and just like that the air between us feels sharper. Brighter. Like we've stumbled into a private joke no one else around the circle even noticed.

We talk for I don't know how long. About everything and nothing, alternating between joking around and watching him play. At some point, I notice that it's quieter, the party having thinned out without me realizing. The only sounds left are the hush of the tide, the occasional snap of wood collapsing in the fire pit, and his smoky, rasping voice.

The fire's burned lower now, more embers than flames, casting the beach in a softer glow. The air feels different. It's thicker, heavier. Like we're the only two people left in the world rather than just this beach.

He plucks a lazy pattern on the guitar, green eyes half-lidded, gaze flicking between the water and me. My pulse trips over itself every time his fingers drag across the strings, every time his lip ring flashes in the firelight. He looks to be deep in thought, mouthing some silent, unidentifiable words as he plays with an unfamiliar melody.

I don't know when it happened, but I've moved closer to him. Or maybe he's moved closer to me. Doesn't matter. What matters is he's close enough now that I could reach out and touch him. Close enough that when he twists to set his guitar down next to him, his arm brushes against mine. He turns to face me, and I feel a pull towards him like the tide is drawing me in.

I don't know who leans in first. Maybe both of us. Suddenly, he's right there, close enough for the smoke and salt on his skin to fill my lungs. His lips touch mine, light and unassuming, soft as breath.

It's… different.

I've kissed people before, but never like this. Those other times felt like an obligation. Like going through the motions so I wouldn't hurt someone's feelings, or because it was what I was supposed to do. What I was supposed to want. There was never any real passion or desire behind it. This is nothing like that. This is slow, careful, like he's purposely making sure I have time to feel every second of it. And I do. Down to my toes.

I don't even realize I'm the one leaning forward until I am. Until the kiss deepens, until his lip ring scrapes against my mouth, sharp and electric, sending a jolt straight through me. The sound I make, low and involuntary, betrays exactly what it does to me.

He smiles against my lips, the curve of it brushing warmly across my mouth. Then, voice rough and slightly restrained, he murmurs, "Are you staying here tonight?"

I blink, dazed. I feel like I'm floating somewhere outside myself. The question hangs in the air, simple but heavy. There's no pressure or expectation. Without thinking, I reach for his hand. His fingers thread through mine, warm and certain, and I lead him away from the fire, up the worn steps towards the house.

The attic room is dark, but not completely. A single beam of moonlight cuts through the cracked window, spilling across the middle of the room. It's just enough to make his skin glow when he steps into it. The night air drifts in with the tide, cool against my overheated skin. Above us, the ceiling fan stirs in slow, lazy circles.

It's so quiet that it's loud. Every little sound comes in sharper—the ocean crashing onto the shore in a steady rhythm outside. My own heartbeat, loud and insistent in my ears.

I look at him, this ethereal, beautiful boy I don't even know, and realize I have no idea what comes next. My body feels heavy, full of wanting, but my mind is blank, stripped bare of anything that sounds like words. I don't want to speak anyway. I don't want to break the spell.

I don't have to. He steps closer, slow and sure, until the space between us thins to nothing but heat. He pauses there, his lips so close I can feel his breath ghost across mine, the air between us buzzing like static. He waits—hovering, patient, a question in the way he tilts his head.

Waiting for me to say yes without saying anything at all.

I take the leap on an exhale, pressing my lips to his. It's not tentative exactly, but it isn't confident either, just a blind step forward into something I don't understand but can't resist.

His lips part under mine, warm and soft, and his tongue flicks gently against the inside of my top lip. I'm not expecting it. The surprise pulls a gasp out of me, and he does it again, slower this time, tongue sliding deeper into my mouth. The second our tongues touch, my body lights up, sparking through me like a live wire.

The way he kisses me steals everything—my breath, my balance, the last edges of hesitation I didn't even know I was holding onto. I delve into the taste of smoke and salt, tangling our tongues together. It feels natural, like we've known each other longer than a single night.

His hands find my waist, fingers slipping under the hem of my shirt, roughened palms caressing the lines of my abs. The more we kiss, the higher his hands climb, until the fabric's bunched tight and we're forced to break apart just long enough for him to tug it over my head.

The look in his eyes as he takes me in makes my skin prickle. The bright green has turned darker in the shadows of the room, edged with hunger. He doesn't hide his appreciation, staring at me like I'm something to be devoured. His hands roam my chest, abs, and shoulders as he kisses me, tangling our tongues together in a way that I feel everywhere.

I want to touch him, too, to see him and feel what his skin feels like against mine. Reaching for the bottom of his shirt, I help him pull it up his body and over his head, pausing to take him in. His body is so unlike mine. He's leaner, but sculpted. Smaller, but strong.

He's unreal. Like something out of a dream I'm not sure I'm allowed to touch. But I reach up anyway, my fingers brushing over warm skin, tracing the lines of ink across his chest, lingering over the hard metal of a barbell through his left nipple.

I'm surprised at my physical reaction to his piercings, finding myself staring at the barbell and wondering what it would feel like in my mouth, how it would taste, if I'd feel it rubbing across my skin the way his lip ring does when he kisses me. I pull him against me, and when our bare chests press together, heat rolling between us, I fall into what feels like a trance.

Some instinct I didn't know I possessed takes me through the motions. I want to feel him, kiss him, touch him… taste him. Forgetting to second-guess myself, I do just that. We tumble onto the bed, our heartbeats beating out a rhythm that feels like music.

His hands are everywhere, mapping me like he means to memo-rize me, fingertips skimming the lines of muscle, pausing in places that make my body jolt, my heart stagger. Every brush of his skin against mine sets fire to something deeper, something I've never touched before.

I follow his lead, undressing and exploring his body. We hold each other close, kissing and touching, hands everywhere, until there is nothing left between us but skin. The sheets blur into shadows, blue-grey against the moonlight, and for a moment it feels like we're floating, suspended above the world, weightless and untethered.

I'm not clumsy, but I feel undone—each piece of clothing peeled away is another revelation. I kiss everywhere I dare, growing bolder as he shows me all the little places on my body that I didn't know could feel good. His tongue on my skin is the cata-lyst to my undoing, bringing me closer and closer to the edge. When his mouth finally reaches my cock, it barely takes more than a broad lick up the bottom of my shaft, and his lips closing around my tip before I'm unloading into his mouth.

I come so hard it takes a moment to register what I've done, and my skin grows impossibly hotter. I'm unsure how embarrassed I should be. I should have at least given him a warning.

My apology is cut off when he presses his lips to mine again. I nearly choke at the rush of arousal that jolts through me when his tongue wraps around mine, coated in slick, warm, slightly salty fluid.

"See how good you taste?" He whispers huskily, and all I can do is moan.

The heat between us grows until it's impossible to tell where I end and he begins. His body slides against mine, smooth and warm, and the contact leaves me dizzy and weightless. Like we are suspended above the tide, caught between stars and waves, existing nowhere but in this single moment.

I'm seriously out of my mind. I'm not me, and it's not possible that he's real, that this is actually happening. This must be a dream.

He seems surprised when I sit up, hold him to me with one arm around his back and the other on his thigh, then flip us so I'm on top of him.

If this is a dream, I might as well make the most of it.

My mouth moves down his body, taking detours to satiate my curiosity. I play with his nipple ring, lick the sweat from his sternum, run my nose through his armpit—twice, because for some reason, it drives me wild. When I nip along his hip bone, his thighs open wide to allow me to trail my lips and tongue down the crease of his groin. I bury my face in his trimmed pubic hair and groan.

Dear God, please don't let this dream run away from me because it turns out I'm a weirdo. I'm obsessed with the way he smells— the salt and campfire and what I can only assume is his natural musk. I glance up to make sure he's okay with everything I'm doing. There isn't enough light to make out every detail of his expression, but I can see his mouth drop open and head fall back when I wrap my hand around the base of his cock and lick him from taint to tip in one broad stroke.

"I got the impression you hadn't been with a guy before, but—" His voice wavers when I run my thumb over the tip of his cock, spreading the bead of fluid there.

Is it normal to think someone's dick is pretty? I've seen enough of them in locker rooms, and I've watched porn before, but this is the only one I've been up close and personal with. He's as long as I am, but thinner, and circumcised where I'm uncut.

"I haven't," I answer him, my voice barely above a whisper. "I don't know what I'm doing. I'm just going with it. You'll need to tell me if I do something wrong or how to make you feel good."

He chuckles, but it sounds almost pained. "I don't really think you could go wrong, but I promise I'll tell you." He moans when I wrap my lips around his crown and give a gentle, tentative suck.

The moment the taste of his pre-cum hits my senses, my brain short-circuits. There's a small part of me that wonders if this is what it's like to take drugs. There's no doubt in my mind that this is something I could get addicted to.

I press my tongue against his slit as my fist strokes up and down his shaft, coaxing more from him. Then I try sucking again, and following the reaction of his abs tightening and hips twitching, I take a little more of him. With my hand around his base, thumb gently caressing the skin where his shaft meets his balls, I experiment with taking more and more of him, suctioning my mouth on my way up and moaning whenever there's a reward.

My gag reflex becomes an issue, but he brushes his hand over my cheek and whispers that I don't have to take him so deep, that what I'm doing is amazing and he's close.

"If you don't want me to come in your mouth, you might want to– *Oof!*" I end up gagging myself hard in my haste to make sure he's not going anywhere.

I want it, alright? I want it so bad.

I'm a goal-driven guy. When I really put my mind to something, I can usually work it out. Now, I'm putting all my focus on licking, sucking, and stroking him in all the ways he's liked most, until he moans low in his throat and tenses up.

Unlike me, he gives a warning before flooding my mouth. But, seeing as I'm lacking much experience in giving or receiving head, I'm not aware of the exact timing or just how much would come out of him. I'd planned on sucking it down like a milk-shake through a straw, but I end up coughing, forcing a good bit of it out the sides of my mouth, and a little up my nose as well.

"Shit," he gasps, hips rocking into my fist as I continue sucking and pumping him through his orgasm, not wanting it to end. When he falls back, I get to work cleaning up my mess, because I'll be damned if I don't get to taste every drop.

I lap at him, cleaning every escaped remnant from his shaft, his pubic hair, his–

"Oh fuck. Did you just suck my–" He falls back, covering his face with his hands, muttering, "This guy," but his hips buck when I suck one ball, and then the other, into my mouth, feeling the weight of them. I work my tongue around them, making sure he's clean. When I pull back to inspect my work in the dim light of the moonbeam, I realize a small rivulet has made its way all the way down past his taint into new territory.

I look up while tentatively brushing my fingertips down towards my new obsession. Because not only will I cry if I can't get that last drop, but I'm realizing there's a lot more to explore down there, and I don't want to leave an inch of him to my imag-ination.

"Is this okay?" I whisper, nearly shaking with nerves and sheer want. My fingers ghost over his crack so he knows what I'm referring to.

He moans. "You can do whatever you want."

I look up at his face, trying to gauge his expression to see if he's serious. He sits up and leans forward, pulling me to rise and guiding my face up to his.

"Baby, you can kiss, touch, lick, suck, or fuck any part of me you want," he rasps before kissing me deeply. My cock doesn't just twitch, it fucking jumps, tapping against the inside of his thigh. He grins wide against my lips. "I have a condom and a packet of lube in my wallet," he says.

I blink rapidly, not believing that this is where the night has taken me. *And to think I didn't want to come to this party.*

"There's some in the bathroom, too," I say roughly. I thought it was weird that they'd stocked those for the party, but damn if I don't understand and appreciate the forethought now.

"Good," he says. "Because I don't think once is going to be enough." He reaches down and palms his growing erection. "I'm already getting hard again."

Releasing a shaky breath, because I am far past hard again already, I guide him to lay back down and take my place between his legs again. Palming the backs of his thighs, I push them up and out a bit, allowing my gaze to fall to his ass, spread open for me.

It's too dark to see as much as I'd like, and an involuntary rumble leaves my throat. That rumble becomes a growl when my tongue finds his perfect, puckered hole. He's so smooth down here. And so small. I have my doubts about fitting myself inside there, but I'm okay with nothing more than this.

I do exactly what he said. I touch, kiss, lick, and suck him in the one place I never in a million lifetimes would ever think I'd put my mouth. I get into it, feasting on him while my hips rut into the bed linens.

He's gasping and moaning, whispering instructions and encouragement. When he begs me for a finger, I drench it in as much spit as I can before pressing into him. He's so hot and tight inside. I work just the tip of my finger in and out, unsure of what to do. But he reaches down and takes my hand, pushing until my finger is all the way inside him, then uses my finger to fuck himself.

I'm panting by the time he coaches me to crook my finger, guiding me to find his prostate.

"There!" he chokes out. "Right there." I work him just the way he showed me until he's whimpering and begging me to stop. "I don't want to come again just yet. I'm not ready for this to be over."

"Me either."

"Want me to show you yours? Your prostate, I mean?"

There's a little bit of fear and apprehension mixed in with my longing and excitement, but I swallow it down and nod. "Yeah, okay."

The beam of light catches his smile. "Lay back, then. I'll grab the lube."

His fingers find my hole, and he spends a moment circling it, massaging around the ring until I relax. "You are the sexiest human being I've ever met in my life," he says as he trails kisses up the inside of my thigh.

I want to tell him that I'm convinced he's not even real, or maybe some kind of mythical creature that turns people into sex fiends because I've never felt like this in my life. But before I can say anything, his tongue swipes against me. It's... *strange*, at first. I have to focus on how much I loved doing this for him to even consider that he'd want to be down there, and that helps me relax. Before I know it, he's pressing a finger inside me, breaching me. It's a strange pressure, but not bad. And then it's good—*really* good. *Too good.*

Suddenly I'm begging him for another finger, then another

because I want to feel the stretch again. I didn't know… I mean, *I had no idea* it could feel like this.

"I want you to do it," I say breathlessly. "Please?"

He looks down at me, three fingers working me into a frenzy. His head cocks. "You want me to fuck you?"

I nod, almost frantically. "Yes. Please."

"So polite," he teases. He pulls his fingers from me and crawls over my body until he's looking down into my eyes, getting close. I'm assuming so he can see that I'm sure, then reaches down to caress me. "You want me to fuck this tight virgin hole?"

"Please…" I say, but it comes out as more of a whine than a word. He reaches over and grabs the condom he'd moved to the corner of the bed when he got his lube.

His eyes stay on mine while he rolls the condom on and spreads more lube over himself, pushing more inside me for good measure. I'm nervous, but I don't want him to stop. He tries to say something, probably to reassure me that we don't have to do this, or that he'll stop if I tell him to, but I cut him off with a kiss that he falls into, blanketing his body over mine.

There's pressure, enough to edge on pain, but he reminds me to breathe and tells me to bear down. He pushes inside me slowly, filling me in a way I never thought possible. It's more than physical. I feel like I'm being stretched to the brink mentally and emotionally as well. It feels like more than I can handle, but my eyes find his again, and I get lost.

When he moves against me, when our bodies fit together, it doesn't feel like a first time or a one-night mistake. It feels inevitable. Like this was always meant to happen. He takes it slow, not fucking me so much as making slow, careful love to me, the way I imagine someone would do with someone special to them.

He makes me feel like I'm the only person on earth.

The rhythm we find is unhurried but unstoppable. Every breath and every sound falling in sync until the room itself feels alive with us. The ocean crashes outside in steady time, the fan circles overhead, our hearts beat at the same rhythm.

Every kiss he presses against my mouth, my throat, my chest, feels like a vow I don't have words for. Whenever he's not kissing me, he's looking deep into my eyes. The moonlight glints off the green of his eyes, a color I can still see when I close my eyes and throw my head back, crying out into the night.

I'm broken apart completely, and I know one thing with a certainty that terrifies me.

I'll never be the same again.

Time bends around us. What begins as a kiss, a thankful prayer into his lips for giving me this gift, this night, this feeling, becomes something larger, a tide that carries us out and back in again, over and over, until I don't know how many times we've touched, or where one moment ends and the next begins.

Sometimes I'm the one leading–pressing him down, tasting the lines of his throat, his ribs, his hip, until his body arches into mine, answering me without words. Other times I'm the one carried, yielding to the press of his hands, the coax of his mouth, the slow, deliberate way he takes me apart as if he's teaching me how to let go of the control I've so desperately held onto my entire life.

Every way we fit together feels different, yet somehow the same. My body burns, but not with strain, with something deeper. A fullness that blooms and settles and blooms again. The rhythm between us shifts, soft and searching one moment, rough and desperate the next, and each time it builds into something that shatters me, I think that has to be the end–until he touches me again and it begins all over.

The hours blur. The fan stirs the humid air, the moonlight slides across the sheets, the ocean keeps its endless rhythm. All I feel, all I see, all I know is him. His mouth, his hands, his weight, his voice and moans rasping against my ear in a way that sets all my senses on high alert.

By the time the night gives way to pale dawn, my body is wrung out, every nerve alive. I've never been held like this, never been touched like this. Never been *known* like this. And the strangest part is, I don't even know his name.

I feel embarrassed about it, feeling too shy to ask despite every-thing we've done. I'm too exhausted to talk. I'll ask in the morning.

We fall asleep tangled in bedding damp with sweat and cum, my face pressed to the hollow of his shoulder, our breaths slowing in sync.

Everything about this night has felt unreal, but what I'm feeling right now is… I don't know what *it* is exactly, but it's real. I feel it in my gut, as sure as the ache in places I've never ached before.

It's something big. Maybe a little scary.

It feels like something I was never meant to have but somehow stumbled into anyway.

I wake up slowly, awareness seeping into me like tidewater. The room is hot, the air conditioning little more than a sugges-tion in this attic room. Sweat slicks my skin, cooled only by the slow, steady rotation of the ceiling fan above. The rhythmic push of the blades matches the steady crash of the ocean outside, almost enough to rock me back under again. Almost. Until the rhythm reminds me of everything that happened last night.

I blink my eyes open, wincing against the bright sun filtering through the cracked window. It takes a moment for my vision to sharpen, the whitewashed beams above me slowly coming into focus. Dust motes drift through the sunlight, suspended, almost shimmering. I smile without meaning to, a faint curve ghosting my lips as the soreness in my body makes itself known in every place he touched me.

The memory rolls in, warm and dizzying, but so does the realization—I still don't even know his name. My first ever hookup, but it felt like so much more. How is it possible that I know every sound he makes and what each part of his body tastes like, what he feels like on the inside and how he feels inside me, yet I don't know something as simple as his first name? How do I even ask without sounding like an idiot?

Not that he seemed inexperienced. He knew exactly what he was doing, every touch confident and sure. Which means this couldn't have been his first time spending the night with a stranger. Unlike me. Hell, the only other time I've ever had sex was with my best friend on prom night, and even that was nothing more than curiosity. Platonic friends checking a box. It was awkward. Mechanical. Nothing like last night.

Last night was… something else. Transcendental.

My cheeks flush hot with embarrassment at my own corny thoughts. *Transcendental?* But honestly, is there even another word for it? What happened last night was more than sex—wasn't it? That couldn't possibly be what it's like all the time, or no one would ever leave the bed. Society would fall to ruin.

I never understood why people made such a big deal out of sex, but maybe now I get it.

I'd nearly convinced myself I was some kind of freak of nature. Shawna says I'm probably asexual. That I just wasn't built like everyone else was.

Last night blew that idea out of the water, that's for sure. Even now, just thinking of his lips on me, my body stirs, blood rushing hot and insistent. My heart thunders in my chest, memory sparking into want.

I'm almost afraid to face him in the daylight, to see if the spell holds when the moonlight's gone. And yet I want to. I need to. I need to see where this goes, if he feels what I do.

Finally, I work up the nerve to turn my head, ready to see him, ready to tell him, clumsy and unpracticed as I am, that I want to know him. *Really* know him.

But the bed beside me is empty.

There's a clear indent in the pillow where his head rested, but the sheets are already cool. Other than the damp spots dotting the bedding and the waste bin filled with used condoms and wrappers, there's no trace of him.

Panic flares sharp in my chest. I drag on a pair of shorts and run, stumbling, down the stairs two steps at a time. Shawna's in the kitchen with her boyfriend and a couple of others, mugs of coffee in their hands, eyes flicking towards me in unison. There's a mixture of expressions ranging from amused to curious to concerned, but none of them knowing. Without asking, I know he isn't here, and they haven't seen him.

His shoes are gone from their space next to mine inside the back door. So is the guitar he'd sat down by the fire pit last night.

I run back upstairs, searching the room, turning over everything. There has to be something—a note, a scrap of paper, anything to prove he was real. But there's nothing here.

Nothing but the hollow ache in my chest as the truth sinks all the way down to my stomach.

He just… *left?*

My heart aches with the realization that I might never see him again, and that he likely didn't feel the way I did about what happened between us last night.

I try to rationalize my pain away, telling myself it's probably for the best. I've got a big future looming, only a week away. It's not like I can afford a distraction from my purpose.

I don't even know his name, but I'll never forget him. I'll spend the rest of my life remembering the way he made me feel.

ONE
JESSE

The noise backstage hums with activity, but it's like static. A chaotic symphony of roadies shouting, cases slamming, and gear being packed up in a rushed frenzy. My ears are still ringing from the set, but it's a familiar ache, one I've grown used to after nearly six years on the road. It's the last night of a series of homecoming headliners after wrapping up the European leg of our tour, and it feels good to be done for a couple of weeks. Not that I'm complaining. I love that I get to be on stage like this for a living. This is my first tour sober, and, if I'm being honest, it's been a lot harder and more exhausting without the drugs to blur the edges and get by. It's… different. More involved. Louder. Busier. More intense.

Naz bumps his shoulder into mine as we cut through the dimly lit hallway, sweat dripping down his temples.

"So what now? You crashing early like a good boy, or…"

I arch an amused brow at him, feeling the familiar tug of temptation. "Or?"

He shrugs, a wicked gleam in his eye that I recognize. Naz doesn't want to stay in, however exhausted he is. We all get restless in different ways. He craves the neon lights, thumping bass to drown out the rest of the world, the thrill of someone's mouth on him before sunrise. He's being polite, trying to gauge my mood.

"Let's go to that club you like," I suggest, more to appease him than anything else. I'm not sure I'm really in the mood, but I don't particularly want to be alone, either. And I don't want to keep the guys from decompressing in their own ways. It's not their fault I haven't settled on a new outlet for all my restless energy yet.

His eyes flick over me skeptically. "You sure? It's not exactly your scene anymore."

Not my scene anymore.

My stint in rehab isn't something the guys bring up often, but it hangs awkwardly between us and probably always will. It's a stark reminder of how hard I've worked to get this far, learning how to exist without pills or powders or drinking until I blacked out every night. Living life without a crutch, especially given our lifestyle, is a never-ending test of my willpower. This tour has been one long test, one I've passed with flying colors—so far. I can't say it's been easy. The consequences of numbing myself just to get by for years have made living life on the road, promoting, performing, and being constantly surrounded by crowds of people that much more overwhelming. There's no quiet in this life.

I sling my arm over his shoulder, the gesture more for my comfort than his. "We're all good. I don't need booze or blow to have a good time. Promise."

Partying and peer pressure were never the problem. It was finding quiet inside my head, calming the impossible itch of my own skin. I'm not tempted by the people around me having a good time. In fact, when someone gets really fucked up and shows their ass, it's an effective reminder of how the drugs turned me into someone I never wanted to be.

From the moment we step into the club, I know tonight will test me more than I thought it would, though. The music slams into me like a wall. Everywhere around me is thick with bodies, lights strobe off mirrored tiles, smoke curls through the air and settles on my skin, in my eyes, over my taste buds and up my nose. It's overstimulation to the max. Even upstairs in the restricted VIP section, where the rich and recognizable get corralled and cordoned off from the masses, I feel a familiar sense of claustrophobia wash over me.

I hate this.

If there's anything I miss about my party days, it's not feeling like I want to burst out of my own skin. I miss losing myself in a sea of strangers, dancing in the chaos, feeling the crowd's energy instead of standing away from it, fearful that my brain will melt if anything or anybody touches me.

The others don't mind or don't notice my off-kilter mood, but no one is drinking as much as I know they normally would. Or maybe they assume that I'm struggling with cravings. I don't know how to tell them it's okay to let loose. Knowing my presence is a burden only makes me feel worse, and I don't need even one more thought in my head right now.

Even if they are holding back on purpose, they've all still managed to find their respective distractions. Naz is grinning salaciously at something a pretty twink is whispering in his ear. Ari is chatting with a guy sitting on the other side of our booth, turned fully around like he's not even with us. And Will is lost in his own world. He's got a beautiful woman straddling his lap, but he keeps flicking his eyes towards his brother. Will's always been protective of Ari, but I still find the way he's glaring at the guy he's talking to amusing. Meanwhile, the girl in his lap is staring right at me.

She's hot, I'll give her that. Smooth tan skin wrapped in a pink bandage dress that leaves little to the imagination. Her blonde hair is pulled over one shoulder, her eyes rimmed with dark blue eyeliner that complements her eyes. It wouldn't be the first time Will and I have shared a woman, if that's what she's hinting at. I consider it, just for the release, if only to shut off my brain for a while. As hot as she is, there's nothing in me that feels interested enough to risk being touched. Even her pink tongue darting out to lick her blood-red lips isn't enough to make me want it. I look away before I give her any ideas.

It takes effort, but I find small, singular things to focus on to calm myself down. I sip my club soda and let the bubbles fizz over my tongue, memorize the rhythm of a single flashing light, find shapes in the haze of smoke. I light a clove cigarette, inhale the spicy smoke, and slowly start to relax.

A flicker catches my eye, and I look over to find Naz watching something on his phone. It looks to be sports highlights of a foot-ball game.

My nose crinkles. "Are you that bored?"

A smirk tugs at his mouth. "Just checking some highlights and stats from last year so I can finalize my fantasy roster for this season."

I blink at him slowly, conveying my lack of interest. I've never been much of a sports fan, although I do strangely enjoy watching random obscure Olympic events, like speed walking and break dancing. Also curling. That is a weirdly entertaining sport for no good reason.

There's a flash of a football player on the screen that registers as familiar. He's probably super famous, but I have no idea who he is. I can't even see his face through the helmet while he sprints down the field, but something about him feels familiar. It unsettles me.

When I drag my eyes away, I notice movement under the table. My eyebrow raises and I look at Naz with a deadpan expression. "Really?" Naz shrugs and keeps talking, like there isn't a guy under the table sucking his dick.

"Have you given any thought to Gavin's pitch?"

Our new manager won't shut up about it. *"It's the biggest stage in America! The biggest audience you'll ever have! An opportunity to immortalize your music."*

I scoff and shrug. "You know I don't give a shit about the Super Bowl."

If the guys want to do it, I'll agree to it whether I really want to or not. I don't care.

Truth is, I don't care about much lately. The stage, the crowds, the screaming. It doesn't have the same sparkle it once did. I don't think it's because I stopped taking drugs, either, because it's not like I needed to be drunk or high all the time—that wasn't my problem. My problem is that it all gets to be too much sometimes. Everything is too much, too loud, too crowded, too excessive. And I'm not sure how much longer I can keep it up, as much as I love it at the same time.

I stub out my clove and make my escape under the pretense of taking a piss. The bathroom's just as overdone as the rest of the place. Gleaming marble sinks lined with hand towels, lotion, and tiny bottles of mouthwash are on one side of the room, coke lines dusting the counter like it's a regular complimentary offering. Mirrored walls reflect warped images of myself. A stranger I barely recognize, with hollow eyes and shit posture, stares back at me. I put a piece of cinnamon candy in my mouth and turn away.

The door swings open, and the girl who was on Will's lap strolls in. She grins and walks towards me, hips swaying, eyes on me. She drops to her knees in front of me like she's been invited.

I let her open the front of my jeans, surrendering to the moment, hoping for a fleeting escape from the tangled mess of my thoughts. She's barely gotten started, but I'm already bored and feeling restless. She moans as she discovers the row of piercings along the underside of my cock, and rubs her tongue over them, which usually does it for me. Instead, the desire to push her off me slithers beneath my skin. I grit my teeth and try to give my body a chance to react. Her mouth is warm and wet and likely skilled, but I feel nothing. No desire. No ache. Nothing.

The door swings open again, and Will strolls in, grinning when he sees us. "Damn, Jess," he laughs, feigning disappointment. "Always stealing girls from me, and guys from my brother."

I chuckle humorlessly, pat the girl on the shoulder, then turn her towards him. "She's all yours." Maybe I should feel bad about treating her like something to be passed around, but she goes happily enough.

Will quirks an eyebrow and starts to say something, but is quickly distracted by the girl's enthusiastic mouth. Not wanting to engage and risk any questions or another invitation, I turn towards the sink and wash my hands, feeling the water rush through my fingers and imagining it rinsing away the whole interaction. I unwrap another cinnamon candy, and I'm gone before Will can so much as moan, the weight of the night pressing down on me.

I wake the next morning with a start, lungs pulling in air like I've been underwater. Sweat clings to my skin, images from a dream flashing in my mind like a strobe light. Memories of pale moonlight casting shadows over tanned skin, desperate gasps for breath, hands gripping my body with a need that left behind more than just marks on my flesh.

Dropping my head, I groan into the pillow I'm clutching so hard I'm surprised it's still intact. Memories of that night still haunt me, sliding into my thoughts and dreams at will, uninvited and relentless. I chase them even when I know I shouldn't, like a moth drawn to a flame–dangerous and painful, yet impossible to resist.

My body stirs, heat building low in my gut as I replay the scenes over and over. The memories are vivid despite it being so many years ago. Almost six years to be exact. I'm probably remembering it being better than it was, over-inflating the raw energy between us. But I still close my eyes and sink into the memory of a feeling that was more than pleasure.

I find myself shifting, absentmindedly rubbing my morning wood into the mattress and imagining I can feel him beneath me. I reach for the top edge of the mattress, remembering the way I'd held his hands above his head as I laid over him and rolled my hips, fucking myself between the globes of his firm, round ass. I'd already had him once, and he'd just finished taking me, his cum dripping down the cleft of my ass, but I was desperate with need all over again. It was like that the whole night, and the next morning when I woke to him in my arms.

I roll onto my back, eyes clenched shut, remembering myself reaching for another condom and pulling him down on top of me. My hand moves down my stomach and grips my cock, slowly sliding up and down the length as I recall the feeling of wrapping my arms around him and holding his body against mine while I slowly fucked him until he got comfortable enough to ride me. The sight of his handsome face, his pouty pink lips open and gasping as he sat up and rocked himself on my cock, will live in my brain rent-free for the rest of my life. I remember it so vividly I almost believe I can feel the weight of him again, and if I open my eyes, I'll see–

Not this.

The sight of smeared lipstick staining my dick makes me freeze. Revulsion claws at my throat, a bitter reminder of all the ways my past has tainted me. A reminder that it's been almost six years, and I likely wouldn't have had a chance even if I had stayed. Why do I keep thinking of him?

It's worse since I got sober. Without distractions and drugs to dull my brain, the memory of that one random night seems to creep up on me more than what feels reasonable. Then again, it felt anything but random at the time. I've never thought twice about a hookup before or since, but I have never been able to forget the stranger from the beach party. Maybe the only way I stopped myself from thinking of him this much before was staying buried balls deep in another person and numbing myself brainless.

I fall back into the pillows, arm draped over my eyes like a makeshift shield. I'd give anything to fall asleep again, to forget my reality for a little while longer. To lose myself in the dreams that take me back to that night and make me believe, if only for a moment, that I'm still there.

Back when we went on our first tour, our manager, Francis, used to give me pills to help me sleep. There were different ones. One of them would knock me out completely and make me groggy for days. The other made me sleepwalk, but I would have the most vivid dreams. I used to take them just to chase those dreams, to keep him alive in the dark.

But I don't anymore.

Pushing myself up to lean back against the headboard and covering my shame with the bedsheet, I drag my journal off the bedside table. Originally, I'd started writing in these journals as an exercise with my therapist, to make sense of my chaotic thoughts. These days, it's a lifeline. I scrawl thoughts across the page, jagged and messy, hoping to capture forgotten details as if I could carve the ghost of him into something tangible. More often than not, I just jot down my thoughts in lines that used to turn into lyrics.

> Drag me under, don't let me wake
> I'd sleep forever for one more taste
> Hold me down in the dark, make me feel love
> Could I change the ending if I sleep long enough...

But it's futile. I can't hold on to it. The words won't stick, sliding through my fingers like water.

TWO
JESSE

The hum of the engines is almost enough to lull me to sleep. I sink deeper into the leather seat of the jet, my knees pulled up against the armrest, notebook open on my lap but blank. I haven't written a single word since takeoff. The thought of going home has my brain stuck between static and silence.

It's been months since I set foot in Raleigh. Even then, the last time was nothing but a quick blur between rehab and therapy. It didn't really feel like I was home. Now we've got weeks off before we're back in the studio, and no major shows until New York at the end of the month.

Rest and recovery should feel like a gift. I know I need them, but it feels daunting at the same time. I don't know how to slow down. I'm used to being shoved forward by deadlines and shows and sound checks. There's always something demanding my attention. If I stop, if I let myself just sit still, I'm afraid of what kind of noise my brain might make in the quiet. Even as a kid, I always needed to be busy. Otherwise, I'd drift aimlessly to anything to entertain myself, finding myself in some kind of trouble more often than not.

Naz drops into the seat across from me. "You ready to be home for a while?"

"I think so," I answer, but I must not sound enthusiastic enough.

"What's up?"

"Nothing's up. I'm just tired. What do you have going on when you get home?"

"Taking my grandparents to see the land and meet with the builders."

"Ah, that's right. Sorry, totally forgot about that." I haven't been the most present friend, and I feel bad about it. There's both guilt and relief in his easy acceptance of my issues.

"No worries, man. We've been busy. I'm ready for a break."

"Hard same," Will calls out from across the aisle. Ari is asleep in the chair facing his, a confirmation of his exhaustion, too.

"What are y'all getting up to?" Naz asks.

"Gonna stick around for a couple days, then we're going to head up to New York early. There are some clubs we want to check out."

I have little doubt that the clubs he's referring to are probably sex clubs. We went to a few as a group before. It wasn't really my thing, but I appreciated the ironclad NDAs and discretion of the clientele. Sometimes I'd go just to enjoy a night out without being bombarded by fans or being followed by bodyguards.

"You're still coming by for dinner, right?" I ask him.

"Definitely. I'm not about to miss out on seeing our band mama."

"I'm pretty sure she'd hunt you down anyway."

"Bet," Naz says, laughing.

Will and Ari don't have any family connections left in Raleigh, but they usually spend at least a day or two visiting old friends and coming by to see my mom. She's always treated the guys in the band like extra sons, and they show her love in return. Naz has been my best friend since elementary school, so he might as well be blood.

I turn back to him. "You didn't tell me how Ted and Linda reacted when you told them about the land."

Naz bought a plot of land about forty-five minutes outside the city, with enough acreage that he can build a house for himself and another for his grandparents, all far apart enough that they won't feel like they live on a compound.

"Ah, you know how they are," he says, shrugging.

His grandparents weren't thrilled about him skipping college for music. Even now, they act like they're disappointed he didn't go into academia like them and his dad, despite being a literal superstar with platinum records and a bank account to show it.

"What have they been up to?"

"Running their nonprofit, writing a book, doing the academic power couple thing, making the rounds speaking at various conferences and universities."

"That reminds me, I know they aren't my biggest fans, but what's the likelihood they'd answer some questions about starting a nonprofit for my mom?"

My mom has been doing a lot of research and has almost everything she needs to get started on opening an after-school program for underprivileged kids and kids with single parents. She won't accept a penny from me, other than allowing me to move her into a nicer condo than the shithole apartments we lived in when I was growing up, and that was only because I agreed to call it *my* condo that she takes care of while I'm gone. I stay there whenever I'm in town. If the time ever comes that my life and schedule are more settled, I'll get my own place, but I really don't need one. We're rarely in one place long enough to warrant putting down roots.

I opened a bank account for her so she could quit working, but of course she never touches it. She did go down to one job since she didn't have rent and utilities to pay for anymore, and the dentist she works for as a receptionist is really nice. If she's happy, I'm happy. I kind of love that she wants to funnel all the money I refuse to take back into a program to help kids get access to music, art, and sports programs after school.

"Definitely. They'd be all about it." Naz nods, serious for a second. "I love that she's doing that, and kinda in your honor, too. You would have been a mess without music stuff after school."

"Correction," I say, stretching out like a cat. "I *was* a total mess. Just… with choir and band as a soundtrack."

I lean my chair back like I'm going to take a nap while Naz pulls a book out. Eventually, I drift off to sleep, wondering how these next few weeks are going to go.

Being home is weirder than I expected, but good. It's given me a lot of perspective, and the timing couldn't have been better. I don't think I realized just how bad my mental health had gotten in the last couple of months. Another week or two on the road might have broken me.

I've checked in with my therapist, done yoga, gone for long walks with my mom. I've even found a good balance of staying busy without overloading my mind by doing physical labor.

After talking to Naz's grandparents, my mom got the idea to look at older historical properties in the city instead of a commercial space. They'd been discussing how rough it's gotten living in the city, how more kids are being left to their own devices or can't afford extracurricular activities. A large part of the problem is that the city is slowly but surely becoming gentrified. Older properties are being bought up by developers, the buildings bulldozed and replaced with overpriced townhomes and apartments. By buying up one of these properties herself, she could not only restore a piece of Raleigh history and prevent the problem from getting worse, but it'll give the program headquarters a homey feel.

It just so happened that there was a perfect house up for sale—a large three-story brick home with a wrap-around porch. It's a fixer-upper, but it's got good bones, and a lot of the work is stuff we can do ourselves.

So every day, I haul my ass out of bed and get to work sanding floors, scraping paint, carrying boxes of tile until my arms feel like noodles. It's honest work, grounding in a way I didn't realize I needed. I thought if I slowed down, the silence would become too loud in my head. It's a kind of noise that eats at me until I want to crawl out of my skin, almost as bad as the overstimulation of having too much going on. And I waver back and forth like a ping-pong ball.

Having a task like this, one with a goal in front of us, has been the perfect compromise. I stay busy but not overwhelmed. The exertion helps me sleep, and it's strangely relaxing. I've become comforted by the scrape of sandpaper, the hiss of a paint roller, the creak of old wood being coaxed into life again.

At night, I crash hard, the exhaustion washing away the restless hum that usually keeps me awake. For the first time in years, I'm sleeping soundly without pills or booze.

Two weeks have passed before I know it.

Today I'm heading out with Naz to a house party at an old friend's home. It's going to be a low-key affair with a small group of people that knew us before *Lest Is Moore* and still see *us* rather than the famous rockstars we've become. No one is going to bombard us with questions, beg to take pictures, or ask for autographs. I'm not a celebrity around them. I'm just the flighty choir geek that smoked a lot of pot. It's comforting, even if I'm not entirely sure I want to be around people.

Naz honks from the curb and yells out the window when I drag my feet. "Careful, Moore, if you keep this hermit thing up, you'll grow a beard, disappear into the woods, and the album we just wrote will never see the light of day."

I flip him off and climb in. "Unlikely."

"You're right. You're twenty-five and still can't grow facial hair."

"Shut it."

We end up having a great time. It's nice to catch up with old friends, eat barbecue, and just hang out. I even end up reconnecting with a guy I hooked up with a few times back in high school. After some flirting and suggestive glances, I run into him coming out of the bathroom, and I back him into a dark corner of the hallway. We make out for a while, passing the candy I was sucking on back and forth, and I'm into it. It's the first time another person has gotten my dick up in a while.

Maybe this is what I needed? Something uncomplicated. Marc is familiar and safe, so it's easier with him. He's in this for the same thing I am and has no expectations from me afterwards. I'm hard, he's hard, and I seriously consider moving this into a more private location.

But when I disconnect my lips from his, I get distracted by a light outside and pull away. My mind reels with familiarity, and I blink back flashes of memory. Whatever desire had flickered sputters out. I crunch down on the candy and flex my fingers.

It'll never be that good again, I think, looking out at the firepit that someone started in the backyard. Flames lick the air, bending and twisting, pulling me backwards in time. Fire always reminds me of my past. Of that night. Fire, and a light breeze. The ocean. A beam of moonlight in a dark room.

My chest tightens. I mumble an excuse and walk away before I unravel completely.

Naz and a couple of guys are sitting in the living room watching a football game. I'm not interested in the game, but it gives me something to stare at while I pretend to be normal. I sink into the couch and zone out, wondering how long Naz will want to stay. He brought us here, but I'm the designated driver to get us back to his place after.

Everyone in the living room erupts in cheers, and I blink, looking up at the television for the first time. The camera pans across the field, zooming in on a player who apparently just made a big play.

The air leaves my lungs.

That face.

That jawline.

That mouth…

The camera cuts away from the player, and I shoot to my feet, heart hammering, muttering, "Go back, go back, come on–"

Everyone looks at me like I'm nuts, but I'm waiting for him to come back on the screen again. The camera cuts again, and there he is, clear as day.

"There!" I shout, pointing at the screen. "That guy. Who is that?"

Someone laughs and rattles off a name. "That's Luke Martín. He's a safety for the Cyclones. He's one of the best defensive players in the NFL."

"Nah, man. It's pronounced *Luce*, like *loose*, or Lucy without the y. I think his full name is Lucien or something. He's on my fantasy team."

Mine, too. For the past six years.

"You know him or something?"

Or something, I think but don't respond. I stare at the screen and repeat his name under my breath. Then again, over and over, each syllable carving itself into my memory.

His name is Luc Martín.

Luc.

It's him.

THREE
JESSE

Naz lets himself in without knocking, the way he always has, keys clinking into the bowl by the door. "You look like shit," he announces, then flops next to me on the couch and tries to peek at my screen.

"Thanks," I mutter, angling the laptop away.

"You've barely answered my texts the last two days," he says. "You wanna talk about whatever that was at the party, or do I need to start worrying?"

"It's nothing."

"Bullshit." He bumps my knee with his. "Come on. I know you."

To be fair, someone wouldn't have to know me to recognize that I'm spiraling.

I've been in what can only be described as a state of dissociation since Luc Martín popped up on the television screen. Despite not being a sports fan, I watched every moment of that game with rapt attention, waiting for them to show his face again so I could be sure. During commercial breaks, I scrolled through whatever information I could find on my phone.

Luc.

I want to say his name out loud, to wrap my tongue around the simple syllable and draw out the sound, taste it. I haven't let myself yet.

The man on the screen is a little different from how I remember him, but he's a few years older. His jawline is sharper, hair cropped shorter on the sides, and his body has bulked out in ways that only time and the intense training of a professional athlete could accomplish. But in one of my first image searches, I found a picture of him exactly as I remember him. When I clicked on the image to open the article, I realized it was taken only a week after the night we'd been together. It was from that year's NFL draft night.

On our way home from the party, I didn't talk much. Naz asked about it, but I was still too dumbstruck to articulate what was on my mind.

As soon as I got home, I did a deep dive, searching for anything and everything I could find about Luc Martín, and I haven't come up for air since.

I've devoured every article I could find. There isn't much outside of stats, game highlights, and mentions here and there. Despite being one of the best defensive players in the league, he doesn't get much press. He seems to keep his head down, hasn't been involved in any scandals that I can find, nor is there any gossip about his personal life. At all. He doesn't even have social media. Seriously, what kind of celebrity doesn't have social media these days? Even if they don't manage it themselves, like our PR team does for us.

Even though I know his name now, the lack of a trail makes him feel more intangible than ever. Maybe that's why I keep scrolling, clicking on every mere mention of his name. Hope is more addictive than the strongest drug.

Naz nudges me and then gestures for me to hand him my laptop. The NFL draft article is on the screen, because it's the one I keep coming back to again and again.

"This the guy you saw last night?"

"Yeah. I've met him before."

He lifts an eyebrow. "There has to be more to it than that."

Naz waits me out, quiet for once. I sigh, trying to think of a way to explain myself.

"Do you remember that Spring Break showcase we played in the Outer Banks, the one where we first met that producer?"

"How could I forget? That was the day everything changed," he smiles.

I nod. "The night before we got that call, I'd gone for a walk on the beach and I kind of stumbled on a small party."

Naz snorts. "Sounds like something you'd do. Let me guess, you met this guy there?" He taps the screen next to Luc's face.

The air leaves my chest in a pained huff and I can only nod to answer his question. He waits patiently, but expectantly, for me to say more. Clearly there's more to it if I'm acting so erratically.

My voice comes out rough. "We talked a lot and, well… more. I spent the night with him, and then the next morning is when you texted that we'd gotten the call. I left while he was still sleeping, and I didn't get his name."

Naz studies me, waiting, but I don't say more. I don't offer up any explanation for this being the one exception to every other hookup I've walked away from without another thought. Nor do I say that the reason I didn't wake him or leave a note was because the rawness of what had happened between us scared the hell out of me. Lying there, watching him sleep, it felt like standing at the edge of a cliff so high I could only see clouds below. And I was suddenly afraid of heights.

"Everything happened so fast after that, I thought it was probably for the best. We left for New York the next day."

Naz's mouth softens. "Jesse…" He swallows whatever he was about to say and shifts closer, shoulder to shoulder. Then he freezes. "Wait. This can't be… Is this who *Remember My Name* was about?"

I stare at my hands and nod.

He lets out a low whistle. "Damn."

If anything, he must understand how much of an impression Luc made on me back then. Everyone, including him, has always remarked how that song had to have come from somewhere deep. And considering it was deep enough that I never spoke about it to anyone, not even my best friend…

Naz looks back down at the article, then leans in. His eyebrows shoot up, and he touches the scroll pad to read more. "New York," he says. "Dude. He was in New York at the same time we were. We were only two blocks away from Radio City Music Hall that night," he says, pointing to the article.

My mind reels. As many times as I'd read this article, and scoured every detail I could find about him, I didn't pick up on that.

A laugh breaks out of me, too sharp. "What a small fucking world."

Naz looks at me for a long moment, and when he speaks again, his voice is careful. "So, what now?"

My pulse kicks. "I have to find a way to see him again."

———————

I spend most of the day still reeling. We have a video meeting with our manager and the other guys to discuss our schedule for the next few months. I'm barely present. I'm there physically, sitting next to Naz in front of the camera. Blake has given up asking me any direct questions. He seems to think I've checked out because he brought up the Super Bowl again, but all my attention is focused on figuring out how to meet up with Luc.

My first thoughts were the easier ideas. I have connections and strings I could pull to get in contact with someone who could get me his number or set up a meeting. Then I think, what if he doesn't remember me? Or what if he does, but isn't interested? My face is in the news, tabloids, and on billboards across the country. I'm really fucking famous. There's a good chance he knows who I am and made the choice not to get in touch with me. Which means he's probably not interested.

What if that night wasn't as memorable for him as it was for me?

Luc.

No. I can't chance having a meetup be rejected. There needs to be a way I can run into him somehow, or otherwise physically be in his presence. After all this time, I'd almost convinced myself he wasn't real or that my memory of him was distorted. I need to know. I need to see him in front of me, with my own eyes, close enough to touch him and know he's real.

Wait…What if I went to a football game? I know plenty of celebrities who are self-important enough to bully their way backstage to meet me. Maybe I can get backstage for one of his games, or whatever it's called for sports arenas. Maybe the team would want to meet me, and then I could walk around shaking hands in the locker room after the game or something.

A visual stabs through my brain like an ice pick. Me making my way through the room. Him half-stripped after the game, wearing nothing but a pair of those tight football pants.…

Damn.

Yes, that's it!

"Where's my phone? I need my phone!" I shove back from the table so suddenly my chair squeals across the floor. Naz jumps in surprise.

"Jesse?" Blake snaps. "Is he okay?"

Naz says my name questioningly.

I don't answer. I'm already grabbing my phone off the counter, scrolling with frantic thumbs, searching for the Shreveport Cyclones' schedule. Cities and dates blur as I flick through. They play in Philadelphia this weekend, and then…

Yes. Holy shit. They play in Buffalo the same weekend as our headliner in NYC! It's perfect.

"Earth to Jesse," Blake's voice cuts in again, exasperated. "What's going on?" Will and Ari are chattering, asking Naz the same thing. He shrugs into the camera.

"I have an idea," I tell Naz.

I walk back around to the front of the computer screen, adrenaline fizzing under my skin. "Blake, I need a favor."

Everyone shuts up at once. Blake's face looks pinched and wary. Will and Ari look mildly curious. Naz leans back, arms crossed, smirk tugging at his mouth because he knows I'm about to blow something up.

"A favor?" Blake repeats.

"Our New York show." I lick my lips. "Could we… make room for some special guests?"

Blake blinks. "Jesse, that show sold out in less than an hour. There's already going to be a mob outside just hoping to get a glimpse of the back of one of your heads. This isn't the kind of night where we slip people in."

"But if I wanted to invite someone," I press, leaning forward, "we could make it happen, right?"

He sighs, already defeated. "I can probably swing a couple. How many are we talking?"

My phone screen glows back at me, the Cyclones' roster page still open. A grin creeps up before I can stop it.

"How many guys are on a football team?"

LeST is MooRE

FOUR
LUC

Practice finally winds down just as the sun dips, casting a warm haze across the field that makes everything look like it's glowing. Coach blows his whistle to call it, and the team jogs off the field, sweat dripping, pads heavy. It was a good practice, one that still has adrenaline buzzing under my skin.

We're all still on a high from a big win against Detroit this past weekend. It was the perfect start to the season. Our team is tight and meshes well. We have high hopes for what could be a monumental season.

By the time we're in the locker room, the guys are already cutting up, the air thick with steam and chatter and the stench of hard work. My locker buddy, AJ León, is in rare form, running his mouth and laughing at his own dumb jokes. When I'm down to nothing but my jock, he snaps his towel across my ass with a loud *smack*.

"Motherfucker," I mutter, turning a scathing look on him, but the corner of my mouth betrays me.

It's hard to stay mad at AJ. He can be irritating as hell, but it's part of his charm. He's one of my favorite people in the world, and probably the closest friend I've got. AJ always sticks around, even though I don't make being friends with me easy. I'm more of a solitary type, and I don't go out much. I rarely hang out with the guys, or even AJ, outside of work. Not because I don't like them or being around them, but because I'm not into crowds and flashing cameras–and wherever these guys are, the fans follow. I'm not cut out for the spotlight the way some players are. I love football, but I don't love the circus that comes with it.

To be fair, I've probably gotten a little too comfortable with my solitude. The habit is too deeply ingrained. After the draft, I barely had time to breathe, let alone socialize. Between practice, games, and the endless travel, I was grinding through online classes, determined to finish my business degree. Dad always said I needed a backup plan, and I promised him I'd finish my degree when he found out I'd be entering the draft instead of graduating. I wanted to make him proud, so I kept at it, night after night, studying on the bus or plane to away games, passing on going out with the guys, and going straight home, alone, every day after practice. It was hard, and it took me longer than it would have if I'd stayed in school, but I did it. And even though I didn't walk across a stage in a cap and gown, that diploma is framed on a wall in my parents' home in a place of honor, above any trophy or award I've won.

Pushing him into the lockers, I roll my eyes at AJ and tell him to go mess with Dez instead. Unlike me, Dez Carter is known to walk around with his ass out. He's practically a nudist. It used to weird me out, but nobody bats an eye at him anymore. Then again, Dez looks like he was carved out of marble, so who could blame him for wanting to show off? This guy has GQ spreads, endorsement deals, the works. He's an Adonis with golden-boy charm that earns him every dime. It doesn't bother anybody, least of all me. We've all got our quirks. AJ is the class clown, always pulling pranks and laughing the loudest. One of our cornerbacks, Treydon Rocke, likes to trash talk government officials on his social media, where he has like a billion followers. Monty Nash, our quarterback, dresses like a rodeo cowboy in boots and big belt buckles despite being far from Wyoming, where he's from. Our running back Connor Laramie is a total golden retriever with an international supermodel girlfriend who he never shuts up about.

Then there's me, the quiet guy. The loner. I get along with everybody, but nobody expects me to do the big media interviews or photo ops. They invite me to everything they do, but no one expects me to show up, and they don't get upset when I decline the majority of invitations.

We're a mixed bag, but everybody accepts each other the way they are. It's a hell of a group to share a locker room with, and I thank my lucky stars every day the Cyclones picked me up. Not only because I get to stay in my home state, close to home, but because I've found somewhere I belong.

I shower fast, ready to get home for dinner. When I come out of the showers, I notice the buzz in the room has shifted. Excited chatter bounces from one end of the benches to the other.

"What's going on?"

AJ leans in, eyes wide. "Check your phone, man. The team got invited to see *Lest Is Moore* next weekend when we're in New York."

Quirking my eyebrow, I open my phone's email app and see a message from the Player Engagement office.

> *The entire roster for the Shreveport Cyclones has been personally invited to attend the Lest Is Moore NYC concert next Friday before our game in Buffalo. Backstage passes included. All players please respond by Monday if interested.*

Around me, the room's excitement grows. Questions are being thrown out, like anyone might have the inside details about the invitation.

"Isn't that concert sold out?"

"I thought the entire tour was."

All the guys are grinning, hyped for the show and making plans for a night out in Manhattan.

I'm less excited, although I'm happy that everyone else seems pumped. Scrolling back up, re-read the subject line. I've heard the band name, sure. They're everywhere, right? I'm not much for keeping up with current music. My playlists are stuck in the '90s, alt-rock favorites on repeat. I almost never bother with the radio.

AJ practically bounces in his seat, shoving me in the shoulder. "Come on, man! Get hyped! It's *Lest Is Moore*, dude!"

I shrug. "I don't really know them."

His eyes bug out. "How is that even possible?" He shakes his head. "You know what, you've gotta go. They're insane live. I think you'd dig their vibe. Trust me, dude. You won't want to miss this."

"I don't know. I'll think about it."

Truthfully, the thought of a packed arena, earsplitting loud music, screaming fans, and cameras flashing everywhere doesn't appeal to me. I live it enough already.

AJ pouts at me like I just kicked his puppy. "Man, you're no fun."

Back home, my place is blessedly quiet. Unlike most of the guys, who live in giant houses in gated communities, I live in the same modest condo I bought when I first started, though it's still more than I need. It's nothing flashy, but there were only so many options for buildings in Shreveport with a doorman that could restrict access to a prescribed list of visitors. Thankfully, I'm not popular enough to attract that much attention off the field, so reporters haven't tried to follow me home. They only bother with me if I brave going out for dinner or somewhere with the team, which is the reason I don't. I like my quiet life.

While I throw together dinner, I decide I should at least listen to this *Lest Is Moore* band and see what the fuss is about. I pull their music up on my phone and push play, the music coming through the surround sound speakers. When the vocals hit, there's a flicker of familiarity, but I can't place it. More than likely, I've heard them somewhere before. In the locker room maybe, or in a grocery store. How could I not? They're global superstars.

Which makes me wonder why the hell they'd be sending *us* tickets. A young team out of Louisiana that hasn't won any major conferences yet. Then again, maybe it's not just us. Maybe it's a PR move? I heard someone say they might play the *Super Bowl Halftime Show*, so that might make sense.

Just as I'm plating some of the quinoa jambalaya I meal prepped on Monday, topped with two big, marinated, grilled chicken breasts, a slower track comes on. I stop mid-motion, spatula in hand, the hairs on the back of my neck prickling. *That voice.* Why is it so familiar?

And then it clicks. A few years back, I'd stumbled on a song. Something about it resonated with me to the point where I'd played it until the repeat button was nearly worn out. I couldn't get it out of my system. It helped me process a lot of what I was going through at the time, the way really good music can sometimes.

The night of that bonfire had left me feeling empty, confused, and more insecure than I was willing to admit, even to myself. As much as I'd wanted to forget and move past it, I couldn't. It took immersing myself in the memories with this song playing over and over to get to the point where I could breathe again.

This must be the same band. I drop the spatula, grab my phone, and scroll until I find the song in an old playlist. *Remember My Name* by *Lest Is Moore*. I push play, and mouth along with the lyrics, remembering every word as if they're burned into my brain.

Your blue eyes cut me wide

In a flickering flame, I couldn't hide

Moon hung low like it knew

What the hell was I doing smiling at you

We touched like it meant everything

Was it all too much

Breathless in a stranger's bed

Heart beating like a threat

I never told you who I am

You didn't tell me about you

Is it stupid I want you to

Remember my name

Even though I never told you

You saw me the night I came alive

For one stolen moment, I couldn't hide

You kissed me like it was the end

Like you knew you'd never see me again

We broke the rules in whispers

With skin we couldn't tame

The morning silence buried

The truth I never claimed

I never told you who I am

You didn't tell me about you

Is it stupid I want you to

Remember my name

Even though I never told you

Remember my name

(The way I'll always remember you)

Remember my name

(Is it stupid I want you to)

Remember my name

(I wish I'd stayed)

Remember my name

(and told you the truth)

The team stands around a cordoned-off area so close to the stage it might be too close. There's a good bit of the stage we can't actually see, and the speakers are so close my ears are already ringing. But we're well-separated from the rest of the stadium crowd and backed up to the stadium for inside access. Nearly our entire roster came. There are at least forty of us plus a few of the coaching and training staff. They've really gone all out, full VIP treatment with drinks, snacks, merch, and private bath-rooms so we don't have to fight the crowds. It's a really nice setup.

Nobody can stop talking about why we're here. Speculation runs wild. The most popular guess is the same one that I'd had, but the idea of the band inviting teams that cross locations with their touring schedule doesn't make sense if the Bills aren't here as well. The other ranking theory involves Connor Laramie's super-model girlfriend, who is a known hardcore fan. If that were the case, wouldn't she be invited, too? Granted, the WAGs rarely travel along with the team for away games, and they weren't mentioned in the invitation. Nobody has a good answer.

The opening acts already have me overwhelmed. The main opening act is a late '90s alt-rock group I know and like well enough. They look old, which makes me feel a little old, even though I'm only twenty-seven and they're a little before my time. I'll probably look the same if I'm still grinding at their age. The act before them screamed a little too much for me, but the first one had a grunge vibe I appreciated, even though we walked in halfway through.

When the final opener announces the band and the lights drop, the entire stadium goes feral. Tens of thousands of people are on their feet, screaming with the kind of intensity and excitement you can feel in your ribcage. My teammates are contributing to the din, shouting and throwing their fists in the air. AJ is posi-tively beside himself. The way he's talked about this concert, you'd think it was the highlight of his entire career to get invited here like this. His enthusiasm is infectious.

From the start, the band is high-octane, relentless energy that resonates through the crowd. Some of the vocals are so high, I imagine the notes drifting off into the stratosphere. This guy could give Steven Tyler a run for his money. I stick to the back of the crowd, back resting on the wall where I can't see as much, but I have to admit they're pretty damn good. I'm even feeling the music, bobbing my head and tapping my foot.

The whole spectacle is well worth all the excitement. The thumping beats, wild riffs, lights, massive screens flashing insane artwork with overtly political messages are really some-thing. But what gets me the most is the lead singer's vocals. A few times I even push myself off the wall, nearly hypnotized by the sound of it, wanting to see what kind of human could possess that kind of raw grit, pain, and sexuality in just their voice.

Eventually, I find a break in the wall of muscle and bobbing heads to get a peek at the stage. The frontman, Jesse Moore, is a blur of motion, energy cranked to eleven, voice cutting through everything with a sharpness that makes the hairs rise on the back of my neck. He's in the middle of the stage, facing away from us, sandwiched between the bassist and lead guitarist. The three of them look close. Like they're all *very* familiar with each other. The crowd loves it, screaming as the frontman reaches around his bandmate's waist to finger the strings of the bass, then leans back on the guitarist's shoulder like he's in ecstasy. I shift on the spot, feeling uncomfortably warm despite the cool September night.

Jesse turns back towards our section, his eyes seeming to pan the crowd as the rasp of his voice makes suggestive words sound downright lewd–

I'm okay with being used

Whatever you want me to do

Break me, make me, twist me up

I can't breathe unless it's rough

When push comes to shove

I wanna be painted with your love

Drip, drip, drip it down–make it enough

His eyes lock on mine in passing, then snap back, a slight hitch in his singing like he loses the beat for a quick moment. And then… God help me, it feels like he's looking at *me*. The suggestive curl of his mouth around the lyrics, the way he moves, it rattles something loose inside me. I jerk my gaze away, but every time I glance back, it's the same. Like he's singing directly to me. Which is insane. I'm just another face in a mass of oversized bodies. But the thought won't leave.

Not only that, but he's so familiar. He reminds me of…

Don't be ridiculous. That's impossible. This guy has an entirely different build, not to mention the rough edge about him that doesn't match the soft, casual vibe of the man I met that night.

The shape of his mouth is so familiar. to the one I've dreamed of…*No. Stop it.* Sure, maybe some of his features line up, but it can't be.

I look away, ashamed of the way my mind finds ways to make impossible connections. It's not the first time I've twisted my obsessive memory to fit the present in a wild attempt to make myself believe it could be possible. Or even just to imagine.

I've imagined scenarios where the stranger from that night all those years ago comes back into my life, each of them more and more impossible. It started with simple daydreams, wondering and visualizing how life would be different if I'd woken up with him still next to me. Or if he had shown up in the next two days that I'd extended my visit, waiting forlornly on the beach for the ghost of a guy I only knew existed from the dwindling soreness in my body and fading marks he left behind.

Then my daydreams became delusions. My heart would quicken if I saw a similar hairstyle from behind or looked into a pair of green eyes. My wishful thinking turned into hopeless imaginings, little "what if" scenarios that I'd make up in my mind. What if he saw me on tv and showed up to a game? What if we bumped into each other at a grocery store or airport?

It's like a sick hobby I've become addicted to.

Though I can no longer remember the exact shape of his jaw or taste of his skin, that night is always at the edge of my consciousness. He's more than just in my dreams, waking me up in the middle of the night, sweat slicked and sticky like a pubescent teenager. He's a fantasy that I've built to give myself comfort and lull myself to sleep at night. One where I can imagine a world where our story doesn't have an end. One where I can feel him against my skin again.

Skin that is currently breaking out in goosebumps as the opening chords of a familiar song start up. The very song that hurt so much to listen to, I'd play it on repeat. The song that helped me heal.

The crowd goes wild, and so does my heart.

Jesse steps out onto a raised platform as the audience gets even louder. "I hope y'all don't mind, but I thought I'd strip this one down a little."

The place detonates. A tech hands him a black acoustic guitar.

He's shirtless, ink sprawling over sweat-slick skin, hair wild, chest rising as he catches his breath from the last number. His voice is hoarse with use, but when he starts strumming and singing, it hits me hard in the center of my gut. The way his fingers move over the strings, the tilt of his head–it's too familiar.

My stomach twists, and I look away again. My head is starting to ache with the effort of not matching his face up to my memory. And every time I look up again, I can't convince myself that he's not looking straight at me. And I can't convince myself that he's an older, more muscular, more heavily tattooed version of the guy I met so many years ago.

Logically, I know it's the song that's getting to me. The feelings the song stirs up, and the energy of thirty thousand people swooning is bound to affect anyone. There is a reason this band is so popular, after all. Everyone in the crowd probably feels it too. I look back and forth from one of the most famous rockstars alive, staring down into the crowd like he sees me, to my sneakers, trying to wake myself up before I need professional help for my delusions.

Then he starts to walk down the platform, faced away from the crowd, back towards the main stage. Directly facing our group. His fingers strum the guitar as he walks, slow and deliberate, his voice rolling over the crowd like smoke. Straight towards me.

I freeze. My teammates shift, some shooting me looks I can't read. My chest is tight. I haven't slept in days, not since I pulled that damn song back into my rotation, and now I'm hallucinating. The crowd, and the noise, and the sleeplessness have all finally taken their toll.

I need some air. Some space to breathe… *Something*.

Muttering an excuse, I tear myself away and slip out. AJ yells after me, asking about going backstage, but I quicken my steps until I'm running through the stadium halls.

A security guard points me towards the back exit, the team bus waiting to haul us away from the chaos. By the time I'm halfway there, the crowd's already flooding into the parking structure. The concert's over.

I'm climbing the steps when someone shouts my name. I turn, expecting AJ or one of the guys chasing me down.

But it's not.

It's him. Jesse Moore. Charging out the back door of the arena, calling *my* name.

My legs stutter, but I stop, rooted, as he closes the distance. Shirt thrown on, unbuttoned, billowing with his stride and showing off his abs, chest, and the edge of a tattoo that makes my finger-tips tingle.

And then he's right there. Just a few feet away.

My eyes drag away from the familiar ink, and I look up into unmistakable, impossible, bright green eyes.

It's actually… *him*.

LeST is MooRE

FIVE
LUC

He says my name again, his voice sounding like it's coming through a tunnel before it sharpens. I blink at the familiar smoky rasp of his voice.

"Luc."

It's breathless, but certain. Like he's been saying it for years. I just couldn't hear him.

He stops before he's within arm's reach but looks poised to move closer. All the times I've imagined an impossible moment like this, and I don't know what to do. I feel weighted to the spot, my feet glued to the pavement and tingling with the absurd instinct to run. Towards him? Away from him? I don't know. My brain feels fuzzy, overloaded with thoughts yet not quite able to process them.

I've forgotten how to move. All I can do is stare at the man standing before me. It's no wonder I didn't recognize him right away. He's changed a lot. The guy I remember from that night was barely an adult, compared to the man he is now. His physique is still wiry, but more filled out than he was six years ago. His shaggy hair, which was dark back then, is longer and dyed a smoky silver color that makes his black-rimmed eyes look wild. His face is more angular and serious rather than carefree and playful. He's almost unrecognizable from the young, flirty guy I remember from the beach, skin and bright eyes reflecting the light of the fire.

Except his mouth. His mouth is the same. The slight curve of a knowing smile. Those lips.

Something knocks loose and rattles around in my chest as I try to breathe normally.

"Hi," he says, then laughs like he can't believe that's what came out of his mouth first. "Holy shit. It's really you."

I clear my throat. "Yeah, I– Uh…" I reach for something solid, anything that doesn't make me look like the bumbling idiot I've become. "I–It's Jesse, right?"

His eyes flicker. Is it possible that he feels the same way I do about hearing my name come out of his mouth? Is he still processing that we're standing right in front of each other? Did he ever wonder if it was all a dream?

"Jesse," he confirms, like he's introducing himself for the first time.

Not sure what else to do, I reach out my hand to shake his, then pull it back because I realize how sweaty my palms are. I awkwardly rake my hand through my hair. "I'm Luc."

"Luc," he repeats, and I get that same feeling again–that he's said my name before. His raspy voice curls around it, elongating the end like a hiss. The sound sends a shiver down my spine.

Somewhere behind Jesse, a door bangs open, popping the bubble around us. I'm suddenly aware of the noise of the crowd leaving the stadium, thousands of people pouring into the night. A man wearing a snug black shirt and black cargo pants steps outside and leans against the wall, thumbing through his phone. He doesn't look at us twice, and neither do the couple of security guards that are walking by to monitor the entrance to the loading dock, where our bus is waiting.

"Bodyguard," Jesse says, gesturing towards the man in black. "He won't bother us."

This is too surreal.

He's sweaty and still catching his breath. After the show he just put on, and then running after me, I'm not surprised. "I ran," he says, laughing a little breathlessly, swiping his hair back from his forehead. "When I saw you leave, I–I thought I'd miss you and I didn't know how else to see you again."

My mind trips over his words. Did he expect to see me here? Wait, does that mean?

"I can't believe it's really you," he says, voice cracking a little like he's just as astonished as I am, except he somehow knew that I might be in the crowd? "I saw you on TV. I thought I might be hallucinating, but there you were, after all these years."

"You remembered?" It comes out softer than I mean it to, which might as well be a confession of my own.

"I never forgot."

My eyes snap up to his, and I really look at him. The careful part of me wants to look over my shoulder for cameras, or team-mates, or paparazzi that probably follow his every move, but the rest of me is twenty-one again, sunbaked and stunned by beau-tiful green eyes and self-assured charm.

The ache of the memory could melt me into a puddle if I let it. My fingers dig into my palms to steady the feeling inflating in my chest, growing larger than what my rib cage can hold in.

My silence seems to worry him.

He takes a small step closer. Close enough that I can smell something sweet and spicy on his breath. It kind of reminds me of Christmas sweets.

"Luc." The way he says my name this time is quieter, softer. More serious. "Can we–" He glances back to the door where his bodyguard is pointedly not looking at us, then up at the ledge of the building, where a security camera is mounted. He winces. "Do you want to come back to my dressing room?"

The question blindsides me. My stomach tightens. "Look, Jesse–"

He lifts both hands, palms out, eyes wide. "I didn't mean… Not like that. I swear. I just thought we could sit down and talk. Privately. Five minutes where it's just us."

Just us.

It feels a little forward, but the honesty in his voice strips away any suspicion. I don't think he's trying to drag me into a room to put the moves on me. He just wants some privacy, which I can appreciate.

I nod once. "Okay."

"Yeah?" He says, looking hopeful.

Before I can overthink anything, he reaches for my wrist and pulls me behind him. The bodyguard opens the door for us, giving me a quick once-over before following us in. Another guy in a similar outfit leads us down a hallway and through a backstage area cluttered with large cases and equipment. Staffers and roadies run around, but no one pays us much attention.

"Thanks Cory," Jesse says to another bodyguard, who opens a door for us.

The dressing room is larger than I expected. There's a sitting area with a small sectional and recliner and a kitchenette. The room opens into another section that has racks of clothes along one wall and mirrored desks along another.

"The rest of the band is probably still with your team," Jesse says, reaching into a refrigerator and pulling out a few bottles of water. He holds one up, offering it to me.

"Yes please," I say, reaching for it. "Thank you."

"Still so polite," he says, a mischievous gleam in his eyes.

My face warms, and I look for something to distract him from my embarrassment. "Shouldn't you be out there, too?"

He shrugs and drops onto the couch, hair damp, shirt still hanging open. It seems like he'd be too wired to sit still, but his shoulders sag with relief. He pats the space beside him, inviting me to sit.

"Maybe. But the whole point of inviting them was to get to talk to you."

I take a seat on the arm of the opposite side of the couch, facing him. "Seriously?"

"After six years, I'd almost thought I'd made you up," he says softly. "I went a little nuts when I saw you on TV. Thought I might be hallucinating or something, so I looked up your team schedule and saw that you were playing nearby. I thought my manager was going to burst a blood vessel when I asked him to invite a whole football team to a sold-out show."

"No one could figure out why we were here, but you made a lot of guys really happy."

"And you?"

I blink back at him, not sure what to say. I decide to go with honesty. "I don't really know how to feel."

"That's fair," he says. "It's been a long time, and I kind of…"

"Ghosted?" I fill in for him. "Absconded like a thief in the night?" I raise my eyebrows, hoping he can see the amusement there and not just my disappointment. I don't think I'm ready to admit just how much that night affected me.

"Look, I…" He takes a breath. "I should have left a note. I wanted to," he adds quickly, words tumbling out now. "I woke up every day for weeks replaying what I should have done, and I thought–" He cuts himself off, scrubs a hand over his mouth, then shakes his head like he's annoyed with himself for rambling. "I don't want it to sound like I'm making excuses, because I'm not. I left myself with nothing but regrets."

"What happened, then?" I can't help but ask.

"We'd played a show earlier that night near the Boardwalk. The next morning, I woke up to dozens of texts. A producer had been at the show and wanted to bring us to New York to discuss a recording contract. Everything went really fast after that."

"My life was pretty busy, too," I say, choosing not to mention the days I'd stayed behind, hoping he'd come back. "I was drafted the next week." I remember the hotel room in the city, how loud it was. I remember lying awake with the air conditioner blasting because sometimes I could pretend that I could hear the ocean.

"We were in New York at the same time and didn't even know it," he says, sounding amused but a little pained.

My chest lurches at the thought, and I almost admit that I'd gone looking for him, that I'd made Shawna call everyone she knew to ask who the green-eyed stranger with the guitar was. That I sat out on the beach for hours and willed him to walk back to the very spot we'd first noticed each other.

"You look different," he remarks. "Bigger." His gaze drops and snaps back up like he didn't mean to say that out loud. His lips stretch into a crooked smile.

Heat flashes up my neck. I want to tell him he seems bigger too. Larger than life, even more than he seemed back then. He's sharper around the edges now. Cockier. Dangerous, even. And gorgeous in a way that makes me feel like the world is spinning too fast. Instead, I say, "You have more piercings," and focus my eyes on the piercings in his nose and eyebrow.

It sounds dumb, considering everything about him, from the color of his hair to the way he holds himself, is different. I'm looking at a completely different person, but I still see the boy I met in the green of his eyes and the shape of his mouth.

"Quite a few more," he says, and either I'm mistaken or he's flirting with me. I try to arrange my face into a semblance of a smile rather than gawking at what he might be insinuating. He winks and I nearly choke.

The door bursts open without warning, saving me from what I'm sure would have been an awkward response to his blatant come-on. A harried staffer pokes their head in. "Jess, they need you back for press photos. Please."

Jesse grimaces but doesn't argue. "I'll be right there."

When the door shuts, he looks back at me with urgency in his eyes. He stands, and so do I, my posture stiffening when he takes a few long strides to close the distance between us.

"Without coming on too strong, I'd really like the chance to get to know you. For real this time. I know we've both got crazy schedules, but maybe we can get together sometime soon?"

"Okay," I say. "Yeah, that might be nice."

"Might be?" He smirks. "I'll take it. Can I see your phone?"

I hand it to him and watch him enter his number and then send himself a text. When he hands it back, I notice he added himself as "Ghost". My breath hitches a little.

Someone knocks on the door, and Jesse groans. He places a hand on my arm and leans in slowly. His breath tickles across my cheek. "Text me. Please," he says, his lips grazing the corner of my mouth.

"I will," I promise.

Because I know I will. Even though the cautious parts of me are screaming that he's trouble, I know without a doubt that I can't resist the man in front of me. This close, he's… inevitable.

And then he's gone, swept back into the chaos that is his rockstar life, leaving me in the quiet hum of a room that smells faintly of cloves, cinnamon, and sweat.

———

The team bus idles outside. AJ leans halfway out the open door like he's been waiting for me and might come haul me in by the ear.

"Where the hell have you been?" He asks the moment I get close enough. His eyes are questioning and weirdly excited. "Dude, it almost looked like Jesse Moore really ran off stage and sprinted after you like some kind of corny rom-com."

"I don't know what you're talking about," I say, because I don't have a better response prepared. "Get on the bus, León." My voice comes out hoarser than I intend, and I can tell he senses weakness. He clocks it and makes a show out of pressing his lips together, but his smile tells me it's not going to hold for long.

I drop into the seat beside him and busy myself with my phone to avoid his gaze. There's already a message from Jesse.

Ghost: If it wasn't obvious enough, I'm really glad we found each other again.

Me: You mean, that you found me, tracked me down, and set up an elaborate ploy to corner me instead of just sending an email like a normal person?

The three little dots that indicate he's typing pop up immediately.

Ghost: Semantics.

Ghost: I considered it, honestly. I was worried you wouldn't respond.

Me: That's fair.

Ghost: OUCH

Me: I probably wouldn't have thought you were real.

Ghost: I'm real. And looking forward to proving it to you.

Me: Forward, much?

Ghost: We've already seen each other naked. What is there to be shy about?

I almost choke. AJ leans over to see what I'm looking at, but I cover the screen.

"Man, mind your business."

"Are you really not going to tell me what happened back there? Do you, like, know him or something?"

"Who?"

AJ glares at me like I'm an idiot. Jesse and I didn't discuss what, if anything, we should tell other people. I know I don't want my relationship with him, or whatever this is, out in public. There's not a chance in hell I could maintain my peaceful, private life if I'm connected to a famous rockstar. Jesse probably feels the same.

Anyway, I don't think I should be talking or even thinking too hard about it when I have no idea where this is going or if it'll lead anywhere at all. Hell, I might never see him again for all I know.

But I hope I do.

Back at our hotel for the night, it takes practically slamming the door in AJ's face to get him off my back. I had to feign being more tired than I am to get him to leave me alone, because he was hard set on coming in and hanging out instead of going out with the rest of the guys. I know he's curious and wants answers, but I don't have any right now.

I shower, pull on pajama pants, and brush my teeth in a daze. Jesse has sent me a couple more messages, but I've put off opening them until I was alone. Now I'm putting them off out of sheer nerves. I can't lie to myself and say I'm not intrigued—or at least a little turned on—by his directness. After all, he's right. We definitely have seen each other naked. And while it might have been six years ago, it's still a memory that burns hot in the back of my mind. Not to mention that Jesse is… *damn*. Jesse is danger-ously sexy.

Before I look at his texts, I decide to search his name and see if I can learn a little more about him. The screen floods with an endless list of fan sites, show clips, paparazzi photos. Gossip sites, especially, are obsessed with him. And it looks like he's given them plenty to work with.

By all accounts, Jesse Moore lives the stereotypical "sex, drugs, and rock and roll" lifestyle people expect from someone in his business. Wild parties, drunken escapades, sex scandals. There are grainy photos of him making out with men and women alike and even articles about him getting caught having sex in public. Article after article. Picture after picture.

Well, there's no worry about him being closeted. I scoff. The thought isn't exactly reassuring. I'm not comfortable with this level of publicity, no matter who he's with.

Every headline and picture documenting Jesse's wild lifestyle makes my stomach twist. It's not that I'm judging Jesse for his lifestyle–he seems to enjoy himself, and that's all fine and good. But it isn't me.

Maybe Jesse wouldn't mind rumors tying him to me, but me being connected to him would definitely blow up my quiet life overnight. It has nothing to do with being outed, either. I've never considered what it would be like to be publicly out, but I don't really care what people think about my sexuality. I just don't want the attention.

And being tied to a hard-partying rockstar who regularly makes tabloid front pages? That's a lot of attention, and the wrong kind at that.

When I finally open Jesse's most recent texts, the flirty words don't give me a fluttery nervous feeling anymore. The butterflies are rocks in the pit of my stomach now.

Maybe I'm more judgmental than I thought. All I can think about is why someone like Jesse–someone rich and famous that could have anyone he wants eating out of the palm of his hand–

would be interested in pursuing me? Then again, maybe our first meeting wouldn't lead him to think I'm as boring as I really am.

I stare at the glow of my phone screen, the words blurring together. My chest tightens. I don't know how to feel. All this curiosity and excitement over reconnecting with this person I've fantasized about for six years. But there's a confused sadness welling up with the realization that there's no happily ever after for us.

What could Jesse even want with me, other than a roll in the sheets? Will the passion that brought us together so long ago still be there? Or will what I have to offer seem boring by comparison?

Do I really want to put myself out there for another one-night stand when my first encounter wrecked me so thoroughly?

LeST is
MooRE

SIX
LUC

The game on Sunday against the Bills is another win. It wasn't pretty. It was one of those ugly, hard-fought games where every yard feels like a fistfight, but we pulled it off. The roar of the crowd is still ringing in my ears just as loudly as the music from the *Lest is Moore* show. My thoughts are still louder.

Between snaps, in the huddle, even in those long seconds when I'm crouched on the line waiting for the ball, I keep wondering if Jesse's watching. He said he would.

It's stupid and distracting, but I can't shake the thought of him somewhere with a TV tuned into the game, green eyes fixed on the screen. *On me.*

After the post-game handshakes and locker room chaos, we shuffle through the after-game obligations. I don't usually talk to the press, but I hang back longer than I normally do, standing in the background of Monty's sideline interview. I get a once-over by the trainers due to a hard tackle in the third quarter, but I'm fine. The coaches pull us in for a quick post-game congratulatory talk, and then we head for showers. Several of my teammates have more press obligations before we head out for dinner, where half the team orders enough food to feed an entire army. By the time we get back to the hotel, it's after nine and my body feels like I've been hit by a truck.

My phone buzzes while I'm peeling off my suit jacket.

> Ghost: Congrats on the win. You were a beast out there.

A grin tugs at my mouth before I can stop it. I thumb back a quick **thanks**, hit send–and nearly drop the phone when it immediately lights up with his name. *Jesse's calling me?*

"Hey," I answer, my voice rough.

"Hey yourself," he says. His tone is warm, teasing. "It sounds quiet where you are, I'd assumed you'd be out celebrating."

"I'm just getting in after the team dinner."

"Where are you headed to next?"

I shake my head, even though he can't see me. "My bed," I grumble. "I'm in for the night."

There's a pause. "Isn't it only eight o'clock where you are?"

"It's after nine," I correct him, amused. I lean against the desk and pull my feet out of my shoes.

"It's still early. Are you sick?" He sounds legitimately worried.

"No, why?"

"I just expected you'd be out celebrating with the guys from your team. Or is that not a thing for football players?"

"It depends on what else we have going on, but a few usually go out. It's not really my thing."

"So the great Luc Martín is a homebody? Or are you just not a people person?"

"Little column A, little column B."

He laughs. "So what is it you do like?"

"I like to read. And I like old camp films."

He chuckles. "I kind of love that. It's not what I was expecting, but also somehow isn't surprising after only having met you twice." I can hear the smile in his voice. "Naz reads a lot too. Maybe the two of you can trade book recommendations."

"Are you not much of a reader yourself?" I ask. It occurs to me how very normal this conversation is, and that in of itself feels strange, but this was what I wanted. We're getting to get to know each other.

"I try," he says. "But I've got the attention span of a gnat. I pick it up, get very into it, then have to put it down for whatever reason, sometimes just because I saw something shiny. Once I put it down, I forget everything and then have to start it over to remember the plot. Rinse and repeat."

"So what do you do with your free time then? What does a famous rockstar do other than the whole sex, drugs, and rock and roll thing?" The words are out before I can stop myself. I don't know why I said it. I guess to remind myself who I'm talking to.

"Well, true free time isn't something I come across often, which honestly might be for the best," he laughs. "I work on music almost constantly, no matter what I'm doing. I'm always jotting down notes of my thoughts or lyrics or even just vibes. And lately I've been swimming."

"Swimming?" That body makes sense now.

"Yeah. Most hotels have pools and can be persuaded to let me use them overnight. It keeps me from climbing the walls if I can't sleep."

"Do you have trouble sleeping?"

"Sometimes," he answers, but the way he says it gives me the impression he has issues more often than not.

"Are you good friends with your bandmates? I mean, I read that you and the drummer–that's Naz, right? I read that y'all have known each other since childhood."

"He's my best friend, and the other guys really are, too. We're all close."

"And where are they tonight? I'm not keeping you, am I?"

"Not at all. It's just after eleven where I am, so they're most likely out at a club."

"You wouldn't rather be off having fun with them?"

"Not really my scene anymore. I still go out with the guys some-times, but I'd rather talk to you."

"Even though I'm an anti-social homebody?"

His laugh is infectious. "Yes, even so."

He tells me about their upcoming single dropping while I get changed for bed and brush my teeth. I usually like to shower again, but I don't want to hang up, so I stay on the line. While I'm settling into bed, he asks me about football and the places I've gone. He seems fascinated by my life, despite the fact that he's had a much more interesting one. The places he's traveled, the people he's met, the things he's seen.

I cannot for the life of me imagine what someone so extraordinary could find interesting about me. But we talk for hours, about everything and nothing, much the way we did the night we met. It's so easy.

If only it could be so easy to associate the man I'm talking to on the phone with the very different person I see in the photos and gossip. I know most of the tabloid stuff is likely made up if not grossly exaggerated. It just feels like there's so much more evidence to support the public image of Jesse Moore than the person he's presenting to me.

Still, I fall asleep to his voice describing the time he purposefully got lost in the crowds of Seoul, Korea. Or at least tried to, but he's six-foot-two and one of the most recognizable people on earth, and it was harder to blend into the crowd than he'd anticipated. Long story short, he made friends with an old woman who runs a street food booth and still sends her cards and visits her whenever they're anywhere close by. She apparently makes the best kimchi pancakes he's ever eaten in his life, and even though I have no idea what that is, I love listening to him talk about all the random friends he's met and continues to stay in touch with.

For the rest of the week, it becomes almost routine for him to call in the evenings when I get home after practice. I find myself looking forward to sinking into the velvety comfort of his voice and hearing what he and the band have been up to.

———

Despite being the beginning of October, the heat index is well into the nineties, making today's practice brutal. All of us are dragging, and it doesn't help that we don't have a game this weekend, so no one has much motivation, either. We're all ready for our days off.

Other than our general sluggishness, it's business as usual. Pads slap, whistles blow, voices bark back and forth across the field. AJ jogs beside me as we rotate through drills.

"How's the fam, Martín?" he asks, tossing me the ball to reset.

I grin. "They're doing well. The girls are keeping Dad on his toes, as always."

"You're probably heading out to visit them for the bye week, yeah?"

Instead of answering, I gesture for him to line up to run the drill again.

I usually head home to visit my dad, sisters, and Shawna when we have any breaks, but I'm not sure what my plans are yet.

I've been talking to Jesse almost every night. Sometimes texts, sometimes hours on the phone until one of us falls asleep. It's crazy how fast it's become routine.

He wants to meet, to hang out in person, since he's going to be within reasonable traveling distance of Shreveport on my bye week. I'm pretty sure he means for it to be a date. He's never once pressed me or made me uncomfortable, but he's nothing if not unapologetically flirty.

I keep going back and forth over whether or not this is a date, and how comfortable I am with it. There's a big part of me that wants it, but worry chews at me. Jesse lives such a loud, public lifestyle. He can't go anywhere without being recognized, and the paparazzi go nuts whenever he's caught spending time with anyone. Every time he smiles at someone, fan theories and speculation erupt. I was surprised to learn, during one of our many late-night talks, that half of the people he's been "shipped" with are barely more than acquaintances. He's a friendly guy, and it gets blown out of proportion a lot. He told me this like it was no big deal. Probably because he's so used to it. Little does he know that it's the one thing keeping me from forming any sort of real relationship with him, platonic or otherwise. I've loved our conversations and getting to know the man behind the fame. I can even trust it when he tells me that the hard-partying lifestyle he'd fallen into is something he's trying to put behind him. He told me about rehab, something that their new manager and PR team were able to keep out of the press.

There is so much to like about Jesse, but seeing him in person makes me nervous. It's easy to get to know him over the phone, to learn about the person he is while keeping him at arm's length. I'm not sure I can maintain that space in person, though. Even on the phone, whether he's being flirtatious or not, his voice does things to me. He makes my skin feel alive and electric, my blood hot, and my libido has never been this strong. Seriously, who gets a boner while listening to a story about the time Jesse and one of his bandmates got arrested for public intoxication?

I definitely don't fit into his world. Still, I can't stop looking forward to seeing him.

AJ tries to catch up more on our way to the showers after practice, but he's easily distracted and I manage to talk around the answer until it's time to go. He tries to ask me if I want to hang out or go have dinner, but I mutter something about being tired and slip away before he can press any further. I know I'm being an asshole friend. I'm just not ready to talk about everything that's been going on, and I know AJ. If he even gets a whiff of me still being in contact with Jesse after that concert, he'll never let it go. He's barely stopped asking me about the night of the concert as it is.

Driving home, I glance up at a digital billboard flashing an ad for a radio station announcing *Lest Is Moore*'s hot new single. Jesse's face, all smoky eyes and silver hair, lights up the sign.

How is it that I never noticed his face and voice everywhere? Maybe subconsciously I did and that's why I could never forget him. Now that I've noticed, it's a floodgate. It's like he's everywhere now. Like I couldn't escape him even if I wanted to.

Almost as soon as I walk through my front door, my phone rings.

"Do you have my apartment bugged so you know exactly when I walk in the door?

"You're predictable," Jesse says when I answer, and I can hear the grin in his voice.

"Am not. I'll have you know that I almost went out with AJ tonight," I lie. He probably knows I'm full of shit, too. He certainly laughs like he does.

"You are, but I love that about you. Have you thought about the weekend?"

I close my eyes. "Yeah. I'm free. Let's meet up."

"Really?"

A little cheer goes up in the background, and at first, I think it's a reaction to my acceptance of the maybe-date, but that would be weird. Then I remember the single dropped today, and they're obviously celebrating.

"I take it the new single is doing well," I say, wanting to make sure he knows it's okay for him to go celebrate instead of talking to me for hours.

Noise erupts on his end—laughter, voices, a cork popping. "Hold on," he says, and my phone beeps. I click the icon to accept a video call, and suddenly I'm looking at his face. His hair is damp, skin glowing, eyes bright. Behind him is a skyline, people bustling around, champagne bottles everywhere.

"You remembered," he beams. "And yeah, we're top of the charts." More cheers in the distance and people waving into the phone around and behind Jesse.

"Congratulations," I say, awkward but genuine.

"I wish you were here," he says simply, and I smile back.

I'm happy for him. I really am, but all the champagne popping and luxury and fanfare around him just remind me of how different our worlds are.

LeST is MooRE

SEVEN
LUC

Come Sunday, I'm a nervous wreck. I'm excited but also overthinking everything. He's picking me up later this afternoon.

He's picking me up.

That definitely makes this a date, right? I mean, it could still be a date if we were just meeting there, but it's more ambiguous. There's no way this isn't a date if he's coming to pick me up. Knowing makes me more excited and more nervous. I'm both. A lot of both.

I'm freaking out a little. I've already tried on three outfits, and I still have a whole day ahead of me, so it doesn't even make sense to be getting dressed yet. Especially since he just called to tell me he needs to switch up our plans because something came up with the band. Several hours before he's supposed to pick me up, because yeah, he's picking me up. *That absolutely makes this a date, right?*

He said there's been a little issue but he promised that he's working on it. I told him we can reschedule. I have tomorrow off, too, and his next big interview isn't until Thursday, but he refused. He insisted he'll make it happen, just that some of the plans are changing.

By the time five o'clock rolls around, I'm pacing my condo. I've probably taken four showers today, and after trying on almost every item of clothing I own, I broke down and went to a department store. A very helpful store associate took pity on me and helped me pick out a nice pair of light grey chinos and a soft, navy-blue sweater that I'm worried is too snug, but she insisted it was perfect.

I'm just about to change out of the sweater and wear the plan white button-up I wear with my game day suits, when my phone rings. It's him.

"Go outside," he says. "There's a car waiting."

Sure enough, a luxury sedan with tinted windows idles at the curb. A driver holds the door open. I climb in, pulse thudding, expecting Jesse to be inside.

The seat is empty except for a single long-stemmed flower, red with edges tipped in yellow, and a folded, handwritten note.

Just go with it. See you soon.

The flower reminds me of fire, and I wonder if it's an intentional nod to the night we met, but that might be a stretch. It was probably just the flashiest long-stemmed flower at the florist shop, and it's doubtful he even chose it himself.

I stare at it, twirling the stem in my fingers while the chauffeur closes me in and walks around to the driver's seat. He gives me a quick introduction, telling me his name is Harry, and that we don't have far to go. My nerves climb with every turn the car makes. Ten minutes later we're pulling onto a tarmac where a helicopter waits, blades thumping in the night air. I gape at the driver when he stops and comes around to open my door.

"You're kidding, right?"

The driver just smiles and escorts me over to the pilot, who buckles me in, puts a headset on me, and gives me a short rundown about safety. He says our flight should be around two hours.

"Where are we headed?" I ask, stunned.

"Dallas," the pilot says with a grin.

Dallas?

"As in Texas?"

He chuckles and straps himself in, flicking a bunch of buttons. The propellers are almost as loud as the blood rushing in my ears. Is this really happening?

As the helicopter lifts, I look back at the hired car that brought me here, still parked to the side of the tarmac, watching us take off. I strongly consider getting out and asking the driver to take me back home, but I stay frozen in my seat. The ground drops away beneath us, lights shrinking, and I dig my nails into the palms of my hands hard enough to hurt.

The helicopter eats up the miles faster than I can process them. The view is unreal. The sun bleeding into the horizon, the world falling away in pinks and golds, but I barely notice. My head is too full of so many questions and doubts. Even more than that, Jesse's smile is burned behind my eyelids.

By the time the pilot's voice crackles through my headset, I'm wound so tight my shoulders ache. "We'll be descending soon."

I glance out the window. Below, a city unfurls in sprawling, twinkling lights. We circle a tall, glassy skyscraper, sleek lines glinting in the dusk. At the very top, tiny figures cluster near a glowing helipad.

As we draw closer, I make out Jesse's two bodyguards, and Jesse himself. My chest constricts.

Wind whips his hair into chaos, strands flashing silver under the floodlights. He's wearing dark jeans and a black button-down, several buttons undone, pale chest and inked skin catching in the glow. My mouth goes dry, heat crawling up the back of my neck. I shift in my seat, restless, as the skids touch down.

The door swings open. One of the bodyguards jogs over and opens my door, steadying me with a firm hand as I step out. We duck under the thundering blades together, and then suddenly I'm standing in front of him.

Jesse.

Time seems to slow, every sound muffled under the rush of blood in my ears. He steps forward without hesitation and catches my hand in his, fingers warm, grip sure. His smile is blinding, so bright it knocks the air out of me.

I blink, dazed, and without giving myself permission, I'm smiling back. I can't help it. Despite every reservation, every warning siren in my head, there's something about him that draws me in.

Jesse leads me off the roof and to an elevator while I stare at the way he holds my hand so casually. The ride is short, maybe a floor or two, but my chest is pounding like we're scaling the whole damn building. The elevator is permeated with the sweet, spicy smell of him.

The doors slide open to a gleaming marble foyer, recessed lights washing the walls in a warm glow. A huge abstract painting dominates one wall, all jagged shapes and fiery streaks of red. My shoes squeak faintly on the polished stone, the sound weirdly loud in the hush.

He guides me into a living space that looks like something out of a magazine. The room stretches two stories tall, floor-to-ceiling windows looking down on a dazzling display of city lights at night. A massive fireplace stands in the center, detached like an art piece, flames flickering low and steady. Candles burn everywhere, soft points of light giving the room an ethereal, romantic glow.

A plush sectional faces the hearth, and on the glass coffee table sits a glass bowl of what looks like candy wrapped in red cellophane, and a vase of flowers–the same red and yellow blooms from the car, their edges glowing like the fire behind them. On the other side of the fireplace, a formal dining area is half-hidden in shadow. To the side, a sleek black wet bar gleams, and something that is either a very uncomfortable-looking stone chair or a sculpture holds a row of candles too.

What grabs my attention is the small table set for two right in front of the windows. Candlelight pools around polished silver, the city glittering behind it like another world.

I stop dead. My heart skips, then stutters into a strange, fast rhythm. *Definitely a date then*, if I had any lingering doubts.

Jesse is watching me, waiting for a reaction. When I can't quite get my brain online fast enough to process the last several hours, he steps in front of me.

"Is it too much?"

"It's…" I swallow hard. "You didn't have to go through all this trouble. It seems like a lot."

He grimaces. "I knew it was too much as soon as Randall called me to say you'd gotten on the chopper. He said you looked terrified."

"Terrified is a bit of an exaggeration." *Terrified isn't strong enough of a word.*

Jesse huffs out a laugh like he knows I'm full of shit. "I really hope I haven't scared you off or anything. I know I can be a lot. I get these little ideas and just kind of--*go*." He throws up his hands a little with the last word, then grimaces again. "Please don't run away." His tone is playful, like he's joking, but the worry in his bright green eyes is real.

"What was the original plan?" I ask with an awkward laugh.

"Well, originally I wanted to come to you and take you somewhere in Shreveport. I rented out a botanical garden and had a catering company set up a table in one of the greenhouses. Right next to those," he says, pointing at the red and yellow flowers.

"That's the same flower that was in the car, right?"

"It's called a flame lily. Anything that looks like fire reminds me of you."

My brow creases. He's really comfortable putting it all out there, isn't he?

"So you sought them out in Shreveport of all places? That's... elaborate. Do you do anything small?"

A wide grin crosses his face. "Not for you, I don't."

"And here I wasn't sure if this was a date or not," I say sarcastically, rolling my eyes at his forwardness and trying not to smile. Damn it, why do I have to be like that?

He steps closer, running a finger along the neckline of my sweater. "Oh, this is *definitely* a date. And for the record, I'm trying to be a good boy. I told myself I wasn't going to try to get in your pants, but then you showed up looking like," he gestures to all of me, "and now I can't control the flirt."

I choke out a laugh. "You're ridiculous."

Jesse cocks his head, then slowly drops his gaze down my body again. "Would you like a drink? The bar is fully stocked."

"I thought you said you don't drink anymore."

"I don't, but that doesn't mean you can't."

"Trying to loosen me up?" I smirk.

He scrunches up his nose like the thought offends him. "Okay, nothing from the bar then. There are a few options in the fridge. I have sweet tea in case you're one of those southerners, and there's soda, sparkling water–"

"Sparkling water is fine, thanks."

I follow him into the darker part of the suite, which seems to go on forever. Recessed lighting comes on automatically as we walk.

Jesse gestures for me to sit at the kitchen island while he prepares two sparkling waters with lime wedges and hands one to me. He holds his up and I tap mine against it, repeating his murmured, "To new beginnings."

I take a sip and look back to where the small table is glowing on the other side of the suite. It looks like something out of a cheesy *Hallmark* movie. The scene feels intimate and deliberate. I can't decide how to feel about how hard he's trying. It's kind of endearing, though.

"You know," he says, catching my attention again by guiding me back towards the table. "Aside from potentially chasing you off with my slightly over-the-top gesture–"

"Slightly?"

"Aside from that," he continues, shoulders shaking with laughter. "I kind of like how this has worked out. I have you all to myself now."

My throat goes dry. "You say that like we're already dating."

His green eyes lock onto mine, steady and unflinching. "I'd be okay with that."

My chest tightens, sharp and aching. Butterflies claw their way up, threatening to spill out. I clear my throat, trying to get control. He's obviously joking.

I chuckle, but I'm sure it sounds strained. "I'm not sure how that would work, considering our schedules. And how would we go anywhere and not get mobbed?"

The whole reason our date was changed is because their fans figured out where they were staying and basically mobbed the hotel. A security guard, as well as a bellhop, were injured in the fray. Not only did the band have to sneak out of the hotel and check into a new place across town, but Jesse and his bandmates went to visit the injured people at the hospital. They actually had to wear disguises and everything. Luckily, everyone is going to be okay, but I can't imagine how scary that would be

His grin tilts sideways, playful but careful. "I'm not gonna out you, if that's what you're worried about. And I'm not asking you to marry me. It's just dinner. I really do want to get to know you."

A beat passes. I nod once. "I want to get to know you too. I just–I don't really like attention. Publicity isn't really my thing."

Jesse chuckles. "Big football star doesn't like attention? How exactly does that work?"

I roll my eyes, but I'm used to getting teased about this. "I'm a football *player*, not a football star. I went pro to help my family, and it's really the only thing I've ever been good at."

He steps closer, heat radiating off him, warm spice curling into my lungs. His hand lifts, cupping my jaw like he's been waiting years to do it. "I'm pretty sure I remember you being good at a lot of things," he says, his voice low.

His green eyes bore into me, and he moves in close enough I can feel the brush of his breath. I close my eyes and lean forward.

When his lips touch mine, my skin ignites. Goosebumps erupt over every inch of my skin, electricity buzzing all the way down to my toes and snapping back up to my scalp. It's like I've been plunged into a pool of static.

The kiss deepens almost immediately, like we've both been holding our breath for six years and finally let it out at the same time. Jesse's mouth is hot and insistent, tasting faintly of cinnamon and something darker I can't place. It's enough to make my knees threaten to give. Surprisingly, I don't notice his tongue piercing right away, but once my tongue touches it, I feel feral. A jolt of pure desire shoots down my spine, and I kiss him deeper, wanting more. I lick deep into his mouth, chasing the piercing like I could wrap my tongue around it. Jesse groans, and I know I'm done for.

He takes the drink from my hand and sets it on the table without breaking the kiss. My hand fists in the fabric of his shirt, fingers brushing the warm skin underneath where it hangs open. His chest is hard under my palm, and I can feel the rapid beating of his heart. He makes a noise low in his throat that sparks something hungry in me.

He presses closer, walking me backwards, our mouths crashing together again and again in sloppy, urgent kisses that make me feel twenty-one all over again. My teeth catch his lower lip. His hand slides from my jaw down to my waist, curling in my sweater like he's daring me to pull away.

I don't. I can't.

The room tilts as he urges me deeper into the suite, surrounded by flickering firelight and glass and shadow. We bump into something solid–his hip hitting the edge of a table, a glass rattling. He doesn't notice, and we don't stop.

By the time my calves hit the edge of the sofa, I'm breathless, pulse hammering like I sprinted from Shreveport rather than flew. He pushes gently, urging me down until I sink onto the plush cushions. He follows, a knee pressing between mine, mouth never leaving mine, hands braced on either side of me like he's caging me in.

It's overwhelming. The city lights blazing beyond the windows, the fire crackling behind us, the relentless spinning of the world's axis as our kiss spirals hotter, rougher. Jesse's tongue slides against mine almost desperately, kissing me like he's afraid I'll vanish if he stops.

I'll worry about what all of this means later. For now, I let myself forget everything–the cameras, the chaos, the way our worlds don't line up. For now, it's just us, tangled in heat and memory and the kind of want that swallows me whole.

With trembling hands, I grip Jesse's body, fingers digging into his thigh as I pull him flush against me. He fits against me perfectly, every angle of him pressing in, melting into the curve of my body like he belongs there. I arch up into him without thinking, a groan escaping before I can choke it back.

He swallows it like fuel, and it ignites him. One hand sliding into my hair, the other gripping my waist where the hem of my sweater has ridden up. His thumb strokes absent circles over my Adonis belt, sending shivers racing up my spine. My hands wander without thought, over his ass and up the firm line of his back under the silky fabric of his shirt.

It's terrifying how easy this is. How natural it feels to touch him, to get lost in him, to ache for more from someone who is still little more than a stranger.

The room blurs. City lights outside bleed into the flicker of candles, the crackling of the fire muffled by the rush of blood in my ears. The only thing I can focus on, the only thing sharp and real, is Jesse. The rasp of his breath against my cheek, the softness of his skin against mine, the way he drags his teeth across my bottom lip before sucking it into his mouth.

My head tips back against the sofa, surrendering myself to his touch. He kisses down my throat, biting softly where my pulse jackhammers. I gasp, hips jerking, and he answers with a growl that vibrates against my skin, grinding his pelvis against mine.

It's too much. It's not enough.

I'm seconds away from coming in my pants. My hands fist in his shirt, tugging him closer, until there's nothing between us but heat and the dangerous wish that there were no layers of clothes between us as we writhe against each other.

I could lose myself in him all over again and never come up for air.

It's a sobering thought that pulls me back just enough for the realization that if I don't stop us now, I won't have the strength to. My self-control is thin and frayed, close to snapping at the feel of his hot, insistent mouth moving down my neck, his fingers reaching between me to unfasten the button of my jeans.

"Jesse–" My voice cracks. I bring my hands up to his chest to push him away, but the feeling of a rumble moving through him has me digging my fingers into his shirt and holding on. I'm not pushing him away like I should, but I've stopped him from going further.

"Fuck. Say it again," he rasps, his voice little more than a desperate growl. "Say my name again."

"Jesse…"

"Luc," he gasps, trembling, like the sound of his name on my lips is enough to push him over the edge. He drops his head onto my shoulder and shudders.

God help me, that makes it even harder to breathe. I move a hand from his chest to the back of his head, gripping his hair to pull him up so I can look into his eyes. His eyes are darker and dilated, wild and desperate. He looks as wrecked as I feel.

I forget all about caution or slowing down. Instead, I pull him down to slam my mouth against his. I suck his tongue into my mouth and play with the ball on the underside. My other hand slides around his waist and down the back of his jeans, gripping his ass and guiding him to grind against me while I roll my hips into him. One thrust, then two, fingernails digging into skin. Three, and…

He lets out a choked moan, and I swallow it down hungrily, giving in to the warm pleasure building at the base of my spine. My release follows his, warm, wet cum drenching the inside of my briefs. We both gasp for breath, moaning as we rub ourselves together, riding out the wave of pleasure unlike anything I've felt since that night six years ago.

EIGHT
JESSE

I lean against the balcony rail, a clove cigarette burning between my fingers, the smoke curling up into the night. Below me, the city sprawls in a scatter of glittering lights, endless and alive, but I can't focus on anything but the echo of Luc's mouth on mine, his body beneath me, the sounds he made as he came undone. My chest still hums with it, like the aftershock of a song that won't stop playing.

I drag in another breath of spice and smoke, let it fill my lungs, then exhale slowly. I should feel satisfied. Instead, I feel restless. I should've drawn it out longer, or something. Thought ahead so he wouldn't be in the bathroom right now trying to clean himself up. I could've done that for him.

With my mouth.

Behind me, the glass door slides open, and Luc steps onto the balcony. He looks damn near perfect again, not a hair out of place, except for the faint blush that hasn't left his cheeks since he excused himself.

He glances at the cigarette in my hand and smells the air. "Clove?"

I nod.

"Makes sense."

"Does it bother you?" I reach for the ashtray to put it out.

"No. I actually kind of like it. You sort of smell like Christmas."

I laugh. My eyes fall to his pants. They're the same ones he was wearing before and not the sweatpants I'd set on the counter for him. I lift an eyebrow.

"They were salvageable," he mutters, clearly embarrassed. "Mostly." I notice him tugging his sweater down a little in the front, and I am desperate to know what he's hiding.

"Well, now I feel underdressed," I tease. I changed into a pair of low-slung black sleep pants and left my shirt unbuttoned.

He shakes his head in amusement, but I don't miss the way his eyes rake down my body. I stub out the clove in the ashtray, forcing my hand to steady, and bite my lip. "Hungry?"

Luc's cheeks darken even more, and I'm pretty sure I hear the slightest intake of breath when I step forward. He doesn't move an inch as I take the few steps to cross the balcony. My hand brushes over his waist as I pass him and walk into the suite.

Walking over to the small table set with our dinner, I wink and pull out a chair for Luc. He shakes his head, either amused with himself or with me, and takes a seat. I walk away for a moment to refresh our drinks, taking several breaths to calm my racing heart and libido. I nearly trip over my feet as I'm walking back to him, though. He's so fucking gorgeous. The dark blue of his sweater makes his eyes look even deeper than I remember, and goddamn if it doesn't fit him like it was made for him. It makes me want to rub myself against him like a cat.

I've already done that, so I set the drinks down and lift the silver domes from our plates. Steam curls up from perfectly seared salmon with lemon-herb sauce, roasted potatoes, and sauteed green beans with heirloom carrots.

Luc looks surprised, or maybe a little confused. I let out a little huff of laughter, realizing that he probably thinks I have some hidden server or had someone in here while he was in the bathroom. It's been nearly forty-five minutes since he arrived, and the food is still hot.

I tap the hidden warming tray beneath the plates. "I wanted to be sure everything stayed warm enough in case you were delayed or I had to talk you into not running for the hills."

"It looks amazing." He grins and digs in hungrily, which makes me feel a little guilty for distracting him earlier, but not guilty enough to stop wishing we were still tangled up on the couch.

"The chefs here are amazing," I tell him. "Very accommodating, too. I told them my guest is an athlete who prefers to eat clean, and they took it from there."

His face blanches.

"Don't worry," I add quickly. "They don't know who my guest is. No one saw you except the pilot and my bodyguards. And the hotel staff sign strict NDAs. You're safe here."

That seems to help, but there's still a shadow in his expression.

"You still look worried," I point out.

He sets down his utensils, wipes his mouth with a napkin, and takes a sip of sparkling water. I can't stop staring at his mouth. The way his tongue darts out to catch the bead of moisture on his lip, the way his Adam's apple shifts as he swallows.

"How do you live the way you do?" he asks. His voice isn't judgmental. He sounds genuinely curious. "How do you deal with being constantly on display, with people hounding you for every personal detail?"

I go with honesty. "For the most part, we're used to it. But sometimes… yeah, it's hard. Especially when something personal gets leaked. People judge fast. Sometimes it's warranted. Sometimes it isn't."

"Like how?"

I take a breath. "Like when I made a personal decision not to attend my dad's funeral, and the media spread wild stories about me going on a drunken rampage."

"That's awful."

I huff a sardonic laugh. "I didn't even know the guy. The idea of mourning his death around a bunch of people I don't know made me uncomfortable. Not to mention the circus it would have caused at the funeral itself. No one needed that."

Luc's brows are furrowed, but he nods with understanding. "That makes sense to me."

Shrugging, I take a long sip of my drink. "To be fair, I did go and get shitfaced the day I found out about it. There might have been an incident with a bathroom mirror." When I blink down at my hands, I can still see the blood on my knuckles.

"It's not fair that you didn't get the privacy you needed to process that. I can't imagine if it had been like that when my mom passed away a couple of years ago. All I had to deal with was a little speculation over why I'd missed a game. If reporters and photographers had followed me home to her funeral, I would have been sick over it." The pain in his eyes reflects that he loved his mother very much. I'm glad he was allowed to mourn her passing in peace.

"I'm sorry to hear about your mom," I say, reaching out to lay my hand over his.

"Thanks. I'm sorry you went through all of that."

"It was a weird time for me. I was already struggling with… stuff." Now is not the time to detail my faults and failures. I was honest about rehab and being sober, but the last thing I want to do is give him another reason not to trust me by going into the details of my spiral. "I didn't know him, and he certainly didn't know me. He called me after he saw me on TV, playing at the Grammy's for the first time. He didn't even know I was a musician," I snort. I'd called my mom and scolded her for giving that deadbeat credit for the guitar I'd been given for my tenth birthday. I pretty much assumed every gift with his name on it had really just been her. Which hurt even more, because I know she must have worked overtime just to afford it. It wasn't super expensive, just a used and beat up old acoustic she'd found at a pawnshop, but every dollar was stretched in those days.

"How long had it been since you talked to him before that night?"

"A few years," I answer. "When I was a kid, I used to call on his birthday and Father's Day, but then when I got into my teens I realized how one-sided it was. As an experiment, I stopped reaching out, and I didn't hear from him for years. And all he had to say was some snide comment about how it looked like I was wearing a skirt. Which I was, and I didn't give a fuck about his opinion on it, either. I remember looking down at the phone to make sure the call was still connected because he'd gone so quiet, and then laughing and saying, 'It was nice to hear from you, Dad. We should check in again in another four years or so, yeah?' and hung up on him. That was the last time we talked."

My throat feels tight. "When he died, the media made it into this huge thing about me being a hateful, ungrateful son for not going to his funeral. Some tabloids even claimed I showed up and wrecked it, the way we supposedly wreck hotel rooms. Which, by the way, is also not true. But really? He'd already been dead to me for years. I'd already grieved. When I cried, I didn't even know why. Why cry over a stranger?"

When I glance up, I catch a flicker of recognition in Luc's eyes. I smile faintly. "Wait a second–you said you didn't listen to our music."

His lips twitch. "I might have looked you up when we were invited to the concert. And I've maybe listened to a few songs since. Once I knew it was you."

I gape at him. "That's not one of our popular tracks. It's practically obscure. Luc, are you a fan?" I clutch my chest and fake a swoon.

He scoffs. "You wish."

We laugh, and then he asks quietly, "Did writing that song help you process?"

"Yeah," I admit. "That and being shit-faced all the time."

His head tilts curiously. "Is that why you wrote *Remember My Name*?"

I freeze. Somehow, after all this time, it never occurred to me that I'd have to answer for those lyrics.

"It's about that night, isn't it? The bonfire, and… after."

For once, I'm not sure how to answer. How much can I divulge without sounding totally obsessive?

"I wrote the hook on a napkin at a diner the morning after," I admit finally. "Finished the rest on the plane. After our first meeting in New York, Naz found me passed out with a vodka bottle and a notebook open to the lyrics. He suggested we use it for the debut EP."

"Wow. Who would have thought?"

My throat tightens. "It's not the only song about you on that album."

"What other songs?" His curiosity is too sharp to ignore.

"*Make Me Real. The Tide. Take It Back. Pieces. Haunted.*" I don't tell him that nearly every filthy lyric I've ever written came from thinking about him.

He mouths the word *Haunted*, looking unsure. Maybe it's not familiar to him, because he pulls out his phone, types, and scrolls. His lips move as he reads silently, then he reads aloud:

You've haunted me since that night

One touch and I came alive

I'm still burning, I can't make it right

Possess me, bury me, take me

From the silence where you left me behind

Luc frowns. "Left *you* behind?"

I lift my shoulders and make a pitiful cringe face. "Artistic license. The guys thought the song sounded better this way, and I wasn't ready to admit just how pathetic I was."

"So they don't know where the songs came from?"

I shake my head. "Naz does now. I told him after I saw you on TV. He said they'd all assumed I'd been through something that I didn't want to talk about and didn't press."

He's quiet for a long moment, then clears his throat. "I wasn't going to tell you this, but it's funny, actually. I heard *Remember My Name* on the radio or something. It must have been when it first came out because it wasn't too long after… And well, it reminded me of that night. I hated it at first, but then I kept listening. And the more I listened, the lighter I felt. Like someone else knew my pain." He chuckles and rubs a hand over his face, pushing his hair back. "Who would have ever thought it was the song he wrote to get over it."

"It didn't work."

His brow furrows. "What?"

"I never got over it. That night. You. I could show you notebooks full of lyrics and thoughts that never became songs."

He swallows. "I'd kind of like to see that."

"Yeah, no. It would ruin the illusion."

"What illusion?"

"That I'm suave and charming."

He laughs, warm and rumbly, like distant thunder. "Do I really think that?"

"Come on. I brought you here in a helicopter and impressed you with my dry-humping skills. You're practically in love with me already."

He cracks up, shaking his head. Damn if that laugh isn't the most beautiful sound.

I grin and nudge his leg with my bare foot. "Let's go sit on the couch. I'll get dessert."

Luc perks up. "There's dessert?"

"Of course. Looks healthy as hell, but the chefs here are magicians."

He carries our drinks to the sofa, deliberately sitting on the opposite end from where we were tangled up earlier. Maybe intentional, maybe not. I grab a plate of mini fruit tarts from the fridge and set it between us.

"These are almost too pretty to eat," I exclaim, pulling off the label card. "Made with almond flour and no added sugar." What the hell kind of dessert did they set me up with?

"They look delicious."

"If they taste like cardboard, I'm demanding sundaes."

"You're ridiculous. Hand me one."

I hold out the plate, and he takes one, biting in. "Oh, damn. That's really good."

"Damn it."

NINE
JESSE

Luc grins and holds up the other half of one of the tarts, the glaze dripping from his fingers. "Here, try it."

I lean in, open my mouth, and let him feed me. I make a point of wrapping my tongue around his finger, sucking the sweetness from his skin, rolling the smooth metal ball of my piercing along the length of it. His pupils flare wide.

"Mmm," I moan. "That is good."

He grabs another tart, breaks it in half, and offers me a piece. This time I take it from his hand, which I choose to believe he looks disappointed about. I hold it up to feed him instead, smearing glaze across his lips on purpose. "Whoops."

He tries to roll his eyes, but the second I lean in and lick the sweetness from his mouth, he shudders. Our lips crash together, sweet and sticky, until the dessert is forgotten, and it's just us again, tangled in the heat of a kiss. I crawl into his lap, straddling him and holding either side of his face to keep him still, licking deep into his mouth. I noticed earlier that he seems to really like my tongue ring, so I make a point to play with it against his tongue, then lick along his neck and ear. *Just wait until I show you what I can do with it.*

Luc holds me against him and shifts, rolling me beneath him. I hook my legs around his hips, hands sliding under his sweater to feel the solid planes of muscle. His mouth is everywhere, urgent and demanding. All I can think is how impossible it feels that I went six years without feeling like this again.

"Luc–"

"*Mmm?*"

"I know you're a little unsure about the dating thing, but… fuck, Luc, I want you."

A sound rumbles out of him, like a moan but almost growly. I feel it through my sternum and in my groin. He drops his forehead to mine, both of us breathing heavily.

"I want you too, Jesse. I don't know if–"

"We don't have to do anything public," I cut in quickly, my voice husky and desperate. "We can keep it just between us, I promise. Give me a chance? I don't want this to be another one-time thing."

"I don't either."

"Oh, thank fuck–" I crash my mouth into his again, wrapping my arms around his neck. "Now say you'll spend the night?"

Luc's shoulders shake. "Give an inch, take a mile."

"I want you to give me all the inches," I say, dropping my hand between us to make it obvious, just in case it wasn't, what I'm talking about. My palm presses down on his bulge, and he thrusts into my hand. "I want to touch you," I whisper into his mouth.

"You want a lot," he teases, nipping my lip ring.

"Are you going to give it to me?" I say, my voice breaking a little as he licks at my pulse point. A low hum of approval rumbles in his chest.

My fingers slip into his waistband, and when he doesn't seem like he wants to stop me, I push my hand inside and wrap my hand around him. Sighs of pleasure and relief come from both of us.

"Fuck, Luc. You aren't wearing underwear."

"I had to take them off. After earlier." He blushes a little, and goddamn if I don't find the juxtaposition between his confident, sexy teasing and timidity to be wildly endearing.

I don't just want to fuck this man. I want to keep him.

The feel of his hot, smooth, bare skin and the realization that he's been commando for the past two hours makes my cock unbearably hard. I'm reminded of how I regretted not getting him naked earlier. He already ruined his underwear enough to need to take them off, so it's only courtesy that I make sure he doesn't ruin these pants, too.

Pulling my hand from his pants, I push him lightly on the chest, guiding him to sit up before continuing to press him backwards. He falls back against the other end of the sectional, where the two sides meet. He adjusts his legs, allowing me to climb over him, and I get a flash of memory from that first night so long ago. The way he let me take the lead, getting to watch and feel him experience things for the first time.

His blue eyes are dark and intense. Despite the blush, I don't detect any wariness or fear the way I did that first night. I'm sure he's had a lot more experience since then, but I'm determined to make him feel so good, he'll be as obsessed with me as I have been with him for the past six years. I'll fuck him better than anyone ever has, and I'll make this man mine.

Keeping my eyes on his, I trail my fingers down the front of his soft sweater.

"Is this cashmere?" I ask, as my fingers reach the bottom hem and push the fabric up so I can caress the bottom of his stomach.

"Um. I don't know? I had help picking it out."

Do professional athletes use stylists? I hadn't considered it before. Both of the times I've seen him before tonight, he'd been wearing jeans and a t-shirt or henley, which he also looked delicious in, but tonight he looks like a GQ model.

"As perfect as this sweater looks on you, I think we should go ahead and take it off. I'd hate for you to ruin it the way you ruined your panties."

He laughs. "I do not wear panties."

"No? That's a shame. You'd look sinful in satin." I push my hand up the smooth planes of his toned abs and chest. He stops laughing abruptly, blinking up at me as his cheeks darken again. *Fuck, I love that.*

I lean down to brush the shell of his ear with my lips. "I rather enjoy wearing lace myself," I whisper. He lets me maneuver him to remove the sweater, gaping up at me when the fabric is pulled over his head.

My fingers lightly scratch down his sternum and stomach to the waistband of his pants. I tease my fingers along the waistband of his pants, from the outside of his sculpted V to the center fly. I undo the clasp and slowly unzip him, revealing trimmed, dark curls and the exposed head of his cock that he had pulled up in his waistband. Leaning down, I trail my tongue down the same path my hands took, until I'm nosing along the length of his cock, pulling his pants lower to expose him fully. The delicate herbal, citrusy scent of the hotel hand soap has me swooning, imagining him cleaning himself in the bathroom. It could only be better if he'd just left the mess for me to clean up.

"Fuck me, it's even more beautiful than I remember," I murmur as I give the underside a few soft kisses.

Luc lets out a soft, breathy sound that might be a cross between a chuckle and a moan. He can laugh if he wants to, but this thing is fucking glorious. It was dark the first time I saw it, so I couldn't really appreciate it in all its glory. It's long and thick, not massively huge but big enough to make you work for it. My ass clenches, remembering how good he felt inside me.

He's uncut, which I find so fucking hot it borders on fetishization. I wonder if he'd let me play with it?

For now, I focus on getting his pants off so I can get on him.

Finally, he's bare before me, leaning back on the back of the couch and watching me. Jesus, just the way he looks at me could drive me wild. It's so obvious how bad he wants it, yet he waits so patiently.

Slowly, I pull my shirt off and drop it on the floor. I keep my pants on for now. I don't want to give either of us any ideas and get ahead of myself again. I want to taste every inch of him before I take him to bed and ride him until dawn.

I move up his body, trailing hot puffs of breath and light kisses all the way from his ankles to his jaw. My tongue licks along the seam of his lips, which he opens for me, letting me inside and groaning into my mouth when our tongues tangle around each other. I fuck his mouth with my tongue the way I plan to fuck his ass with it, and he rocks his hips, his bare cock rubbing the seam of my ass through my sleep pants. He's hard enough I almost think he could break through the thin material. The thought makes me whimper.

Luc's hands move down my back and into the back of my pants, pushing lower than he did earlier, fully cupping my ass in his big hands. The way he moves me against him makes my cheeks spread enough to feel his hardness against my hole and then close around him. The friction of my cockhead rubbing against the soft waistband of my pants, and his hard cock against my ass has me fucking feral.

Fuck me, I should have taken these fucking pants off!

One hand moves back to the small of my back, then dips low again, this time skimming my crack. Oh, holy hell, I'm a whimpering mess, out of my mind with desperation. One big finger plunges deeper, rubbing right over my hole but not trying to breach it. *Fuuucckkk* I want him to though.

Bringing my hands to his chest, I push myself up, curving my back and pressing against his hand.

Luc groans and I look down into his eyes to say something dirty, but he's not looking at me. His eyes are on the bottom of his stomach, where the tip of my cock has escaped the confines of my sleep pants and left a little puddle of pre-cum on his skin.

Leaning farther back, I dip a thumb into the mess, smearing some of it across his skin, and then bring it to his mouth. I press against his bottom lip, and his eyes dilate.

"If I remember correctly, you liked the taste of my cum," I say, pushing my thumb in a little and then drawing it back. He lifts his head and takes my whole thumb in his mouth, sucking hard and swirling his tongue around the tip.

I push my thumb farther into his mouth, rubbing the back of his tongue. I hope he hasn't gotten so much experience that he doesn't still gag for me. Fuck, I loved him all enthusiastic and unsure like that. His inexperience made it the best oral I've ever gotten. Or maybe it's just him. Even dry humping on the couch was the hottest thing I've done since that night, and I've done some wild stuff.

Luc removes his hand from my ass, and I want to cry. He swipes through the remaining mess on his stomach and returns his finger to my hole, rubbing it in small circles and pressing. I push back and hiss out a "*yesss*" as the tip of his finger breaches me, then whine when he pulls it back out. *Tease.*

His free hand pushes the waistband of my pants down around my balls and wraps around my cock. He pumps me once, then pauses, eyes widening with confusion and maybe a little shock. I bite my lip and give him my most seductive smile, while in the back of my head I say a little prayer that I don't scare him off.

Replacing his hand with my own, I watch his reaction as I pull my cock up to my stomach, showing him the rows of metal balls along the underside of my shaft, starting just below the crown. He gapes, then swallows.

"How does that feel?" he asks huskily, gently running his fingers over each ball.

"For me or for you?"

He blanches, as if he hadn't thought of both of those possibilities, but he definitely looks curious.

"For me, they feel good. I'm more sensitive," I say, rubbing my thumb through the evidence leaking from the tip. "And they make me feel good. More confident, I suppose."

"Just what you needed, more confidence," he teases, still fingering each row of studs. "Why so many?"

My lips quirk. "Well, what looks like ten is actually five," I explain. "Here..." Taking his fingers in mine, I guide him to press on the space between the studs so he can feel the horizontal barbell beneath the skin. When he wraps his hand around me fully and rubs his thumb up and down the space between the studs, I shiver. More pre-cum dribbles out of me, and he uses it to glide his hand up and down my cock, paying special attention to the pierced area. In no time, I'm rocking my hips, thrusting into his hand. After gathering more pre-cum, his finger returns to teasing my hole.

"You didn't answer me," he says, watching as I roll my body on top of him, still trapped in these God-forsaken pants. Damn it, I wish he'd just tear them off of me. The fabric is so thin and soft, he could do it easily. "Why so many?" He repeats, bringing my attention back to the question at hand.

"I, uh–*mmph*–I like them. I got one and then couldn't stop, kept going back every year for another."

"How many do you plan on getting?"

"Luc, I can't think with your finger teasing me like that," I whine, then gasp when he pushes it all the way in, which at this angle is only to the second knuckle.

"Shit, sorry, was that too much?" He tries to pull back, but I lift my hips and all but sit on his hand.

"Don't you fucking dare," I growl, rocking back on his finger. Luc grins salaciously and moves his finger in and out of me.

I have completely lost the plot. I'm supposed to be swallowing his cum, not getting finger-fucked and questioned.

"Answer, Jesse."

"Uh, I–it depends."

"On what?" he asks when I don't clarify.

"On you."

He pauses for a moment and locks a curious gaze on me.

"I'm due for the sixth piercing this coming spring. We'll see if you want me to continue or not."

"This spring?" His brow furrows, some unnamed emotion swirling in his blue eyes. Is he calculating what I meant?

What did I mean? Did I mean if we're still together come spring, because I'm confident we will be. There's something about him, about how this feels, that's right. I think we're meant to be together. That's why I've been haunted by his memory all these years. It's why the universe brought us back together.

Or did I mean that I won't need to mark another year since the night we spent together? I got a tattoo on the anniversary of that night, got high while getting inked, and decided to pierce my dick as punishment for screwing up so badly. Then, in a mixture of liking the piercing more than I anticipated, but also overdramatic pity for myself, I decided to mark each year that went by. I'm not sure what I planned to do once I got to the bottom. Start along the top? Pierce myself until I ran out of surface area and my dick looked alien? No idea. Thinking that far ahead isn't really a habit of mine. It's possible I didn't think I'd live long enough to worry about it.

None of that matters now.

I lean down to kiss him, and he continues his delicious torture. I mewl into his mouth, wishing I had lube out here so he could keep going until he fit all of his fingers in there. And then he could fuck me right here, bent over right in front of the fireplace.

Like he can hear my internal begging, he pulls his finger out of me and spits on it, then holds his hand up for me to do the same. *Goddamn.*

With his spit-drenched fingers, he reaches around me again, pushing not just the one, but two fingers inside me. I moan loudly. He looks at my cock hungrily, his tongue darting out to lick his lips.

"Want to know what they taste like?" I huff, breathing heavily as Luc fucks my asshole with his fingers, a little too close to finding the detonation button. I won't be able to last.

"I want to know what they taste like, and I want to know what they feel like."

Whoa.

The pulse of lust that just went through me was like a shock-wave. It started in my core and radiated to my ass and the tip of my dick. I let out a cry and grit my teeth, not wanting to come yet.

"I'm going to make you feel like you've never felt before," I say, flicking my tongue ring out before forcing it into his mouth again. His groan is deep as he sucks on it.

Before I can pull myself away from him to show him what I mean, his fingers slip out of me. He hooks his arms beneath my thighs and flexes his arms, bringing my cock up to face level. I grip the back of the couch behind him before I fall ass over head onto the floor on the other side and try to get my bearings, but he sucks my cock into his mouth. I tremble.

"Who's showing off now?" I snark weakly through my moaning as Luc continues to get an arm workout, flexing his biceps to hold me up while he fucks his own mouth with my body. "I wanted to do that," I whine, trying to look down. "And I want to see."

Luc slides down the back of the sofa and lets my legs down so I'm hovering over him. My vision goes hazy seeing him like this, his mouth open to take me. I scramble to take my pants off and straddle his chest again.

"Goddamn, Luc. You could not be sexier than you are right now." I rasp and hold myself around the base of my cock. I'm too fucking close. "Stick out your tongue."

He does, and I guide my cock back into his mouth, rubbing the pierced underside along the flat of his tongue. I suck in a breath, trying to hold on just another minute, but then he looks up at me, closes his lips around my cock, and sucks, rolling his tongue along the underside of my shaft, over the piercings.

I shout, and my hips buck, pushing me farther back in his mouth than I meant to go. He gags, then moans, and I'm done. I unload into his throat, vision whiting out.

It takes me a few moments to get my composure after pulling out of Luc's mouth. I all but collapse on him, and he maneuvers us so I'm draped over his body. His hard cock is against my hip, and I can't stand it for long. It's my turn.

Getting off of him and the couch, I boss him into the position I want him in, leaning back in the corner of the sectional. He complies, but he's amused by it.

"Don't get too cocky," he says. "I'm pretty sure I'd sign over my entire life's savings to get your mouth on me."

I bark out a laugh, getting to my knees in front of him, then grabbing his hips and yanking him down farther before guiding him to place his feet on either side of the couch. "I'll get you to sign over more than that by the time I'm through."

He looks like he might try to snark back, but I take his cock in my hand, opening my mouth to let spit slide off my tongue onto the tip of his cock. I use it to pump his cock, finding just the right spot to wrap my fingers around him to get the most movement of his foreskin over his cock.

"Someday," I tell him. "We're going to fuck each other raw, and

I'm going to stretch this deliciousness all the way over my own cock and jack us both until I come inside it."

"Jesus, Jesse," Luc exclaims, leaning his head back. "Fucking hell. Is that something you've done before?"

"No," I say, leaning in to lick at the spurt of pre-cum that tells me he doesn't hate the idea. "But since meeting you, I watch a lot of porn with uncut guys."

"Is that a thing?"

"Fuck yeah, it's a thing." I put my mouth around just the tip and slide my tongue down the underside of his head, rubbing the ball of my tongue ring against the sensitive spot. "What do you like?" I ask before taking more of him into my mouth, sliding all the way down his shaft.

"What? Like what porn do I watch?"

I nod with my mouth around his cock, grinning when I feel his hand comb back my hair. I flick my eyes up to his when he's pushed it away.

"Um… *Uh*…" He's too distracted watching me to answer, but I don't change my pace. I just stare into his eyes curiously, waiting for him to answer. "I like the amateur stuff mostly."

I pop off, letting more spit run out of my mouth. My fingers gently fondle his balls, teasing under them, coaxing wetness down his crack. "Mmm, me too. I hate the scripted stuff."

"It's funny rather than sexy," he says, trying to chuckle through his arousal.

"What topics do you look for? Like, are you watching jock porn where the big, buff football player pounds the pretty cheerleader or the nerdy twink or…?"

Luc is shaking his head, face flushed dark red. Is he blushing or holding back an orgasm already? I should move this along.

"I–I like– Um… I usually only watch gay porn. And I like… *unghh*… first times." He says it quietly, breathlessly, caught between embarrassment and distracted arousal over all the ways I'm touching him.

I've moved on to swirling my tongue around his tip, slithering it around the edge of his foreskin before pushing my tongue inside.

He bucks, knees rising, and grips my hair. "Shit!" Then he gasps and drops his hands and legs, leaning forward to take my face in his hands. "Shit, I'm sorry!"

I can't help but chuckle. "It's alright. I don't mind, I promise." I push up to kiss him. "Was that a good reaction or are you not a fan?"

"Good," he says quickly. "Too good. I wasn't expecting it though."

"Thank fuck because that is way too much fun to not do, like, all the time," I say, pushing him back into position.

This time, I don't waste time torturing him. I give his cock the full treatment, making it wet and sloppy. He really seems to love when I suck and tongue his foreskin. I think it feels best when I put my whole tongue inside and swirl it around, but the visual of me using just the tip of my tongue so he can see my tongue stud really seems to turn him on.

When my thumb finds his hole and starts massaging small circles, he doesn't act shocked or jump. He was probably expecting it, he's obviously had more practice with a guy. I'm trying not to hate it, because God knows I've done my fair share of fucking around. It's been almost a year since I've been with someone, though, because it turned out I did need the drugs and alcohol to pretend they were as good as him. I'm glad it's been that long. Hell, part of me wishes I'd been celibate since that night, because no one ever measured up.

I lick, suck, and kiss down to put my tongue where my thumb has been playing with him. He's relaxed enough that I could easily slide the tip of my thumb in, but I want to tongue fuck him until he shakes and then milk him for all he's worth.

His breaths get heavier as I suck and kiss and lick his ass. When I spear the tip inside, he moans, but he hasn't felt anything yet. When I push my whole tongue inside, piercing and all, he sucks in a breath and curses. Every time I push it in, his breath hitches as the balls of my piercing push through. When he's soft and pliant under my tongue, and his hips are rocking, I replace my tongue with two fingers and take his cock in my mouth again.

My eyes nearly roll back when he moans my name and runs his hand through my hair. I reach up to cover his hand with mine, wordlessly instructing him to push and guide me the way he likes. Once he takes over, I return my hand to the base of his cock and pump while I take him deep, pushing my fingers all the way inside and curling them up, stroking his insides while I stroke his outsides. He doesn't push hard, but he finally loses enough control to put pressure on my head, rocking his hips to get deeper.

"Jesse!" He cries out my name three times before spilling into my mouth, and I swallow every drop, stroking his prostate and sucking him through the aftershocks until he's curling in on himself.

He falls back on the couch cushions, legs falling to either side of me. I rest my cheek against his thigh, giving his cock gentle kisses and licks as it softens while he strokes my hair. We sit like that, silently soaking in the afterglow and waiting for our heart rates to go down.

"There's no way I'm letting you go now, Luc Martín."

LeST is MooRE

TEN
LUC

I wake in the middle of the night. At least, I'm assuming it's the middle of the night. I'm not sure how long we've been asleep.

The past day has gone by in a haze of good food, good conversation, and a lot of really good orgasms. A *lot*. I'm not sure I've come as much in the past year as I have in the past twenty-four hours.

We spent most of Sunday night cuddled up on the couch naked, staring into the firelight or at each other, talking and laughing. I'm still surprised by how easy conversation with him is. I forget that he's a rockstar, or that we're basically strangers. It feels like catching up with someone I've known forever. We made each other come with our mouths and fingers two more times before Jesse led me to his bedroom and went to start the shower. But apparently when he came back to get me to join him, I'd fallen asleep. I woke up late the next morning to his mouth on me, using my body against me to persuade me to stay for the day before turning me around and fucking himself between my thighs. I was close to begging him to just do it, but we both seem to be holding back.

I don't know why I'm nervous about it. It's not like it's my first time. And even though it's been six years, I know the pleasure is going to overshadow any discomfort.

I think my nerves have more to do with the emotional effect of whatever is budding between us. I'm not sure I could handle waking up to an empty bed again after opening myself up this much.

Yeah, he said he wants us to date, even if that means he has to hide his relationship. But what does that mean? And what do I have a right to ask for? It's bad enough to expect him to basically closet himself to be with me. Is it fair to expect exclusivity when our schedules will make it impossible for us to see each other often?

Not to mention that he's Jesse fucking Moore. He's one of the sexiest men on earth and a goddamn rock god. *But, oh hey, I'm basically in love with you even though I barely know you, based purely on the memory of one night years ago, and a single date turned weekend together, so could you keep it in your pants. For me?*

Yeah right.

I know that the media and tabloids lie or grossly exaggerate what they report on celebrities. The story about the coverage of his father's death was heartbreaking. No one should have their lives under a microscope like that, and then over-inflated for the world to pick apart.

He is a rockstar though, and he's admitted to living a rockstar life. It seems like he's calmed down a lot since getting sober, and that's encouraging, but if he's given up drugs and alcohol and nearly every other vice, how could I ask him to give up sex, too? It'd be one thing if I were around to give it to him, but I won't be. We'll be lucky to see each other once a month during game season and when he's on tour. They're at the peak of their career, too, with no signs of slowing down.

Who am I to ask him to give up anything? Especially if it might bring him happiness or comfort.

If anything, it's too soon to expect anything from each other.

I know myself, and I know that if we cross this line, I'll latch on harder than I ever have.

Then again, it might be too late. I think I was screwed the first time we had a real conversation. And every time we touch, it's… I don't know what it is. I've never felt like this before, with anyone. Even when I've found other people attractive here and there, it didn't work. There wasn't anything real between us, and I simply cannot perform on command, socially or sexually.

I'll never forget the blind date AJ set me up with once. It was a good friend of the girl he was dating at the time, and he begged me to go on this double date. She was objectively extremely hot. She was a brand ambassador for some celebrity line of makeup products or something like that, and she was legitimately a kind person. I let it drag on for over a month, simply because I felt bad, and AJ's girlfriend was way too invested. I knew he wanted to make her happy, so I just went along with it. On our last date, she surprised me and came to my house. I was confused when the doorman had called up to tell me I had a visitor. AJ, that fucking bonehead, had given her my address because he thought I'd like to be surprised by the beautiful girl I supposedly liked. And a surprise it was. She walked in wearing a white wrap dress and matching strappy heels, and soon after I let her inside, she unwrapped and dropped the dress to the floor. She was wearing a white lace teddy and garters. She was an utter fucking angel and looked like a lingerie model. But when she walked over to me, my stomach dropped with every click of her heels on the hardwood floor. Even with her heels, I had to bend down to let her kiss me. And I did let her. I had let her before. I felt too bad not to, and I kept hoping something would change, that I'd grow to like her in more than a friendly way.

When I didn't get hard, even when she pressed into me and stroked me over my athletic pants, she seemed concerned at first, but when she looked up into my eyes, the concern turned to sadness. Tears welled up in her pretty amber eyes. She could tell that I was a lost cause. I didn't know how to tell her it wasn't anything to do with her. The whole "it's not you, it's me" thing didn't help.

I realized too late that I shouldn't have led her on out of concern for hurting her feelings.

She left my place in tears, and that doorman hasn't treated me the same since. I'm sure he thinks I was mean to her. Maybe I was. I tried to be direct, but gentle. Turns out I'm shit at explaining myself.

Maybe I'm missing whatever biological or neurological component that makes you connect with other people on a deeper level. It's just not in my nature to open myself up to other people. There are few people in my life that I've felt truly close to, and aside from Shawna, they're all related to me.

And then there's Jesse. It doesn't make sense how connected I feel to him. Even with Shawna, it took until the sixth grade for me to warm up to her. I took one look at Jesse and swooned like some kind of cartoon damsel falling in love at first sight. I can feel the fucking hearts in my eyes when I let my guard down. Luckily, he's probably used to people looking at him like that and probably doesn't notice. I mean, not only is he famous, but he's gorgeous, and has this effervescent quality about him. He doesn't just light up a room, he outshines the stadium lights he performs under night after night. He's extraordinary.

How can someone–especially someone so different from me, with this big, public life that I wouldn't touch with a ten-foot pole–burrow so fully into me with zero effort?

"What are you thinking about so hard?" Jesse's voice is rough with sleep, the gravelly tenor resonating in my sternum.

I look down at where he'd rested his head on my shoulder and see him gazing up at me. His smile catches the dim light flickering from the battery-operated candles still scattered all over the suite.

Instead of answering, I bend my head down and kiss him. It's a gentle, light touch of lips, followed by the barest flicker of tongue. The electricity that shoots through me from that one touch makes my breath catch. He reaches up and cups my jaw, then slides his hand around to the back of my neck. I follow the pressure of his reach and roll over his body, deepening the kiss.

He writhes into me, and our cocks harden with the friction of rubbing ourselves together. I reach for the bottle of lube on the headboard and pump some into my palm, before wrapping my hand around both our cocks the way Jesse did in the jacuzzi tub earlier today. I love feeling our cocks pressed together, especially when I can feel the pulse of Jesse's release.

"Luc?"

I lift my face from the crook of his neck and smile down at him. He looks earnest and maybe the slightest bit sad or worried. I can't quite read it.

"What's wrong, beautiful?"

"Nothing could be wrong in the world right now. I just want you." He leans up and licks along the column of my neck to my ear. "Inside me."

My lips part on an exhale, and he uses it to his advantage, licking into my mouth. He knows I'm weak if that tongue is involved. The things he does to me with that thing.

Is this going to be too much? Maybe. Am I still going to do it?

How can I not?

Even after lying here in the dark, agonizing over all the reasons this relationship can't work, I can't say no to him. I can't say no to myself.

Every part of me wants to be wrapped up in every part of him.

Releasing our cocks, I reach up for another pump of lube, then lower my lubed fingers to rub against his hole. He's still soft and a little slick inside from the multiple times we've touched and played in the last twenty-four hours. Two fingers slide in easily, and he clenches around them. God, to feel that around my cock again.

Jesse lets out a low moan and writhes, rocking against my hand as I work them in and out, spreading my fingers to open him. I lean down to flick my tongue over the barbell in his nipple, then suck it into my mouth as I add a third finger.

"Luc, please," he whines.

Pulling my fingers from his body, I trail my kisses up his neck, across his jaw, to his soft, pleading mouth. The way he looks right now is something I want to commit to memory—eyes dark with lust, lips parted, disheveled hair spread out on the pillow. I want the image burned into the back of my eyes so I can see him this way every time I close my mind.

It's hard to look away from him for even a moment, but I have to if I want to get inside him, and if I don't soon, we might both combust. I reach for the box of condoms sitting just behind the lube and end up struggling with it. It takes me far too long to get the box out of the impenetrable shrink wrap, and then the damn thing is welded shut with a baffling amount of clear stickers that are impossible to see in this light.

Why does this stupid box have more security than prescription drugs? Shouldn't this be easier to get into?

I'm just about to rip the whole thing in half like a gym bro with a phonebook when Jesse takes it out of my hands.

"Let me help with that," he says through a laugh and pushes himself up to sitting.

I lean back on my heels and watch him use a knife from the snack plate we ate and set aside earlier. That was smart. Not being able to think past my throbbing dick is just another example of how gone I am.

"I guess I should have thought ahead a little better. It took three days to even talk myself into getting them. I wanted to be prepared, but I didn't want to be presumptuous," he says, finally releasing the spoils of my battle with the cardboard and tearing one open.

Does he not keep them around?

He notices my confusion and answers my unspoken question. "I've had a bit of a dry spell, but I always use protection, I'm on PrEP, and I get tested regularly."

I nod my understanding, distracted by his touch as he rolls the condom down my shaft, then realize this is the part where I'm supposed to share my status in return. Should we have done this before swallowing so much of each other's cum? Hell, six years ago I didn't give it one bit of consideration before or after. Jesus. I guess it's too late for that now.

"Um, me too. I mean— I get regular health checks, and I've never had sex without protection. And it's also been a minute." *And by a minute I mean six years.*

Jesse leans forward and kisses me while his hand coats me with lube. He uses my cock like a joystick, guiding me to sit. He climbs in my lap and sinks down, his hot, tight body enveloping my cock and pulling a long, deep moan from both of us. When he's fully seated, his arms wrap around my neck, legs around my waist. We stay like that, just kissing and touching, barely rocking together until neither of us can stand it anymore, and we have to move. Wrapping my arms tightly around his middle, I help guide him while his strong, lean muscles use my waist as leverage to ride me slowly. The whole time, his mouth never leaves mine.

It's intense. It feels fucking amazing, but this is so much more than sex. The slow glide of his body, the sweat slicking our skin between us, the desperate way we hold on to each other, the gasps and cries that echo in the room… It's powerful.

Way too soon, I'm crying out a warning into Jesse's mouth. He answers with his own cries, body tightening, and I know I can't hold on. Keeping one arm wrapped around him to hold him close, I move the other to his ass, keeping him steady as I switch positions, laying him on his back.

With Jesse's legs looped tight around my hips, I prop myself on one forearm, holding myself steady above him. My palm cups the back of his head, thumb stroking through his hair, while my free hand caresses down his body to wrap around his cock. I roll my hips, thrusting in long, slow, firm strokes.

Jesse's moans and little cries increase until he's calling my name. And I swear, nothing other than the sound of him singing to me sounds sweeter.

LeST is
MOORE

ELEVEN
LUC

Something startles me from what might be the deepest sleep of my life, but the muffled voices I thought I heard blur into the background of my consciousness and whatever fleeting dream I was having. The first thing I see when I open my eyes is the beautiful man lying next to me, sprawled out on his stomach. There isn't a stitch of clothing on him, miles of creamy skin etched with random designs. The curve of his ass calls to me. Memories from last night, or maybe it was early this morning, have my cock ready to greet the day before I've even stretched.

Jesse breathes in deep, shifts, and a soft, sleepy smile curves his lips.

"Morning," he rasps without opening his eyes.

God, this man wrecks me. I press a gentle, reverent kiss to the corner of his mouth, and he sighs contentedly. He snuggles in closer to my side, face tilted up for more kisses. His hand skims my chest, fingers wandering lower to wrap around my stiff erection.

"Is this for me?"

I groan. It pains me to remember it'll be weeks before we can wake up like this again, so I push it far from my mind. We still have a few hours before I have no choice but to leave. Technically, I should have left yesterday, but the day melted away and I ended up back in bed with Jesse. Nothing short of a natural disaster could pull me away from this even a moment before it's absolutely necessary.

Or at least that's what I thought.

I hear the voices again. They're louder, right outside the bedroom. Before I can process or cover myself up, the door swings open.

I freeze, sheet tangled low around my hips. Too low. There's nothing but Jesse's hand covering my very obvious erection. Heat floods my face as I register just how much of both of us is on display, and that we've been caught. We didn't even make it through one weekend. I pull the sheet up, covering my dick and Jesse's bare ass.

Weirdly, Jesse doesn't seem to care. He just looks mildly irritated. Likewise, the man in the doorway doesn't blink. He's wearing black slacks, a tan silk shirt, and an expression of obvious exasperation. Other than a fleeting glance, I might as well be furniture. His eyes are locked on Jesse.

"You haven't answered your phone all weekend, Jesse," the man says flatly, like barging in on people's privacy is his job.

"I turned it off," Jesse says simply, and sits up. I adjust the sheet again to cover his groin, and Jesse smirks. "I was enjoying my weekend off."

"I can see that," the man deadpans. "But had you kept your phone on, you would have remembered that you have a fitting with the stylist this morning."

A mousy little guy pops his head over the man's shoulder, cheerfully waving to Jesse. "Hi, Jesse!"

Jesse's lips quirk. "Hey, Emmy. I'll be out in a few, okay? I need to take a shower."

"Okay, Jesse! Take your time."

"Absolutely not. If you're not out here in ten minutes, I'll simply bring the whole team to you. There is too much to do for the photo shoot tomorrow. And then you need to look over the questions and answers for the radio interview, or did you forget that was being taped tonight, as well?" He purses his lips.

Jesse rubs a hand over his face and looks like he's counting to keep his temper in check.

The man sighs. "Look, Jesse, I'm trying to work with you here. You know that, right?"

"Yeah, Blake, I know. And I appreciate it. I'm sorry I turned my phone off, I was…" He looks at me, and his eyes soften. "…busy. It was important."

"I can give you twenty minutes," the man, Blake, acquiesces. "But we really need to get started. Everyone else has already been fitted, otherwise I'd try to give you more time." He moves to leave but pauses again. "If there are any accommodations I can assist you with to ensure your *friend* gets home safely, just let me know."

I blink at him as he gives me a clipped nod, acknowledging me for the first time before he finally backs out of the room and closes the door.

Wow.

Talk about a blast of cold water. Suddenly I feel cheap and exposed.

I flinch when Jesse's hand covers mine. "Luc…"

"I should go," I say with a tight smile. It's all I can muster, and I can barely look him in the eyes.

"Luc," he says again, and cups my jaw to turn my face his way. I'm not ready to let him see me like this. I have too many thoughts and feelings to process.

"I just need a minute. Let me take a quick shower, and then I'll head out so you can do what you need to do. We can talk about it later."

"Luc–"

"Jesse, I said I need a minute!"

Suddenly, I'm tackled onto my back, body blanketed by Jesse, his knees on either side of my hips. He holds my face in his hands. "Then you can take a minute with me," he says firmly, then crashes his mouth to mine.

For a few seconds, I'm too stunned to react. Then my body reacts instinctively, kissing him back with equal ferocity.

The sound of a door closing somewhere in the suite pulls me back to reality, and I manage to unlatch our mouths. I sigh and throw my head back.

"I'm sorry," Jesse says. "I got so wrapped up in you I forgot what day it was, and this fitting wasn't supposed to happen until later."

What time is it, even? After being awake and active for a few hours in the wee hours of the morning, there's no telling how late we slept. I find my phone and check the time.

"It's after eleven."

"Shit."

Yeah, *shit.*

"Look, Blake isn't going to tell anybody, and neither will anyone on the styling team. Everyone that works with us has to sign strict NDA's, and Blake's interests are tied to my success and happiness, even if he's a pain in the ass sometimes," he says, raising his voice so anyone outside the door can hear him call Blake a pain in the ass. "No one here is going to out you."

I scoff and try to sit up. He tries to hold me down, but I have at least fifty pounds of muscle on him. It doesn't take a whole lot of effort to pick him up and throw him on the bed.

"Goddamn," he says, and I look back to see him staring up at me, eyes wide and hungry. "Is it wrong that I liked that?"

I have to look away to keep from laughing, and walk over to the closet, where the clothes I arrived in are all cleaned and pressed. Jesse sent them out to be laundered yesterday morning–I washed my underwear in the sink first, because the idea of sending my dry cum-crusted underwear to someone else to clean was morti-fying. And we spent the whole day naked or in robes anyway.

Before I head into the bathroom, I turn around and look Jesse in the eye.

"It's not about being outed, okay. Who I choose to sleep with isn't something I broadcast, but it isn't something I go out of my way to hide, either. And that goes for any gender." I clear my throat. "What I care about is my privacy. I don't like crowds, or answering questions, or having attention pointed at me. I never have. The only reason I joined the draft was to help my family, and I've stayed because I love football and my team, and I've found a comfortable balance there."

"We can keep you out of the public eye."

"Maybe." I look towards the door, wanting to mention what the whole incident this morning made me feel, but I know I need to put my big boy panties on and get over it. I don't want to cause Jesse more stress.

Jesse climbs off the bed and comes over to hug me around my waist. I wrap my arms around him and kiss the side of his forehead.

"Come on," he says, taking my hand. "Let's go get you cleaned off."

As soon as we're under the shower spray, Jesse drops to his knees. It takes almost no time at all for him to suck my soul through my dick. Then he stands up, flips me around, and spits my cum between my cheeks before using them as a cock sleeve. He licks up my spine and bites my shoulder to muffle his groan as he shoots all over my ass and thighs.

After taking another minute to wash his hair and body, he kisses me, then steps out, leaving me still trembling in the shower.

Once I'm dressed and feel like I've gathered enough of my dignity, I open the bedroom door. I can hear Jesse arguing with Blake about me, and my face heats all over again. I just need to get out of here.

Walking out into the main living space, I'm surprised how many people there are bustling around. None of them pay me much mind. The smell of Jesse's clove cigarette hits me before their hushed voices do. Blake and Jesse are still arguing, albeit in quieter voices, on the balcony while Jesse smokes. I catch his eye, and he winks, holding up a finger to say he'll be with me in a minute.

It's not until he's stalking back towards me, popping a piece of his candy into his mouth, that I notice Jesse is wearing nothing but tight, black boxer briefs. *Around all these people. Like it's nothing.* Meanwhile, I have to avert my eyes in case anyone who missed the first show gets a second chance.

"He's kind of hard to look at, right?" A small voice beside me says.

I look down–literally, he's at least a foot shorter than me–to see that perky little guy from before. Emmy?

He answers my raised eyebrow with a huff of laughter. "He's just so hot. It's like looking directly at the sun."

He's not wrong, but I don't appreciate hearing it from someone else. Specifically, someone who gets to spend a lot more time with him. Not to mention he's cute and rather pretty.

"I'm Emerson, but everyone here calls me Emmy." He reaches out a hand, knuckles up like I'm supposed to kiss them.

I shake the proffered hand awkwardly. "I'm Luc–"

"Luc Martín, #14, defensive back for the Shreveport Cyclones. I know who you are," he says cheerfully.

I raise an eyebrow.

"What? Twinks can't watch football?"

I laugh and try to relax. He can't know how off-putting I find being recognized, especially in this situation, but he's very friendly, asking me if I'd like anything to eat or drink, which I politely decline, even though I'm ravenously hungry.

"I'm going to be getting on my way here in just a minute," I say, eyes locked on Jesse, who was interrupted on his way over to me.

When he gets to me, his hand cups my elbow. "Are you sure I can't persuade you to stay a little longer?" He says in a low voice only for me, although I have a feeling the pretty little one is listening.

"I don't think that's a good idea," I whisper back, trying to look anywhere but at him. The problem is, no matter where I look, I'm reminded of the things we did all over this hotel suite.

"And why is that?" Jesse drawls, and I'm pretty sure he knows what I'm thinking about when his eyes land on the end of the dining room table. There's a blonde woman sitting in the exact chair he pulled up to make a meal out of my ass, a stack of what looks like scrapbooks on the table where I was bent over. I'm pretty sure I can still see a stain on the ornate rug beneath the table.

Jesse grins salaciously, confirming my suspicions. He leans in, breath caressing over my ear. "Do you have any idea what it does to me when you get all red like that?"

Without thinking, I let my eyes drop to his bulge, which is definitely even more noticeable than it was before.

"Can you put some clothes on already?"

"Now why would I do that?"

I shoot a sideways glance at Emmy, who looks like he's trying to look busy. I narrow my eyes at the back of his head.

"We've barely started dating and you're already so possessive," he coos. "I don't hate it."

"I am not. And we're not dating. Officially… yet."

Jesse snorts. "If you say so, baby," he says teasingly.

I blush harder and look around. "Don't do that."

"Do what?" His grin is so wide, it's evil.

"Call me baby like that."

"But you like it when I call you baby."

"Not in public!" I whisper-shout.

Jesse laughs loudly enough to get everyone's attention. I look at the floor and try to pretend I'm invisible. Unfortunately, I'm the largest person in the room by far, so it's not that easy.

Someone comes up behind me, and Jesse rolls his eyes. "Luc, I want you to meet my manager, Blake Holland. He's a bit of a tyrant sometimes, but it's only because he's seen me at my worst. He's a genuinely good guy if you overlook his whole band-daddy shtick. Blake, this is my *friend* Luc."

Blake rolls his eyes, but gives me a genuinely apologetic smile. He reaches for my hand, shaking it firmly. "It's nice to meet you. I'm sorry about earlier. I was rude. I get a little in my head when things get behind schedule."

"I understand," I say, too embarrassed to say more. "It's nice to meet you, too." I look up at Jesse. "I really do need to go. I've got to get back to Shreveport, and you have work to do here."

"Shreveport?" Blake asks, concerned. "Do you have a flight out? Need me to call a car?"

"No need," Emmy says, stepping into our circle. "I already called a car for you, and the jet is waiting."

Blake looks like he's trying to swallow his objections and they taste bad, but he manages a grin and nods. "Very good. Well, it was nice to meet you. Jesse, Myra is ready for you. Try not to make her wait any longer, will you?"

"Yes, sir," Jesse snarks. He looks at Emmy. "On point as always, Mr. Keller. Thank you for pulling that together so quickly."

Emmy preens at the praise. And honestly, I get it. I can't even fault the little guy. Hell, I even like him, but I still kind of want to punt him.

Said little guy turns his sunny demeanor on me. "Your car should be here any minute," he says, checking his phone. "Take the penthouse elevator down to the basement level, and the driver will meet you there. It's a private entrance, so you won't have to worry about meeting any fans." He holds up a to-go cup and a folded paper bag. "I know you said you weren't hungry, but I didn't believe you, so I made you something for the road."

I blink down at him. "Um, wow. Thank you." I accept the goodies and smile at Emmy. He's impossible not to like, and I kind of hate it. "I really appreciate you," I say, and I'm surprised to see him preen the same way he did at Jesse's praise.

Jesse chuckles and places a hand at the small of my back to guide me out of the hotel room and back into the marble foyer. The elevator opens immediately, and he steps on with me.

"Myra is waiting for you," I remind him, even though I have no idea who Myra is. "And you're still only in your underwear."

He smirks. "Myra can wait."

The moment the elevator doors are closed, he's in my space. He grabs the bag of food and drink from me and sets them on the floor, then presses me against the wall and absolutely ravishes my mouth. Fuck, I'd be such a slut if kissing was like this with everyone.

My eyes catch the glowing number over the elevator. We're only about a third of the way down, with no chance of being stopped since this is a private elevator.

So I bend down and pick him up, wrapping his legs around my waist and turning us around so I'm pressing him into the wall. I rock into him, barely able to keep myself from whimpering because my dick is desperate for him already.

It's not just my dick, though. I'm going to miss him. His company, our conversations, his presence.

The elevator dings, and I let Jesse down as the doors are sliding open. Cory stands on the other side.

"Morning, sir," he says, but turns around to give us privacy while we try to straighten our clothes.

Well, my clothes. Jesse looks positively indecent now, with his puffy, kiss swollen lips, beard burn from my stubble, and his cock trying to escape his tiny underwear.

I take a deep breath and take a step back, but Jesse follows me, not allowing more than an inch of space between us. He guides me with a hand on my waist as I walk backwards from the elevator to the car, stealing kisses and telling myself it's the last one every time. My butt hits the back of a car, and Jesse pins me to it, kissing me deeply, not giving a fuck who's watching. I can see the driver in my periphery when I flutter my eyes open. It's time for me to go.

With one… two… three last slow pecks, I hold Jesse at arm's length. He looks as wrecked as I feel, not just because of the semi-public make-out session, but because I feel so fucking sad to be walking away from him.

"This sucks," Jesse rasps.

I nod. "It does." I eventually pull away, and try to pretend I'm not blushing as I thank the driver who has been holding the door open for me this whole time. He shuts the door, and Jesse raps on the window.

"Call me when you get home?" He says, bending through the window once it opens all the way, kissing me again. And again.

"I will. I promise."

Cory steps up and hands me the breakfast Emmy made me. "Have a safe trip, Mr. Martín."

"Just Luc. Thank you." I side-eye Jesse, who still hasn't let go of the window. "Try to keep this one out of trouble?"

"I'll do my best, sir."

I chuckle and look up at Jesse. He's biting his lip, like he's trying to think of any excuse not to go back to the real world, but he surprises me again.

"You'll think about it, right?"

"Think about what?"

"Being mine."

He kisses me one more time, so sweetly, and I inhale his spicy scent.

Then the car is pulling out, and I turn around in my seat, watching Jesse's nearly naked image disappear as we pull out of the hotel's private entrance.

"You'll think about it, right?"

"Being mine."

TWELVE
JESSE

The moment the taillights disappear, I feel hollow.

For about thirty-six hours, my head has been clear. I've felt light and unburdened since the moment I saw him climb out of the helicopter. I didn't crave oblivion or feel like peeling off my skin even once.

Now that he's gone, that realization alone is making the walls feel like they're closing in.

"Mr. Moore?"

I glare at Cory. He clears his throat. "Jesse," he corrects. He's only ever used my first name when I was at my worst.

Shit. Am I that transparent?

"I'm fine," I say, and give him a weak smile. He nods, but I don't think he believes me. He leads me to the elevator and rides back up to the penthouse suite with me. It's a long, quiet, and somewhat awkward ride. Compared to the ride down, which happened in the blink of an eye. If only it had gotten stuck. Just for a little while, at least.

The moment the elevator opens, Blake points in the direction of Myra, all but kicking me to get me moving faster. "We're behind, Jesse."

"I know."

I can't look at him right now. If I do, I'll see him standing in my open bedroom door all over again. I'll have to relive watching all the love drain out of Luc's eyes, and morph into insecurity while my overprotective manager reamed me like an errant teenager and treated Luc like he didn't exist.

I feel sick. Empty. Afraid. But I let Blake lead me to the dining area, where Myra has spread out the concept ideas for our photo shoot tomorrow.

Myra does so much extra work to print out photos and pull fabric samples to make physical scrapbook-style mood boards because I have a hard time visualizing the concepts as a whole. Normally, I have a lot of fun with these kinds of shoots and enjoy picking out which coordinating pieces I want to wear. And because she's amazing, Myra always includes an edgier, provocative feel for me, like crop tops, corsets, and plunging necklines.

I can almost see the wind go out of her sails when she sees me, and it makes me feel terrible. She's been waiting for me for an hour, and then I show up in a piss-poor mood.

"Sorry, Myra," I say, kissing her on the cheek. She wraps an arm around my waist and tells me to shut up.

"Wanna tell me about it?" She asks.

"I wouldn't even know where to start."

"You could start with that blushing beefcake that walked out of your bedroom."

I huff out a laugh, then pull out my phone and change his contact name. That's just too damn good.

"I really like him."

"I can tell," Myra says, bumping my hip. I look at her curiously, and she rolls her eyes. "Well, for starters, he clearly spent the night. He was still here when all of us rolled in."

"Unfortunately," I mutter.

"It's a good thing that he seems the timid type," she says. "Otherwise, I can't imagine that he wouldn't have put Blake on his ass."

I snort. "Luc isn't like that." Though I might have liked to see it this morning.

"Luc?" She rolls the name on her tongue. "Interesting pronunciation."

"His full name is Lucius, but that's his dad's name, too. He just goes by Luc."

"I like it."

"I like him."

"You said that already," Emmy says, coming in with my pants draped over one arm.

"You." I point at Emmy and look him dead in his pretty sky-blue eyes. "Flirt with my man again and I'll tell Daddy Blake that thing you don't want him to know."

"You wouldn't," he says, narrowing his eyes at me.

I narrow mine right back at him. "*My* man, Emmy. Mine."

Emmy raises an eyebrow, ready to snark back, but Naz chooses this very opportune moment to slink in like he smelled gossip, shades on, twirling a drumstick between his fingers.

"Did I just hear you say *your man*?"

"Mind your business."

"Bro. You've known him for what, five minutes? All the years in between boning him the first time and the couple of days you spent with him don't count, you know."

"One, don't call me bro when I'm emotionally fragile. Two, when you know, you know. And I know." The trouble is whether or not he knows. "Third, you look like the worst kind of stereotype."

"My dude, you're the one who waxed his dick to wear assless chaps backwards."

"You're just jealous because you wouldn't be able to pull it off."

"Yeah, 'cuz my dick is too big."

"Oh please, I've seen your dick."

"So have I," Myra says.

"Me too," says Emmy.

Naz crosses his arms and stares at all of us with narrowed eyes. He's silent for nearly ten whole seconds before he says, "You're all a bunch of assholes," and moves on. He looks at Emmy and pumps his eyebrows. "What kind of secret are you keeping from Daddy Blake?"

"I'm not keeping any secrets!"

"Is it that you want his dick? Because you're right, it's not a secret."

Emmy gapes and nearly drops the pants. Myra catches them and pats her assistant's shoulder. "Don't worry, honey, he's too oblivious to realize."

She passes the pants to me. "Alright, let's see how they look."

I'm determined to let Myra enjoy this moment and try to act normal. Despite my shitty mood, the banter, and getting to try on badass, sexy-as-fuck pants does help me feel a little lighter. Especially since I get to drop my underwear and show everyone my ass while I slip them on.

Myra walks over once I get everything tucked away and makes some adjustments to the belt before stepping back. "Not bad," she says. "I wouldn't do any sort of jumping around, and watch yourself whenever you have to get up and down, but they look damn good. Do you want to put the boots on before you take a look?"

Emmy passes me a pair of socks and the boots before I can even nod, and I slip them on. Myra was right about being careful about which way I move, because my junk is definitely in danger of making an escape.

I turn and walk towards the standing mirrors that have been set up and give Myra an appreciative nod in the reflection.

The pants are a soft leather, tight fitted from my hips to just below my knees, where they flare into a bootcut leg. The fit alone is sinful, hugging every centimeter of my body and leaving nothing to the imagination. The fun feature of the pants that makes them so daring, though, is how the front dips into a deep V shape. On the woman who originally modeled this design, the tip of the V came down so far, she was *this close* to showing lip cleavage. Myra modified them somewhat to allow for my dick to be contained, but the hem is barely concealing the base of my cock. I have to tuck my dick down one leg to keep it secure, and the imprint is clear as day. There's a thin belt made of the same leather that goes around the waist where the hem would be, creating a sort of triangular cutout. The belt gives a subtle bondage feel to the pants and accentuates the plunging waist-line. My boots are heeled shitkickers, which elongate the legs and lift my ass.

"These are the best pants I've ever worn," I say. "Can I keep them?"

Sometimes the clothes for photoshoots are loaned, but custom pieces are sometimes gifted or sold. Myra had to customize these to accommodate my bare dick fitting inside, so I'm hopeful I'll get to take these home.

"There's a good chance you could, but I'll check with the designer."

"Thanks, Myra." I give her a genuine smile. "You killed it, as usual."

"Where the fuck else would you wear those?" Naz asks.

I shrug. "If I do a tuck and tape, do you think I could wear them on stage?"

"With the right tape–" Myra starts.

"Absolutely not," Blake cuts in, barely looking up from his phone to give me a cursory once-over. He blinks and shakes his head, but he knows these photos are going to be fire. Normally I'd make a snarky comment or ask if he wants to try them on. Which would be hilarious, since he's such a buttoned-up stiff, but he's my least favorite person right now.

"Go away, you're bumming me out."

"I said I was sorry," he exclaims. "And I was sincere. I am sincere. I'm genuinely sorry."

"Sorry means fuck-all if he doesn't come back."

Blake drops his arms, defeated. "What can I do to make it up to you?"

"Whatever it takes to keep him," I say seriously.

Naz looks confused. Myra and Emmy are looking at me with pitying expressions.

"If I can help, I will. If it means that much to you."

Rolling my eyes, because I'm a sucker and too easy, I cross my arms. "You could also… put on the pants and helicopter dick for thirty seconds."

Myra's hands come up to her face. Naz snorts. Emmy blushes when I give him a wink.

"I would sooner get a job jerking off Minotaurs or whatever the fuck you people were reading last month." He says it so seriously, I have to hold my breath to keep from laughing out loud.

He leaves us to laugh at him, and Myra helps me out of the boots and pants.

"You know he means well, right? Not that it excuses how he behaved."

"I know. And I truly believe he's sorry and won't ever do that again, I'm just feeling a bit sensitive. When Luc drove off, I could feel it in the pit of my stomach, you know?"

She nods and places a hand on my arm. "You're raw right now, but it's because he just left. That's a normal thing to feel in a relationship, Jesse. You've just never experienced it before."

"No, I have. That's why it scares me so much. Because the last time I felt this way, I walked away and ended up losing him."

I take a drag from my cigarette and lean back on the patio chair. I'll regret smoking this much during this weekend's show, but I only have so many vices left. I can't bear to be inside the suite for too long. All day it felt too loud and too crowded. Now every-one's gone, and I still can't breathe.

Expelling the lungful of smoke, I watch the clove-scented cloud dissipate into the night sky.

I finally found quiet, but it's too loud.
Nothing makes sense now that you've come around.
The stillness is too heavy, every breath is too loud.

Ugh. I'm annoyed by my own angst, but I stub out my cigarette and head inside to find my notebook. Sometimes even a shitty idea can take shape when I write it down, or if I come back to it later.

Eyeing the candy dish, I opt for gum instead. Maybe having something to chew on will help.

The notebook is on the bedside table, but when I walk into the bedroom I pause. The sheets are still tangled in a heap, the pillows still have indents from where we slept. There are ques-tionable stains everywhere, but I don't care. I climb into the bed and crawl over to the last spot he was lying in, pressing my face into his pillow and taking a deep breath of his lingering scent mixed with mine.

When Luc first arrived, he smelled like clean laundry, *Irish Spring* soap, and something earthy, like he's spent so much of his life out in the sun that the grass and soil soaked into his skin. By the time he left, he smelled more like my spicy shampoo and body wash, which made me feel a bit like a caveman.

Right now, though, it just makes me feel lonely. I'm not usually one to get very lonely, although I do occasionally need a distrac-tion from my own thoughts. But today, even goofing off with my best friends, I felt disconnected.

I never knew there was such a gaping space in my heart until I met you.

Rolling over, I grab my notebook and jot down the last few thoughts. I'm not in the headspace to write anything but sad emo ballads. I flip through the last few pages, at all the lovesick scribbles about how he sets my veins on fire, how I could live on the press of our skin together, never needing to eat or drink anything but him. It's honestly gross.

Fuck, I miss him.

I glance at my phone and note the late hour. He texted to let me know he was home earlier, but was feeling tired and had a headache. We've texted on and off throughout the day, but it doesn't feel right. With every text, I feel him pulling away as viscerally as I did when the car drove him away from me.

Staring at our text thread until my vision swims, I finally type something out. The only thing I can do is make sure he knows the ball is in his court.

> ME: My day is finally over. I hope you're getting some rest and feel better in the morning.

To my surprise, he texts back immediately.

> Blushing Beefcake: I feel like I got hit by a truck.

Same. My heart kicks as I try to type out how I'm feeling, then delete it and go with something simpler.

> ME: Physically or emotionally?

Instead of texting a reply, my screen lights up with an incoming call. He's calling me?

"Luc?"

"Both," he says, not bothering with hello. There's a breath, then a chuckle, low and worn.

I lie back on the pillow he had his head on only twelve hours ago. "Tell me where it hurts."

"You really want a list?"

"Read me your injury report, Mr. Safety."

He huffs a laugh. "Points for knowing what position I play, but it's called that because I'm the last line of defense. I'm not the team nurse or anything."

"I know that." *Sort of.* "Quit deflecting."

"Well, there's the obvious aches and pains from a certain overzealous rockstar keeping me busy for the last two days." I smirk, pleased with myself. "Bit of a headache and overall tiredness, but I can't tell if I'm coming down with something or just feeling…Weird."

"Weird how?" I know how, but I need to hear him say it. I need to hear him say he feels even a fraction of the loss I do, like phantom limb syndrome, there's an ache in an empty space.

Hmm… I open my notebook again and quickly jot down a thought.

> You're my phantom limb, I can't cut clean
> Ache in an empty space, I can't breathe
> Whole on the outside, wrecked underneath
> I still feel you moving inside me.

"I feel like something has shifted," he says. "In my brain, or maybe something deeper. I can't name it."

It's love, baby. It's love.

"I miss you," is what I say out loud.

Luc lets out a heavy breath. "I miss you too. And I'm sorry about this morning. I didn't mean to cause any issues with your manager."

"You didn't."

"I did. I heard you arguing on the balcony."

I sigh heavily. "Did you hear what we were saying?"

"No, but considering how sincerely Blake apologized to me, I know you talked to him."

"I did. I was pissed. It wasn't okay for him to treat you like that. There's no excuse, but it's my fault he reacted like that."

"How was it your fault? I get that you missed some calls, but he shouldn't treat you like that."

"Me? He was upset with me for a good reason, that was fine. I'm talking about how he treated *you*."

"That was… whatever. I'm fine."

"You're not. Or at least you weren't. I feel like I need to explain, at the risk of pushing you farther away."

"I don't need to know all your private business, Jesse."

"I want you to know the real me, Luc. Even the ugly parts. And I have a lot of ugly parts. I told you about rehab. It was Blake who got me there. He came into our lives when I was at my worst and helped me. I might not be here at all if it weren't for him."

Blake didn't just help me wean off the pills, he made sure I got the help I needed. He was the one who found out our old manager was paying off multiple doctors to write me prescriptions. The dosages were too high and too frequent. There were pills to wake me up, pills to make me sleep, pills to treat the headaches, anxiety, and restlessness that the other pills were causing. Add partying like a literal rockstar, and I was on a dangerous path.

Telling Luc all of this is both terrifying and incredibly freeing. If he can accept me as I am, then every ounce of effort I put into this relationship is worth it. And if he can't, it's better to know now.

"I didn't tell anyone other than Cory and Tad that you were coming, so he had no idea you weren't just some random guy I'd met on a bender. He was worried that I'd relapsed."

Luc is quiet the whole time I'm talking, which makes me ramble more. Eventually, I cut myself off, afraid that he's trying to find a way to tell me I'm not good enough for him. I know I'm not, but I'm also trying to be better every day. I want to be good enough. And I want him.

"That makes sense. I didn't even think about that. I guess because I didn't know you then, I don't think of you that way."

"It's refreshing," I say honestly.

"I need to know if I'm contributing to a problem, though. Not just to be courteous to the people in your life that are clearly worried about you, but also because I wouldn't want to compromise your safety or stability." He's speaking in a measured, careful tone, weighing each word as he says them.

"You're like a sexy Southern Boy Scout."

"I was an Eagle Scout."

"Of course you were."

He chuckles. "Thank you for sharing all that with me, though. I imagine it can't be easy. I'm glad you felt comfortable enough to be honest with me."

"Have I scared you off yet?"

"I'm not any more scared than I was before."

"Well at least there's that." There's a long moment of silence where I wonder if Luc has fallen asleep. "Luc?"

"Yeah?"

"You're thinking about it, right?"

"Yeah, beautiful. I'm thinking about it. I'm always thinking about it."

LEST IS
MOORE

THIRTEEN
LUC

"Alright boys! Shut 'em down!" Coach claps and breaks the huddle, sending us out on the field. I settle into my spot just outside the line, scanning the offense.

We're up by five and there's only a couple of minutes left in the game. The ball is on our forty-yard line, and if Miami gets in the end zone, they'll be able to turn the score in their favor with little-to-no room on the clock for miracle plays to pull off the win.

But they have to get through us first.

Miami's quarterback shouts and the line shifts. I know this look. I've spent hours reviewing game footage. He shifts to his right, a slot receiver stacked inside. Rocke is tracking him. Good. Ninety-nine times out of a hundred, he uses this play to bolt straight downfield, looking for a quick strike.

The ball snaps. AJ Leon bursts through their line like a bulldozer, blowing their protection apart. On the edge, Dez Carter bends around the tackle, hell-bent on a sack. The quarterback senses the pressure, but he's calm. He sees his window–a receiver sprinting open down the seam. But I see him, too, and I'm already moving before the ball leaves his hand. It cuts through the air, a perfect, smooth spiral.

I dart towards the receiver, ready to drive into him the moment the ball touches his hands, but I get there just a fraction of a second before he does. Diverting my attention at the last moment, I break across and step right in front of him. Leather smacks into my chest and I lock my arms around the ball just as the receiver crashes into my back. I stumble but maintain my footing and take off the other way, towards their end zone.

Ten yards fly by under my feet. Then fifteen. The sideline opens up, and the crowd detonates, a wall of noise so loud it rattles my helmet from here.

Two of Miami's players drag me down near the thirty-yard line. I hit the turf, ball cradled tight, a smile behind my facemask.

I stand, eyes wide at the madness around me, bracing as a wall of white and gold comes rushing towards me. AJ knocks his helmet into mine and screams like an absolute maniac. Dez whoops, and Treyden Rocke is slamming his fists against his chest pads, yelling, "That's right, baybee! That's right!"

As we head back to the sideline, Monty rips my helmet off and kisses the side of my head before taking the field. "Dinner's on me, Martín!"

I pick up my helmet, more aware than ever of the cameras following me as my teammates and Coach congratulate me on a great play. One gets rather close, and I wonder if Jesse is watching. I shift my eyes to the camera briefly, as if I could see him there, then look away, smiling to myself.

We end up winning 46-34 after Monty makes a clean drive to the end zone, and our kicker puts up the extra point.

Tonight is not a night where I'm able to keep my head down. Coach Harrick actually shrugs when I'm immediately pulled to the side for a post-game interview, after being forced to endure a quick ride on my teammate's shoulders. I keep my statement quick and to the point, and then I'm thankfully torn away from the cameras by an overexcited defensive tackle who mutters, "I got you," under his breath as he manhandles me.

Once we're in the tunnel, I smile at AJ gratefully. "Thank you," I say sincerely.

"Anytime, my man. I know you hate that shit," he says, locking his arm around my shoulders. The moment we step into the locker room, everyone starts clapping and cheering. A ball hits me hard in the chest, and I almost don't react in time to catch it.

Is this–?

"Game ball, Martín. You fucking deserve it."

"Oh." Wow. I'm speechless. Everyone's staring at me, though, so I'm not sure what to do other than tip my head and say, "Thanks."

Monty chuckles, then looks at AJ. "René's on it."

"Nice–you already tell everyone?"

"They're all in."

"What are you two talking about?" I ask nervously, because AJ looks like he's up to something. Hopefully, if he's involving our team captain and René, our team travel manager, it can't be too bad.

"Go take a shower, Lucy," he says. "We're taking you out to celebrate."

"A–"

"–Just dinner, and René is setting us up with a private room. I told you, I've got you."

I huff a laugh and shake my head. "Alright. But stop calling me Lucy."

A mischievous grin stretches across his face, and I turn away to go take a shower before he starts his stupid Ricky Ricardo impressions.

———

Ghost: Was that smile for me?

ME: You caught that?

Ghost: Kind of hard to miss. I'm not the only one, either. I'm afraid to tell you that you've become America's sweetheart over the last half hour.

ME: Shut up.

Ghost: For your fame-hating sake, I wish I was. You can't help it, you're so goddamn sexy.

A link comes through, and just by the title, I decide not to click on it.

"The smile that launched a new football fandom: America has a new heartthrob, and his name is Luc Martín."

ME: That's just absurd. They'll forget by tomorrow.

Ghost: Doubtful. They're in love 😍

Ghost: Not gonna lie, I love knowing that half the country is losing its collective shit over you right now, but I'm the only one who knows who that smile was for.

Ghost: Me. It was for me.

Ghost: *GIF of Scarlett O'Hara swooning*

ME: You're ridiculous.

Ghost: I'm also riDICKulously hard.

ME: Don't tell me that. I'm about to get on the bus.

Ghost: Headed back to the hotel to order something bland from room service and wait for your dashing boyfriend to call?

Wait... *Boyfriend?*

ME: I'm actually going out for dinner with some of the team.

Ghost: GASP 😱

Ghost: Tell AJ to check your temperature.

ME: Don't get too excited. It's a private room.

Ghost: Baby steps. You'll be dancing on tables and doing blow off a stranger's dick in no time.

ME: ...

Ghost: Just kidding. I've never done that.

Me: ...

Ghost: Okay, once.

Ghost: For the blow thing 👀

Ghost: I've danced on a lot of tables.

Ghost: Okay, I'm done digging my own grave now.

———

Shawna: THAT WAS INSANE!!!

Shawna: Congrats on a great game!

Shawna: Um. DO NOT get on the internet right now.

ME: Too late. I already saw the article.

Shawna: THE article? Oh, honey… There are so many.

Shawna: So, so many…

ME: How much shit are you about to give me?

Shawna: How much time do you have?

ME: I'm actually headed to dinner.

Shawna: What, with people?

ME: …

Shawna: Did you hit your head? Tell AJ to take you to get a CT.

ME: Why is it always AJ?

Shawna: Because he's your only friend.

Shawna: Other than me, obvs. I'm your BEST friend. He's your work bestie. It's a caste system.

Shawna: Has HE seen the articles?

God, I hope not.

I look around at my teammates, shuffling onto the bus. They're mostly talking among themselves about the game. People keep slapping me on the shoulder or fist-bumping me, but no one is being over-hyped.

Well, no one except AJ. He comes bounding towards the bus just as I'm about to get on. The people behind me let him cut in because we all sit in pretty much the same spots anyway. He's practically buzzing, lips rolled in to keep from letting too much joy out. It's disturbing.

I groan. "You saw it, didn't you?"

"Oh. My. God. Lucy, you're an internet sensation!"

"I am not. It'll die down by tomorrow."

"Unlikely. The clip that ESPN showed went viral immediately, and then so did your very boring post-game interview. Those things never get much replay unless the player says something offensive. But your boring ass, 'Well, we played a great game. Despite the stick in my ass, I ran fast,'" he says in a poor impression of Forrest Gump's voice, "is now viral.".

I roll my eyes. "It'll die down." It will. Right? *It has to.* I wonder if I can get Jesse to do something to distract the masses, like release a dick pic or something. There are pictures of his dick on the internet. I've seen them. They were all before he got sober, though.

Jesse Moore dances on tables at the Louvre and exposes dick to passing convent. Three nuns faint, and the rest strip out of their habits on sight. One nun joins him, and they perform an impromptu duet that becomes an immediate world sensation.

That should do it.

I snort a laugh and open my phone again to send Jesse a text telling him my idea, when AJ looks over my shoulder. *"Ooooh,* is that Shawna? Tell her I say hi."

"She's not interested," I sing-song.

"How do you know? You asked her?" He pauses. "No, really, have you asked her? Because if I'm not her type, I can change."

"León, she's not even *your* type." AJ almost exclusively dates models and influencers, extremely beautiful women who dress to the nines in couture and wear stilettos with jeans. The type of women who wouldn't be caught out of bed without the latest fashions, their hair and nails perfectly done, and a full face of makeup.

Shawna goes to the grocery store in an old, ratty pair of my sweatpants that she stole from my gym locker in high school. Her daily wardrobe is a pair of leggings and a baggy t-shirt that is likely also stolen from me. In the winter, she sometimes accessorizes with a hoodie that's usually covered in profanity and snark. I've never seen her wear a stitch of makeup, even at our senior prom. Her hair is almost always in a ponytail pulled through a hat that–you guessed it–bitch stole from me.

She farts and burps more than any man I've ever met, has a crippling caffeine addiction, and spends all her time reading gay smut novels.

Shawna Landry-Ryan–*middle name redacted because she hates it*–is, put quite simply, awesome.

She's my best friend in the world. My brother (because I have two sisters and don't need another) from another mother. My platonic soulmate. My inspiration for who I want to be when I grow up because she does not give a fuck.

There's no one better. That doesn't change the fact that she's not AJ's type. Not only that, he couldn't handle her.

We're still bantering back and forth about it, or rather he's kicking ideas about the different ways to woo my best friend and I'm repeating the word, "No," while looking at the menu and paying very little attention to him.

Mention of my viral embarrassment doesn't get mentioned until after we've all ordered and gotten drinks. Monty stands up and instructs everyone to lift their glasses for a toast.

"To tonight's MVP, Luc Martín, for a game well played and an interception that will make highlight reels for seasons to come. A truly impressive play that is overshadowed only by a dashing grin hidden behind his surly mask. Let it be known that tonight's meal and drinks are being paid for by the merchandising rights for the smile that got the Shreveport Cyclones more than one hundred thousand new fans in a matter of hours." He lifts his glass and winks good-naturedly. "To Luc!"

"To Luc!"

"Y'all need to stop," I grumble, bringing a palm to my face to hide how red I must be turning based on how hot I feel.

"We haven't even begun to start, darlin'," Monty says. "Treyden, our resident social media guru, has made a short list of highlights that he would like to share."

Snapping fills the room. Treyden is known for his occasional pregame poetry readings. They're usually snarky or sarcastic, but sometimes they're serious or inspirational. He's internet famous for trash-talking conservative media figures and going on insightful rants about the state of the world.

Treyden clears his deep voice and begins.

"Forget the interception, I'm intercepted by that grin. Melted face emoji." Everyone snickers, but he has, in fact, only just begun.

"Top five defensive plays of the year. Top one smile of all time." A chorus of "*aww*," fills the room. I drop my face into both hands.

"He shut down the offense, then shut down the internet." That one gets snaps of appreciation. Dear God.

"Did anyone else just feel their ovaries twinge? #sexiestsmile #impregnatemeplease" The room explodes into laughter.

"Are we done yet?" I ask over the rumble of laughing men.

"Just one more," he says. "Stats don't lie: One interception, one grin, one million new fans. #SportsCenterSpotlight"

The table stands to applaud both me and Treyden. I suppose that's an exciting one for the team overall. Since our team is still relatively young and we haven't won a championship yet, new followers are welcome. *For them.*

"Alright, now we're done. I know you don't like attention, but you really killed it tonight," Monty says, tipping his glass towards me one more time.

"Killed the ladies!" AJ calls, which gets more laughs.

"I hate you."

"No, you don't. I'm your best friend."

"Shawna is my best friend."

"Well, I'm your work best friend," he says. "But since you brought her up, is she still coming to the Carolina game?"

"Yup."

"Staying with you after?"

"For two days."

"Can I come over and hang out?"

"Nope."

"This is bullshit," he says, pointing an accusing finger. "What kind of friend are you?"

"What kind of friend are *you*?" Will Phillips, one of the offensive blockers, jokes. "Has it ever occurred to you that being all up in her face might be cock-blocking your bro? Luc could be into her, and that's why he doesn't date."

Whatever face I make must say enough about that idea. I feel like my eyes are going to pop out of their sockets. Laughter bubbles out of me. "Hell no." She knows too much. I've seen too much.

Despite the fact that Shawna and I lost our virginities to each other, it's not like that. It wasn't even like that when we did it. It was just a thing we did out of curiosity. Like a science project that had really underwhelming results.

Shawna told me to take it out and then looked at my dick like it was a dead fish.

"Isn't it supposed to be… bigger? I mean, not bigger, but like, stiff or something?"

I ended up having to jerk myself off while she watched on curiously, which made it really hard to get well, hard.

"Whoa," she said, staring at my crotch like she was doing calculus. "It really does grow a lot bigger. That's kind of a neat trick."

"Does yours do any tricks?"

She shook her head. "Nah, but I watched a video once were this lady shot a ping-pong ball out of her cooter. So there's potential," she deadpanned.

I scrunched my nose. "Don't say cooter."

She pointed at my wilting dick. "You don't look very excited."

"You don't exactly look like you want to jump my bones, either," I pointed out.

Shawna deflated. "I'm just curious, and you're the only boy I trust."

"I'm curious, too," I admitted. All I'd heard for the past four years was sex talk in the locker rooms. I liked to jerk off like any other teenage boy, and I was curious, but I didn't see the appeal of involving another person. "And you're the only person I like."

She laughed then, and we both relaxed. "Okay. So we're doing this?"

I swallowed nervously and shrugged. "I guess."

We both masturbated for a while until it seemed like we were both ready enough. Then she handed me the condom. "Can I be on top?"

"Yeah, obviously." I sure as hell didn't want to be in charge.

"Do you want me to undress more?" She was wearing one of my Cane Ridge High School football department shirts. It came down to her thighs, and she wasn't wearing anything underneath. "You can touch my boobs or whatever if you need to." Shawna was so serious and to-the-point that it was endearing.

"Let's see how it goes like this, and if it escalates, it escalates." I'd watched porn before. And it got me hard, but I didn't really see how

Shawna being naked, and likely less comfortable because of it, would help either of us.

Shawna nodded and walked over to where I was sitting on the couch. "Just… Stay still." She climbed onto my lap, straddling me. "Um, so, hold it still, and I'll do the rest?"

"Okay," I said, but before anything could happen, I grabbed her hand. "Shawna. You're my best friend and the only person I would allow myself to feel this incredibly awkward with. Don't be afraid to do whatever you want to do, or stop, or do something you think might be embarrassing. It's just you and me here."

Those would be words she'd repeat to me the morning after my night with Jesse. When she found me sitting outside, staring at the spot around the fire where we'd kissed, she sat next to me and held my hand.

"You're my best friend and the only person I allow myself to be honest with, because you're my person. Don't be afraid to cry and then tell me whatever you're going through. It's just you and me here."

In the end, neither of us got off. Shawna didn't disgust me by any means. She was gorgeous and smart and amazing. Hell, sometimes I wished I *could* feel that way about her so we could just go through this life together, always. I could even say she was objectively hot. It just wasn't like that. Never has been. Never will be.

"You know, usually when someone has a super hot friend that they're best friends with, they're either secretly in love with them or one of them is gay."

Our end of the table erupts in argument. To his credit, I don't think Will meant it with any malice, but we have a standing rule about 'phobic language, and that edged the line. Joking about someone being gay or calling someone gay used to happen all too often in the locker room, as it sometimes does when a bunch of macho athletes get together to prove their masculinity is more toxic than the others. I grew up with two sisters and Shawna for a best friend, so a lot of the typical locker room bullshit didn't sit right with me. In this case, it was Dez Carter who put a stop to it. A slur got thrown out, and he turned white as a sheet right before he snapped and said he'd had enough. He came out as bisexual to all of us, and said if anyone had any problems with that, they could say it to his face.

No one did. A few guys apologized. A couple kept more to themselves and seemed uncomfortable around him in the locker rooms and showers, but the rest of us rolled our eyes and told them to get their heads out of their asses enough that they eventually relaxed. There's only one guy left on the team I'm not really sure about, but he doesn't cause any problems.

I don't want to lie about my sexuality, because that gives the impression that I'm ashamed or embarrassed. I'm not at all. Coming out to my teammates wouldn't be a big deal. My issue is solely about my privacy. I don't want a bunch of publicity, and for some reason, the public is obsessed with the shock of finding out that a professional football player could be anything other than straight.

I'm not even sure gay is the right label. I think I'm as attracted to women as I am to men. Which is to say that I'm not, really. I can see someone and appreciate their attractiveness, but I don't want to sleep with any of them.

I just want Jesse. He's the only person who's ever made me feel like this. I can't think of another man or woman I've wanted or even noticed. I've just floated through life, oblivious to everyone, until there he was. Jesse is who I want, and Jesse is a man, so I think using the label is probably fine. It's easier than explaining myself.

"So what if I am?"

Everyone who heard me freezes. Then, slowly, one by one, each person at the table notices that the person next to them has gone quiet, and they do the same. Once again, everyone is staring at me. Damn it.

I look at Will first, since he was the one to bring it up. He shrugs. "Okay. I didn't mean anything bad by it," he assures me.

"I know."

A few seats down, Dante Briggs whispers to Treyden. "What's happening?"

"Martín is gay."

"Oh, word." Then he goes back to whatever conversation he was having, and eventually the room goes back to normal.

I feel AJ staring at me. When I turn my head towards him, he's grinning ear to ear.

"What?"

"I'm proud of you, man. Good for you."

"What the hell are you talking about?"

"I figured it out a while ago, I was just waiting for you to get comfortable to share." He pats me on the back reassuringly.

"How the hell?" Unless he's been snooping through my phone in the past month, I don't see how that's possible.

"Sonya told me about what happened with Ava." He says, eyebrows raised. "I figured you gotta be super gay because that girl in lingerie? She's so hot, dude."

I smack him on the back of his head. "Ouch! What was that for? I didn't tell anybody, did I?"

"I wasn't hiding it, it just didn't come up. It's nobody's business and the last thing I need is my name in the news and a qualifier attached to my stats. I don't want any of my private business out there."

Dez nods. "I get it. I'm not media-phobic like you are, but it gets really annoying to have your sexuality attached to everything you do. As if liking the occasional dick has anything to do with my win rate or how fast I run."

We laugh, but it's not really funny.

When Dez came out, there was some backlash from fans. We are in the deep south, so it was expected, but he got more positive attention from the fans who appreciated him publicly living his truth than anything else. He got more endorsement deals and magazine spreads, too.

Except I don't want positive attention, either. I've turned down every endorsement deal and every media event that isn't required. This smile thing is bad enough. I don't want to be America's heartthrob, gay or straight, or a conversation piece used for news fodder.

Why the fuck does it matter so much?

"Y'all know that when I came to play for the Cyclones, I didn't plan to stay past the initial contract. I love the game, but being a celebrity isn't for me. I stayed because I found a comfortable balance, and I love this team."

Before anyone can say anything else, Monty stands up again. He tells us all to listen up, but he didn't have to. The moment he stood up, with his big shiny belt buckle and black cowboy hat, he had everyone's attention. Monty is our leader, and we all have a lot of respect for him, even if he likes to embarrass his team members on occasion.

He looks at me pointedly, and then at Dez. "Both of y'all have all our support, no matter what." His gaze moves around the table, settling on every player. "I ain't about to have anybody on this team go off tellin' your business to nobody, you hear?" I give him a clipped nod, and then he stares everyone down again, as if to make sure they understand the unspoken threat. Everyone murmurs their agreement, or support, or nods. He nods his approval and sits back down.

"I told you, man. I've got your back," AJ says, echoing what he said when he saved me from the journalists after the game today. "We all know you're a private guy. Although honestly, I thought you were afraid of the publicity because you were in the closet."

I shake my head. "No, I'm just an introvert, I guess. I'm comfortable with most everyone here, so it's easier to be social, but I just don't… What?" I ask, looking around at more than one pair of raised eyebrows.

"Aside from today, you think you're social?"

"With you, yeah," I shrug.

Monty laughs. "I'm pretty sure you've said more in the last half hour than you have since you joined the team."

My face burns, and I laugh uncomfortably. I guess he's right. "Sorry. I'll try to–"

"Nah, man," AJ cuts in. "You be you. Who you are is part of what makes this team great. And we're going straight to the top this year!" AJ holds up his glass, and everyone cheers.

"Well, not *straight* to the top," Dez says. I roll my eyes, but my shoulders are shaking. These guys are something else.

Dez ends up ordering the whole table a round of *blowjobs*, a milky white shot with whipped cream on the top. Most everyone takes one, minus me and one or two other guys, but no one pressures anyone to drink. Dez explains how you take the shot, then demonstrates. I get a kick out of watching each of them take their turn putting their hands behind their back, putting their mouths around the shot glass without getting it on their faces, and then tipping them back without using their hands.

Connor Laramie, who must be a lightweight, informs me right before his turn that he likes it when his girlfriend pegs him. Which, good for him, but I didn't really need to know that. Then he's laughing too much and ends up choking when he tips his back. Some of the shot comes out of his nose and the sides of his mouth, getting all over his face.

He sputters, still laughing and coughing, and I pat his back.

"You gotta open your throat," I say, not giving it much thought.

The whole table dissolves into raucous laughter. AJ has his hands on either side of his face, practically screaming, "*OHMYGOD*! Did Luc just make a joke?! A *dirty* one?!"

I can feel my ears burning, but I can't stop laughing. By the time I get back to my hotel room, my face is actually sore from smiling so much.

LeST is MooRE

FOURTEEN
LUC

Ghost: So how was dinner?

ME: It was equal parts mortifying and awesome.

Ghost: Let me guess, they ribbed you about being nominated for Sexiest Man Alive?

ME: Shut it.

ME: But yes. Treyden read quotes from the internet.

Ghost: Ohhhh. Wait, is that the guy that reads poetry and tells off state senators on TikTok?

ME: That's the one.

Ghost: I like him.

ME: He's pretty great when he isn't sharing my biggest embarrassment in front of the whole team.

Ghost: THAT'S your biggest embarrassment? Damn, we've got to get you out more.

ME: Ha. Ha.

Ghost: We got our proofs from the photoshoot
back today.

ME: Yeah? How'd they turn out?

Ghost: You tell me…

The next message is an attachment. I open it up and… *Oh, Holy
Night.*

I have jerked off to many pictures of Jesse. Especially ones where
he's performing and he's all sweaty, or the selfies he takes after
he gets off stage.

But this…

Jesus.

It's a shot of Jesse, alone, with no background and simple, muted
colors. He's wearing the most obscene pair of leather pants I've
ever seen. The front of the pants has a plunging waistline, leading
straight to his dick, which is a hair's breadth from being exposed.
I can actually see the shape of the base catching the shadows, and
the full shape of his cock down the inside of his right leg. His
hand is resting over the bottom half of his shaft, not quite gripping, but curled around enough to be suggestive. His other hand
cups the back of his neck, feigning a timidity that doesn't reflect
in his eyes at all. The pose and the placement of a thin belt
around his natural waist, lengthens his body, accentuating the
nakedness of the front of the pants. He's standing with his legs
just a little more than shoulder-width apart and leaning slightly
back, making his hip bones and Adonis belt pop. He's looking
down at the camera like the photographer was on their knees.

He's not wearing anything else. His chest, arms, and throat are completely bare. His hair is wet or gelled and looks darker than usual, and his green eyes are rimmed in black eyeliner that's smudged just enough to make it look like he's had a wild night.

Goddamn he's so fucking hot. Otherworldly hot.

I have to unbutton my pants to get comfortable, adjusting my cock against my waistband and absentmindedly stroking myself while I stare at the photo.

I'm zooming in to look closer at how his cock is possibly fitting in those pants when the screen lights up with a video call. I'm so surprised, feeling caught red-handed zooming in on Jesse's dick-print, that I almost drop my phone.

I don't have time to make myself look less completely shook, so I answer and give him the brunt of the state I'm in. My face is flushed, I'm sweaty, and my hair is falling in my face.

Jesse, of course, looks flawless. His hair is damp, so he might be fresh out of the shower. I can almost smell his shampoo, the herbal scent that reminds me of mulling spices and sex. I consider the stupidly expensive bottle of shampoo in my shower at home and wish I'd replaced my travel bottle of *Irish Spring 3 in1* that I keep in my away bag. I don't smell like him after showering when we're on the road.

"You went quiet on me, heartthrob."

I give him a look. "First of all, just no. Second of all, you kind of shorted out my brain."

"Yeah?"

"Uh, yeah. Those pants defy physics. And decency. What the hell were these photos for?"

"*Rolling Stone.*"

"I love how you say that so casually, like it's nothing to be in *Rolling Stone* magazine."

He smiles and shrugs, and it occurs to me that, to him, it probably isn't that monumental. I know he's been on the cover at least one other time.

"I can't imagine they'll get away with having this on the cover."

"I'm wearing the pants on the cover, but not this pose. And the rest of the band is in it, too."

"What are they wearing?"

"Nothing quite so extra," he laughs.

I blow a huff of air at a lock of hair that's fallen onto my forehead. "Well, you look…" I swallow, not really having the words.

"Show me."

"What?"

"Show me how much you liked it."

Blinking rapidly, I look down at myself. I'm wearing the same pants I wore on our date in Dallas, and a long-sleeve black button-down. The shirt is tucked in, but I've undone my pants to give my raging erection room to breathe. It's poking out of my underwear, leaking pre-cum all over the bottom of my shirt.

"Come on, baby. Don't be shy."

I shiver at the low tone of his raspy voice. And then I tilt my phone screen down, showing him what he's done to me.

Jesse whimpers. "God, just look at that. Fucking gorgeous, and so wet and messy. You're going to have to explain that to the dry-cleaner, you know.

I close my eyes and let out a pained chuckle. He might be right. Although I'd probably toss the shirt before I did that. But hearing him admonish me for getting cum on my clothes is insanely sexy.

He knows it too.

"Take it all the way out," he tells me. "I want to see just how messy you are."

Slowly, and with trembling fingers, I switch the camera around and point it down at my lap. Jesse hums.

"So wet from just one little picture? *Tsk*."

I huff a laugh. "That wasn't just any picture, and you know it."

He laughs. "Well, I'm glad you like it."

"I don't think that's a strong enough word for it."

"Now you have some idea of how I felt when I saw you smile into the camera for me. I knew you were thinking of me, just like I was thinking of you when I had that photo taken."

I groan and prop my phone up on the dresser and sit across from it. It's clear where this is going, and I'm here for it. I'm hard, and I miss him, and I want to feel close to him. I've jerked off while he was talking to me, telling me things he wanted to do to me. I want him to do that now while I can see him.

"Let me see you, Jesse."

He bites his lip and grins like he was waiting for me to say just that. He moves around, setting his phone up to face his bed. Then he crawls onto the bed, wearing just a black button-down shirt and–

"Jesse."

"Hmm?"

"Don't act all innocent. What exactly are you wearing?"

"Just a shirt. And…" He slowly unbuttons his shirt as he talks, opening it to reveal red lace. "…some panties."

"Panties," I croak. My hand stalls mid-stroke.

"Do you like them?" He asks, looking almost legitimately sheepish.

"Let me see them closer," I demand, smoothing pre-cum down my shaft. Jesse knee-walks to the edge of the bed, close enough that I can see him from nipple to thigh. "Goddamn, beautiful. You are…" I take a breath. "Fucking stunning." He's wearing a pair of blood-red lace boy shorts with a black waistband. The lace is doing nothing to contain his erection, the lace pushed out from his body.

"Turn around," I beg. "Let me see the rest of you."

He obliges, slowly turning around, and I nearly choke on my own spit. His delectable ass is cupped perfectly by the scalloped hem of the lace, and the fabric at the back is held together with strings that look like corset ties.

"Sweet Jesus, what are you doing to me, Jesse?"

Instead of answering, he slowly bends forward until he's on his hands and knees, then lowers himself even more to put his face to the mattress. The corset strings are tied together at the base of his balls for easy access to his hole that he's presenting to me with his back curved and pert ass sticking up like an offering.

My mouth waters. My dick leaks, and I have to pinch the base of my crown to keep from blowing my load before I even start stroking myself.

It can't be legal to be this sexy.

While I'm trying not to come, Jesse reaches around himself to untie the bow at his taint, and the middle of the panties unravels to show bare skin, lace framing the perfect view of his spread cheeks and perfect, tight pink hole.

"Goddamn Jesse," I groan, as his body starts to rock, his right arm shaking with the movements of jerking himself. I start stroking in time with him, quickly working myself up to an edge.

Jesse rolls over on his back, with his feet on the bed and knees bent. He starts thrusting up in to his hand, and the dirty words come tumbling out of his mouth.

"I miss you so fucking bad, baby. I want you so much. Fucking me, filling me up. I want your cum dripping out of me," he rasps, voice getting higher and shakier as he gets closer to release. "And I want to fuck you. I want to feel you squeeze my cock as you cum so hard for me, you scream my name and milk the cum into your tight ass."

"Oh, fuck, Jesse—"

I'm half bent over, with one hand on the dresser so I can get as close to the phone screen as possible, not wanting to miss a single detail. My orgasm is coming, but I try to slow down, to stave it off until he's pumped the last bit of cum from his balls. I don't want to chance my eyes crossing when I finally bust.

"Fuck. Come for me, Jesse. Soak those pretty panties."

"Loooooosssssssss—"

He lets out a long, guttural moan and strokes faster, until he shoots into the air and spills down the sides.

Shit. Shit. Shit. I can't hold it anymore.

"I can't see!" he cries, scrambling to his knees to watch me, and I have just enough cognitive function to adjust how I'm sitting right before I spray all over my chest and stomach.

"Fuuuuucckkk," he moans, still stroking himself, and we ride out the aftershocks of our orgasms together, muttering barely intelligible things to each other.

I almost want to cry from the release when we come down. It's still a pale shadow of what it's like to be touched by him in real life.

When I can breathe a little easier, I unbutton and toss my filthy shirt away and scoot back onto the bed. For a while we just lie there, both lying on our sides as if we were in bed next to each other.

"I came out today. To my team."

"No shit?"

I shake my head, smiling as my cheeks heat.

"Ugh, don't do the blushing thing. It's too adorable. I'll just get hard again, and I am close to chaffing with how much I've jerked off since the smile that broke America's brains."

I scoff and put a hand over my face.

"Luc?" I open my fingers to peek at him, and he laughs. "Did you really?"

"Yeah. It was kind of an accident," I say, and give him a brief rundown of the conversation. "I didn't want to lie. And it's not even that I'm closeted, I'm just a private person and don't like talking about myself. Besides, I didn't really know for sure until now anyway."

"What do you mean?"

"I never really thought about what label to use. It's never been important. Will made a joke, and I thought about it, and I'm definitely into you in a big way, so I think it's okay to use gay as the closest thing."

"I assumed you were bisexual. I know you'd never been with a man our first time, but what kind of people have you dated since then? Just women? Or was it a mix?"

I clear my throat and avert my eyes, trying to think of how to say I'm not into anyone else that I've met so far in my twenty-seven years.

"Luc?"

"I mean, I went on a few dates with someone, but there wasn't a connection for me. Besides, I only went out with her in the first place because AJ set us up."

"What about hookups?"

I shake my head. "No. You're the only hookup I've ever had."

"Really?"

"Jesse, you're the only *anything* I've ever had."

"What do you mean?"

"Don't laugh."

"I would never."

I give him a look, and he returns it with a cheesy grin.

"Before the night I met you, I'd only had sex once, and not to completion."

"Not to…completion?" he repeats under his breath. "You mean you didn't come?"

"Uh-uh. She didn't either. It wasn't right. Parts of it felt okay, I guess. I mean it's a dick, if you rub it, something's going to happen. But I didn't really find it enjoyable. I just never liked sex."

"You seem to like it well enough with me," he says, sounding rather cocky. "But there's not been anyone else since that night? At all?"

I shrug. "I've never met anyone else I felt interested in."

"Ever?"

I shake my head. "Maybe it's because I didn't really put myself out there. Or maybe it's because I was still so overwhelmed with the memory of you. And not just the sex. I felt something the first time I saw you. A recognition or awareness that I'd never experienced before and haven't since."

"So I'm the only one you've ever come with?"

Why does he sound proud of that? I want to die, but I nod, holding my breath and looking away from the screen so I don't have to see him process what a loser I am.

Jesse groans.

"Sorry."

"What? What are you sorry for?"

"I dunno, bringing the mood down. Making it weird. That's probably too much to put on something so new, and we barely know each other."

"You didn't make it weird. What's weird is how much I like the idea that I'm the only one who has ever had you this way."

He pumps his eyebrows and I hide my eyes with my hand. "Pretend I didn't say anything. I'm still delirious from what you put me through with that picture and then those panties."

"These panties?" Jesse holds up the panties with one finger, and I can see they're completely drenched.

"You're trying to kill me."

"No," he says simply. "And you're not allowed to die, anyway. I think we might be soulmates, Luc Martín. I'm keeping you."

"Soulmates?" I say skeptically. "Really?"

"I never believed in that sort of thing before," Jesse says, laying his head on his pillow and blinking up at me with earnest green eyes. "But tell me what else it could be."

FIFTEEN
JESSE

The power in the arena flickers, rain pelting the roof so hard it sounds like it might cave in. Me, Naz, Ari, and Will are camped out on couches in the greenroom, waiting to find out if we'll be doing sound check any time soon. Blake is pacing one end of the room, playing middleman between his director and the venue manager, who is standing just inside the door looking stressed. Gage, our equipment manager, is sitting with his feet kicked up on the small dining table, scrolling on his phone.

The energy on the couch is different. Strained, maybe, but I'm not sure why. Ari and Will are sitting farther apart than they normally do, with Naz between them. He's holding his e-reader and trying to read, but he must feel the vibe, too, because he keeps looking up to cut eyes at each of the brothers.

I'm texting Luc. He just finished up with a positional meeting, whatever that is.

ME: If you wanted to learn new positions, you could have just said so.

Blushing Beefcake: Don't even try it. I am NOT letting you give me a boner before I get on the plane again. The ride home from Miami last week was awful.

ME: Aw, I'm sorry.

Blushing Beefcake: No, you're not.

ME: Not even a little bit. I jerked off three times to your whining about how hard you were.

Blushing Beefcake: I hate you.

ME: You already know the Milk and Water Embrace.

Blushing Beefcake: Do I even want to know? Is it safe to look this up?

Blushing Beefcake: Never mind, I saw the words Kama Sutra and bailed. Did I mention that I'm getting on a plane?

ME: The Rowing Boat is my personal favorite. We've done something similar, but you probably don't remember it. I'll have to refresh your memory.

ME: It requires some strength and flexibility, but you really get in there so deep...

Blushing Beefcake: I'm going to turn my phone off.

ME: No, you're not.

ME: ...

ME: You know, I've always wanted to try Congress of a Cow. Look that one up and tell me what you think. You're an athlete. I think you could pull it off.

Blushing Beefcake: Can't this wait until I'm in the hotel at least?

ME: You're blushing right now, aren't you?

ME: Have a nice flight! 😇

"Alright, enough! What the fuck is going on with you two?"

I snap my gaze up to see Naz with his arms crossed, e-reader in his lap, glaring back and forth at Ari and Will. They're both just as stunned as I am with Naz's outburst.

"Nothing is going on–" Will starts.

Naz cuts him off. "Bullshit."

While those two are bickering, I watch Ari. He seems to be avoiding Naz and Will's gazes. He must feel me staring, because he flicks his eyes up to mine.

I give him a curious look and mouth the words, "Are you okay?"

He shrugs first, then nods. "It'll be fine," he mouths back.

"What are you all bickering about?" Blake asks, putting his phone down for the first time today.

"Nothing important," Ari says quickly. "Will is just pissy about his costume."

"Still?" Naz asks. "Come on, man."

"The bald cap makes me sweaty."

"Then you wear the wig cap like Myra suggested," I say, then look back at Blake, redirecting the conversation. I'm about ninety-five percent sure Ari's excuse is bullshit. Will has been in a mood lately, but that seems like a petty reason to be so on edge. "What's the word?"

"The storm is supposed to get pretty bad tomorrow night. NOLA is battening down the hatches. There's no other choice but to cancel the show."

Everyone deflates in a series of groans, heavy sighs, and curses.

Our annual Halloween concert is not only our favorite because it's so much fun, but it's also one of our top charity events of the year. The concert is live-streamed, and people make live donations throughout the set. Large donations get on-screen shout-outs and song requests, plus we let the audience make one-dollar votes for what songs we play as we go, based on social media polls run by our PR team. It's something we started three years ago and has become a huge social media event. Last year we raised hundreds of thousands of dollars for *The Trevor Project*. It's a huge loss.

Everyone is silent for a few minutes, processing having to cancel our best event of the year, and trying to think of a miracle solution.

"Can we reschedule? It won't be Halloween night, but this is our last full concert until after the holidays. All we have next month is a bunch of promo and a studio block. There's got to me something we can move around," Naz says.

Mr. Hebert, the venue manager, chimes in. "I have an idea, if it's alright."

Blake gestures for him to go ahead. "Let's hear it, Vic."

"We have a hold for next weekend, but I think I could persuade them to work with us if the band might be willing to let them co-sponsor the concert."

"Who is it?" Blake asks.

"Have you heard of the *Waves* app?"

"No way," Ari and Will say simultaneously.

"That's actually kind of perfect," I say.

"I thought so, too," Mr. Hebert says. "Would you like me to put out a feeler?"

"Yes," I say, echoed by Naz, Will, and Ari.

Blake says, "Hold on."

"Call PR, and if they don't tell you to jump on this opportunity immediately, I'll never talk back to you again," I say. "*Waves* a progressive social media company. They're new but growing fast enough that they're showing real promise of competing with the big companies."

"They were just in the news for turning down a massive payout from Nark 'My Skin Suit Is Itchy' Fuckerbird," Gage says. I flinch a little because I forgot he was here.

"They're legit, and align with a lot of what we're about," Naz says. "They'd be a huge boost to the concert, and we'd actually be contributing to their success as well."

"Which is why I feel very confident that they'll want to collaborate," Mr. Hebert says.

"Okay," Blake says. "See what they say, and I'll do a little research before pitching it to PR."

Mr. Hebert nods excitedly and lifts his phone to his ear on his way out the door. Blake pulls out his laptop, and we all shuffle to make room for him on the small sectional. He does some basic internet searches to read about the company.

"The social platform where music and activism collide. Make waves, be heard," he reads out loud.

Ari hands him his phone. "They've already got over ten million followers." Blake thumbs around the app, looking mildly impressed. "All of us and the label have accounts with several million followers."

Blake hands Ari's phone back. "I hate social media, but I might download this one just based on their mission statement and activism."

Mr. Hebert bursts into the room, looking flushed and excited. "They're in! Zero questions." He hands a sticky note to Blake. "That's the number to call for their events management team. They're waiting to hear from you." He looks at all of us. "Kit Quinley, one of the co-founders, is a huge fan, and they are very much looking forward to meeting all of you."

"Alright," Blake says, standing. "Let me make a few calls and make sure the label is on board. Then we can start getting things in motion."

Gage gets up to follow him out. "Cory just texted that they ordered pizza. Want me to grab a couple for y'all?"

"Hell. Yes," Naz says. "See if they got any with–"

"Cory also said that Scott ordered one with extra peppers just for you."

Naz pauses. "Oh. Tell him I said thank you?" His voice lilts up at the end, making it sound like more of a question than anything else.

Gage smirks like he knows something the rest of us don't and nods. "Any other requests?"

"I'll eat anything except onions," I say.

Will says, "Veggie, please." Just as Ari asks for, "Something with a lot of meat."

"You would want that," Will snaps, and it doesn't sound like their usual friendly banter.

"Yeah, because it's good."

I point at Ari. "100% facts." Will narrows his eyes at me, and Ari's eyes swim with amusement. "You were talking about dick, right?"

"Will you shut up," Will spits. "Let's talk about how Scott clearly wants Naz's dick."

Gage snorts on his way out of the room.

"Wait, he's the new bodyguard, right?" He confirms with a nod but doesn't say anything else. In fact, he's pointedly ignoring me. Which means it's probably true. "How have I missed this?"

"You've been a bit distracted lately," he says pointedly.

"You would be too."

He rolls his eyes and is getting ready to say something else when Scott walks back in with a stack of pizzas. Everyone goes quiet, watching Naz act completely out of character. He sits stiffly, refusing to make eye contact with anything except the screen-saver for his e-reader.

"Yours is on bottom, boss."

"Thanks, Scott," he murmurs. Ari snorts and says, "Yeah, I bet it is."

Naz peeks up to watch Scott leave the room, raising an eyebrow when he notices me watching. *Yeah, I saw that.*

He gives me a look. *Not now.*

I narrow my eyes. *Better be soon.*

Letting him be–*for now*–I open the pizza boxes, taking a slice from both Naz and Ari's requests and wrinkling my nose at Will's onion-infested veggie pizza.

"Aww, poor thing. Do you need me to pick them off for you?" Will snarks.

"You think you'd be in a better mood now that you don't have to wear your costume," I snark back, my tone very clearly suggesting that I know that excuse was bullshit.

We dress up in coordinating costumes every year. Last year we wore variations of black suits and elaborate skeleton makeup on our faces and bodies. The year before, we dressed up as Batman villains. I was Poison Ivy.

This year, I convinced everyone to dress as characters from *The Rocky Horror Picture Show*. Will was supposed to be Riff Raff, but he was being a little bitch about the bald cap. Meanwhile, Ari's Magenta wig is huge, and he hasn't complained once. Naz's costume is nothing but a pair of tiny, shiny gold briefs. I, obviously, was going to be Dr. Frank-N-Furter. It's a shame, really. I was looking forward to hearing Luc's reaction to our costumes, since I know he's a fan of the film, and also recently became a fan of seeing me in lingerie.

Blake comes back in and lets us know we're on for next weekend. There are still a lot of logistics to work out, so he's heading back to the hotel where he has an office set up in his suite. "PR wants you to record a video for your socials about the changes. It'll be a good way to soothe the hurt of the cancellation and get the fans hyped for next weekend. Send it over to Charlene, and we'll post it as soon as the logistics are worked out. And since we're going to miss Halloween, we decided to do a subtle resistance theme. Emphasis on subtle." He gives me a pointed look.

"What?"

The guys snicker.

"Anyway, the label rarely polices what you wear or display on stage. However, with the addition of *Waves* to the event programming, and because this will probably reach double the home viewership, we'd like to keep it a little more family friendly than usual. No one expects you to change your lyrics or performance, but let's keep our protest positive. "*Pro*-Women, *Pro*-LGBTQ, *Pro*-Immigration, *Pro*-Prison Reform," he says. "Yes, Naz, you can wear your *Read Books, Punch Nazis* shirt. And Will, hard no to the guillotine shirt, but your *No Kings But Drag Kings* shirt would be a winner."

"Can I wear guillotine earrings?" Will asks.

Blake sighs. "How big are they? Wait. No. Better safe than sorry."

"Fine. At least I don't have to wear the bald cap."

"Actually…" I say, giving him my most angelic grin.

"That's creepy," Ari says.

"Hush. I have an idea. Tomorrow is Halloween, and the fans always make a big deal out of our costumes. The makeup and wardrobe crews are already going to be here, so why don't we make the most of it and do something fun for the fans by recording the video in costume? Will, you'd only have to wear it for a short while."

"Yeah, no, for sure. I'd be cool with that."

"Alright then," Blake says. "It's settled. I'm going to head back to the hotel to get some of this work done if anyone wants to ride with me."

"I wouldn't mind going for a swim," I say. The other guys nod and decide to leave too.

We pile into our rented SUV, Blake sitting up front while Tad drives. "So, it looks like you all are free after about two p.m. tomorrow. Any plans for what you guys are going to do with your unexpected weekend off?"

"I think I might head home and check on construction. I should have at least the framework of a house up by now," Naz says.

Ari and Will say, "New York," at the same time and then pout. They share a condo in the city and usually go there during any time off we have.

"Atlanta," I say, smiling to myself.

"What's in Atlanta?" Will asks.

"There's a football game I'd like to see."

"Since when do you like football?"

Naz snorts. "Since he found himself a *boy-friend*," he says, singing the word like a bully on a playground.

"What? Since when?" Ari shrieks.

I shrug. "About… six years-ish?"

Ari, Will, and Blake are all staring at me in confusion. I shouldn't have said anything. Nosy bastards. I give them a brief rundown without much detail, just that we'd met at a party the night before the band got picked up by the producer. We lost contact and recently reconnected. That's all. No biggie.

Blake huffs thoughtfully and turns back around. Ari and Will, however, are still giving me dubious looks.

"Y'all haven't seen him walking around with that goofy-ass smile on his face, always typing away on his phone?" Naz asks. "Suddenly requesting a penthouse suite all to himself, and staying locked away in his own room when we share a suite like usual?"

"Wait. Is that why you were all distracted in Dallas?" Ari asks, with an almost sad crinkle in his brows.

"Uh, more importantly, when I walked out on the balcony yesterday morning, did I or did I not almost catch you taking a dick pic? Because you threw your phone down like you were doing something sketchy."

"When have I ever been shy about showing anyone my dick?" I ask.

"Since you traded in your fuckboy status for *The Smile That Broke The Internet*," Naz laughs.

"WHAT?!" Ari's outburst is so loud, Tad slams on the brakes and nearly gets rear-ended.

"Shit. Sorry. Are you okay back there?"

I give him a thumbs-up in the rearview.

"Jesus, Ari, calm down."

"I fucking can't, *William*," he says, over-enunciating his name. "Did you hear what he said?" Ari looks at Naz, then points at me. "You're telling me that *he* is dating Mr. Colgate?"

"Don't call him that. He hates that." After his newfound fame, Luc was approached to do a toothpaste endorsement, which was mortifying for him. I was amused, though. I thought he should do it.

Ari blinks. "You're actually serious?"

My face breaks out in a grin. How can I not smile? I'm getting to lay claim to my man.

Will shakes his head. "Only you, man. Wait. Is he out?"

"No. He's extremely private about his personal life."

I don't miss the looks of pity on Naz and Ari's faces. They're looking at me like I'm some kind of sad sap falling for a toxic closet case who will only break my heart by rejecting me publicly, just like the field hockey player I secretly hooked up with my junior year of high school.

"Don't look at me like that. He's not *closeted*, he's just private. And don't judge him either. We live in very different worlds. I can screw whoever I want and its entertainment news, at most. If he gets outed publicly, it follows him and overshadows his entire career. I get to be Jesse Moore, rockstar and sex god. He'd be Luc Martín, *homosexual* defensive back for the Shreveport Cyclones. *He's one of the best defensive players in the league, but I don't know, Chuck, I'm just not comfortable being in the locker room with one of them queers.* Reporters would hound him almost as much as they do us, follow him home, to the grocery store, bother his family. All things he's spent his entire career avoiding even before he knew for sure that he was gay."

"Jesse, how can you date a guy who isn't out and doesn't want to be out with your level of fame?" Ari asks gently. "How does it work?"

"Well, right now it's a lot of late-night phone calls and dick pics, but we'll figure it out." We have to.

"If Luc doesn't want to be famous, he might want to reconsider making eyes at you through a camera lens," Naz jokes.

"I'll let him know you said so," I laugh.

"Ooh! When do we get to meet him?" Ari asks excitedly.

"Hard no."

"What?" All three complain.

"It's not going to happen. You'll scare him away with your heavy breathing. Ew. Stop. Also, you're meddlesome, and you know it. You can't be trusted not to scare him away. It's precarious enough just because of who I am."

"Damn," Will says. "Can you imagine how many broken hearts there are going to be if it does ever get out? People might actually send you death threats. You could get booed off stage."

Ari nods, agreeing with Will for perhaps the first time today. "He's right. I even kind of hate you right now. I don't want to admit how many times I've watched that GIF on repeat."

Same, Ari. Same. But he's mine.

"Well, you're definitely never meeting him now. Stay away. He's mine."

SIXTEEN
JESSE

Cory pokes his head into the stairwell, gesturing for me to move quickly. "Alright, you're clear."

"Thanks, Cory," I whisper.

"No problem. Call if you need anything. And Jesse–"

"Don't leave the room without alerting you first. I know the drill," I say, taking my bag and guitar case from him. "I don't plan on leaving tonight for certain, so go have some fun for once. Throw some axes, or whatever lumberjacks do these days."

He chuckles and stands back, watching and waiting until I'm safe.

My nerves are buzzing. He was alone and about to hop in the shower a few minutes ago when we talked on the phone, but what if someone showed up since then? Cory said he could get fined or even suspended if he's caught with someone in his room, so I'll just have to make sure not to get caught. It's been agony to be so far apart these last few weeks, and I'll be damned if I'm not going to take advantage of any amount of time off.

I rap on the door quietly, hoping it's loud enough for him to hear, but not loud enough for anyone else to get curious. He said most of the guys were going out to do some touristy stuff in downtown Atlanta for promo opportunities, so there shouldn't be many people around.

My heart jumps when I hear the door handle move. Darting my eyes up and down the hall, I only see Cory walking in the opposite direction. I pull the belt of my knee-length trench coat open, and position my hands on my hips, praying to every deity anyone's ever prayed to that I got the room number right.

"Trick or treat," I say, watching his eyes widen comically.

He's frozen for a long moment, eyes taking me in from my heels to my garters, to my curly black wig.

"Jesse? You…You're not supposed to be here." *God, this man is precious.*

I smirk and finger the large pearls around my neck. "I'm a wild and untamed thing," I quote, winking.

That seems to jolt him back to the here and now. Luc gasps, reaching for my wrist and hauling me inside the room, checking both ends of the hallway as he grabs my things and closes the door. Spinning to put his back against the door, he surveys me again, blinking rapidly as if he doesn't believe I'm real. I drop my trench coat to the floor. He lowers my bags.

He opens his mouth to say something, but can only gape. We take each other in. My eyes fall down his body, drinking in his wet hair, bare chest sprinkled with little water droplets that make me thirsty, and the dark grey sweatpants sitting low on his hips. Every inch of him is perfectly sculpted, as if a divine creator carved him in the perfect image of every one of my fantasies.

My eyes catch on the very prominent erection tenting his sweatpants, and I flick my eyes up, finding his eyes on my garters. He notices me watching him, and then, with a sharp intake of breath, we collide.

His arms wrap around me, pulling me against his hard body. My hands grip both sides of his face to hold him still, and I thrust my tongue into his mouth, moaning and whimpering because, holy fuck, how have I gone almost three weeks without his touch?

Luc's fingers play with the garters running down the backs of my thighs, and I hook one leg around his hips. He holds it there, massaging my thigh and ass, pulling me tighter against him and rocking his hips into me.

"Luc… Please fuck me. Right now."

"Right now?"

"Right fucking now," I say, and jump up. I'm a couple of inches taller than usual, thanks to the heels, and my balance is off, but he catches me and wraps my legs around his waist. He walks into the hotel room and sets me on the bed, where I immediately start pawing at the drawstring on his pants to tug them down.

No underwear? We're going to have to talk about answering the door like this when he's already on the *Most Wanted* list. Later. Because even my possessive musings are put on hold when his cock is free from his sweatpants. It bobs up, hitting me in the chin. I can't even laugh about being dick slapped–that's how fucking horny I am for this man.

Instead, I close my eyes and nuzzle it like a cat trying to get him to pet me. I rub my face and consequently, my makeup, all over it. My nose runs up and down the length of him, breathing in his earthy musk and–

Is that my body wash?

Just to be sure, I bury my nose in his trimmed pubes and huff. Sure enough, the subtle hints of ginger and shea are there, mixed in with his natural scent. There's no *Irish Spring* soap detected.

When I flick my eyes up to him, there's a deep blush painting his face and down his neck to his chest. *Oh, my.*

"I can't wait to find out what that blush is for," I say, my voice gravelly with lust. "But I'm shivering with–" I grip the base of his cock. "–antici…" A little lick at the tip, a gentle nibble on his foreskin. "…pation."

He huffs a breathy laugh that turns into a guttural moan as I take him down my throat. Wrapping a hand around the back of my head, he grips my wig and holds me where he wants me to fuck my face.

Fuck *yes.* The way he's taking control has me leaking into my tight black briefs. I moan and look up to find him gazing down at me reverently. One finger swipes the tears from my cheeks, and I can't imagine how wrecked I look with this much eye makeup melting off my face.

Before I'm ready for it, he's pulling out of my mouth. I whine as his cock moves over my lips, and my tongue chases it. I'm rewarded with a swift thrust back into my mouth, Luc grunting and riding my throat for another few seconds before he pulls out fast and bends down to kiss me.

"I don't want to come too soon," he says against my lips before lowering to his knees, trailing his kisses down my jaw and neck. His fingers play with the strings of my corset all the way down to the bottom. I lean back on my hands to stretch out my torso, and he licks along the top of the garter belt, and then up both creases at the apex of my thighs. I'm already panting by the time he's pressing his mouth against my cotton-covered cock, sucking on the wet stain soaking the front of my underwear while running a finger under the hem.

"Luc," I pant, rocking my hips to get more friction because he's barely touching me and it's driving me wild.

"I thought you liked the anticipation," he teases, lips pressed on the inside of my thigh. Then finally–*finally*–he pulls the crotch of the briefs to the side to let my poor cock escape. He licks and sucks me, flicking his tongue over my piercings. It's hard to hold on, to keep myself from giving in and succumbing to the pleasure, but I know it'll be worth it when his fingers start moving over my taint and I know that at any second, he's going to find–

Luc snaps his gaze up to mine, eyes turning dark and stormy, before he guides me to lean back more, spread wider, and tip my hips so he can get a better view. He pulls my underwear to the side and drags his fingers lower until he exposes the deep red heart-shaped jewel sitting flush against my asshole. He makes a sound like a cross between a cough and a whimper, then drops his head to my thigh. Sitting up a little, I reach down to comb my fingers through his hair until he looks up at me with an almost pained expression.

Except it's not pain, I realize. He's trying to get control of himself, but I want him to take all the frustration of the last couple weeks out on me in any way he desires.

I pull a condom and a packet of lube out of the front of my corset and toss it down on the bed next to him.

"I'm ready for you, baby. Take me. Take me and make me yours again. Use me. Again and again and again until you've ruined me even more than I already am."

Luc closes his eyes, and I watch a shiver work its way down his body. When his eyes pop open again, they're nearly black with lust and spent control.

In one fluid move, Luc grabs me by the hips and flips me over onto my stomach. His thumb presses into the fabric over the base of the plug, and I whine until he takes the back of my underwear in his big hand and rips them from my body.

"Oh, *Fuck!*" I cry out, clenching my body to keep from coming.

The bed dips as Luc presses a knee onto the bed next to me, lowering himself so his lips are hovering just behind the shell of my ear.

"As much as I want to hear you scream," he says, fingers tracing down my back to my now exposed ass. "You're going to have to be quiet, or you'll get me in trouble. Do you think you can do that for me?"

I fist the blanket near my head and nod, not trusting myself to speak. He slips his fingers into my crack, rubbing and pressing against the plug. The mattress absorbs my moaned curse as he pulls the plug partway out and pushes it back in, fucking it into me a few times.

"Jesus, Jesse, how big is this thing?" He exclaims as he pulls more of the plug out of me.

"Not as big as you— *Nnyggh!*" I shove my face back into the mattress and cry out as he fucks me with the toy and I shake, on the edge and losing control at a rapid pace. He might be too, if the pool of pre-cum dripping on my lower back and ass is any indication.

I breathe a sigh of relief when he gives me a short reprieve to open the condom and squirt the lube on himself and directly in my hole, pushing it into me with the plug before he finally removes it entirely, dropping it on the bed where I can see it.

Luc grabs me by the hips to maneuver me into the position he wants, with my ass in the air and my face flat against the mattress. He snaps the garters at my thighs and runs his fingers down the back of the corset.

"God, you're so fucking beautiful," he says, holding his cock and rubbing it through my crease. Even that has me trembling and moaning. Luc rips the rest of my underwear off, balls them up, and shoves them in my mouth. "Shhh," he whispers, sweetly kissing my cheek before licking behind my ear. My eyes roll back, and I whimper as heat builds in my core, getting hotter and stronger the more Luc teases my hole with the tip of his cock. My orgasm is already sparking to life by the time he sinks into me, and I'm shaking uncontrollably.

"Fuck, Jesse. You make me feel like an animal," he groans, pulling out and slamming home again. He picks up his pace, pounding into me harder and faster, hitting my prostate with the precision of a machine. It's all I can do to fist my hands into the bedspread and hold on for dear life as the heat in my body overtakes me. The underwear gag is barely muffling my cries. He doesn't let up, pushing me past the point of orgasm and into a full-body meltdown, my muscles contracting so hard my scream is silent and I'm in danger of my vision blacking out.

Luc holds himself still for a second while my ass clenches around his cock. We're both breathing like we've run a marathon, sweat pouring out of us. He stays buried inside me, helping me lift my chest off the bed and cradling my back against his chest. Somehow, my cock is still hard. Luc thrusts, and I scream. Actual tears fall from my eyes. The angle is too intense, I'm too sensitive.

Still moving inside me, Luc's hand comes up to cup my jaw, turning my face towards him. He licks up some of my tears and runs kisses over my jaw to my mouth, pressing his lips to my gagged mouth. "Are you okay?"

I whimper through the gag, sucking air through my nose with the small reprieve. I nod, and he smiles. His lips and tongue move down my neck, and his hand covers my mouth. His other hand wraps around my aching cock. Every time he thrusts into me, a whine leaves me. The faster and harder he moves, the more I cry, until I'm screaming again. Screaming for him to stop, to keep going, to slow down, to push me over whatever edge is looming. He muffles the sound with his hand and keeps going, pulling out and slamming into me, the angle hitting the already pulsing pressure point inside me. Despite not coming down from the first orgasm, the relentless assault on my prostate forces a second wave to hit me hard and fast. I sob, spraying the bed.

Luc pulls out, and I collapse on the bed, but he's not done yet. He tears the wig off my head, and the wig cap, and threads his fingers into my hair. His other hand grips my thigh and pushes one leg up like a frog, then he's there again, pushing inside my swollen, aching ass.

He uses me like a life-size cock sleeve, fucking into me with reckless abandon, harder than I knew he was capable of. He's never been quite like this before, and I am all the more wrecked because of it.

Luc lets out a warbled grunt and slows his thrusts to a smooth, rolling motion that has me moaning. It hurts so fucking good.

"Jesse," he murmurs. "Jesse. Jesse…" He shudders, emptying the last of himself into the condom, and I wish desperately that I could feel his cum flooding me.

Luc gently pulls his cock from my body, falling to my side, still catching his breath. He pulls the underwear from my mouth and hikes my leg up over his hip for easier access to run his fingers over my abused hole, soothing and massaging.

I'm in a daze. Where did my big, shy, gentle giant go? And how did he learn to fuck like that?

He kisses my neck and shoulder and collarbone while he soothes my aches and whispers, "How is it so good with you, Jesse? How do you make me feel this way?"

LeAST is MooRE

SEVENTEEN
LUC

A text informs me that my room service has been delivered and is just outside my door. I asked for a no-contact delivery to avoid anyone getting a peek at what I'm hiding in my room.

My sexy as fuck rockstar is lounging across the bed like some kind of erotic Victorian painting, his long limbs stretched out, beautiful face lying on one arm. He's watching me hungrily, and not because of the food. He's insatiable, even after everything I put him through when he first arrived. I didn't even know men could have back-to-back orgasms like that. We're both young and healthy and have an active libido, or at least I do when I'm around him, but it usually takes us at least twenty to thirty minutes to rally.

He passed out almost immediately after rasping just how good and perfectly wrecked he felt. I stroked his hair while he slept, chuckling at how wrecked he looked, given the costume makeup smeared all over his face. Wanting him to be comfortable, I untied the corset and loosened it as much as I could without rustling him. I followed him into sleep with him hugged against my chest, and we took such a long nap the sun was going down when we woke up.

The bathtub here isn't anywhere near as massive as the one in the Dallas penthouse, but it's big enough that we fit in together with my back against the porcelain and Jesse's back to my chest. I washed and massaged him while he scrubbed the rest of the makeup off, and told me about the New Orleans cancellation. It's ridiculous how choked up I feel that he went through all the trouble to come see me.

He soothes that ache by teasing me about my recent change in body wash. "In all seriousness," he says, turning in my arms, "I'm completely obsessed with your dick smelling like me." And that's how we ended up getting hot and heavy again so soon after I was rough with him. I was supposed to be helping soothe the ache, and here Jesse was trying to coax me into fucking him again.

He's so swollen down there, though. He needs a rest. Jesse keeps insisting that he loved every intense second and would do it five more times tonight until he was bleeding and unable to walk. I feel guilty for going that hard on him, but it's like my mind left me. I'm a bit weirded out by how much I like the rough talk, although I'll admit that the intense session was exactly what I needed after being deprived of him for weeks. I've been taut as one of Jesse's guitar strings, and I can feel the tension released from my body. That said, I love our passionate, drawn-out make-out sessions and slow lovemaking even more. I can't wait to really show Jesse how much I missed him with every inch of my body.

I got us off with my hand wrapped around both our cocks and water sloshing all over the floor, making him come for me when I told him tonight it would be me taking his cock. He's been looking at me with those bright, calculating eyes ever since, like he's trying to decide all the different positions he'll bend me into.

Shaking out of the dirty turn my thoughts have taken, I pull the room service cart inside and gesture for Jesse to join me on the couch.

"I was just thinking that I'd rather eat you for dinner," he teases, climbing into my lap to kiss me.

I groan and squeeze his ass through the sweatpants I was wearing earlier, which are comically large on him. I don't think of him being that much smaller than me, but we had to cinch the drawstring and flip the waistband to get them to stay on his narrow hips. Holding him against me, I shift us so he's lying on the couch beneath me and get lost in his devilish tongue. Then his stomach growls, and I remember what we were supposed to be doing.

"Behave," I say, like I'm not half the problem. "You need to eat. And we can't just fuck every moment that we're together." I reach for the domes covering our dishes–grilled shrimp and chicken with a brown rice broccoli-cheese baked casserole and collard greens for me, and chicken carbonara for Jesse. Plus two bottles of sparkling water and a crustless apple pie for dessert.

"Why not?" he pouts, drawing a laugh out of me.

I kiss his neck. "I want to do things with you, and get to know you in person like we were in Dallas."

"Between all the sex," Jesse said, pointing at me with his fork. "I suppose we'll have to come up for air, and we can't have you all sore for your game on Monday. Aside from that, I fully plan to be buried inside each other as much as possible for as long as possible. It's been too long since Dallas. I miss you."

"I know. I miss you, too." I don't understand it. I've lived alone for all these years now, and not once have I ever felt even the slightest bit lonely. Until I got back from Dallas, that is. Then suddenly I'm feeling cold without his body next to mine, missing the touch of his skin like a lost limb. My condo feels cavernous and empty. The only time I don't feel like I'm missing something vital is when he's on the phone. At least then I can close my eyes and pretend it's him, or set my phone in front of me and get to see his pretty face.

We eat in comfortable silence, both of us putting away a lot of food in a short amount of time. I've been surprised by how much food Jesse can eat with his wiry frame, but he told me he actually has a fluctuating appetite. When he's writing or in the studio, he tends to forget to eat for entire days sometimes. But when he's been with me, we've been so *active* he's constantly starving and eats almost as much as I do.

When we're done, we sit back and just talk a little. These are my favorite minutes with Jesse, outside of being physically connected to him. Our conversations, no matter how long or short, are never lacking. I love hearing about his experiences, not just the rockstar parts of it, but the little detours he's taken along the way. He gets me to download the *Waves* app, even though I don't do social media at all, and makes me a fake profile. He names me BB Smiles and giggles almost manically about it. He makes my profile picture a zoomed-in photo of my smile from one of what seems like dozens of GIFs and stills of my embarrassing camera incident.

"Are you sure they won't be able to tell it's me?"

Jesse gives me an amused look and types my name into the search bar. There are at least a hundred profiles that have my name and a random photo from the internet, more than 80% of which are from the stupid smiling thing.

Ugh. I'm never going to live that down. I hope Shawna never sees this, because she's already relentless. She sent me a box of random Colgate branded items, including a vintage-looking Colgate advertisement, a "tooth bank" for little kids, a t-shirt and hat, a car magnet (just why?) and a bunch of other bullshit no one needs, especially me. Even if I did want an endorsement deal, which I don't, it wouldn't be with them, for multiple reasons. The first being that this is the single most embarrassing thing to ever happen to me, and the second being that the Colgate company apparently found out where my family lives and gifted them a lifetime's worth of Colgate products. I asked my dad to burn them, but he doesn't see what the big deal is. This is my penance for choosing football over doing something with my business degree.

I hand the phone back to Jesse with a frown.

"Oh, nooo," he says, laughing. "Don't do that."

"Do what?" I say, having to hold back a smile at the way he crawls into my lap and cups my face, pushing the edges of my mouth up into a smile.

"You can hide this from the rest of the world if you want to, but never me." He drops sweet, chaste kisses all around my mouth. The left corner. The right. My cupid's bow. The tiny childhood scar just below my bottom lip on the left side of center. "I want every part of you, but especially your joy."

Straightening my back from where it was leaning, I capture Jesse's mouth in a slow kiss.

It never ceases to amaze me how much I love kissing Jesse Moore. The way our lips fit together so perfectly, the energy I feel buzzing between us.

Jesse presses me into the couch again, taking control of the kiss, mouth hot and hungry against mine. I get swept up in the rush of him, like I always do. His weight, his scent, the way his tongue drags over mine and makes every nerve in my body light up.

My hands wander, sliding down his sides until I brush over the bulge pressing into my stomach. I palm him over the sweat-pants, massaging, and he groans into my mouth. The sound goes straight to my spine.

I slip my hand under the waistband, greedy to have more of his skin on mine, and the second my fingers close around him I remember.

Oh. Shit.

The Jewelry. Five distinct bumps slide against my skin as I stroke down the middle of the studs.

"Um, Jesse?" I ask against his mouth.

"*Mmm*?" he hums, eyes half-lidded as he nips at my lower lip.

I lick at his lip ring, tugging on it with my teeth.

"How do they work, exactly? How much will I be able to feel them?" I trail off, face hot.

He pulls back just enough to give me that smirk, the one that says he knows exactly what I mean. "How does what work?"

I groan, pressing my forehead to his. "You know."

Why can't I say it? After everything we've done together? After the way I held him down, gagged him with his own panties, and fucked him into the mattress earlier?

"No, I don't." His voice drops to a purr. "You'll have to be more specific, baby."

I lean my head back on the couch and cover my face with one hand, muttering, "Why are you like this?"

"Because watching you squirm is my favorite pastime," he teases. "You're so fucking sexy when you get all bashful."

Jesse rolls his hips, thrusting his hard cock through my light grip. I feel the studs rolling over my palm. He leans in to take another kiss, this one deep and filthy. "I plan on making sure you feel each," *kiss*, "and every," *kiss*, "one."

I groan, and his tongue plunges in my mouth, curling around mine in a way that sends goosebumps skittering over my heated skin.

I can't breathe.

I can't think.

All I can focus on is Jesse's mouth as he moves down my body, trailing a path of heat from my neck all the way to my waistband, making detours on the way to nip and suck each nipple and lick into my belly button. Slowly pulling my sleep pants down my thighs, he continues the path down to my ankles, even licking the ticklish arch of my foot when he removes the pants entirely and starts making his way back up.

I'm panting, nearly out of my mind with want, by the time he makes it to the apex of my thighs and licks up the crease.

"Get on the bed and spread yourself for me," he demands in that raspy tone of his.

It doesn't even occur to me to be embarrassed or shy about holding my knees up to my chest so he can reach every inch of me. I want him too badly to feel anything other than searing lust and pleasure. Jesse can make me forget everything but the way he feels against me—his skin, his mouth, his cock. I want it all.

The first swipe of his tongue has me moaning already, and I wonder if I'm going to need a gag for this. We were lucky most of the team was out and about when he arrived here, but now there are people sleeping in the rooms on either side of us. If I'm not careful, we're absolutely going to get caught.

Still, when his mouth closes around my cock, and a lubed finger pushes inside me, I can't keep from shouting. Jesse only chuckles, the bastard, and takes me deeper. He works me over, adding a second finger before he pops off me.

"Are you ready for another?" He asks me, trickling more lube down my crease and working it inside me. "I need to get you nice and stretched to take me. Get you good and wet, and sink my cock inside you, piercing by piercing, until they're all swallowed up."

"*Fuck me*," I exclaim under my breath.

"Oh, baby, I am going to fuck you. I'm going to fuck you so good."

A whimper leaves me as he continues to torture me, fucking and stretching my ass while taking leisurely licks of leaking pre-cum like my cock is a melting ice cream cone. He plays with me, alternating between stimulating my prostate and stretching me out. I keep climbing to the edge and slipping back down until I'm dizzy with need and have no fucks left to give.

"Jesse–"

"*Shhh*, soon, baby."

"*Now*, Jesse, *please*." I let out a shaky breath, and look down at him biting his lip, playing with his lip ring. Does he do that because he knows it turns me on? Or is it just something he does?

Finally, Jesse takes pity on me. When he pulls his fingers out, I can feel a trickle of lube leaking out of me and wonder if he went overboard. I get distracted by watching him carefully roll a condom down his length, eyes locked on mine. It's familiar, bringing me back to the night we were together almost six years ago, when he awakened something inside me.

Like then, I'm a little nervous, maybe more so. Not because I'm worried it will hurt or that I won't like it. I have zero doubts that he'll play my body like his guitar. But because I'm already so enraptured by this man, I'm not sure how I'll ever recover if it doesn't work out. I was splintered the first time, and the cracks never faded.

I'm pretty sure I'd crumble if it happens again.

I no longer feel like I have a choice. I remember feeling this way the first time he pressed himself inside me. That this is inevitable.

"I think we might be soulmates, Luc Martín."

I think he might be right.

With his eyes on mine, one hand holding the back of my thigh, and the other guiding his cock, he presses against my hole. There's very little resistance after how thoroughly he's worked me open, only a little pressure as he presses through the first ring of muscle, and it feels divine. With the way he's worked me up so much, even the slightest stimulation has a low moan of pleasure rumbling deep inside my chest.

He pushes in a little more, and my eyes go wide, the studs of the first barbell pushing through.

"Alright?"

I nod. It's a lot more noticeable than I thought it would be. Even the small balls are enough to add a different kind of friction from what I remember before. It's definitely different than his fingers. Just like with his tongue, the metal is harder, unyielding in a way that sets it apart from flesh. The piercing grazes the sensitive, electric skin of my rim as it pushes through. I don't just feel his length and girth pushing inside me, but every bump of the ladder that stretches and rubs me from the inside.

"Breathe, baby," Jesse rasps, massaging the back of my thigh.

"I'm okay," I tell him, but my voice sounds more strained than I want it to. He hums and wraps a hand around my flagging erection, the stimulation causing me to clench around him. The muscle movement aches, but in a good way, and I nod that I'm ready for more.

Doing as he says, I pull in a deep breath and let it out, feeling myself relax further. Jesse pulls out slightly with each inhale, and then in a little deeper with each exhale. I count each bump, groaning the deeper he pushes inside me.

Three.

Four.

Five.

I feel full. Stretched beyond capacity, and we've only gotten past the barbells, which means he's just over halfway in.

Instead of pushing in further, he slowly pulls out again, each of the five barbells popping free, and then back inside. Slowly, so slowly, he saws in and out of me. The studs massage my rim from the inside out and back again, little by little.

My eyes flutter, and my cock hardens in his hand again. I feel flushed and breathless, overstimulated from the extra friction and still wanting more, climbing higher and higher as Jesse fucks into me in short strokes while lazily running this thumb up and down the vein along the bottom of my shaft.

"One day," he says, eyes locked between us where he's moving in and out of me, "one day I'm going to fuck you raw so you can really feel every bit."

His words send a barrage of primal urges ping-ponging down my spine and back up to my prefrontal cortex, where every inhibition and complex thought crumbles into a primal need to be fed, fucked, and filled. Fed every inch of Jesse's pierced cocked, fucked raw in every way imaginable, and filled with cum.

"Oh, fuck," Jesse grunts, then thrusts in deeper.

"Yes," I groan back. "All of it."

Holding my dick like a joystick and bracing his other on the back of my thigh, Jesse adjusts himself and thrusts inside. An electric shock of pleasure sparks from deep inside me, and I cry out. Jesse curses and does it again, and I suck in a breath, my body tightening.

The combination of the new angle and depth, the added friction of his hardware, and the way he's pumping my dick creates a perfect storm of mind-bending pleasure.

"Shhh," Jesse reminds me, but he's barely holding his own grunts and groans in, either.

I know he's right, but he's pushing the sounds out of me. A cry when he thrusts inside, a moan when he drags his cock out of me. I barely have the cognitive function to care, but I pull a pillow down over my face and hold it there to muffle the sound.

"Fuck, baby, you feel so good. Just as hot and tight and perfect as I remember. I don't want to come yet, but I don't think I can hold back much longer."

My only intelligible reply is the way my ass clenches and ripples as my orgasm snakes its way up my spine. Jesse keeps cursing under his breath, fucking into me harder and faster, pegging the sensitive tissue inside me.

I come first, thankful to have my face covered because I know my eyes are crossed, face contorted into something ugly that doesn't match the beauty of the energy between us. The force of the orgasm ripping through me has every muscle in my body tightening, and my face is no exception.

"Ah, fuck!" Jesse chokes out, then slams into me harder a few more times before falling over me and pressing his face to the other side of the same pillow. He moans almost directly against my mouth, twitching as he fills the condom. I wish he were filling me instead.

When it seems like we've gotten past the need to scream out our releases, Jesse yanks the pillow from between us and crashes his mouth to mine, still rolling into me until our bodies stop pulsing.

One thing's for sure, my memories didn't exaggerate a single thing about Jesse. If anything, they pale in comparison to the man nuzzling his nose against mine and whispering words of praise into my lips.

LeST is
MooRE

EIGHTEEN
LUC

As much as Jesse insists he's going to be fine, I don't like the idea of leaving him here alone all day. I'm not going to be back until this afternoon, and then I'll have to leave again for a team dinner later tonight.

Him showing up here was a surprise I never could have seen coming, so I had zero expectations for how long he'd stay. While the risk of getting caught is pretty terrifying, I love having him here. I slept better last night than I have in weeks. I had some initial soreness this morning, but it was nothing a little tongue massage in the shower couldn't take care of.

"You're going to be late," Jesse mumbles against my lips, smiling and doing nothing to actually deter me from stripping down and fucking him into the mattress again. He's still fully naked from the shower, pressed against me and making it impossible to leave.

"Yeah, I'm going," I say, not moving from where I have him pinned to the door. "I'm going right now."

Instead, I lift him by the backs of his thighs and wrap his legs around my hips and rock into him, dry fucking him through my gym gear. He leans his head back against the door, exposing his throat to me. I latch on and suck.

Jesse hisses out my name and writhes. We're both panting, time and responsibility long forgotten. My cock is throbbing against his ass, and I'm moments away from taking it out and going into a rut. The only thing that stops me is not wanting to hurt him.

That, and the banging on the other side of the door.

"Yo, Martín! You up?"

Every curse word I can conjure leaves my lips in a string of frustrated whispers. Jesse scrambles down and runs to hide in the bathroom while I tuck my aching boner into my waistband and consider swapping my shirt out for something more loose. But AJ is incessantly banging on the door.

"Yeah, yeah, I'm coming!" I quickly reach for my bag and pull the door open just enough for my body to pass through.

"Are you sick?"

"What? No. Why?"

"You're ten minutes late. You're never late. Everyone's worried that you weren't the first person down for the team breakfast."

Shit. This is what I get for being overly responsible. "Well, I'm coming now."

Like he has a sixth sense for bullshit, AJ leans in and tries to peer into my room. I shoo him away and step out into the hallway, only to pause.

"Shit. Hold on, I forgot my watch."

Not giving him a chance to step into the room with me, I shut the door in his face. When I turn around, Jesse is there, wrapping his arms around me and pressing a kiss to my mouth. He licks at my smile, and I groan, pulling away.

"Psst!" Jesse gets my attention before I open the door again and tosses my watch to me. I catch it, then take three long, quick steps to wrap my arm around his lower back and pull him into me again for a deeper kiss.

I finally manage to leave the room, hoping the feverish flush living on my skin isn't too noticeable, but considering the way AJ keeps looking at me like he's confused, concerned, or both, I don't think I'm so lucky.

———

The morning creeps by. The team breakfast is awkward, with everyone sending me strange looks. The longer it goes on, the more I'm convinced everyone heard me getting fucked last night. I can't decide if it's worse for them to think I was in there doing something to myself to cause those sounds, or if it's worth the trouble I'd get into if they knew I had somebody in my room.

When Langley, one of the team trainers, taps me on the shoulder, I nearly jump to my feet and confess everything, but he only takes me into the hallway to check my temperature.

"Any fatigue, lightheadedness, head or body aches, or sore throat?" He asks, making a relieved face when my temperature registers as normal.

"No, sir. I just forgot to set my alarm and slept in a little later than usual." I cringe, realizing that I'm probably over-explaining and making it worse. "I'm sorry for being late," I add on, because I can't help myself.

"It's no biggie, Luc, really. As long as you get here before the bus leaves, no one's going to have a problem. It's just unusual for you and you're looking a little…"

"Flustered?" I supply for him and nod. "Just embarrassed."

Langley smiles and thumps me on the shoulder. "You're alright, kid. Go finish your breakfast."

Shortly after, we load a bus and head to the Falcon's stadium to do a walkthrough and very light scrimmage. Then we head back to the hotel for a catered lunch and film session to review game strategy. It's really only about six hours total, but it feels like it drags on forever.

Finally, we're on our own. Normally I'd have a treatment with one of the massage therapists, but I opt to cancel my time slot in favor of a nap. Which is to say, I feign a headache so I can get out of socializing for the rest of the day and head back to my room.

I smile at the faint strumming of a guitar that can barely be heard through the door. If anyone heard it, it could easily be blamed on a television, so I don't worry too much about anyone over-hearing.

"Don't stop," I tell Jesse when I enter the room.

He's sitting on a bench seat in front of the window overlooking downtown Atlanta, wearing the same pair of sweatpants he borrowed from me last night and a wide, boxy black t-shirt cut into a crop-top. He grins up at me when I walk over to brush a gentle kiss against his lips. Sitting down on the edge of the bed, I pull my shoes off and settle back against the headboard to watch Jesse as he casts more spells on me.

Stealing time in a world that won't wait,

Two hearts beating together.

If these moments are all we get,

I'll cherish them forever.

No spotlight, no crowd, just you and me,

Hiding quietly in plain sight.

The world keeps turning endlessly,

But I'm yours tonight.

The morning's gonna come too fast,

Sunlight bleeding through the blinds.

Love like this was made to last,

So let's keep stealing time.

The song is slow and heartfelt, almost folksy compared to the music *Lest Is Moore* typically plays. He bends the strings of the guitar like he's bending them to his will, making their notes sound as raw as his voice. The verses repeat, with refrains about stealing time woven throughout, until eventually the last notes reverberate quietly into the silent room. I blink back at Jesse like I'm seeing him for the first time again. Even though he looks so different from how he did back then, it's like having the echo of past Jesse blended with the current version. It reminds me just how impossible it is that we've found each other again, and how his voice and the way he strums his guitar can bring me back to that night so thoroughly.

"Is that the same guitar?" I ask, looking at the faded black acoustic.

Jesse nods. "This is my favorite instrument to write with. She always helps me find inspiration in the wildest places."

"Oh, really? Like where?"

"Busking on street corners in disguise, in the middle of some woods I wandered into once when our tour bus got a flat. On a beach, where I found a bonfire and sang the corniest song I could think of to get this guy's attention." He grins widely.

"You had it before you started playing, but I'll admit to being a little impressed."

"Only a little?" He pouts.

"Well, until you played Rage," I laugh. "Do you ever wonder how things might have been different if we–"

"I did. But not anymore," Jesse says, putting his guitar down gently and walking over to the bed, crawling up to put his face in front of mine. His green eyes look back and forth between mine intently. "All the what ifs drove me so far out of my mind that I lost myself. I was lucky enough to get a second chance to make up for walking out that morning, and I'm not going to take a single breath for granted." He smiles against my lips and kisses me softly, humming that ridiculous song.

"Can you stay again tonight?" I whisper, pulling him closer so he's straddling my lap and kissing up the column of his neck.

"Don't you have a team dinner or something?"

"Yeah, but I've got this terrible headache…"

Sweat pours down my face under my helmet. Too much sweat considering this is a night game in the middle of fall. My nerves are the most likely culprit, but I'm trying to keep my head in the game.

I blame Jesse. Or I'd like to blame Jesse, but I'm the one that begged him to stay last night. I should know better than to assume I'd have any sort of willpower. How could I waste all those hours sleeping when I don't know how long it'll be before I see him next?

Of course, he waited until morning to surprise me with the news that he'd be at today's game. I thought he was out of his mind, but he just petted me like a silly, but very pretty dog and told me not to worry so much. No one would notice he's even there, and even if they did, it's not like they'd have reason to draw any sort of connection between the two of us. I'll give him credit for the second point, but did he forget who he is? He's Jesse *fucking* Moore. He's basically this generation's version of Mick Jagger. Of course he was spotted right away, sitting up in the owner's box, and wearing my goddamn jersey for fuck's sake!

I'm going to kill him.

Every time he jumps up and cheers–usually when I'm part of a big play, considering he knows little to nothing about football–I can see my number 14 emblazoned boldly across his chest. My only saving grace, and the silver lining to the smile, is that more of my jerseys have been sold lately. I didn't even know I had merch before I accidentally hit the viral pages for something so stupid. *Yes, I'm still salty.*

I'm having a lot of conflicting feelings and nerves about his audacity. I'm on edge. Every time they show Jesse on screen, they pan to me like they're hoping for a reaction. *Never again, bastards.*

On the other hand, there is a not insignificant part of me that kind of loves seeing him in my number. Now just imagine him wearing a cropped version of it, with a pair of black lace–

"Martín!"

Shit.

Fucking Jesse. I scowl up at the owner's box before I settle into my stance, focusing on the Falcons' quarterback across the line. We're at fourth and five and getting too close to the red zone for comfort. So far, this game has been neck-and-neck. If we don't keep them from driving forward, we'll basically be handing the game over to them. This drive is our chance to stop them in their tracks and hand the game back over to our offense.

Head in the game. Head in the game. Don't look at Jesse. Keep your head in the game.

The ball snaps, and the line shifts. Dez explodes off the edge, and AJ rushes the guard, putting pressure on the quarterback right away. His eyes shift downfield, shoulders twisting to find his window. I check the field, but my eyes are drawn up, Jesse's face is blown up on the halo board, his attention riveted on the field. On me.

My pulse stutters, a sudden flutter of nerves in the pit of my stomach at the thought of him watching me. Here, in person.

A receiver bursts off the line, the movement pulling me out of my momentary distraction. My hesitation almost costs us, but I recover quickly. I drop my weight, launch myself off the turf, and drive my shoulder into the oncoming receiver. A sharp twinge of pain lances down my arm, but I grit my teeth and shove, forcing him back and cutting off his lane. Meanwhile, AJ and Dez take advantage of the scramble and crash the pocket to sack the quarterback.

The stadium explodes, not just from our sideline whooping or the Cyclones' fans screaming their lungs out in enemy territory, or even from the wall of boos raining down from the Falcons' fans.

It's the music.

Typically, music plays for the home team victories, and very rarely for the visiting team. It's not even one of our fight songs. The stadium DJ drops a *Lest Is Moore* track right in the middle of a hard-hitting chorus, bass shaking the whole damn place.

My breath catches, and I look up at the screen to see Jesse pumping his fist and cheering, my name on his back while his voice reverberates through the stadium. The crowd has lost the plot, even the Falcons' fans are getting into the song, thousands of strangers singing along while my teammates whoop and slam helmets against pads.

I meet AJ and Dez on our way off the field to congratulate them on a great play. AJ jumps on my back, putting weight on my shoulder, and I wince. Once he's bounced over to celebrate with another teammate, I shake it out and roll my shoulder. It's nothing, just a tweak.

When I take a seat on the bench to drink some water, my eyes gravitate back up to the halo screen around the stadium. Jesse is still up there celebrating, singing along with the crowd and raising his arms in the air, hyping up the crowd like he's part of the team.

Like he's mine.

LEST is
MOORE

NINETEEN
LUC

"You're so full of shit," Shawna drawls, taking another bite of pizza and screwing up her face. "And so is this nasty excuse for pizza. What the hell is this, Luc?"

"I told you it's not traditional pizza. The crust is made out of ground chicken breast. It's healthy."

"Gross."

I roll my eyes. My best friend has a deep aversion to healthy food. She won't eat a vegetable unless it's deep fried or slow cooked into a stew, like the good Louisiana girl she is. "There's a bag of chips and salsa in the pantry."

Shawna perks up, then narrows her eyes.

"They have salt," I clarify, not waiting for her to ask. "And I got you that off-brand restaurant-style salsa you like, not the 'bullshit from the deli' with actual fresh vegetables."

"You're my favorite."

I laugh as she runs off to find more acceptable snacks. I miss Shawna's antics like crazy some days. With everything that's been changing in my life, having her here on her normal bullshit is a breath of fresh air.

When she gets back, she folds herself back into the corner of my couch and proceeds to eat her chips and salsa directly out of the bag and jar. And then, true to form, she waits until she has a mouthful before again asking the question I already answered because she thought I was kidding.

"So anyway, I didn't peg Jesse Moore for a football fan," she continues.

"He's not."

"*Pssht*. Except he invited your team to a concert *and* came to one of the games. Wearing your number, no less. That's going to mean more jersey sales, you know."

I resist groaning. She doesn't understand how I could not care less if people are wearing NFL merch with my name and number on it. She was excited to *finally* get one, like I was holding back on her.

"Remember the beach party right before the Draft?"

Shawna frowns. My uncharacteristic behavior and stressful sexual awakening, as she called it, has always been a sore spot. I've never been the one to bring it up the very few times it's been necessary to mention.

"What about it?"

"Remember the guy?"

"I mean, I don't remember meeting him, but I remember that you did. And I remember… you know, after."

I cut my eyes to the television and back to her, trying to give her a hint. Which of course, she doesn't catch. Why would she?

"Why are you doing that with your eyes?" She asks, reaching for her soda to take a sip.

"It was him. Jesse. Jesse was the guy."

Dr. Pepper sprays across my living room furniture. Shawna clenches her eyes and pinches her nose. "Oh God, I snorted it."

"Still better than hard drugs," I deadpan, quoting her snarky response to anyone mentioning how much caffeine she consumes.

"Fuck you," she says, and it's even funnier because her voice sounds like she has a bad cold. Her eyes are streaming with tears from the sting.

"Want some water?"

"Water? Like out the toilet?" Shawna will take any opportunity to quote the movie *Idiocracy*.

A laugh huffs out of me, and I shake my head, getting up to grab her a kitchen towel. When I come back, her big, grey eyes are fixed on me.

"You're really serious?"

It takes a minute to remember what we were talking about. I shift my eyes back to the television, where Jesse is on his knees at the edge of the stage, head thrown back and screaming up into a mic. He's wearing torn black skinny jeans and an almost sheer white t-shirt with the words "You'll Have To Go Through Me" in the colors of the trans pride flag.

My lips quirk. I'm so fucking proud of him and his band for what they're doing. They've barely started, and they've already raised over half of their goal. Their partnership with the social media company is giving them a huge boost, as is the rising discord with American politics.

Taking out my phone, I use the QR code on the screen to open the donation link, making a large anonymous donation.

I notice Shawna has been quiet for a little too long and lift my eyes to meet hers. She's gaping at me.

"Lucius Barrett Martín," Shawna says slowly. She gestures at the screen. "Him? Really?"

"Yeah." I shift in my seat. "Him."

"Jesse fucking Moore."

"Jesse fucking Moore," I repeat affirmatively.

She makes a strangled noise, somewhere between a laugh and a groan. "Holy shit." Her eyes narrow. "Wait," she says, and I can see the cogs whirring as she rewinds all the way back to the beginning of this conversation, when I said I wanted us to watch this concert. "You're actually, like *actually,* seeing him? Currently?"

I glance at her, then back at Jesse. The cameras sweep the crowd, colored lights illuminating the smoke. Jesse's voice hits a high note, cutting through the air, sharp and raw. With my surround sound and this ridiculous TV AJ talked me into buying, it feels like we're right there at the concert. Minus the crowd, which is a huge plus. But it's also minus real-life Jesse, and that sucks.

"Sort of," I answer finally.

"Sort of," she repeats, and then snorts. "Babydoll, you're gonna have to give me more than that, and you know it."

Babydoll. He calls me baby. I'm bigger and taller than he is, but I melt into a puddle of goo when he calls me baby.

"What more is there?" I say indignantly.

"I am your best friend. I tell you all of my–"

"Nuh-uh. I don't ask for the dirty details of whatever you get up to. You force those on me against my will."

"I will comb my cooch with your toothbrush."

"That's disgusting."

"What's disgusting is you not sharing any details about your rock god boyfriend with your best fucking friend!"

"Dude, calm down. He's not my boyfriend."

"We'll circle back and unpack that later. I can't calm down, bro. This is serious beans."

"I'm not going to kiss and tell, Shawna. I'm a gentleman."

She barks out a laugh so loud it almost drowns the music out. "You? Puh-lease. But fine. You just have to answer one thing…" My best friend leans in, eyes gleaming with mischief. "Is it good?"

"Is what good?"

Shawna swats me with the kitchen towel. "Oh my God, I've never seen you blush that hard." She collapses sideways onto the couch cushions, kicking her feet like she's won the lottery. "That's an emphatic yes if I've ever seen one."

"Shut up," I groan.

Shawna continues snickering to herself while on screen, the band finishes their song. Jesse is bent over his guitar, sweat dripping from his hair, chest heaving.

"So are you going to come out?" Shawna asks in a quiet, surprisingly serious tone.

"I'm not in."

"You know what I mean."

I sigh. The halo of lights on the TV cuts to a closeup of Jesse's hand sliding down the neck of his guitar in a way that sends shivers down my spine like I've been touched by a ghost. My chest tightens with the weight of what Shawna's asking.

"You hate publicity," she says gently, straightening the hem of her oversized Colgate toothpaste t-shirt. The big red letters stretch across her chest, obnoxious as hell against the teal leggings she paired it with.

I give her a long side-eye.

"What?" she says innocently. "I'm just making a point. Keeping a relationship between the two of you, a massive superstar and a famous NFL player–"

"–I'm not famous."

Shawna gives me a highly unimpressed stare. "Okay, smiley. Sure. Maybe you weren't, but even before you dazzled everyone with your thousand-watt killer smile of sweet babydoll shyness, you couldn't have escaped public scrutiny if you were dating that guy." She points to Jesse on the screen, playing an electric guitar and looking like the sex god he is. "And here I thought you were always chasing a *normal life*–whatever the fuck that is."

"Normal doesn't exist in my world, Shawna, you know that. I mean, look at your stupid shirt, for fuck's sake. Dad's got a life-time supply of toothpaste stacked in my old room like some kind of doomsday prepper. That's not normal. And even if I wasn't in love with a rock god, it's not like I could have a normal relation-ship anyway."

Shawna's nose twitches, the only indication that she caught my little slip-up. She ignores it for now. "Why not?"

"Well, for starters, I've never wanted one before. I've never wanted anyone before. Certainly not like this. Even if lightning struck twice or Jesse wasn't a superstar, it couldn't work, because then everything I've done, everything I've accomplished, will all be reduced to my sexuality."

"Maybe if more people came out publicly, or even just started living their lives without ever making a public statement, it would start mattering less," she points out. It's a good point, but I don't think I'm the guy to step up and be anyone's poster boy.

"Isn't there an out player on Carolina's team?" Shawna pulls out her phone and starts to type.

I wrack my brain. "I don't remember. I don't pay attention to players' personal details, just their game footage."

"Jack Perry!" She announces.

"Wide receiver."

Shawna snorts.

"Really?" I deadpan.

"What? It's funny and you know it."

I refuse to give her the satisfaction.

She squints down at her phone. "But yeah. Apparently it was a big deal when it first came out, mostly because there was some drama involved. But he didn't bother with the trolls and did his job well. Now no one gives a fuck, and he's happily married to some big-shot sports agent."

"Good for him," I say. And I mean it. I wish I could do it. But all I can hear is–

"You know what your problem is, right?" She doesn't wait for me to answer, probably because she knows the answer. Her nosey ass always has to be right about shit. "You're too much like your dad. And you know I love me some Daddy Lucius, but he's got a few outdated ideas that I think you take too much stock in."

I scrunch my nose and turn away from the TV. They're having a short intermission to make announcements about what the fundraiser is up to, so Jesse and the band are no longer on screen.

"Tell me how many times you've heard your daddy say," she clears her throat and tries to imitate my dad's voice, "I don't care what somebody's got goin' on behind closed doors, just keep it to yourself."

"What's wrong with keeping your personal business to yourself?"

"You ever hear him say the same thing about a straight person or a straight couple?"

I open my mouth to defend him, but I stop short. As usual, she's right. Not that I'd tell her that to her face. I'd never hear the end of it.

"I'm not saying he's a bad person, or that he'd be outright homophobic to someone. People say shit like that all the time and don't even realize how fucked up it is, but that's exactly why more of us need to put on our big girl panties and speak up, correct them, point out their mistakes. Because people are going to stay set in their ways until they're taught better."

I snort. "I'm not sure Dad can be taught anything." He's a good man, but he's old and stubborn as hell.

"Maybe, maybe not. But when or if it comes up someday, especially if you're serious about this guy and have to weigh the risk of getting publicly outed, what do you want from him?"

"From my dad?"

"Yeah. You want him to be okay with it, right?"

"Of course."

"And you want him to be okay with you bringing Jesse home, and him being welcomed and treated the same way a girlfriend would be, right?"

That's when I take a pause. I see where she's getting at.

"It is not enough to be tolerated. Especially when that tolerance comes with the caveat of making yourself smaller. Tolerance is bullshit. You deserve and should demand acceptance. You can't hide who you are to protect small minds."

"You're right." I know she is, but that doesn't mean I want to get mobbed by reporters every time I leave my house or place of work.

"Duh."

I focus on my phone a bit, sending Jesse a text now that I know he's probably sitting backstage, taking a breather.

ME: I wish I could see you in person, but I think I'm sold on live-streaming for concerts. It's way better watching from my couch. Less people-y.

Ghost: Next time you can watch from side stage. You'd only have to deal with crew.

Ghost: Well, and Blake.

ME: Tempting.

Ghost: Good. It's happening.

ME: Ha. Ha.

Ghost: So cute how you think I'm kidding.

Ghost: Are you having fun with Shawna?

ME: Yeah. Except she's a know-it-all and a slob.

Ghost: The love you have for this woman is astounding.

ME: 🤣

ME: I told her about you.

Ghost: Really?

Ghost: What'd she say?

ME: She didn't believe me at first. But she might be a little over-excited.

I don't want to tell him about all the realistic worries she brought up. It's too early to be worried about what kind of future we could or couldn't have, or whether I'm brave enough to step outside my comfort zone in such a big way. Right now we're just getting to know each other and enjoying each other's company when we can manage to get together.

Ghost: I am too. *winky face emoji* *heart hands emoji*

Ghost: Tell her I said hi.

"Jesse says hi," I say, not looking up from my phone.

The kitchen towel hits me in the face. "You jackass."

"What? He's not allowed to say hi?"

"Not that. *That*," she says, pointing to the television screen.

A banner flashes across the screen:

$50,000 donation made by Luc Martín!!!

Wait. What? No! "Th–That was supposed to be anonymous!"

Shawna cackles. Loudly. Like an old, evil witch. "That's definitely going to help y'all stay incognito!" There are actual tears streaming down her face.

"This isn't funny, Shawnnnaahhhh!"

My phone pings several times in a row.

> Ghost: Did you mean to do that?
>
> Ghost: You know what, I don't even care.
>
> Ghost: The next time I see you, I'm going to drop to my knees and worship your cock until you're trembling. Then I'm going to bend you over and tongue fuck you until you cry.

"Ooh, spicy–" Startled, I accidentally smack Shawna in the face. But to be fair, she shouldn't have been creeping over my shoulder like that.

"What is wrong with you?" I ask.

Shawna folds her arms. "You're the one sexting your boyfriend when I'm busy making fun of you! I just said that you should hire a third grader to teach you how to work your phone so you don't do stupid shit like this, but if y'all are gonna be nasty over text, that's probably not a good idea."

My phone pings again, and Shawna's eyes light up a little too much for my liking.

"Is it a dick pic?"

"What? No! It's AJ."

> AJ: You meant for that to be anonymous, didn't you?

Shawna snorts. "Can I have his phone number so I can have someone to talk shit with?" Then she stops and makes a face. "Wait, if he knew about Jesse first, I'm going to riot. That's bullshit."

"He doesn't know about Jesse."

"You mean he *didn't* know about Jesse."

I fall back against the couch and cover my face with my hands. "You know what, you two are made for each other."

"Whatever. I'm loveable as fuck."

"I'll remember that when your life implodes."

"Wouldn't happen. I have no secrets. I give away my bullshit for free. In fact, I give it away so freely that nobody really wants it, so it's not interesting enough to anyone to be newsworthy."

"You're the worst."

She nods solemnly and pats my hand. "If it makes you feel better."

Ping.

AJ: We got you, fam.

What's happening?

Ping.

Ghost: How many people did you recruit to do this?

Ghost: Oh, baby. I'm going to do so many delicious, depraved things to you. When's your next day off?

Ghost: I hope you're still watching. We have a surprise for you now.

I look up at the screen and watch the crowd going wild over the on-stage screen lighting up like a slot machine hitting a jackpot.

$50,000 donation made by AJ León!!!

$50,000 donation made by Desmond Carter!!!

$50,000 donation made by Monty Nash!!!

$50,000 donation made by Connor Laramie!!!

$50,000 donation made by Giselle St. Vincent!!!

$100,000 donation made by The Shreveport Cyclones!!!

The screen doesn't stop flashing, alert after alert of my team-mates, their friends, and even the organization as a whole. One after the other, other NFL players and teams start donating. And it becomes more than just a couple of my friends supporting me, it becomes a huge statement. Because these big-name NFL players and teams aren't donating to just any charity, they're donating to organizations on the frontline of fighting for the LGBTQ+ and BIPOC communities. And that's a hell of a statement to make given the current political climate.

My eyes get so blurry, I almost miss what the band is wearing when they come back on stage to a roar of cheers and applause from the crowd. Jesse has replaced his t-shirt with my jersey, *because of course he has*. At least the rest of the guys are wearing our colors, too. Will is wearing a Shreveport Cyclones shirt, Ari is wearing a white tank top with gold cuffs around his arms, and Naz has the top half of his body painted gold and is wearing a Cyclones trucker-style hat.

"Let's give a shout-out to our friends over at the Shreveport Cyclones, and all the NFL players out there showing support for things that really fucking matter!"

The crowd screams, and I have to smile. Despite my awkward mistake, it actually ended up being a good thing. I'll have to thank AJ for stepping in. He clearly did something to start that chain reaction. All these guys make good money, and most make a lot more than I do since they typically do endorsements and appearances, but that's still a lot of money to throw out. It's pretty amazing that they'd recognize I wouldn't want my name flashing on a screen alone like that, even if they don't know the real reason. I'll definitely explain it to him one day soon, but I'd prefer to have a better idea of what is going on between me and Jesse before I tell anyone other than Shawna.

"I think this deserves something special, and it just so happens we've been working on something new that sort of fits the Cyclone's team colors. Do y'all want to hear it?"

They scream again, but Naz shakes his head and yells into his microphone. "That's bullshit, we can do better than that. My man asked you if y'all want to hear a new song!?"

The crowd screams even louder, and Naz hits the drums hard, beating a throbbing rhythm that builds into a rapid-fire drum solo. Then all at once, Jesse and Ari join in, a crescendo building before they abruptly stop. A spotlight hits Will, and he leans into a sharp guitar solo. Ari comes back in with a rhythm that sounds like a heartbeat. Jesse's guitar joins in, and then Naz, and everyone falls into the rhythm of a sensual melody.

Jesse steps up to the mic, eyes closed, and my pants get a little tight.

> *I'm painting myself in your colors tonight,*
>
> *Brushstrokes burning under neon lights.*
>
> *Drip, drip, dripping in your gold,*
>
> *Paint me a new identity, so we can lose control.*
>
> *Your name–*
>
> *A secret I'll take to the grave.*
>
> *Your touch–*
>
> *Something that I'll never claim.*
>
> *You're pushing back, can't hold the line,*
>
> *Pressure building under different lights.*
>
> *Drip, drip, dripping in my love,*
>
> *Don't let me go, don't give me up.*
>
> *Your face–*
>
> *I see it when I close my eyes.*

Your love–

A burning, aching fire inside.

We're tangled up in lust and memories,

Don't want to come up, don't need to breathe.

Drip, drip, dripping in our sin,

Where you begin, and where I end.

The last notes of the guitar reverberate into silence, and then the crowd goes about as wild as my heart is.

Shawna lets out a long, low whistle. "You're so screwed."

She's right. I know I am. This thing between me and Jesse has gotten too real, too big, and it's starting to bleed into the outside world. I'm scared, but not enough to stop. Because maybe, just maybe, what we have together might be worth it.

TWENTY
JESSE

I'm wiggling in my seat, feeling antsy as hell as the small plane finally touches down on the tarmac. It's all I can do to stay in the car. There have been more paparazzi than usual lately, including a few sightings of drones popping up where they shouldn't be. Cory and Tad are working on a few strategies to take them down so we can trace the culprits, but in public spaces, there's not much we can do.

Rumors have been stirring, and while it's nothing worrisome yet, I don't want Luc to be put off from getting closer. The more I have of him, the more I need. I probably wouldn't tell him this, because it's not his responsibility and it's also probably super weird and would scare him off, but I've felt more like myself than I have since we went on our first tour. And I attribute it mostly to Luc. Talking to him every day, and touching base throughout the day when we are able, keeps me tethered.

It also helps that our schedule is a lot less hectic right now, and being sober definitely helps me appreciate the little things. I'm not feeling as overwhelmed as I was when we first got back to the states. Even on our longer stretches of press rounds and concerts, I haven't gotten to that itchy, overstimulated place where it feels like I'm outgrowing my skin.

More than anything, I feel happy–truly happy–and hopeful for the future. I'm motivated and enjoying life like never before. I look forward to every day that I get to talk to him, and every night brings me one day closer to the next time I'll see him. I know it's corny as fuck, but it's how I feel.

I'm pretty sure I'm in love. Like the gross, swoony fairytale kind.

Right now, I'm so excited that I'm about to vibrate straight through the seat. I can see him stepping off the stairs that lead down from the jet, and now he's walking across the tarmac towards the car. I told him I was sending Cory to pick him up. The consensus was that it was safer to travel separately, but there was no way I was going to wait even five more minutes, much less half an hour, to get my hands on him. So, here I am, tucked back in the corner of the limo SUV I originally thought was overkill, but am about to make very good use of. Let's just hope Cory doesn't feel the need to peek back here before letting Luc into the car.

My heartbeat ratchets up the moment I hear voices getting closer. I adjust my position so much that I worry I might be shaking the car. Luc slides in, thanking Cory before the door is closed.

I can't even manage a hello. For some dumb reason, I feel like I might cry if I try to say anything. Gone is the plan to pose myself all sexy and give him a seductive welcome. Instead, I pounce.

Luc sucks in a little breath of surprise, but recovers quickly, kissing me back and pulling me tightly against him. Considering I shoved my tongue in his mouth right away, it doesn't even take a full second before things get heated, and I'm moaning into his mouth, writhing on his lap. His hand moves up and down my spine before finally settling on my ass.

He pauses and pulls back. "What are you–fucking hell, Jesse–what are you wearing?"

Not much. I'm wearing his jersey, a lacy black jockstrap, and a plug.

"I didn't want to waste any time," I say, sucking his bottom lip into my mouth. He groans and brushes his fingers down my crack, groaning even louder when he touches the plug. Just one press and the sound of his lust, and I'm on edge already. "Take it out," I tell him. "Now. I fucking need you," I say, slipping a condom and a packet of lube from under the garter strap.

There's a flurry of movement as we work to get Luc undressed enough. He unzips his jeans and lifts his hips to push them down his thighs while I remove his jacket. I press myself closer to him so I can wrap both our cocks in my hand and jerk them together. I'm not the only one leaking pre-cum like a drippy faucet. I barely need any lube.

My hips rock, both thrusting into my hand around our dicks and pressing back against Luc's fingers as he teases me. I moan and whimper into his mouth, begging him wordlessly to let me ride his cock all the way to our hotel. I need him inside me.

Not want.

Need.

Now.

Luc slowly removes the plug, but slips it back in, fucking me with it and enjoying the way it pops through my rim. I used a lot of lube, so the wet, squelchy sounds only add to the sex in the air.

"Goddammit, Luc. *Please!*"

I try to tease him by moving so his shaft is between my cheeks, rubbing up and down. Finally, he seems to get on my level, writing against me, cock leaving sticky streams of pre-cum all over my ass. Then finally, finally, finally he stops teasing me. He lines his cock up to my hole and holds my hip, guiding me to sink down his length. We both let out a long, low moan, and I shudder.

"Oh, fuck," I say, voice trembling. This isn't going to take long.

I start to move with purpose, needing release. Not just any release though. The release only he can give me. The person he is, this body, this fucking perfect cock. He's the only one who can make me feel like this. Hot and cold simultaneously. Flushed and frantic.

I ride him hard and fast, Luc rocking his hips up to meet me as I bounce on his cock. I put each hand through the handles on either side of the roof and use them for leverage, not bothering to temper my sounds because I couldn't even if I tried.

"Fuck, Luc, I'm going to come!" I know it's fast. We've barely been here five minutes, but I was too desperate to make it last, too needy for the feeling he's giving me, for the wet squelch of my ass slamming down on his cock.

"So. Fucking. Gooood," I moan, and detonate. I cry out and my movements stutter, then I'm spraying cum all over Luc, all over his shirt and the expanse of abs showing where his shirt rode up. Luc moves my hips and rolls up into me until I'm through most of the orgasm, then lifts me up and flips us, moving me to bend over the seat before he thrusts into me again and sets a punishing rhythm. He fucks me hard and fast, my spent cock pushing out little bursts of more cum that Luc works out of me.

I can tell when he's getting close, when his body gets tighter and his movements jerkier than usual. He slams his orgasm into me, then holds himself inside and rocks, riding it out.

"So hot. Wet. Ah… *Fuck*, Jesse. Oh, God." His orgasm seems to go on forever, pumping what feels like stream after stream of…

Oh.

Oh shit.

When he pulls out and pushes back inside…

It's wet. Very wet. And when he pulls out all the way and I bear down the slightest bit, I feel his release trickle out of me.

Luc hisses a curse. Instead of freaking out like I worried he might, he pushes his cock back inside me, pulls out until it starts to seep out of me again, and then pushes it back inside me. He does this again and again, slowly, until he's fully hard again and fucking me through another orgasm, until I paint the seat and he paints my insides again.

I collapse onto the seat in front of me, wet and sticky with cum, and wince as Luc pulls all the way out. His thumb gently circles my rim, and I figure it's the least I can do to give him what he seems waiting for. I bear down again and push some of his load out.

Luc makes a sound I can't describe. It's a barely-there sound that doesn't quite fit his deep timber or overall size. Something like a, "hah" crossed with a squeak. A tiny sound of surprise mixed with alarm, considering how he quickly catches the stream and tries to push it back inside me.

I look over my shoulder and find Luc sitting back on his haunches, looking a bit dazed. *Does my sweet, gentle, blushing beefcake of a man have a breeding kink?*

My fingers actually cross.

"Use the plug," I rasp, my voice wrecked.

Luc shakes himself out of whatever trance he was in. "Huh?"

"You can use the plug to keep it in, if you like."

He looks down, searching around for where it might have fallen. "It's dirty," he says, then looks down at himself. His jeans are pushed down his thighs, cock lolling out, half hard and wet with lube and cum. The front of his shirt is drenched and he's all sweaty and flushed, looking thoroughly wrecked.

After realizing the state he's in, Luc notices we aren't moving anymore. I'm not sure how long ago we arrived at the hotel. Cory is likely standing somewhere nearby, waiting patiently for us to finish what's obviously happening in here. Not that he hasn't been witness to worse, but I'm a different person than I used to be, and I know Luc will probably be embarrassed.

I should probably text the guys to make themselves scarce until I can get him in my room and cleaned up. He will *not* want to meet everyone like this. I already explained that he's not much of a people-person and that they shouldn't grill him or anything, so they already know he's a bit shy.

"We're here," he says.

"It's okay, there's no rush. There are probably some antibacterial wipes in here somewhere, or you can just fill me up again once we get upstairs," I suggest, a smile tugging at my lips. I don't want him to think I'm teasing or making fun of him. The sight of him like this makes the butterflies I always get around him do backflips, and his cock isn't the only one trying to twitch back to life at the thought of him breeding me like a show dog in heat.

We straighten ourselves up the best we can. I slip on the sweat-pants I wore on the way to the airport and shove my feet into slides. Luc ends up taking his t-shirt off and using it to wipe me down, and then the leather seats. He puts his jacket on to hide his bare chest, zipping it up to his throat, then puts the balled-up t-shirt in his pocket.

When we finally open the door and step out of the vehicle, Cory is nowhere to be seen. The basement entrance is deserted aside from us. I open my phone to a text.

Cory: Mr. Martín's bags are in your room, and I've taken the liberty of asking Mr. Lester to distract the others in the rec room until you give the all clear.

ME: You're the best.

He responds by liking the text, and nothing else. Double bonuses this year, I think.

"Come on, baby. Let's get you upstairs and in the shower so you can stuff me full of your cum again."

____

It's nearly an hour before I pull Luc out of the bedroom. His palm is warm against mine, and he looks composed, but I can tell by the way his jaw ticks that he's considering how many escape routes there might be to get out of this.

"I told you, it's going to be fine." I squeeze his hand both in comfort and in warning. I'm not letting him run away. "They already love you."

He doesn't say anything, just follows me down the hall, giving me a side-eye that says he's humoring me for now, but I should be on alert.

I'd meant to warn him that my bandmates would be here. We usually share the penthouse suite. I'd only requested my own so we could be alone on our first date, but now I really want the most important people in my life to meet each other. The next time we have a break that coincides, like maybe Thanksgiving, I want to take him home to meet my mom.

It wasn't intentional to surprise him with meeting the guys. In my defense, the moment he slipped into the car, I lost the capacity to think past getting as close to him as humanly possible. Once we arrived, it felt like getting him relaxed before springing anything new on him was the right move. Plus, we had to talk about what happened in the car so I could reassure him that I'm negative and not sleeping with anyone else.

The rec room is loud when we step in. Music, laughter, and the clack of pool balls fill the space. This suite is bigger than the one I had in Dallas. It has five bedrooms, a full kitchen, formal dining and living rooms, a screening room, and this rec room. It's an open space with a fully stocked wet bar along one wall, pool and poker tables, plus a large, plush sectional surrounding a wall-sized television. Opposite the bar is a stunning view of Seattle at night.

"Well, look who finally decided to join us," Will drawls, leaning one hip against the pool table. He gives us a slow once-over, a smirk tugging at his lips. "I worried you might stay in there forever."

Luc stiffens. I cut Will a sharp look, reminding him to be nice.

He raises his hands in mock defense, grinning mischievously. "I'm just kidding."

Ari doesn't say anything, and remains sitting on the edge of a bar chair with a wide, appreciative smile that makes my skin itch. I know he'd never make a pass at someone he knows I'm serious about, and I made it very clear just how serious I was when I discussed bringing Luc here during his bye-week, but I still don't like his eyes on him like that. I glare at him until he drops his eyes, still grinning like the cat who ate Tweety Bird.

Naz, bless him, saves the night from getting too awkward before it even starts. He pushes up from his seat at the bar, crosses the room with a light, easy smile, and offers his hand to Luc. "It's good to finally meet you," he says. "We were starting to wonder if Jesse was making shit up."

Luc chuckles, shoulders relaxing a little. The tension leaks out of me all at once, chest loosening as I watch the two most important men in my life get to know each other for the first time. The other two, once they've met their quota of bullshit, join in on the easy conversation. The guys thank him for contributing to the fundraiser. Thanks to his donation sparking a chain reaction among his NFL friends, we raised almost double what we did last year. Over four hundred thousand dollars was distributed among several local and national LGBTQ+ organizations.

Luc's cheeks flush, insisting that it was his friend AJ who set the chain of donations in motion. He even admits to them that his was supposed to be an anonymous donation, but that AJ and a couple other close teammates were watching the live-stream of the concert at a bar together and saw Luc's name flash across the screen.

"I, uh, kind of have a complex about publicity. I'm a very private person, so they knew something was off, and all decided on the spot to donate right away so it would look like a team effort. AJ and Dez would have donated anyway, but I'm not sure about the others. It worked out for the best."

The guys laugh at Luc's blunder and cut glances at me over his shy demeanor. Ari puts a hand up to shield his face and mouths, "OMG he is precious!"

"I know right?!" I mouth back.

Naz is the only one who seems to temper his excitement, and I can tell he's deep in thought about something. He still worries about Luc not being open about his sexuality.

I squeeze Luc from the side and whisper in his ear, "Do you want anything to drink?" He shakes his head, and I kiss his cheek before walking over to the bar to pour us both sparkling waters. Naz follows me.

"Alright, Naz, out with it. Lay it on me."

"I didn't say anything."

"Your face did it for you."

He lets out a huff of laughter and looks back at Luc, who is chatting amiably with Will and Ari despite not saying much, and is clearly keeping me in sight.

"I don't think I realized how serious it was," Naz finally says. "Not just how deep in the closet he is, but how deep the feelings are."

"He's not in the closet," I say defensively.

"He's not out of the closet, either."

"His teammates know he's gay. He told them. It's just not something he feels comfortable broadcasting to the world, and I think that's fair."

"I don't disagree with you, Jess. What I'm worried about is how closely we're being watched right now, how much effort is being put in to discredit and expose us for any perceived drama."

Our fundraiser-protest concert did well. *Really* well. Maybe too well. Ever since our live-streamed protest, we've been trolled by conservative news outlets and even called "lame" and outright threatened by the president of the free world on his social media accounts. He's promised to shut us down—that by the year's end, there won't be a venue or record label willing to work with us. And wouldn't you know it, two of our concerts at the end of the year were cancelled because the parent companies that own the venues bowed to the pressure of conservative media outlets and threats of violence at our shows.

Not that we're backing down in any way, shape, or form. In fact, we've doubled down on our media presence, sharing photos of us shaking hands with the CEOs of the organizations we donated to, as well as making appearances at LGBTQ+ centers, shelters, and food and blanket drives in the week since the charity concert. These are things we've always been involved with, but we're being a lot more public about it, to show the contrast between the hatred and threats being thrown by the religious "right", and the good we can do to counterbalance it. We aren't even reacting or responding. We're simply leading by example, and other celebrities and companies are starting to do the same.

After all, what better show of protest is there than love?

Naz is right though, we're under a lot more scrutiny than usual, which could put Luc's privacy at risk. We need to be extra vigilant.

"I'm just worried about what would happen if he got outed because of his connection with you. There are already rumors."

"There are always rumors."

"Would your relationship survive if it were to get out?"

The truth is…

I don't know.

TWENTY-ONE
JESSE

I am on fire,

Burning from the inside out.

On the tip of my tongue I taste your desire,

Your big, strong arms holding me down.

This overwhelming desire,

A fever scorching through my veins.

Your sex sets me on fire,

It's burning me up, I'm lost in the flames.

I am on fire,

Burning from the inside out.

Your sex gets me drunk on desire,

Panted breaths keep me bound.

I am on fire, for you.

Burning from the inside out, the way that you do.

Let the flames burn higher, I'm gone.

I'll burn in hell, just to fuck until dawn.

Luc watching from the wings as I finish out our encore is truly setting me on fire. On top of the heat of the stage lights, and the exertion of playing what might be one of my most energetic shows, I am flushed with arousal. Having his eyes on me while I sing lyrics that I wrote while thinking about him is a heady combination, and I'm about to give Seattle a show they didn't ask for.

I had to come three times before I could even get myself into these pants. Luc's reaction to seeing what I would be wearing tonight was enough to put me on edge before I even got them on. I tried not to look over at him too many times, especially knowing that he's prepped, plugged, and ready for me to take all my after-show adrenaline out on him the moment I get into the dressing room. I can't seem to keep my eyes off him, and the way he's watching me has me lit the fuck up.

Thank fuck for my guitar, because I had a half-chub through more than half the show, and I'm full-on hard right now in anticipation of what's to come. I'm lucky my dick hasn't sprung free from the plunging deep V of the hemline.

"Thank you, Seattle!" I scream to the crowd, before turning on my heel and making a beeline for him.

Luc was supposed to head to my dressing room as the band and I took our final bows, and I was supposed to meet him there, but I have zero self-control when it comes to this man, and I hot-footed it off the stage like I was being booed off instead of being begged for more. So now I'm basically chasing him, and he probably knows I'm likely to fuck him wherever I catch him.

Luckily, he's an athlete, because we make it to the dressing room before I tackle him. He wastes no time passing me the small bottle of lube, unfastening and dropping his pants before I push him over whatever hard surface we land on first. It's dark, only a sliver of light coming from a bathroom light that was left on.

Freeing my cock from the confines of the leather, I pass a lubed hand up and down my shaft before pulling the plug from Luc's ass and replacing it with my cock in one quick thrust. His hands hit the counter, and a choked breath is expelled from his chest with the force of it.

I hold myself still for a moment, a full-body shiver working its way down the back of my neck and spine. This is the third time I've been inside him without a condom, and I'm not sure I'll ever get over how hot and sensitive everything is bare like this. The first time was slow and easy, opening him up bit by bit to accommodate my piercings. There was also the fact that the moment my tip pushed through his tight ring, I was in danger of losing it. I came before I could even work myself fully inside. The moment Luc felt me tensing and emptying inside him, he slammed himself back and worked himself on my dick while all I could do was hold on and spasm. His orgasm swallowed me whole, held my cock inside him from the base, and milked every ounce of cum I had to give until I felt dizzy.

The second time was about thirty minutes before showtime, when I was working him over with the plug, so he'd be ready for me after the show. It was a pretty big one, but the stretching and opening got us both so worked up, I couldn't help but fuck a load into his needy, gaping hole before plugging it up.

Luc's hand comes back to grip my ass, encouraging me to move and letting me know I didn't hurt him. His ass pushes back at me at the same time, telling me he can take it. I can give it to him harder.

I rock against him for a moment, relishing the searing heat of his insides and the tight clamp of his hole around the base of my cock. I pull out slowly, and push back in, slowly increasing speed until we find a rhythm that has us both panting. I was already sweaty, but now it's ten times worse, streaming off my body and dripping onto his skin as I fuck him.

The sweat, lube, and leftover cum inside him provide a decadent slide and delicious squelch that adds to the cacophony of illicit sounds filling the room. Heavy panting, moaning, the rhythmic slap of our bodies coming together, the beat of his hand moving up and down his cock, and the sloppy, wet proof of our insatiable desire for each other is fucking inspiring. It's music to my ears, especially since I can barely see the outline of our bodies.

"Flashlight," I say, and Luc hands back my cell phone. I blink at the bright beam of light before my eyes focus, and the sight of my cock moving in and out of his wet, stretched hole is… "Fuck, baby. This is the hottest thing I've ever seen in my life."

He straightens a little, I push his black tank top up to his ribs, so the fabric doesn't block my view. The slight change in angle squeezes my cock tighter. My balls draw up tight to my body. "*Nnygghh*–I'm going to come."

"I want to see," he pants. "Record it so I can see."

Quickly, I push the button to record, aiming the phone and light to get everything. My fist is balled into his shirt, using it for leverage. His back is curved, two dimples popping up on either side of the small of his back. His firm, round, tanned ass is turned out, my pelvis bouncing off the tight globes. My cock disappears inside his stretched-out ring, strokes slowing as my orgasm tears through me. I hold the camera closer, close enough to see the base of my cock pulsing, pumping cum inside Luc's perfect ass. I work myself in and out, extending it for as long as I can, before pulling almost all the way out. My cock is glossy with cum and lube, and the studs of my piercings are coated and dripping.

"Fucking hell," I growl, dipping my cock back inside and pulling it out again, watching more cum seep out of him.

I stop the video, then place my phone on the counter in front of Luc and push play. Immediately I feel him clench. I'm oversensitive almost to the point of pain, but I know he's close, and I want to feel him react to the sight of my cock inside him. He comes to the sight and sounds of me coming inside him.

"Next time I want a video of you breeding me," I say against the back of his neck, biting down on the back of his shoulder to muffle my grunts as he uses me to work himself through his orgasm.

We're breathless. Boneless. Reckless. When I stumble over to the door to turn the light on, I realize we didn't even lock it. I wet a washcloth with warm water and bring it over to Luc to help him clean up, but I just tuck my filthy dick back in my pants and make sure there aren't any drops or smears of anything visible on my exposed pelvis or torso. I wash my hands and wring out the washcloth for Luc to use again. I lean back against the wall, trying to regulate my heart rate and breathing before someone comes looking for me to do the backstage meet and greets.

Luc pulls his pants up, but leaves them undone and falls onto the couch. He leans back against the cushions, sweat beading at his temple, smirking at me like he knows exactly how undone I am. His eyes rake down my body.

"Those pants are trouble," he mutters, voice rough.

I laugh and walk over, leaning down to brush a soft kiss across his mouth. "You're trouble," I say, popping a piece of candy in my mouth, which Luc steals.

I open the door just before Blake can knock, Cory and Tad standing guard. Triple bonuses. I shoot a wink back at Luc before I shut the door behind me. He rolls his stolen candy on his tongue, and I walk away grinning like a lunatic. Blake doesn't even attempt to chide me, he knows it won't do any good.

Sunday is a blur of tangled sheets and lazy beams of sunlight trickling in around the edges of the hotel's blackout curtains. We watch our video on repeat so many times we're both beginning to chafe. Luc records each time he pumps me full and plugs me.

It's definitely one way to make memories.

We head to New York on Monday. The city is alive as ever, even as the cold weather sets in, crisp winds biting at every spot of exposed flesh.

Having Luc here with us while we record is almost just as heady as having him watch me on stage. He sits in the corner of the studio, quiet and watchful as always, while we lay down some of the tracks we've been tinkering with lately. I feel his eyes on me like a physical thing, it sends little zings of awareness over my skin all day. Before I know it, I'm scratching down lines, humming out a melody that's coming together like a puzzle in my head.

"What's that?" Naz asks.

I sing a little for him, a broken fiber of an idea, and it builds from there. Ari fills in some of my missing lyric fragments to build a solid hook, Will tinkering with the tune until it fits, then Naz gives it a heartbeat.

> *Keep looking at me like that,*
>
> *I know what's burning behind those eyes.*
>
> *Keep watching me like you do,*

You make me feel alive.

It's raw and messy, but I think we all know right away that this is our next big hit.

When we leave the studio hours later, we're all buzzing. We laid down a completed track for the tentatively titled *Eyes On Me* and sent it off with Blake to test it out with the higher ups. I let it be known that I won't be taking no for an answer, although I don't think it's likely the song would be given anything but a fast track to our next single.

We're not the only ones buzzing. The crowd outside is thicker than usual, cameras flashing before the doors swing open. Security clears a path for us, but this crowd is aggressive, and more than once I'm jostled on my way to the car. It feels louder than usual, the bulbs brighter, the shouted questions more intrusive.

I give Cory a panicked look. *Where is he?*

Luc had left with him to go get the car while we finished up with Blake, discussing plans for tomorrow. If anyone in the crowd had seen him, they'd surely be throwing questions out about him and not just my reaction to the latest Twatpost from the shit-stirring poor excuse of a man we currently have leading the country. Doesn't he have anything better to do?

Cory's hand squeezes my shoulder reassuringly, and I duck into the car. Naz, Will, and Ari file in after me. Blake rides with the rest of the security team in the car behind us. Tad is sitting in the back seat. The door shuts behind us, muffling most of the din. Before Cory can pull away from the curb, they start hitting the windows and roof of the car. He lays on the horn and revs the engine, a clear threat to get the fuck out of the way, which they do when they realize they can't see much through the dark tint of the windows, even with their faces pressed up against the glass.

"Where is he, Cory?" I bark, my agitation ramping up.

My knee bounces uncontrollably, my nails dig into my palms, and I nearly rip my lip ring out. I do pull some hairs out, aggressively pushing my hair back from my forehead. The space in the car shrinks, air too thick and heavy to breathe. It's too hot. My skin feels stretched too tight, and my eyes are dry. My heart is beating so fast I cough and gag.

"It's alright, man. Breathe," Naz says, placing one hand firmly on my chest and one on my back like he can hold me together.

"Where. Is. He?" I grit out.

"All clear," Cory yells back.

There's a sharp intake of breath, and Luc pops up in the very back row, next to Tad. My stomach flips, and I fold myself in half, burying my face in my hands.

"I'm here, baby, I'm here."

Seamlessly, Luc maneuvers himself into the seat next to me, while the others shuffle down, Ari taking the seat Luc just abandoned. He pulls me into his arms, and I can feel him trembling almost as hard as I am.

"Fucking fuck!" I yell, muffling my frustration in his chest.

Cory's phone rings over the speakers, and he clicks to answer. "Mr. Holland, you're on speaker."

"Good. Is everyone alright? I'm assuming Mr. Martín was stowed away somewhere safe?"

"Yes, sir," Cory answers. Luc chimes in and says he's fine, but I think it's more for my sake than Blake's.

"This is getting out of hand," Naz says.

"You're threatening the imbalance that certain government officials are trying very hard to cultivate. You're a big enough name to pull attention away from the circus and direct it towards the real problems. They're going to do whatever they can to discredit you."

"You think they're purposefully trying to provoke us?" Will asks.

"It's not uncommon," Blake answers.

"Did anyone notice that most of the paparazzi back there weren't the usual crowd?" Tad asks. I think hard, trying to separate the chaos.

"He's right," I say. "I saw one or two of the usual guys that always follow us around, but they don't usually give us much trouble. These were all new people."

"Hired, maybe?" Cory asks, flicking his eyes up to the rearview mirror. Tad nods.

With a deep sigh, I look up at Luc. He's clearly shaken, even though he's trying to put on a brave face for my benefit. "I should probably take you home. Maybe we can hide out at your–"

"I agree that Mr. Martín should go back home," Blake says, his voice sounding legitimately regretful through the car speakers. "But it's probably best if you don't go with him."

I sit up straight. "What?"

"I think it's a good idea if Luc heads home alone and makes a point to be seen somewhere in Shreveport while you are recorded and photographed in New York at the same time. So far, any rumors about the two of you have gone nowhere, but I wouldn't put it past the news outlets and politicians to look into every single fan theory and rumor just in case they can make something of it, even if it isn't true."

"Better safe than sorry," Naz says, giving me a serious, worried look. His words from the other day come to mind. *Would your relationship survive if this were to get out?*

"Mr. Martín, you should be extra vigilant. Watch what you say in public, there could be recording devices anywhere. Keep your curtains closed and tell your Coach and stadium security to expect drones."

"Isn't it illegal to record people in their homes, or their private conversations?"

"There are ways of getting around that, and if the news is big enough, they'd consider it worth the risk."

"Jesus," Luc mutters under his breath.

"I'm so sorry," I mutter, feeling sick to my stomach.

He pulls me tighter into his side. "This isn't your fault," he says, pressing a kiss to the top of my head.

Tad arranges for an unmarked, unassuming vehicle to be waiting for us in the private basement entrance of the hotel. Luc and I are given twenty minutes to pack up his things and say our good-byes. The quicker he's seen back in Louisiana, the better.

I cling to him, feeling a hundred times worse than the first time I watched him drive away from me. Parting from him never feels good. But this time…

It feels ominous.

LeST is
MooRE

TWENTY-TWO
LUC

Once again, I'm confronted by how fucking lonely my condo is. How did I never feel how thick the silence is?

My keys clatter too loudly against the counter. My footsteps echo. There's barely any light filtering in through the windows from the moon and streetlights outside, still I close every blind and curtain in the condo before turning on any lights.

I consider calling Jesse. He hasn't seen or replied to my text that the plane landed and I got home safely, so I'm guessing he's asleep. I just want to hear his voice, so I put *Remember My Name* on repeat before sinking onto my couch and rubbing my hands over my face.

Before Jesse, my life was orderly. Routine. I went to practice, I worked out, did my grocery shopping twice a week, played through the seasons, and went home when I had breaks in between. That was it. It was simple. But now I see that it was lacking. It was hollow.

Because now I know what it's like to wake up next to someone that fits against me like a puzzle piece. Whose laugh lights up more pleasure receptors than the sex does, and the sex is pretty fucking mind-bending. Now I know what it is to look forward to talking to someone all day, to feel my heart skip a beat when I find a text or video message waiting. To plan for the future, when we'll next see each other, and count the days until that happens.

Now I don't know when the next time will be.

I wake up to a text from Jesse, but it's just another apology. I don't know how to make him believe that I don't blame him for any of this. Even if they find out Jesse and I have been in the same place at the same time and put it together that we like each other, does it matter that much? I'm starting to think that denying myself happiness isn't worth the opinions and comfort of others.

ME: I miss you.

Ghost: I miss you, too.

As Mr. Holland suggested, I call a couple of teammates to meet up for lunch. AJ is the first to arrive, and he wastes no time plopping down in the chair across from me and crossing his arms.

"Alright, what's this about?"

"What?"

"You sent a group text. To have lunch. In public." He gestures around us. We're sitting on the screened-in outdoor patio of one of the more popular cafes downtown.

His glare looks annoyed, but also a bit hurt. I consider telling him something, not all of it, just enough that he doesn't think something's wrong with me or that I'm playing some kind of prank. Then I remember Tad's advice about being vigilant about what I say in public, even if I trust the person I'm telling.

Dez and Monty show up, staring warily as they take their seats.

"Thanks for joining me," I say, trying to sound casual. "Have any of y'all actually eaten here before? I've heard it was good but never tried it myself."

I raise my eyes from my menu to the three men staring back at me.

"What the fuck is this?" Monty says to AJ, who shrugs like he's given up trying to figure me out.

Dez just blinks at me.

"Look, I'm just… I'm trying something new. I–I want to get over some of this phobia I have." It's not untrue. Especially as I consider what it would be like having to stress and hide like this for the rest of my life. I do need to come out of my shell a little bit. If I truly want to be with Jesse, I need to take the possibility that I'll never have a quiet life seriously.

The guys nod, Monty thumps my shoulder, and AJ throws a napkin at my face. "You could have just said that, dipshit."

A camera flashes, and there's chatter outside the enclosed patio.

"That was quick," Dez says, cutting his eyes at me, concerned.

"Where'd they all come from?" Monty asks, and I chance a look. There are only five, which is a lot for me, but it's nothing compared to yesterday's scare.

Apparently it's a lot, even for Dez, unless he's at a scheduled press event. "Most of the time it's just fans snapping pics, and an occasional pap. I've never seen it like this."

AJ watches the photographers for a minute. "I think they're here for Mr. Colgate," he says, grinning.

"Stop that shit," I say, throwing his napkin back at him. "Don't encourage it."

I know what they're really here for, and as soon as we're done eating and are heading home, I'll text Jesse that the mission was accomplished.

———

"Hey."

"Hey," I repeat back to him, voice soft. It's all I can do not to sigh contentedly hearing his voice and seeing his face, even on a screen.

"You alright?" Jesse asks.

"I was just about to ask you the same thing."

"Could be better, but I suppose it could be worse."

"Yeah, I'd say about the same." I smile at him, half embarrassed at the urge to stare into his green eyes and sigh and smile like a brainless idiot. *Who am I?*

Jesse chuckles. "I feel ridiculous."

"Why?"

"Because I'm just so relieved to see your face, I almost don't even have anything to say. But I also want to keep you on the phone."

"Would it help if I said I was thinking something similar?"

"How similar?"

"Honestly, probably worse."

"Oh. Then yeah, that helps. Thanks."

"No problem," I laugh.

"How was practice today?"

"Slow. I'll be glad to get on the plane tomorrow to head to Tampa."

"You, Mr. Homebody, are looking forward to a work trip?"

A laugh bubbles out of me. "If you can believe it."

"Did I break you, baby?"

"In more ways than one," I tell him. "Life will never be the same again. But I'm thinking that maybe it's a good thing."

"Is it?" Jesse twists his lips, like he's not sure he agrees. "I feel like I've screwed up your whole quiet, peaceful existence."

"You shook it up for sure. But it was necessary. I didn't realize how empty my life was before I met you, and then before I met you again the second time." I smile.

"But now you're practically in hiding, having to distance yourself from my chaos."

"Well, about that. It seems like these people are going to be relentless. And maybe it's not ideal, but…"

Jeesh, why is my heart beating so fast? Like I'm about to start confessing everything to the whole world right away.

Jesse's brow is furrowed with worry, so I decide to rip the bandage off. "Maybe I should come out."

"What?!"

"Maybe I should come out. Or at least stop hiding."

"Luc, you can't let them bully you."

"We could look at it that way, but I'm thinking of it as a push in the right direction. I'm giving them power by caring what anyone else thinks of me. If I let them take it from me and expose me, then I'm letting them make news and publicity out of my life. I'd rather do it on my terms and not give them the chance to make a big story out of it."

"So you want to…"

"I want to be spotted with you in public. On purpose. Holding hands or hugging."

"Luc, have you really given this enough thought?"

"Why are you trying to talk me out of this when I know you want it, too?"

Tears slip out of his eyes, and he looks off to the side, wiping them away and laughing.

"I'll talk to Blake and the PR team. If you're okay with it, of course. They can help us plan something that will give you the best optics."

"That sounds great. I just need one thing from you."

"What's that?"

"Come home with me for Thanksgiving? Well, technically the two days before Thanksgiving because I have to be back in Shreveport Thursday, but I think I should give them a heads up, and I'd like them to meet you."

"Really?"

"Yeah really."

"I've never met anyone's family before. Should I be nervous?"

I scrunch my nose. "My dad can come off kind of cranky, but he means well. I know I'll have some preconceived notions and outdated ideals to contend with, but I truly believe he'll love and support me–*us*–no matter what."

"And your sisters?"

"Shawna says Talia has a poster of you on her wall, so things might get awkward."

He laughs. "I think I can handle that."

We talk for a couple more hours, about our families and pasts. We touch a little on our hopes for the future, but I think we're both feeling a bit tender in that regard. Everything feels too good to be true. But now we have a plan.

"I have to get to bed, long day tomorrow," I tell him. "But I have a present for you."

"A present?" His eyebrows lift, and he looks wary, excited, and confused all at the same time.

"Yeah. It's not quite as good as showing up out of nowhere and fucking you senseless, but since it'll be another five days before I get to see you again, I thought this might help us pass the time."

I send over the file on the encrypted app that Tad installed on my phone. I hear his phone chime and watch his face carefully as he navigates to the app to open the video link. Immediately, his eyes go wide and then glaze over with lust. I can hear the sounds we're making in the video, the dirty way we were talking to each other.

It's a compilation video of all the times I fucked him on Sunday, filled him with my cum, and plugged him up. The last frame of the video is when I finally let it all pour out of him, pooling and squelching.

"I think I might love you," Jesse groans.

We run off the field, feeling high. We're undefeated this season so far, and today we absolutely annihilated Tampa Bay, 38 to 7. It was almost a shutout, but their quarterback threw a hell of a Hail

Mary in the last quarter to put some points on the board before it was over for the Buccs.

I'm all smiles and feeling good. Jesse and I have a plan, and I'm taking him home to meet my family in two days. It feels like my whole life is about to start. Really start, since I've been coasting through the last twenty-seven years like a ghost. In the locker room, spirits are high, and I even sing along a little as my friends and teammates dance around to our unofficial new team song by *Lest Is Moore*.

After a shower, I'm ready to join the guys for a celebratory dinner. I'm getting more and more comfortable with testing the waters of public appearances.

I get dressed and pull my phone out of my bag, my heart slowing to a sluggish, slow-motion thump-thump that I can hear in my ears. There are dozens of missed calls in just the last few hours, and texts from Jesse, Shawna, and Mr. Holland. Ignoring all the other calls and not reading any of the messages, I dial Jesse's number. When he answers, his voice is rough like he's been screaming. He sounds wrecked.

"I'm so sorry."

TWENTY-THREE
JESSE

"Luc, baby. I'm so sorry. I–"

The line goes dead. He… *he hung up*.

"No, no, no." I fumble with the phone, staring at the screen like I can will him back. There's a fist in my chest, squeezing so tightly my stomach gets pulled into the knot, twisting and tightening until the weight of it all slams into me all at once.

My knees hit the carpet, the phone clattering beside me.

I'm so fucking stupid.

I fall forward, fists beating the floor, a wail ripping from the depths of my soul until there's no air left in my lungs. I crumple in on myself, pulling my knees to my chest in an attempt to stem the flow of my heart leaking out through my throat. There's nothing left in my stomach to throw up, and I've barely any voice left to scream with. All that's left are tears and heartbreak.

No one runs to check on me this time. I've screamed at them all to leave me alone more times than I can count. I've pushed everyone that loves me away, and I ruined the only man I've ever loved enough to want to be a better person.

Too worn out to move, I stare straight ahead, the wet bar taunting me from across the room. Tears leak from the corners of my eyes, and I squeeze my knees harder, trying to blot out the merciless droning of the news anchor on TV.

"Breaking now: international rock phenomenon Jesse Moore, frontman of *Lest Is Moore*, appears to be the victim of a targeted cloud hacking attack. Personal information, as well as several explicit photos and videos, believed to have been hacked from Moore's personal devices, surfaced online early this evening. At this time, Moore is the only known victim of the breach. While some are pointing fingers at the recent barrage of right-wing media attacks on the band *Lest Is Moore* and their unwavering support of the LGBTQ+ community, many seem to be more focused on the content of the breach, specifically intimate photos and videos of what appear to be Moore in explicit encounters with another man. While the superstar has always been open about his sexuality, fans and critics alike are already speculating about the identity of the partner, though no names have yet been linked."

The words rattle around the room, jarring my bones. The reporter's voice is too bright, too loud, too sharp with her words. All I can do is lie there and take it, as clip after clip and quote after quote are played and played and played again.

"Sex, drugs, and rock and roll: Targeted hack exposes rockstar Jesse Moore."

"Private videos leaked online: Who is the mystery man?"

"Tonight at ten: Jesse Moore's history of drug use, rehab, and descent into sex addiction."

"Conservative news outlets blast Jesse Moore for explicit videos, suggest the breach has exposed Moore for the depraved, immoral person he is."

"The president weighs in: In a post earlier today, the president said, "I don't know who hacked the failed rockstar's phone, but I'm glad they did. What a loser. Now the world can see what a twisted guy he really is. This isn't the kind of guy you want as a role model for your kids.""

"This just in, TMZ releases a list of twelve possible matches for the leading man in Jesse Moore's homemade porn videos. From athletes to actors to industry insiders—the names might surprise you."

The sound of my name being repeated on a loop, of my weakest moments and dumb shenanigans that, in this context, paint me to be the worst kind of deviant, get louder and sound worse every time they're replayed. I can't make it stop. I can't hear anything over their voices, over my own voice, over the billion tiny microphones and cameras set on every facet of my life.

Finally, I gather the strength to get off the floor. I look for the remote, but I can't find it anywhere. I walk to the bar in a daze. My fingertips drag along the bottles, the memory of oblivion imprinted on the pads of my fingers. My hand closes around a heavy, whitefrosted bottle. I feel the weight of consequence in my palm, consider the burn of cold liquid, the lie that makes everything louder and quieter at once, that numbs and hurts. I lift the bottle from the shelf.

And fling it across the room.

The bottle leaves my hand and arcs across the room. It hits the center of the television screen with a sound like a gunshot, glass fracturing into a million tiny veins under the impact. The screen blooms white and then black as the circuits die. The whole TV, almost the size of the wall itself, rocks off its mount, weight tilting. It tips and crashes to the floor with a thunder that rattles the glasses on the bar next to me.

The bottle lies intact on the ground. Nausea fills my mouth with saliva, and my chest squeezes tighter.

Silence falls over the room in a moment that feels suspended, but isn't quite long enough. Finally, the voices commentating on my downfall are quiet, but now there's another sound. Boots on marble flooring, bodies crashing through the French doors. Cory and Tad have remained outside, trying to give me space, trying to be respectful of the pain I'm in, and likely glad to escape the rabid wounded animal I'm acting like. The crash left them no choice but to intervene, though.

"Jesse?" Cory's voice is hard and careful as he steps inside the suite, eyes sweeping the mess as well as my proximity to the bar. I know he's concerned by the way he says my first name instead of my last, but that just gets under my skin, too.

I should be stronger than this. I should be smarter than this. I should have known I'd ruin it somehow.

Cory steps closer to me while Tad opens his phone and steps back into the hallway.

"Are you okay?"

"No," I answer, pressing my palms into the cold, hard marble of the bar top, vertigo threatening my equilibrium. It feels like I stood up too fast, but I was already standing. "I'm not okay," I say weakly.

The fist closes. And the room goes black.

———

Fingertips brush across my forehead, the familiar, comforting scent of home seeping into my sleep-addled brain. There's a rhythmic beeping.

"Jesse," my mother says, her voice low and smooth and melodic. She should have been a singer. I love her voice.

She says my name again, and my eyelids flutter. I'm so heavy and warm, this doesn't feel real.

"Mom?" My mouth makes a clicking sound it's so dry.

I try to open my eyes again, but it's so bright. I hear my mom's voice talking to someone, a lower timber that's familiar as well. Naz, I think.

Someone lowers the blinds or curtains, and I try again to open my eyes. Why am I so tired? I–

Fear spikes through me. The beeping gets louder and faster, an alarm going off. "I didn't– Cory told them not to–"

I want to sit up, but I'm too heavy.

"It's okay, baby. They had to sedate you, but they used a non-addictive sedative. You're going to be groggy for a while until it wears off."

A nurse runs in and shuts the alarm off, watching my heart rate settle. It's still too fast for her liking, but she sets a warm hand on my arm and encourages me to breathe. There's a tube shooting cold oxygen straight into my nostrils, and I focus on breathing in one heavy lungful through my nose and back out through my mouth until the beeping settles.

"Good." The nurse smiles down at me. She's around my age, has bright, clear blue eyes and a pixie cut. "Welcome back, Mr. Moore. I'm Annie. I've been helping take care of you since you came in last night."

"How long have I been here?" I ask, fumbling over my words and wincing at my sore throat. Naz appears at my side with a cup of ice water and a straw. Annie helps adjust my bed so I can raise my head, and I suck down the water thirstily.

"About twelve hours," Annie says. "Your bodyguard, I think Cory was his name?" I nod. "He advocated for you really well. He told the EMTs and the hospital staff what you needed as far as your sobriety. We gave you a high dose of hydroxyzine to sedate you after you had an acute panic attack."

I blink rapidly, trying to recall the night before. My brain feels slow, like my thoughts are wading through molasses. But I remember the voices on the news. The TV crashing to the ground.

"Luc," I whisper, eyes filling with tears.

The heart rate monitor picks up again, and my mom climbs into the bed next to me, careful of the tubes and lines connected to me everywhere, and pulls me into her arms.

"Let me know if you need anything. I'm just outside," Annie whispers.

"Sometimes you just need a good cry," Mom says, and holds me while I do just that.

———

Blake, Will, and Ari visit later in the day, when I'm a little more clearheaded but still quite groggy. I've slept most of the day and cried the rest. I'm feeling pretty numb, so I feel safe asking Blake how badly I've screwed up.

"First of all, you didn't screw anything up. Someone violated your right to privacy, and you had an involuntary panic attack. None of that is your fault," he says firmly, then sighs.

"Just tell me," I say flatly. "I'd rather know than be surprised by it later."

"Unfortunately, quite a few of the major news outlets are getting excellent ratings by sensationalizing everything, and none of what they have to say is beneficial. The paparazzi were camped outside the hotel when EMTs arrived, and they're reporting that you overdosed."

I open my mouth, but Blake gets there before I do. "I've been in contact with Mr. Martín. He knows you're okay, and I let him know that the reports were false. I hope that's okay. I figured you wouldn't want him to think the worst."

I nod. "Thank you. Is he…"

"As far as I know, he's fine. He was concerned about you when he saw the news, beyond that we didn't discuss much. I offered him legal counsel if he ends up needing it."

I nod again, feeling like a swimmy-headed bobblehead doll.

"I've been in meetings with PR and legal. Given the public uproar over the reports, and to protect your health, we think it's a good idea to cancel the remainder of the tour. Luckily, there were only a couple more shows. I can keep the private holiday shows on the schedule for now, and we can make decisions as we go."

"And what about you guys?" I ask my bandmates, who have taken up residence in chairs at the end of my bed. Naz has his legs up on the bed next to mine.

"Seems like the best thing for now," Will says, and Ari agrees.

Naz nudges my foot with his. "No one blames you for this, man. It's fucking bullshit, and it's a hell of a mess to clean up, but it's not your fault."

If only Luc saw it that way.

LeST is
MooRE

TWENTY-FOUR
LUC

"You're a goddamn idiot is what you are," Shawna says, standing with her arms crossed in my kitchen.

"Don't you think I know that?! Who invited you here again?"

"I'm your best friend. I don't need an invitation. I have a fucking key," she says, holding it up and sticking her tongue out at me.

I can't help but huff out an exasperated laugh. "What's it going to take to get you to go home?"

"You getting your head out of your ass," she says, dropping her duffle bag on the floor. "I expect I'll be here a while."

Shawna and I have been at odds about what to do about the Jesse Moore situation. When I went home alone for Thanksgiving, she laid next to me and let me cry it out. She let me mope around for a couple days, making excuses for my odd behavior to my family.

My sisters still managed to figure it out. Unlike my dad, who pretty much exclusively watches the *Weather Channel*, my sisters are as keyed into the latest celebrity scandal as most teenagers, especially as fans of *Lest Is Moore*. The two of them came to me my second night home and told me that they know I'm Jesse Moore's lover.

If I have ever felt sicker in my life, I can't name the day. I've had food poisoning that didn't tear me up as much as finding out that my little sisters saw my sex tapes. Thank God Georgia let me know that neither of them had seen the actual videos, only the blurred-out screenshots shared on the mainstream news sources. My smart, sensitive sisters informed me that, under no circumstances would they look at anyone's private photos or videos that had been leaked without their permission.

"Looking at them would be like violating that person physically. Do unto others, and all that," she said.

They'd seen a few of the gossip rags mention my name as a possible love interest before, and had "Maybe been a tiny bit hopeful that those rumors were true," Talia said, blushing.

When I asked why, Georgia said, "First of all, he's hot. Second of all, he was so cute cheering for you and wearing your jersey, and third of all, he's hot." Talia added, "Oh, and you've never had a person. We figured it was time."

All of that, combined with my surly attitude and moping around during my two-day break, made them feel strongly that I am the lover Jesse Moore is hiding.

I didn't even correct them, or bother asking them to stop repeating the word *lover*, because it sounds weird when they say it. "I was going to bring him home for Thanksgiving," I said. Seeing as I've rarely ever shared anything other than a strong front to my sisters, it was a breaking point for me.

I tried starting a conversation with my father but lost the words. Too much of a coward to let my dad find out that there were videos like that of me, splashed all over the news and internet.

Enter Shawna, who is bound and determined to get me back in Jesse's good graces. Not only am I unsure I can handle the pressure, but I don't deserve his forgiveness. I shut down. He called and poured his heart out to me, took all the blame for something that wasn't his fault, and begged me not to leave him. And I shut down.

I didn't mean to. It wasn't my intention to hang up on him and leave it like that. I was standing in the locker room, listening to him tell me how his phone was hacked, and that the photos and videos we'd shared with each other were out there. The video of him fucking me. The video I made of me breeding and plugging him over and over. A multitude of pictures of our dicks, recordings of ourselves jerking off together. All of that out in the world.

I froze. Then my phone fell from my hand onto the tile. When I pulled myself together and stopped panicking, which admittedly took a while, I bought a new phone. By the time I was able to call Jesse back, it was too late. He didn't answer.

When I saw the report about Jesse being taken to the hospital by ambulance, all the speculation that he'd overdosed, I felt responsible. If he'd spiraled and hurt himself, it was my fault. I didn't say anything to him. I didn't ask him how he was doing, the one who was actively being torn apart by the media. My name has been mentioned here and there in speculation, and a few reporters have tried to question me about it, but Jesse is facing worldwide scrutiny and I've said nothing.

I finally got in touch with Mr. Holland, who assured me Jesse hadn't overdosed, and offered me legal counsel should the truth be revealed. He advised me to not talk to the press and to be vigilant about my security. If I had anything saved to the cloud, now would be a good time to delete it.

"Where is he now?" I asked.

"He's still in the hospital under observation. He's stable. It's the safest place for him to be right now."

I wanted to ask Mr. Holland if I could talk to Jesse, but I didn't.

I wanted to go there and be with him, but I stayed put.

I wanted to go on a rampage and shout from the rooftops that these stupid talking heads needed to get Jesse's name out of their mouths and move on to real news, but I just watched, numbly, as the rhetoric got worse and worse.

I've been stuck in an endless cycle of worry, shame, and self-hatred for being a coward. And Shawna is here to make sure I'm reminded of my cowardly behavior until I crack.

"I've tried calling," I tell her. "He's not calling me back. Mr. Holland told me he was discharged from the hospital yesterday and that he has access to his phone. He doesn't want to speak to me."

Shawna stays for another week. I only get away from her when the team travels to play Washington, but the pressure of knowing she's right and still being too chickenshit to do anything about it still follows me. There's gossip on the plane about Jesse disappearing, and the likelihood that he was in rehab again after overdosing. I couldn't even bring myself to correct them. I just sat there and swallowed back bile.

I don't deserve him.

———

The game against Washington is long, drawn out, and hard fought. We barely manage to eke out the win in overtime. The win clenches our place in the playoffs, but I'm not in the mood to celebrate anything. All I want to do is shower and get on the bus back to the hotel so I can wallow some more.

AJ is thumbing through social media on his phone when I get out of the shower.

"Oh, shit," he says, sounding worried. "Did y'all see this? Our boy Jesse Moore is losing it."

"What? What happened?" I demand, pushing through the guys and snatching his phone, even though I could have just looked it up on my own.

EXCLUSIVE VIDEO: Jesse Moore Loses It On-Air

Afraid of what I'm about to see, especially with half a dozen guys surrounding me, I push play. At first, it's a pretty normal interview. Jesse, looking thin and haggard with dark circles under his eyes, talks about struggling with his mental health after his privacy was violated. He's decided to be more open about his past struggles with addiction and how rehab and the support of his friends and family have kept him alive. The host is annoying right off the bat, grilling Jesse about whether or not his recent hospital stay was related to an overdose, as was reported.

"I did not overdose. I had a panic attack and legitimately felt like I was dying. My chest seized up, and I couldn't breathe–"

"Is it true you went on an alcohol-fueled rage and trashed the penthouse suite of the hotel you were staying in? Reports from the scene noted severe damage to the premises."

"I broke the TV," Jesse admits. "But I wasn't drinking. It was an accident. I've paid for the damages and decided not to sue the hotel for one or more of their employees breaking the ironclad NDA it has with their clients, and releasing over-exaggerated details to the tabloids."

The host, who is known for being an aggressive troll, either doesn't believe Jesse, or is baiting him. Unfortunately, it works.

He digs and digs and digs at Jesse, who is attempting to set the record straight and be open about his struggles with addiction and mental illness, but this guy won't stop pushing about the sex videos and who the other man is. He asks if Jesse has a sex addiction in addition to drugs and alcohol, and starts naming names, mine included, as to who the "lucky man" could be. He asks what kind of future Jesse sees for himself, if the recent exposure of his personal escapades were, in fact, orchestrated by Jesse himself for attention. He asks if Jesse is ashamed of himself.

I feel myself flush with anger. I'm not a violent person, but there's no possibility I wouldn't lay that man out if he were in front of me now.

That's when Jesse snaps. He stands up, tears the headphones off and points at the host.

"You're the one who should be ashamed. I am a person–a fucking human being–who is being repeatedly violated by people like you. You use my pain and mental anguish to boost your ratings while perpetuating misinformation for entertainment value. That makes you no better than the criminals who stole and published my personal moments.

You want a quote for your show. Here's one–"

He leans into the microphone, anger burning in his green eyes.

"Fuck you. Fuck you and your criminal invasion of people's lives. Fuck you for making a mockery of someone's mental health and history of addiction. And fuck you for ruining the one real thing I had in this life. Fuck you for chasing away the only person I've ever loved."

Jesse starts to walk away, but the interviewer, calculated as ever, says, "So this guy just walks away from you and lets you take all the pressure for what you both were clearly part of, doesn't that piss you off? Shouldn't he take the heat just as much as you?"

Chest heaving, Jesse steps forward and upends the table between him and the talk show host. The mic stand clatters and papers fly everywhere. The host flinches back, but Jesse does nothing more than give him a cold look and storms out of the room.

Shit.

"When was this? When did it happen?" I scroll up to find more information. The story broke earlier today, but the actual incident happened early Friday morning.

Still dripping wet from the shower, I pull on the easiest clothes I can and leave the locker room in search of Coach. I explain to him that I was just informed of a family emergency, and I need a few days off. Coach, clearly seeing my panic, tells me to be back in time to fly out for the Atlanta game. I nod, and leave the stadium, finding an uber to take me to the airport. On the way there, I call Mr. Holland and Jesse repeatedly. Neither of them answers.

Just as I make it to the airport, I get a call from an unfamiliar number that has the same area code as Jesse's number. I answer it straightaway.

"Jesse?" I ask hopefully.

"No. It's Naz."

"Is he okay?"

"Not really, man."

"What can I do? I've been trying to call him, but he won't answer."

"He's been trying to fix it so he'd be worthy of you or some shit. Though, to be honest, you fucked up, too, man."

"I know I did. Let me make it better. Please. Naz, tell me where he is."

"I know I did. Let me make it better. Please. Naz, tell me where he is."

TWENTY-FIVE
JESSE

I'm pulled out of a restless sleep by the incessant ringing of the doorbell. It's a chiming, high-pitched tune that bounces off the walls and makes my brain feel like it's vibrating. I roll onto my back and stare at the ceiling, trying to breathe through the vibrations. Now that I'm awake, I notice my stringy hair dangling in my face, the way the sock on my left foot has come off my heel, and the weeks' worth of scratchy stubble on my face and crotch. My teeth feel like they're wearing little sweaters. The sheet is damp with sweat and creased at the small of my back.

Every little feeling is compounded and adds to my discomfort.

Cory's on the landing. I know that. He checked in with me when he took over for Tad, who had first watch this morning. They've been trading shifts until we can get full-time security now that the paparazzi have figured out where my mom lives.

Whoever's at the door was approved to come up, so it's got to be one of the boys, or Blake, or my mom. Naz has a key. Mom has a key. If it's someone who doesn't, not my problem. I don't want to open it. I don't want to see their faces. I don't have the energy to talk about any of it anymore.

I am bone tired in a way that's not just a lack of proper sleep. It's a hollow, under-the-ribs exhaustion, a heavy pressure on my sternum. The last week has been a treadmill of approved interviews, of careful phrasing and pre-cleared questions. I hoped we could move past the deep dive into my personal life by acknowledging my struggles with mental health and addiction. Maybe if people could see my face and hear my voice, they'd remember that I'm a real person who has experienced a deep violation.

Then I went on *Keep It Real* because PR thought that reaching Zach Lawson's audience was worth the risk. He signed the agreements and the list of approved topics like everyone else. Unlike everyone else, he did not stick to the list. It was barely five minutes before he went off it. I waited for Blake to pull me out of it, but I couldn't see him behind the glass walls of the recording booth. Zach dug in hard in the most disrespectful way possible, bound and determined to pull the worst out of me. I knew I was being baited. And I still let it happen. I got up to leave. I did. I was walking out, but then that bastard poked at my greatest weakness. He questioned my relationship with Luc. He questioned Luc's devotion to me if he wasn't willing to stand in the fire with me. He poked and poked at that bruise until I felt myself unravel, and I snapped.

I won't lie and say I didn't get a small amount of pleasure out of seeing that troll cower. Part of me wishes I had hit him, so the assault charges he's trying to file would have been worth it.

I regret losing control, though. Not because of Zach Lawson—fuck that guy—but because the entire purpose of the press tour was to pull the focus away from the scandal and towards healing. I wanted to quiet things, not add gasoline.

I can't help but picture Luc out there somewhere, hearing the same headlines and looped footage of my name being dragged through the mud and being asked on repeat if he's my mystery man like my life is some kind of game show. I've been hanging by a thread, holding on to the mere idea that I might be able to make things better for Luc so he can stay out of the public eye.

Mission failed. I just made it worse.

So now I've run home to Mommy with my tail between my legs. I'll probably rot here in this bed, too tired to even get up to pee until it hurts too bad to hold it. My throat is raw. I haven't eaten. I haven't showered. Despite not leaving this bed since I arrived, which was... What day is it? I crack an eyelid and see that it's dark outside. So it's probably Sunday night? Or is it Monday night? It's been a few days. All I've done is sleep, but I haven't actually gotten any actual rest.

"WHAT THE FUCK?!" I yell when the ringing graduates to frantic banging on the door.

Flinging the duvet off, and stomping to the door, or more like stumbling because my muscles ache. How long does it take for muscles to atrophy?

The hallway light outside the condo door is blinding after lying in the dark for so long. I squint as I throw open the door, ready to tear into Naz or whoever the fuck has the nerve to keep making so much racket.

It's no one I expect.

It's Luc.

He stands in front of me, looking objectively like shit with his clothes disheveled and wrinkled, his hair past the point of needing a haircut, one side sticking straight up while the other is plastered to the side of his head. Dark stubble casts a shadow over his lower face, almost as dark as the circles under his eyes.

Where is his coat? It's fucking December.

I can't breathe at the sight of him. Everything in me goes

stupidly quiet, like he found the pause button on the screaming feed in my head.

"Luc?" I question, testing the waters of whether this is a hallucination or not. My voice cracks, and I hate that it cracks. I hate that I care if it cracks, because even if he's not a hallucination I'm mad at him for hanging up. For giving up.

For breaking my fucking heart.

Luc huffs out a ragged breath that puffs white in the air. He swallows. "Jesse–"

My name on his lips is just as raw and pained as I feel. He takes a small, tentative step towards me, then drops to his knees and wraps his arms around my hips.

"Jesse, I'm so sorry. I'm so, so sorry. Please forgive me."

What?

My knees wobble, and I lower myself to eye level with him. I open my mouth to say something, but I can't find the words, so I surge forward and wrap my arms around his neck instead. He pulls me close and breathes in at the base of my neck. He probably regrets it. I really need a shower. And a toothbrush.

We haven't discussed or decided anything, but heat and relief radiate in my chest so strongly I almost mistake it for pain.

He's real. He's here.

I stand up, not trusting myself to think clearly when I'm so close to him, and gesture for him to do the same. Clumsily pushing the door open wider, I gesture into the entryway. "Let's go inside. It's cold as shit out here. Why aren't you wearing a jacket? Are you insane?"

He shrugs and gives me a tired, exasperated little half-smile. His eyes catch mine, and the blue of his irises seems dimmer. The look he gives me is full of complicated things. Exhaustion is probably paramount. There's fear, some anger. And there's just enough hope that we can find forgiveness with each other.

There's a lot to talk about. We both know it. But for now, I step into him and wrap my arms around his waist. He smells like cold air and clean laundry and hope.

I, however, probably smell like shit, so I pull away. Or I try to. Luc is holding on to me too tight.

"I smell. I've been lying on the same sheets, in the same clothes, since yesterday morning."

"Why?"

I shake my head, and he grabs my chin to direct me to look at him. "Why, Jesse?"

A small flare of anger has me spitting out the truth before I can think better. "I gave up hope that I'd ever see you again, and it hurt too much."

His shoulders move forward almost imperceptibly, like he can shield his chest from an ache.

"I know we have a lot to talk about, but right now, I just need to take care of you," he says, voice strained.

He wants to… take care of me?

"Okay," I whisper, because honestly, I need that too.

He has me point him towards the bathroom, but other than that I don't lift a single finger. He starts running a bath before stripping me out of my dirty clothes, tenderly but clinically. He actually sits me on the toilet, turning away to give me privacy, adding some random bath salts from a row along the edge of the tub to the water.

I can walk, but he still lifts me to lay me in the tub.

He washes me, rinses me, dries me off, and dresses me. I insist on brushing my own teeth, feeling a little better now that I'm clean, and he's here. In whatever capacity, he's here. Luc makes me some toast and changes my bedsheets while I eat. I can't handle much. I'm not really hungry, but I eat one whole slice with butter, and Luc finishes the rest.

When he tucks me into bed, he murmurs against my forehead that he's sorry again. I'm too tired to tell him this isn't his fault. This is just how I am. I tend to feel it all or nothing.

I'm not sure where he thinks he's going when he stands to leave me, but I hang on to his hand and pull him into bed with me.

"My clothes–" he starts.

"Just take them off, you can borrow some of mine in the morning," I say. "Don't worry, I'm too tired to get hard, so you won't be bothered."

His quiet huff of laughter is sad. But he strips down to his boxer briefs and socks and climbs into bed behind me, pulling me securely against his chest.

***

The next time I wake up, it's light out. I have a moment of panic that Luc showing up last night was a dream, but there's a deep indent in the pillow next to me, and I feel almost rested. I haven't felt that since the last time I slept with him next to me, the night before the paparazzi mobbed our car.

I hear movement in the kitchen, dishes clinking, and low murmured voices. The smell of coffee wafts in with the understanding that Luc is in the kitchen with my mother. Just weeks ago, we were talking about introducing each other to our respective families and going public with our relationship. Now he's probably in there discussing my well-being.

After brushing my teeth and pulling a hoodie over my shirt and boxers, I pad into the kitchen. I pause, staring at the comfortable, weirdly domestic scene in front of me. Luc, wearing a pair of my sweatpants and a t-shirt that's baggy on me but almost obscenely tight across his chest, is also wearing one of my mother's aprons, the one that looks like a big-breasted woman in a bikini. He sets a plate with what looks like an omelet in front of her, and she thanks him. Without looking up, he sets a coffee cup that says, *I'm A Fucking Rock-star, That's Why*, in front of the seat next to my mom and fills it, adding the perfect amount of cream and sugar. Warily, I enter the kitchen and take a wide berth around the island, but it's not wide enough.

Luc hooks an arm around my waist and pulls me against his chest, rubbing his nose in the back of my hair. "Much better," he mumbles, and I don't know if he means that he feels better because he could hug me this morning, or if it's because my hair smells better.

My mom tries to hide her grin but fails. I roll my eyes at her.

"So…you two have met then." I hate feeling so awkward about it when I was so looking forward to them meeting. "This wasn't really how it was supposed to happen."

"Things rarely happen the way they're supposed to," my mom says, pushing a lock of hair off my forehead.

Luc slides a massive omelet onto a plate and cuts a small portion off one end, putting it on a separate plate and sliding it to me wordlessly. I pick up the fork, thankful he didn't give me too much. My stomach won't tolerate much.

"So, Luc, how long are you able to stay? You mentioned you play in Atlanta next week?"

"Yes, ma'am. I'll need to be home Friday to pack and get on the plane, but I could stick around until then if I'm not in the way. I can get a hotel or–"

"Absolutely not," I say, interrupting him. "You're lucky you weren't spotted getting here last night." He wasn't. Blake would have called. He has all kinds of alerts set up so I don't have to look at my phone and fall down a rabbit hole of hate and vitriol. "You should probably not leave unless you have to, and when you leave–"

"Jesse. If I were worried about them seeing me, I wouldn't have come. I'm not doing that to you anymore."

"Don't suck up to me," I tell him lightly. "Whether you're ready to come out or not, I don't think this is the right time. The paps and even the mainstream news are feral right now. It's not safe." I want to tell him to discuss it with our PR team, but I don't want to subject him to a bunch of rules just so he can be with me. "We also don't even know what's going to happen. With us, I mean. We haven't discussed it yet."

Luc wipes his face with his napkin and nods. "You're right, we haven't. So let's discuss."

TWENTY-SIX
JESSE

"Finish that," Luc says, gesturing to my still mostly uneaten omelet. "I'm going to have a quick shower and borrow some clothes if that's okay." I nod. His lips quirk. "You wouldn't happen to have any more of my hoodies lying around, would you?"

I narrow my eyes at him. If he thinks he's getting all his clothes back, he'd better think twice. "Top left-hand drawer," I admit. *Wait until he sees what else I keep in that drawer.*

"Thanks." Luc kisses the top of my head before loading his plate into the dishwasher and reaching for the pan.

"I'll do that," I say, sending him off to the shower. I can't decide if I need space to think before we talk about things, or if I'm not ready at all. I watch him walk away, the muscular globes of his round ass and thick thighs testing the limits of my sweatpants.

My mother's silence catches up to me, and I tentatively flick my gaze to her. She pointedly looks down at her cup of coffee, rolling her lips in.

"I can see why you like him so much," she finally says.

We both crack, laughing for the first time in weeks.

"In all seriousness, baby, I like him for you."

"But?"

"No buts. Well, his butt, obviously. It's a nice butt." She grins and pumps her eyebrows.

"I'm not letting you hang out with the guys anymore," I grumble, but her antics never fail to make me feel lighter.

"Anyway," she says, "You've changed. It started with rehab, I think. But since you've started seeing Luc, it's even more noticeable. Look at what's happening around you. All of this stress and what the media is putting you through. I'm not sure you would have cared this much before, or if you did, you wouldn't have owned it. You would have made light of it and even forced the bad boy narrative to cover whatever hurt you felt. You've always taken the price of fame with a grain of salt, but you're taking this seriously."

"It was easier when I could brush it off," I admit. "I could convince myself I didn't care that much. But when it comes to Luc, it feels like something was stolen from me. From us. And I'm terrified we can't come back from it."

"It seems like he might be willing to make some pretty big changes himself. Hear him out. Decide where your priorities lie and do what it takes. If this is going to work, you both have to face it head-on and do the work."

I finish most of the omelet in silence. Mom shoos me away from the kitchen when I start cleaning up.

When I open the door to my room, Luc is standing at my dresser with his back to me. I step in quietly and shut the door behind me with a soft click, turning to rest my back against it and just look at him. He's just out of the shower, hair damp and his wide, muscular back dotted with drops of water. The towel he's got wrapped around his waist looks like it's holding on for dear life. I can't decide if I hope it loses the fight, or if I want to keep a clearer head for this.

It wouldn't be fair to fuck him when we're trying to make decisions about our future, would it? I can't trick him into staying with my body, and I want him to prioritize me–*us*–without sex being the motivator.

I want him to love me the same way I love him. I want him to be willing to give up the quiet, comfortable life he's built and step outside his comfort zone. I want him to know that I'm willing to give it all up to keep what we have safe.

Luc turns to eye me, a pair of black lacy panties hanging off his finger. "You have an entire stash of my clothes, and you keep them in your panty drawer?"

My lips twitch. "It's the drawer of all the things that make me feel beautiful."

His chest expands with a deep inhale, and he steps towards me, crowding me against the door. He tips my chin up to look down at me, and breathes, "You're always beautiful."

Priorities be damned, I can't not kiss him when he's looking at me like that. Not just hungrily, but like I'm something precious.

When his lips meet mine, his kiss is almost reverent. He doesn't deepen the kiss or open to let my tongue do more than lick at the seam of his lips. I think we both understand that this conversation is more important than how carried away we can get when our bodies do the talking for us.

He steps away, but it looks like it costs him. I do everything in my power not to notice the way the front of the towel is slipping, pushed away from his body by his rising erection.

Luc finds an entire set of clothes, including underwear, in the drawer of things I've squirreled away. He seems amused but not like he minds.

"Don't think you're leaving here with those," I say, watching him pull a pair of joggers over his thighs and ass. "Those are mine."

"Are they now?" He chuckles.

"Yes. And you have to admit it's convenient that I keep such things."

"It's cute is what it is."

"If you keep calling me things like beautiful and cute and keep looking at me like that, it's going to make this conversation a lot harder."

"How am I looking at you?"

"Like you love me," I blurt without thinking. "The way I love you," I add, figuring I might as well get it out there.

Luc looks pained, and it's a good thing I have my back to the door otherwise I might feel like I'm careening backwards like I've been struck. What is *that* look for?

He reaches for my hand and leads me to sit on my bed. I perch on the edge, but what I really want to do is run far, far away.

Luc drops to his knees on the floor in front of me, settling his hips between my knees. His hands move from my thighs, up my hips and waist, all the way to my neck, where he cups my head and keeps me facing him. He waits until I can bear eye contact. Once I look, I can't look away, sucked into pools of deep blue emotion.

"I'm sorry," he whispers.

I tense, ready to bolt, but he holds me there, anchored to him.

"Hear me out," he says, pleading with me. "I need to say this." I don't want to look him in the eye while he tells me this is too much for him, so I let my eyelids fall shut, a tear escaping down my cheek. Luc kisses it away.

"I screwed up, big time. Not just because I let you down when you needed me the most, but because if you really don't know, then I was an idiot for far longer than just the last couple of weeks."

His lips brush mine gently, and I taste the salt from my tears. I want to open my eyes and beg him to just put me out of my misery, but I don't think I can hold back the barrage of tears behind my eyelids.

"I love you so much," he says, unlocking a flurry of butterflies that thrash violently in my chest, forcing me to breathe in short, panting breaths. "I've loved you for far longer than the three months we've been trying to get to know each other. But…" The word makes my throat close up, choking the butterflies trying to make their escape. My face grows hot with the effort of holding my breath. "I've been so stupid and so fucking selfish from the beginning. All I've ever worried about was myself. How being with you would impact *my* life, *my* family, *my* skewed sense of security."

I want to open my mouth and tell him I never blamed him for that. All his worries and the fear over how his life would be impacted by being with me were all valid. But he presses a thumb over my lips so he can continue.

"When you called me to tell me about the leak, you called to warn me, and to apologize when you didn't do anything wrong. The violation of your privacy wasn't your fault, Jesse. You were a victim. And what's more, all you were worried about was how it was going to impact *me*. Again, it was *my* feelings, *my* future, *my* welfare. Instead of being present for you and holding your hand, facing the storm together the way it should be, I froze and only thought about myself as well. You're in those videos too, and unlike me, you weren't anonymous. The world has picked you apart, kicked you down, and dealt you blow after blow, and you've not only continued to protect me, you opened up about the pain and struggles you've held close to your chest. And that's not fair. It's not okay."

A slow tide of heat spreads through me. At first, it's a relief, because he doesn't blame me. He said he loves me. Then it twists into something like grief, because it feels like a bad omen that we let the first real threat to our relationship tear us apart and send us to opposite corners, leaning into our own panic instead of each other. We could have been, should have been, weathering it together like he said.

His hands flex, thumbs wiping away more tears. I give up trying to hold them back and blink my eyes open, seeing his eyes red and leaking heartache just like mine. He seems smaller, kneeling on the ground and looking up at me. Human-sized instead of the towering mythical god I think of him as.

"I meant what I said this morning, and it's not something I take lightly. I feel the same way I did before the leak, Jesse. I want to be with you, and I don't want to hide. I'd like to talk to Mr. Holland and the PR team about how to do this right so I'm not a burden when the narrative has been taken from us like this." His eyes bore into mine, pleading and sincere, a deep ocean of regret and pain and hope all at once.

"I love you, Jesse. Please let me make this right."

I don't even remember what I wanted to say to him. I'm too overwhelmed with a mixture of relief, gratitude, and fear that something bad will happen to change his mind. All I can do is sob and nod. The fight and tension leave my body, leaving me feeling wrung out and limp.

When Luc presses his lips to mine again, I cling to him, desperately trying to fuse our bodies together. Luc stands, lifting me with him, and lays me across the bed, his large body blanketing mine.

"I love you," he repeats, over and over, between frantic kisses and tears and snot and me trying to climb inside his skin. To burrow there and never come up for air. I finally tear my hoodie and shirt off and press my chest to his, the skin-to-skin contact calming some of the restlessness clawing through me.

"Whatever happens from here on out, I'm with you. I'm not saying I won't have moments of fear or nerves, but I will never leave you to face it alone again. No matter what happens, I'm fully in this with you, and nothing will change that."

I believe him. I can feel the honesty in every word, the thought and sincerity behind them. This isn't some grandstanding apology to stay in my good graces. He means what he says and intends to charge forward, hand in hand, into whatever battle is placed before us.

I wish I could promise him things that I can't be sure of—safety, a tidy fix that will erase headlines and allow us to live our lives with a modicum of peace. All I can give him is my forgiveness and gratitude and my own steadfast promise that I'll do everything in my power to protect him and the love we've found together.

We lay there, kissing and touching, putting our broken pieces back together. Despite both of us being hard and clearly desperate for each other, we hold back and focus on just being there for each other. Eventually the exhaustion of the emotional release catches up to me, and I fall asleep in Luc's arms.

Where I belong.

Luc stays for two more nights, spending the days in an odd sense of domestic bliss. He orders groceries to be delivered and teaches me and Mom how to make gumbo. The guys come over to eat, and we watch some of our favorite movies. Luc picks *Monty Python and the Holy Grail*, I pick *Amelie*, and Naz chooses a *Star Wars* film that I end up sleeping through. I also sleep through whatever Will and Ari picked, and so does Luc. We wake up after the guys have gone, covered in a blanket, and a picture of us sleeping waiting in our group chat.

It's ordinary, and miraculous in its own way, because I don't know that either of us knew we could have this.

We have a video meeting with Blake and the PR team, who confirm that holding back until the worst of the flames are out is our best bet. With my management team's help, we come up with a realistic plan for the near future that allows Luc and I to spend the most time together without risking media attention. Luc agrees to allow the label to discuss added security and privacy arrangements with his building's management company. To my surprise, he even agrees to hire a driver from our security firm to help manage crowds if or when it comes to that.

He leaves late Thursday to fly home overnight when it's less noticeable. Paparazzi and news vans are still surrounding the property, but Cory sneaks Luc out by having him dress in the security firm's uniform with a hat pulled low over his eyes.

"It's not fair to leave when you look that hot." Not gonna lie, I'm starting to understand Naz's fixation with his bodyguard.

Luc chuckles and kisses me deeply. "I'll see you Monday night, okay?"

While Luc is in Atlanta for a Monday night game, I'll be sneaking into his condo under the cover of night to be there when he returns home. The rest of his games this month are all home games, so he won't have to travel. The plan is for me to lie low at his place and then go home with him for his holiday break until I have to fly to Nashville for a private concert on the 26th.

"Call me when you get home? And good luck in Atlanta," I say, smiling at the memory of the last time he played there. "No surprise visits this time, unfortunately."

I'm a little less afraid than I was the last time Luc had to fly home in the middle of the night. We have a plan, and we're both in this. That's all I can ask for.

LeST is
MooRE

TWENTY-SEVEN
LUC

I don't get home until nearly two o'clock in the morning. Our flight out of Atlanta was delayed due to reports of drone activity near the airport after one was seen following our bus from the stadium to the private terminal.

The team has been getting a lot of press. We're headed to our first post-season games in franchise history. The game against Atlanta was hard fought, but we pulled ahead by a field goal in the fourth quarter and maintained the lead, making us undefeated in the regular season. We're headed for the playoffs and favored to win the conference title, putting us one step closer to the Super Bowl.

That could be why the drone was following us. Championship teams and players obviously tend to get more press attention. There have been multiple occasions where sneaky photographers or drones have been used to leak practice footage leading up to championship games. I've caught a few side-eye glances from curious teammates, but I don't think there's any reason to worry that the press is on to me and Jesse.

I know he's here. He texted around midnight that he'd arrived safely and quietly. There weren't any obvious photographers around my condo when I was dropped off, and if the doorman was aware that Jesse is here, he didn't breathe a word or give any indication he'd seen him.

I tiptoe inside, not wanting to wake him up if he's asleep. After stashing my away bag in the laundry room to deal with tomorrow, I sneak down the hall and push open the door to my bedroom. He's not in my bed, but there is a flickering light coming from the cracked bathroom door.

Quietly, I poke my head in and find Jesse in my oversized tub that rarely sees any use. There are candles everywhere. The glass panes of the shower are fogged with humidity, the air thick with the scent of cinnamon and vanilla.

"Welcome home," he says huskily, his wet, naked body hidden from view by a layer of bubbles. The candlelight catches on his glistening skin, making him glow like some kind of otherworldly being. A siren, maybe.

The last four days without him melt off me, and in an instant, I'm on my knees at the side of the tub, kissing him. His wet hands grip my biceps before moving to the hem of my hoodie. He pushes the fabric up my torso, splaying his fingers over my abs, and up my chest, until I reach back to help him pull the hoodie and my shirt over my head. His hands move to my hips next, pushing his fingers under the waistband of my athletic pants. Chuckling, I take the hint and stand, stripping out of the rest of my clothes and slipping in behind Jesse. He relaxes back against my chest, and I wrap an arm around his waist, pulling him in closer.

"I missed you," I mumble into his hair that he's trimmed and re-dyed so his dark roots aren't showing.

"I can tell," Jesse chuckles, pushing his ass back against my involuntary reaction to his presence, which is aggressively jabbing him in his lower back.

My shoulders shake. "Sorry." I'm really not trying to make everything about my dick, in fact we both spent the entirety of last week making a point not to have sex so we could connect on a different level. But he's here. In my lap. Naked. And wet. There's not much I can do about my dick other than put space between us. But I don't want to. "Ignore that. I want to be close to you."

"The hell I will," he says, turning his shoulders to look at me. "Luc, I miss you. I need you. Please touch me."

Barely holding in a growl, I pull him even tighter against my chest. One hand presses him against me, while the other moves over his abs and down to wrap around his hard cock. He hisses and bucks, laying his head back on my shoulder and moaning when I begin to stroke him.

"I'm– *ungh*– I'm prepped."

It takes me a moment to process what he's saying, but my eyes cut to a bottle of silicone-based lube sitting on the edge of the tub. I move my hand lower, feel the base of a plug nestled in his ass, and groan.

My lips trail along the back of his neck. As hard as it is to deny him anything, I'm not sure what the rules are about all this bath shit getting inside him. "I don't know–"

"You don't have to fuck me," he says quickly. "Just let me feel you inside me. Please."

Does he think I don't want to fuck him? Does he think I'm rejecting him?

A mixture of emotions, from heartache to lust, settle in my chest and make it hard to breathe, much less speak. Turning his chin towards me, I open my mouth to explain myself, but I can't get the words out. The look in his eyes and the desperate way he kisses me renders me incapable.

It takes some finagling to get adjusted, but soon we're both letting out heavy breaths as Jesse sinks down until his ass is flush against my hips, my cock fully engulfed by his tight, hot body. We don't move for a while, content to be connected like this, as close as humanly possible. Jesse's body, half out of the water now that he's on top of me, begs to be touched. My hands caress and massage him everywhere I can reach, roaming over his shoulders and chest, down his stomach and between his thighs. He whimpers and clenches whenever my fingers play over his nipples or trace along the V of his abs. When it almost becomes too much, I take him in hand, wrapping my fingers around his cock and slowly, gently stroking, teasing him until he's writhing and grinding, wordlessly begging for friction.

The pulsing of his rim around the base of my cock becomes its own kind of slow torture, but I sink into it, hungry for the contact, relishing the closeness of being connected this way. I edge us both until the water cools and it hurts too much to hold off any longer.

Jesse's cry echoes off the tile, his hands white-knuckling the edge of the tub while he shakes in my arms. Cum shoots up his chest, splattering in the water, and coating my hand as I work every drop from him. My thighs flex, grinding my cock deeper as he pulses around me, and I spasm almost violently, biting into my bottom lip hard enough to break skin, unloading inside him.

Along with the physical release, the orgasm jostles something inside me loose. I'm thankful his back is to me as I hold him close and tremble. My eyes leak an emotion I've never named out loud before this man broke me into pieces and rebuilt me into what I am now.

A while later, when we've rinsed and dried off and I'm listening to the sounds of Jesse's rhythmic breathing next to me in bed, I whisper into the nape of his neck.

"I love you, Jesse Moore."

———

Our first loss of the season is my fault. Or, at least, I blame myself for it.

I'm too tired, too distracted, to do much more than stumble around on autopilot. Neither my heart nor my head are in the game. My heart is back at home where Jesse is waiting for me. My head is bogged down by the pressure of the upcoming play-offs and the unrelenting circus Jesse's life has become.

The press still hasn't let go of the possibility that I'm the mystery man in Jesse's leaked videos, and speculation continues to grow even though Jesse has stepped out of the public eye for the time being. I'm trying to be strong. I meant what I told Jesse. I care more about being with him than I do keeping our relationship quiet, but the attention is starting to affect the team as well. Press and paparazzi constantly congregate outside the team's facilities, hounding the coaches and staff and other players, yelling intrusive questions about how they feel about me and my private life.

Even worse, it's following me to the field, where opposing players have made it their mission to shake us any way they know how. Just before the snap, the player opposite me makes a joke about getting shafted by the last flag that was thrown. His teammate next to him says, "At least it wasn't pierced," and throws a knowing smirk in my direction.

"Keep it together, Martín," Treyden calls as the line moves.

I stumble on the snap. My foot falters as I lurch forward, and I find myself at an awkward angle when a linebacker slams into me like a bus. The wind is knocked from my chest, my feet are taken out from under me, and I land hard on my shoulder. Pain ricochets through me so sharply I worry I've dislocated it. It's not, thank God, but it's bad enough to put me on the bench for the rest of the game. Dallas keeps their momentum and pushes forward through the end zone, landing a 17-24 loss squarely on my swollen shoulder.

After the game, I see the trainers and sit in an ice bath long enough that most of my teammates have cleared out of the locker room by the time I'm done. Coach is waiting for me when I'm dressed and ready to leave. He pulls me into his office and shuts the door behind us.

"How's the shoulder?" he asks, voice low.

I know him well enough to know he already knows everything there is to know about my injury, but I take the opportunity to bullshit my way through my assurances that I'll be fine for the next game.

"You might be fine for next weekend, but if you take another hit like that, you're going to be on the bench for the rest of the season. I need you in top condition for the playoffs."

"Yes, sir," I say robotically, knowing I'm likely to get benched for next week's game. Whether it's best for me or not, no player likes riding the bench when their team needs them. Especially when it's late in the season and we're all exhausted. These last couple of games won't take us out of the playoffs, but they can still mess with our stats and confidence this close to the end.

"You've got a lot going on right now, and a championship season just around the corner. I'm going to recommend that you take some time off."

My head snaps up to look at him. He has to be kidding, right? "What?"

"Go home, Luc. Go see your family, spend time with your loved ones, work your shit out." He doesn't say the words, but I can read between the lines. I've got a mountain of very public bullshit that I need to figure out. "Get some rest over the holiday and come back ready to win that ring."

There's no room for argument. I can't decide if this is a favor he's doing for me, or if it's a warning of things to come. Either way, I know he's right.

When I'm unlocking my condo door less than an hour later, there's part of me that is thankful for the break. Not just because of my shoulder, or because it'd be nice to hide from the public eye for a little while, but because I can spend some more time with him.

Jesse waits for me, sitting on the edge of the kitchen counter with an ice pack in one hand and a look of concern darkening his bright green eyes.

"I'm fine," I assure him, but let him dote on me anyway.

Over the week that he's been here, I've learned how much he likes meeting me at the front door with a cold drink, his warm, wet mouth, or a song to welcome me home. I could certainly get used to seeing his smiling face every day.

I refrain from nipping at his concerned, pouty lip while he strips me of my jacket and shirt to survey the damage. My shoulder is bruised and sore, but it's really nothing to worry about. Coach sending me home has more to do with my personal life bleeding into my professional one than anything else. I don't complain or argue when I'm led towards the bedroom for a massage.

Yeah, I could get used to this.

———

"It's a good thing that wasn't awkward at all," I groan, leaning my forehead against the back of the door I just closed behind us.

Jesse chuckles. "I don't know, I don't think it was too bad. Not sure your dad is a fan, though," he says, twisting his lips. "He didn't seem the type that could be easily bought with concert merch and a video call with Naz, but it was worth a try."

"It worked on my sisters, though, so you have that going for you."

I'm not sure what I expected when I brought Jesse home for the holiday break. I knew my sisters would be cool, they let me know as much when we talked over Thanksgiving. Jesse really didn't have to put any effort into winning them over, but he's Jesse, so of course he went above and beyond.

My dad is a different story. If anything, Jesse's attempts to win everyone's favor with grand gestures and an arm full of presents probably put him off more than the tattoos and facial piercings. Or, you know, that he's a guy.

To be fair, I never once said a word about anything that's been going on or that I was dating anyone other than letting him know I was bringing someone home for the holiday. I didn't even ask permission. I just said it was happening and showed up with Jesse's hand wrapped in mine.

Dad, not surprisingly, didn't really react at all other than to stare wide-eyed at my sisters, who took it upon themselves to jump up and down and scream excitedly.

Not embarrassing at all.

"I should probably go talk to him," I say quietly, wrapping my arms around Jesse when he steps into my space. His arms snake around my waist and his head nuzzles against my neck.

"Want to take the edge off first?"

My chuckle turns into a groan as Jesse palms my growing bulge and kisses down my neck and chest, slowly dropping to his knees.

TWENTY-EIGHT
JESSE

"Oof, don't let Daddy Lucius catch you doing that," a voice says.

I nearly fall off the tire swing I'm sitting on. The unlit clove cigarette falls out of my mouth and into the pile of leaves I helped Luc rake earlier today before he and his sisters went to volunteer at a soup kitchen. I've been slowly feeding them into the small bonfire we've had going since this morning, but I spaced out for a minute there.

"Jesus, what the fu–"

"That kind of language isn't going to get you on his good side, either," the woman says, cackling like a witch.

I stand and turn towards the woman walking through the Martin's yard. She's got dirty blonde hair piled on top of her head and a wide, devious smile across her face. She's wearing a Shreveport Cyclones hoodie, leggings with mermaids, and polka dot rain boots.

"You must be Shawna," I say, standing to greet her.

"The one and only," she says, her sassy tone accentuating her Southern accent. Rolling her eyes exaggeratedly, she accepts my hand and pulls me in roughly. She smells like coffee and baked goods, which makes sense. Luc told me she owns a café and bookshop.

"It's nice to meet you."

"I know."

Immediately, I can tell that this woman takes no shit and gives zero fucks.

I love her already.

She matches my grin and wraps an arm through one of mine.

"Come on now, you and I have some gossiping to do and I don't want Mr. Martín to know I'm canoodling with the enemy."

I laugh out loud. "We definitely can't have that."

Shawna and I walk to the end of the property and along the fence line, where it dips downhill towards a small creek and backs up into some fields Luc told me were sugarcane that's recently been harvested. She climbs up on the fence and sits down on the wooden railing, staring out at the vast fields of churned ground and stubble.

"Just wait until you come back in the summer. It's hotter than hell, but the fields are gorgeous. Like a rolling sea of green." She looks at me and tilts her head. "Almost the same color as your eyes, actually. Maybe that's why he likes them so much."

"Because they remind him of home?"

She shrugs. "Honestly, who knows what that man gets up to in his head. I can't make sense of him sometimes. Twenty-one years of not taking an interest in nobody and then BAM, there you are."

The way she's studying me like some kind of anomaly has my

face heating. And since when do I blush? That's Luc's thing, not mine!

"You love him."

It's not a question. It's probably obvious to anyone paying attention. Still, I dip my head, in case she actually needs the confirmation.

"Good. He's going to need that when all this hiding explodes in y'all's faces."

A sardonic laugh huffs out of me. She's not wrong. It's unlikely this thing is going to stay under wraps if we're going to keep going in any serious capacity. The way I feel about him, there's no way I'm willing to give him up.

"I'm worried about how he's going to handle it if, or when, more likely, our relationship comes out. He's trying so hard to be cool with the press he's getting from just the speculation, but once it's officially out there? I don't think there's a way to prepare him for how insane it's going to get. And, well, I don't want to lose him. I'd give it all up if it were even an option, but..."

"You can't change who you are. Luc knows that. And likewise, you can't change who he is. But I have to say, the amount he's come out of his shell for you is pretty impressive. The fact that he's still in this, that he's willing to risk the publicity and brought you home to meet his family, it says a lot about how much he cares about you. Seriously? A fucking sex tape? The fact that he even went there at all is an entire conversation on its own, but that he hasn't noped out and run for the hills must mean he has it bad for you, Jesse Moore."

"I don't know how I got so lucky."

"Maybe it's the piercings."

If my eyes got any wider, they'd fall right out of my head. "*You watched them?!*"

"Well… yeah. My best friend just had all his business put out there for the whole world to see. It's part of my job to assess the damage and find out how bad it was."

"And?" Maybe I shouldn't ask, but I have to know.

"I mean, honestly…" Shawna shrugs and gives me a wry look of approval, followed by a slow clap. "As far as leaked nudes and sex tapes go, it could have been way worse. If it were my ass getting cream-pied on the internet, I'd barely be embarrassed about it."

"Luc was right," I say, laughing incredulously. "You really are something else."

"I'll take that as a compliment, thank you," she says, a glint of mischievous laughter in her eye. "But in all seriousness, what is the plan for when shit hits the fan?"

"The plan is to focus on the positive. I'm in love with Luc Martín and that's that. My PR team is armed and ready for the relation-ship to go public. We're hoping to wait until some of the press has died down so we can do it on our own terms and not in response to a scandal. Either way, we will not engage with any questions or conversations regarding the leaked tapes."

"America's sweetheart and the consummate bad boy? It's a love story for the ages."

"I'd like to believe so. I just have to hope he doesn't get chased away before we can find the happily ever after."

"Just be patient with him, give him time to process when things start heating up. He's never gone this far outside of his comfort zone before. You've met his dad now, I'm sure you can see where he gets some of his stoicism from."

"Yeah, that man does not like me."

"If it helps, I don't think he expressly dislikes you. If that were the case, you wouldn't be in his house. That man does not fuck around when it comes to his kids."

"I suppose I should feel lucky he's shooting eye lasers at me rather than a shotgun, then?"

Shawna laughs. "Mr. Martín is intense, but Luc can be too. They're alike in that way. And there's the stubbornness, can't forget that."

"I was going to make a joke about Luc's teen years, but I have a feeling he was a model son that rarely talked back or got in trouble."

"You're pretty well on the nose, although his mama used to credit me for his good behavior back in those days."

"How so?"

"He was so busy trying to keep me out of trouble, that he rarely had time to find his own," she snickers.

"That doesn't surprise me," I laugh.

"Come to think of it, I think the only time Luc went against his father's wishes was when he joined the NFL."

That takes me by surprise. "What? Really? Did he not approve?"

"Oh no, definitely not. Football was meant to be a tool to pay for college and nothing more. Luc only pursued it because the Martín's were having some troubles with the house and were at risk of losing it."

I look back at the modest but gorgeous home with white-washed siding and pale green shutters. Luc mentioned once that the house has been in his family for something like three generations. I can't imagine that his dad could have been upset with him for doing what he needed.

"He wasn't mad about it, though. Was he?"

She shakes her head. "How could he be? He's a proud man, but he's not an idiot. It's not like he could turn down Luc's help when the alternative was losing their home. The girls were still young, and Mrs. Martín had just gone through her first round of chemo. Times were hard. But I think that's part of the reason Luc worked so hard to stay out of the public eye, and old habits die hard, you know?"

"I suppose that makes sense." I think quietly for a few long moments, tilting my face towards the warm afternoon Sun. "Luc cares a lot about his father's opinion."

"Right or wrong, he always has. And yeah, he has some back-wards-ass ideas, but Mr. Martín is a good dad. Hell, he stepped up for me more than a time or two when I needed a father figure. I think very highly of him, even if I like to give him shit for being a surly old grouch," she says, twisting her lips into a grin as she looks back at the house and shakes her head. "When it really comes down to it, what he cares about most is that you're going to do right by his son. The rest is just a matter of getting used to new ideas. He'll come around."

We sit outside, chatting and laughing, until the fire has died down too much. Mr. Martín walks out to join us while Shawna and I shovel more leaves into the flames. He hugs Shawna and wishes her a Merry Christmas, asks about her mother and the store. It's the most I've heard him talk at once since I've been here. I perk up when he mentions he's making gumbo with the leftovers from last night's turkey.

"You like gumbo?" Mr. Martín asks me. Shit, this might be the first time he's addressed me directly. Why are my palms sweaty?

"Uh, yes sir. Luc made some when he came to visit me and my mom a few weeks back."

Mr. Martín makes a *hmph* sound. "Did he make you real gumbo or did he make you some of his health food nonsense?"

I chuckle nervously. "I honestly have no idea. It tasted good, though."

"He use lard or some avocado oil bullshit?"

"Definitely the avocado bullshit."

"*Hmph*," he says again. "Figures."

"I bet Jesse would like to learn how the real stuff is made," Shawna says, nudging me in the ribs. "I don't think we can let him leave here thinking that's how we do things."

Mr. Martín lets out an exasperated breath before turning and walking back to the house. "Well, come on then," he calls back just as he reaches the front porch steps.

Shawna grins widely and pushes me towards the house to follow him.

"What are you doing?" I whisper-yell as soon as Luc's dad is in the house. "Are you crazy? I can't cook worth shit!"

"Well, you're about to learn," she laughs.

I'm on my third attempt at making a roux when Luc and his sisters return home. All three of them stop talking and stare at me in the kitchen with their dad, whisking flour and melted butter while he watches on, ready with a large ladle of the home-made stock that's been simmering all day to add when it gets to just the right color.

I flick my eyes over to them just in time to see Luc making a very obvious *what the fuck* expression at Shawna, who's been sitting back reading a fucking tabloid magazine with mine and Luc's faces plastered on the front while I'm subjected to an intense cooking lesson. I do not let my eyes leave the browning mixture for long, though. This man takes his food very seriously, and I'm paying serious attention, because I know that his dad's gumbo is Luc's favorite food in the world. Part of the reason he loves it is that it's different every time. Using different ingredients and never measuring anything will do that. If I can get the basics down, maybe I could actually cook for Luc instead of setting off the smoke detector every time I've tried to do more than order in or heat up those gross pre-made frozen health food boxes. *Blech.*

I thought I'd said too much when I admitted to my failed attempts at making his son dinner, but Mr. Martín seemed… well, pleased is too strong a word, but maybe interested or mildly approving of the idea that I would want to cook for his son. At the very least, my pathetic rambling about wanting him to come home to a home-cooked meal I'd made myself seemed to make him pity me enough to give me pointers.

"There you go," Mr. Martín says, and a zing of excitement makes me straighten my spine. "Don't get too excited," he mumbles disapprovingly. "You gotta keep stirring so I can add the stock."

Later that night, I'm lying in Luc's childhood bed reading the stupid tabloid I stole from Shawna when Luc crawls over me and plucks it from my hands, tossing it across the room.

"How did you do it?" He asks, his voice strained, nuzzling his nose against my jawline.

"Do what?"

"You charmed my dad. I didn't think it was possible."

I scoff against his lips. "I think the credit for that should probably go to Shawna."

He shakes his head. "She gave you a push, maybe. My dad doesn't share his kitchen secrets like that with just anyone."

"He doesn't?" I still don't think I'm Mr. Martín's favorite person. I got maybe a little too excited over the tiny bit of praise I got when I finally managed to not screw something so simple up, and he begrudgingly let me look through one of the recipe books that have been in their family for longer than their house has been passed down.

Luc huffs a laugh and kisses the tip of my scrunched-up nose. "Well, first of all, Lucius Martín Senior is notoriously indifferent to most people, and he gave you the time of day despite looking like a hooligan. Second, that recipe book has a history that you don't understand. The Martín men have been known to woo their partners with that recipe book."

I sit up straight. "Say what, now?"

He laughs and sits facing me, leaning over my lap and taking my face in one big hand. "It's hard to tell with him, I know. But that was basically his seal of approval."

"Really?"

Look, I have never in my life cared this much about someone else's approval. But I do care. A lot. And I know how much it means coming from a man like Luc's father.

And yeah, okay, honestly, if Mr. Martín had decided he hated me and banned me from entering the house, it wouldn't have stopped me from pursuing his son to the ends of the earth, but I feel all warm and fuzzy inside in a way I'm not sure I've ever felt before. Visions of an entirely tangible future flash behind my eyelids. The Martín's and my family getting together for the holidays, my mom and Luc's dad cooking together, Will and Ari showing his sisters how to play poker, Naz and Shawna comparing books.

Is that the happily ever after Shawna and I were talking about earlier today? Because it feels so real. Like a window into our future.

"I'm going to level with you right now," I tell Luc seriously. "I am all kinds of high on life right now, and I need you to fuck me, but we can't do it here, so you and I need to take a drive or climb up in that big barn or something."

He chuckles and kisses down my neck. "We can do it here," he whispers over my left nipple before sucking the barbell on the right into his mouth. "You just have to be quiet."

"Listen to me, Luc Martín," I whisper-shout, pushing him off me so he knows I mean business. "You think you're cute, but I got your daddy's blessing today. I cannot, *will not*, sully a thing like that by engaging in premarital sex under his roof, lest he change his mind and chase me out with that shotgun Shawna warned me about." I take a breath. "So take me out back and fuck me like the respectable gentleman I am, goddammit."

TWENTY-NINE
JESSE

The last chords echo through the night like a heartbeat. My lungs burn, chest heaving. The mic feels hot in my palm as I hold it up, the voices of thirty thousand people singing the final chorus. The energy in the stadium is palpable, a living thing that takes hold of my very soul and reminds me this is why I do this.

There's only one other thing on earth that makes me feel this alive. And he's leaning on a support beam offstage, watching me like I'm the only thing that matters.

I raise my arm, music swelling as the band joins in for the last lines of *Wreck Me*.

Every time I close my eyes,

I still see you–

The heat, the sweat, the way you move.

Baby just wreck me,

The way you always do.

With a drop of my arms, the band hits the last notes hard, and the lights go out. Blackness engulfs the stage. There are gasps and mutters from the crowd, then the excitement sparks as flashes of light shoot into the sky above. The screens all around the stadium light up with the New Year's countdown, marking one minute until we ring in a new year.

"It's been a fucking year, hasn't it?" I shout into the crowd to cheers and applause. It's not as if I need to specify all that we've been through, especially these last few months. Everyone in the world knows we headed out on tour when I was fresh out of rehab, and everything I struggled with. They saw my very public meltdown and celebrated a triumphant return to the stage tonight. There are still questions, and the press will probably never stop hounding us for answers, but tonight we're surrounded by a different kind of energy. "I can't tell you all how thankful I am to get to ring in a new year, new opportunities, a new fucking me, with all of you here today. We wouldn't be anything without you, without this energy right fucking here!"

My voice echoes over the raised hands, screams, and signs from our fans. "This year is going to be the one that blows them all out of the water. New energy. New songs." *Cue the screams of excitement.* "New love?" I smirk as the words are swallowed by the rising thrum of enthusiasm matched by a steady rise of drums, the thrum of the bass, a guitar riff vibrating into the air.

"So let's bring in this new year right! Grab the person next to you, be it friend, lover, or consenting stranger–don't be a fucking creep, alright."

I peel off my shirt, and the crowd roars again. It's already saturated, barely effective as I wipe my sweaty face and throw it to the side. My wet hair lies flat back as I swipe my hand back through it.

Ten!

I run, breathless, to Naz's drum set. He lifts one arm enough for me to climb into his lap and plant a quick, ridiculous kiss on his cheek before rolling off the other side and running towards Ari.

Nine!

Ari swings his bass to one side and pulls me against his bare chest, grin wide and toothy. He presses a kiss to my temple that gets a few laughter-fueled boos. Our fans have been shipping us from the beginning.

Eight!

I sprint around to Will, waiting with a saucy grin. He turns his back to me and I hop on, wrapping my arms around his shoulders and pressing a rough kiss to his cheek.

Seven!

"Blake, you shit, where are you!?" I shout.

Six!

Blake steps out, only a few feet from where Luc is hiding in the wings. I run up and wrap my arms around him, getting his pressed blue button-down and grey slacks wet with sweat that he wipes from his face, laughing.

Five!

"Behave," Blake says, when he catches me side-eyeing the shadows hiding Luc from the view of the crowd.

Four!

Blake relaxes as I run back to my mic stand. "Come on!" I scream, and the crowd chants louder

Three!

Two!

I glance offstage once more and lock eyes with Luc. Gorgeous, steady, stoic, strong Luc, who has been my rock for weeks now. He'll go back to practice next week, and I'll have to start Super Bowl prep later this month, but I'm staying with him for the time being. I never want to leave.

As electric as being on stage is, it's nothing compared to the way every nerve ending in my body and brain comes to life when I so much as look at him.

"Fuck it," I mutter audibly as the crowd finishes the countdown.

One!

I beeline off the stage and tackle him, my lips on his before the crowd can scream, *"Happy New Year!"* Fireworks explode overhead, and maybe it's the planned pyrotechnics, but it feels like they're going off inside me.

Luc wraps his arms around me and holds me against his body, not caring about the sweat or the crowd on the other side of a flimsy wall and curtains. We're going public after the Super Bowl, and I can't wait. I may never get the chance to drag him on stage and lay claim to him in front of the whole world, and that's okay. Just knowing he's going to be mine is enough.

"Happy New Year, baby," I breathe against his lips.

He laughs and wishes me the same, setting me down and encouraging me back on stage. "You better get back out there," he says, pulling me in for one more kiss before physically pushing me back on stage.

I stumble out to massive cheers and wipe the corner of my mouth with my thumb. My teeth clamp down on my bottom lip at the fire burning in his eyes, the one that promises he'll make it up to me later.

Giving him one last wink, I run back out to the mic for one last encore.

———

"Are you listening to me?" Blake says through my phone screen as my eyes stray to the television again.

"Can this wait until halftime?"

"Not really, Jesse. Did you hear anything I just told you?"

Thankfully, there's a commercial break so I can convince Blake that the divisional playoff game is more important than a bunch of conservative assholes playing games because they were butthurt by our charity concert two months ago.

"So you don't want to do anything at all about the calculated attack on your personal information? It doesn't bother you at all that those photos and videos, and information about your time in rehab, were released by government officials that wanted to discredit the good work you did with that concert?"

"I didn't say I don't want to do anything about it, Blake. I said that I have more important things going on right now than to have this conversation right this second."

"It's a football game," he deadpans.

"It's the divisional playoffs," I say slowly, enunciating the words like I know what I'm talking about.

Truth be told, I still don't know enough about football to explain anything of importance. Sports knowledge doesn't happen by osmosis, or through the transfer of copious bodily fluids. All I know is that they have to win this game to qualify for the next one, and then if they win that one, they play in the Super Bowl. And since *Lest Is Moore* is also going to be at the Super Bowl, we'll be in the same place for the first time in weeks.

"Look, I'll be back Monday afternoon. Can we put it off until then? In the meantime, we can come up with some strategies for how to handle this. I definitely don't want them to get away with that shit, but I'm also not going to let them ruin the last two days I have here with Luc."

Blake sighs heavily but agrees to direct his nervous energy at legal for the next two days until we can discuss it in person.

"There's one more thing," he says warily.

"If you're about to tell me that the new single wasn't approved to be debuted at the Super Bowl show, I'll riot. I mean it, tell your boss, and your boss's boss, and your boss's boss's mom that I'm singing that song whether they like it or not. They can't fucking stop me."

Blake sighs. "No, that isn't it. I'm pretty sure no one would dare tell you not to do something at a live show unless it was something they specifically did want you to do." I don't know why, but that brings a prideful smirk to my lips.

"There's a chance that there's an issue with the company we use to hire additional security." I bristle immediately. "None of our regular guys," he assures me. "But don't go off with anyone you don't know personally just to be safe."

"What about—"

"The guy we hired for Luc was personally vetted and is safe. It's the extra hires for stadium security and events that seem to be the issue. And it's more a matter of backstage information and photos being sold, nothing that would risk your physical safety."

I blow out a breath. "Well, that's shitty, but I suppose it could be worse. I'll see you Monday," I say pointedly.

I'm practically vibrating by the time Luc gets home. I nearly take him down in a tackle of my own the moment he walks through the door.

"You won! You won!" I squeal, kissing him all over his face and neck while I hurriedly unzip his jacket and slip it off his shoulders.

"Miss me much?" Luc laughs as I strip him out of his hat, jacket, hoodie and shirt. He stops laughing and lets out a heavy breath when I drop to my knees to take off his shoes and socks for him. I smirk up at him, loving what the sight of me on my knees does to him. I wasn't even down here for that, but now that it's in front of me…

I rub my face over his growing bulge. "I've been getting hard off and on all day, watching you kick Arizona's ass. Every time you bend over in those light pants…" I shudder and hook my fingers in the waistband of his athletic pants. "I made you dinner, but I'm going to need you to feed me first," I say, pulling his pants and underwear down to mid-thigh.

Luc cups my face in one of his big, warm hands and runs his thumb over my bottom lip. His gaze is heated, but also sweet, almost reverent.

I wasn't kidding when I said I'd been on edge all day. I need him to fuck me in the worst way. Blake's call reminded me that I only have one more full day and two nights left here before we have to be apart for a few weeks. I plan to spend every moment of that time naked and one of us stuffed inside the other until we can't move.

I run the flat of my tongue along the bottom of his cock, tracing the thick, pulsing vein that feeds blood to his erection with my tongue ring.

Then I tip back my head and open my mouth wide, tongue out, and beg him with my eyes to fuck my face.

LeST is
MooRE

THIRTY
LUC

I'm panting harder than I was during the game when Jesse leads me over to the kitchen island. My legs are wobbly, and my clothes have been haphazardly thrown on the floor in the entry-way. It's all I can do to follow his swaying ass, barely covered by one of my dress shirts.

Jesse mentioned dinner, and it smells good in here, definitely something that smells like spices my dad would have taught him to use, but he doesn't tell me to sit or take anything out of the oven. Instead, he pulls a sports drink out of the fridge and sets it in front of me.

"Drink this," he says. "You're going to need it."

Before I can open the bottle and get more than a few swallows down, Jesse moves behind me and pushes my shoulders, so I'm bent over the counter.

So, he's in one of those moods? I gulp down as much of the sports drink as I can before I have to brace both hands on the marble countertop. Jesse grips my ass cheeks and spreads them open, spitting directly on my crack before laving his tongue through it, sucking and teasing my hole until I'm hard and moaning all over again. He spears me with his tongue, teasing my rim with the metal stud of his barbell.

"Please tell me you're getting me ready to fuck me," I groan, pushing back on his tongue. I hiss when he pushes a finger inside me. "Yesss." I moan, clenching around his finger, wordlessly begging for more.

My eyes nearly roll into the back of my head when Jesse stands, licking a stripe of sweat from my spine as he leans over me and purrs into my ear. "I have a different kind of surprise in mind for you. If you open up for me real nice, I promise it's going to be so good."

Jesse reaches for a small gift box and slides it over to me, instructing me to open it. Inside is a bottle of lube, and two black silicone devices. One is shaped a bit like a joystick, not much bigger than my thumb and first finger with two rings at one end. The other is an oval disk.

He lifts the joystick out of the box and brings it to my mouth, pushing the soft, yet firm silicone between my lips. I open for him, my eyes on his as he rubs the toy along my tongue before taking it out and replacing it with his tongue instead.

We've played with toys here and there, but nothing quite like this. For Christmas, we made each other custom replicas of each other's dicks. It was a fun, if not slightly awkward, activity to do in the days between visiting my family and his New Year's Eve concert. The original thought was that we could have a part of each other when we're apart for weeks at a time, but we've had fun playing with them together as well. Jesse likes to use plugs to prep himself so he's ready for me when I get home from practice., but I have no idea what this contraption is that Jesse is now lubing up and cinching my balls through. I'm a little concerned it might be some kind of pseudo-sexual torture device. It doesn't hurt. It's just weird how he pulls my balls through one of the rings. It's like the way he gathers his hair in a ponytail. I shouldn't be surprised when the joystick part is pushed inside me, but I was distracted by the band around my balls.

Jesse moves in front of me and lifts himself up onto the counter, smirking as he reaches for what I'm pretty sure is a remote. I have just enough time to brace myself before he pushes the button, and I gasp, knees shaking. "Shit."

"Oh, that is fun," he says, and wraps his legs around me, holding me close and kissing me while the device vibrates, sending a jolt all the way up my spine. It's stimulating me from the inside out, so intense at even the low setting that I can barely do more than gasp for breath and try to stay upright every time he presses the button.

"Damn, baby, you look close to coming again already," Jesse says, looking down at my cock. The red, angry looking tip exposed and leaking profusely. "I thought if I drained you first this would take longer."

He presses the button again, and I growl. "Jesse…"

"I just can't decide if I want to keep playing with you or sit on your dick and ride you until you scream."

"The second one," I choke out, pulling one of the counter-height chairs over. "Right now," I demand. I don't even want to walk to the bedroom. I need to come now, and I need to do it deep inside him.

With a filthy smirk on his face, Jesse begins to unbutton his shirt, but I reach over and rip it open. Buttons fly everywhere, and his slim, cut, pale body is on display for me in nothing but a white lace garter that circles his waist and both thighs.

"Fuck, you're in trouble now," I growl, pulling his hips towards me and engulfing his cock in my mouth. My fingers trail behind his balls, and I'm pleased to feel the base of a plug there. Sometimes I like to complain about not getting to prep him myself, but I'll be damned if I'm not grateful this time. I twist and play with it for a few moments until a jolt goes through me as the vibration starts up again. I choke around Jesse's cock and pull off, eyes locked on his *I dare you* stare.

I pull the plug from his ass and drop it to the floor, pulling Jesse on top of me and guiding my cock inside him. He lowers himself on top of me and starts with a slow roll, throwing his head back and moaning loudly. Thank fuck he did a good job prepping, because I barely give him time to adjust.

"Luc, baby…" Jesse holds onto my neck and pulls my lips to his. "So good."

Holding him around his waist, I guide him up and down my cock, his thigh muscles flexing. But as soon as he pushes the button again, I falter. It's all I can do to hold him down, jerking and moaning, until he releases the button again.

"Fuck, I can feel you vibrating inside me," Jesse pants.

"You need to be careful with that thing," I say breathlessly. "I'm likely to lose control and jackhammer you." I cough out a laugh and move to resume Jesse's easy ride when I flick my eyes up to his and see that stare again.

My mouth drops open as Jesse not only presses the button, he turns it up and locks it before tossing it across the room. I can't fathom a thing past the rattle in my brain and the overwhelming, screaming sensation inside me as the toy vibrates against my prostate and taint at once, while squeezing around the base of my cock and balls. Jesse's ass tightens around me, and at first all I can do is let out a low, guttural moan as my entire being vibrates with the toy.

My control shatters, my mind driven wild with the need to release the impossible energy inside me. Hooking my arms beneath his legs, I stand and tip Jesse back so he's lying across the kitchen island, jerking violently as he's fucked hard and fast. My arms flex, holding his legs open and his ass at just the right angle, pulling him against me as my hips pound into him so hard, he'll probably have bruises. He doesn't seem to mind, though. If anything, he's abandoned his better sense the same way I have, surrendering to the sensations pulsing through his body.

A loud, continuous cry pours out of him, broken only by the staccato rhythm of my cock slamming into his body, driving air and sound from his chest. The harsh smack of our bodies coming together, the squelch of lube and cum. Drool drips from my open mouth, and my own feral grunts mix with the relentless buzz of the vibrator.

Sharp, piercing pleasure rips down my spine, and I choke as my cock engorges, the rings tightening painfully around my balls. I increase the speed and force of my hips, and a scream tears out of Jesse as his cock erupts, spraying so hard cum hits me in the face and flings across the kitchen. He clenches so hard it throws my never-ending orgasm into overdrive, making me roar through another wave of relentless pleasure-pain.

Jesse and I are coming violently, while I'm pounding into him like some kind of wild beast. Cum is spraying through the air, and we're screaming and grunting and basically frothing at the mouth.

And that's when my front door opens.

AJ's wide eyes pass through a multitude of emotions all at once, and he scrambles backwards. His foot lands on the discarded butt plug that I threw to the floor earlier, and his legs fly out from under him. The bags he was holding fly into the air, and everything comes crashing down. He lands in a heap on my discarded clothes, covered in food and crying, "Oh, God! I'm sorry! Oh My God!"

Worse yet, the prostate massager is still moving violently inside me, my brain short-circuiting with the continued assault of over-stimulation on every nerve ending, and I'm completely unable to make sense of anything that's happening. I have half a mind to cover Jesse's naked body, but all I can really do is lean over him, slack-jawed, drool and cum dripping from my face, while my hips keep jerking uncontrollably, still hard and rutting inside him involuntarily.

AJ scrambles back through the front door, slamming it multiple times to try to get it to close, but my pants are bunched up in the doorjamb, so it just keeps bouncing open again. Finally, still crying out that he's sorry and that he did not need to see that, AJ abandons the door. We can hear his footsteps beating a path to the elevator, muttering to himself until the ding of the door opening sounds.

Shaking uncontrollably, I manage to release my cock and balls from the restraints, pull the deadly weapon from my ass and fall onto the floor with my arms and legs splayed wide, panting and staring wide eyed at the ceiling.

What the fuck just happened?

"Shit. Fuck. Shit!" I can't articulate much past a string of repeated curses and unintelligible frustrated noises.

It's another twenty minutes before I'm able to get my shit together enough to be able to walk, much less think clearly enough to work through everything that just happened.

AJ isn't answering his phone, but from my balcony, I can still see his car in the parking lot.

"Shit. Fuck. Shit!" I turn my head to look at Jesse, who is still sprawled across the kitchen island, watching me with an unreadable expression. "I'm going to have to go out there. Are you alright?" His lips quirk, letting me know he's more than fine. I kiss his forehead and give him a weak, pleading smile for moral support as I pull on my pants and the torn open dress shirt and head downstairs barefoot.

AJ makes a high-pitched noise of surprise and flinches a full foot off his seat when I knock on his window. He fumbles with the window button, which doesn't work until he starts the car, which takes two tries.

He looks down at his hands twisting together in his lap. "Dude. I am so sorry. I didn't know… I heard… And I thought…" He blows out a heavy breath and brings his hands up to cover his face. "I'm so sorry."

I notice a photographer trying to get a good angle, and figure that as awkward as this is, it's better for us to talk inside.

"Why don't you come upstairs?"

He squeaks. This dude is almost the same size as me, maybe a bit leaner, but not a small guy by any means. Somehow, the squeak doesn't seem completely out of character for him.

"AJ. Come upstairs. I'd like you to meet… my boyfriend."

His fingers separate and he makes momentary eye contact before looking away again. "Your boyfriend?"

I sigh. "Yeah. My boyfriend."

"His boyfriend. Who he was just plowing on the kitchen counter while making sounds like someone was being murdered."

"AJ," I snap, cutting off his muttering. "Are you coming in or not?"

He clears his throat and nods, still not looking me directly in the eye. Trusting that he'll come up on his own time and wanting to have an extra minute to warn Jesse or carry him to the bedroom if need be, I turn on my heel and head inside.

I nod to the doorman on my way back to the elevator. "Mr. Hill," I say in greeting.

"Mr. Martín," he says back. "Making your friends cry again today, I see."

I rub a hand over my face, and the elevator closes just as AJ enters the lobby again. That should give me a couple of seconds to make sure my condo is fit for company. Or at least I thought it did, because while I was taking my sweet time and allowing myself an extra minute to take several deep breaths in and out, AJ was running up seven flights of stairs. He's right behind me when I'm stepping inside.

Luckily, the place looks nothing like it did when I chased AJ out of the building. The discarded clothes and food are all picked up, every surface is gleaming, there's a container of disinfectant cleaning wipes out on the counter, and Jesse, fully dressed in my t-shirt and a pair of baggy jeans, is pulling something that smells delicious out of the oven.

"Oh, thank God," I mutter as AJ comes barreling in behind me. He takes a moment to look around, possibly questioning if he's in the same home he walked into not that long ago.

Jesse walks over and kisses me on the cheek, wrapping one arm around my waist and extending the other to my friend.

"Hi AJ, I'm Jesse. It's nice to finally meet you."

AJ, still apologetic and embarrassed, accepts the handshake before flicking his eyes up to meet Jesse's. Then his jaw drops open.

"Jesse, his boyfriend. His boyfriend Jesse…*Jesse Moore*?"

Still clasping Jesse's hand, AJ's eyes bounce rapidly between us before finally settling on me.

"You're fucking serious right now?"

"Do you want to leave and come back again?" I ask, rolling my eyes.

"Uh, no. Definitely not. I'm so sorry. You've never had anyone over before, and I heard… sounds. I didn't know what was happening." AJ averts his eyes again and turns several shades of red and purple before Jesse bursts out laughing.

"Well, now you know."

"Yeah… I definitely do."

THIRTY-ONE
JESSE

Stepping out of the car, I feel immediately bombarded and overwhelmed. It's hard to believe there was a time when New York City was my favorite place. There aren't even paparazzi here. It's just the overwhelming noise and busyness of the city that is such a contrast to the long Louisiana afternoons, lazy sunsets, and nights spent wrapped up in Luc's quiet, calming presence. It's sensory overload the moment I step out onto the sidewalk.

The faint chemical tang of floor polish tickles my nose as I make my way through the lobby and to the elevator, where I head up to the top floor. Naz is slouched on a massive leather sofa in the waiting area outside the executive offices.

"Long night?" I ask.

"Hey, stranger. I thought you might never come back." He reaches out for me to pull him up, and I yank him into a hug.

"I strongly considered moving in with Luc's family and getting a job harvesting sugarcane," I tell him, only half joking.

"I'm not sure manual labor is your thing."

I shrug, then eyeball the conference room. "Kind of feels like it'd be preferable to this, though."

"Nah, it'll be alright. We got you," he says, wrapping an arm around my shoulders and leading me inside.

Will and Ari are already here. Ari has his feet propped up in Will's lap, both thumbing through social media until they notice me. I walk over to them, so they don't have to get up, bending down to give them each a hug.

"Missed you, man," Will says.

"It's been quiet," Ari adds. "Too quiet."

We laugh and catch up a bit, then break out in catcalls and appreciation when Emmy appears, carrying a huge tray of bagels and fruit. A receptionist follows with a coffee and tea cart, and finally Blake arrives. He seems surprised that we're all here first, to which Emmy smirks and informs us that he had us be here an hour earlier than the meeting actually started.

"Well done," Blake praises. Emmy blushes.

The rest of our management, PR, and legal team arrives and take over the conference room with their pressed suits and grim faces. Our main security team, including both Cory and Tad, Scott, Zane, and Eric, file in along the back wall. Cory filled me in on the drive from the airport that all of our main security team would be here. We're all hands on deck for this mess, it seems.

"Thank you all for joining us," Blake says, officially starting the meeting. "Jess, welcome back. I hope you're feeling better. We have a lot to fill you in on."

He starts from the top, including some of the details he already told me or that I've discussed with the guys here and there.

"The source of the leaks has been identified as Curtis Howard. He's a far-right conspiracy blogger who runs a gossip site that frequently spins stories to fit a particular narrative. Some of his spicier opinion pieces suggest that *Lest Is Moore's* music lures in innocent souls for the devil himself."

Emmy gasps. "OMG, you guys are like the real-life Saja Boys."

Blake stares at him. "What the hell are you talking about?"

"You haven't seen *K-Pop Demon Hunters*?"

I sit up straight. I might have watched it with Luc's sisters, and maybe once or twice more when I was home alone while Luc was at practice. "I'm putting in a heavy suggestion for our Halloween costumes next year," I say.

Emmy reaches over and pats Blake's hand as if to say, "It's okay, I'm here to help." Blake pulls his hand away and motions for Emmy to zip it.

He clears his throat and continues. "Mr. Howard has some reach, but there isn't a lot of crossover between your fan base and his. The main issue is that he's been known to feed hacked information to certain politicians, which is what is exacerbating the current issue."

Laura, one of our PR managers, speaks up. "What we need to decide is if pursuing charges and going public is in your best interest, or specifically, the best interest of your friend. From what we've discussed, there could be more in the material hacked from your phone that could lead to identification."

I nod. "Mr. Martín is comfortable with everyone in this room knowing his identity. Most of you know already, but I want it to be known that his privacy and protection are my top priorities. I don't care what this Howard jerk says about me."

"Dude, did you see this video where he accuses us of drinking the blood of young boys? And apparently you keep women chained as sex slaves in your basement?" Naz laughs.

"I didn't know you had a basement," Will says.

"I don't."

We're all laughing, but no one else seems to think it's very funny.

"There's also the issue of the security company. Scott was the one to figure this one out," Blake says, gesturing to Naz's bodyguard.

Scott stands, since the security detail is sitting in the back of the room. Beside me, Naz noticeably straightens up in his seat but looks away as if he doesn't notice his bodyguard is speaking. He catches my eye, and I raise an eyebrow, but he shakes me off.

"I noticed something off about one of the hired security walking around backstage at the New Year's concert, he seemed familiar but wasn't one of our guys, so I kept a closer eye on him. Later, I pulled him to the side and confirmed he did have a phone on his person."

"All employees outside the main security team and management are prohibited from carrying phones or any type of recording devices backstage," Blake explains.

"I'm not even allowed to have one," Emmy confirms.

"So what happened with the guy?" Naz asks. "Could you confiscate the phone and check to make sure he didn't record anything? Or how does that work?"

"Legally, the most we can do is ask for the employee to show that no photos were taken or videos were recorded, however we cannot technically search someone's personal phone without their permission," one of the legal team answers. "There are clauses in some of our stricter agreements that would legally grant consent for inspection of private property on the premises, but these clauses can be a grey area, and were not part of the contract with this particular security company, as they were hired by the stadium and not through us."

Scott nods. "I did try to get him to hand over the phone, but he refused, which seemed like a red flag. We got all of his information, blacklisted both the employee and the company from future events, and informed the man, in writing, that any potential leaks would be followed with swift legal action. Afterwards, I did some more digging and confirmed that this same employee was on staff at multiple concerts, all in different cities, hired by the same company."

Naz groans. "So we've had a mole following us around since when?"

"Since the charity concert at least," Scott confirms.

Well *fuck*.

"Luc was at the New Year's concert," I groan, digging the heels of my palms into my eyes. "What's the likelihood this guy is sitting on something that could hurt him?"

"If he didn't have something, why wouldn't he hand over the phone as proof?" Naz says.

"But if he did, why haven't we heard anything? It's been almost three weeks since the New Year's Eve show."

"We threatened legal action against both the individual employee and the company as a whole," Laura says. "Hopefully that will be enough to dissuade them from leaking anything, and that's assuming they have something worth leaking."

"Or they're shopping around for the right incentive," Blake says. "There are quite a few people with deep pockets that would be willing to pay a lot of money to watch you break again," he says, looking at me directly.

My hands clench into tight fists. I want to rage. To scream and throw things and light shit on fire. More than anything, I want to crawl back to Luc on my hands and knees and beg him to run away with me. Because as much as Luc says he's ready for whatever comes our way, I'm not sure he is.

"We're going public after the Super Bowl," I say, as much a reminder to myself as everyone else. "We just need to do whatever it takes to keep this quiet until then. It's just a couple more weeks."

"Is there anything we can do to distract the press from Jesse and Luc until after the Super Bowl?" Ari asks.

"I can't think of anything more interesting, unless anyone else is having an illicit affair," Laura deadpans. "That's sarcasm, by the way. We don't need any more scandals, please."

The room goes oddly silent. Ari pulls his legs from Will's lap and reaches for a bottle of water. Naz crosses his arms and huffs indignantly. Even Blake looks uncomfortable. I don't need a room full of people feeling sorry for me when I'm the happiest I've ever been.

"Calm down, everyone," I say. "It's fine. It'll be fine. What more could happen in just a couple of weeks?"

Famous last words.

Every breath feels like the calm before the break.
Are we strong enough to bend, or will this be it?
Hold on, hold on—don't let go now.
Even if it's hard, we'll figure it out.
Something's coming. I know you feel it, too.
Will it tear us apart, or make us bulletproof?

Hold on, hold on—don't let go now.
Don't be afraid, we'll figure this out.
Hold on, hold on—don't let me go.
Hold on, hold on—don't leave me alone.
Hold on, hold on—don't let me go.
Hold on, hold on—we're stronger than we know.

LeST is MooRE

THIRTY-TWO
LUC

AJ has my arm in a vice grip. We're on the sidelines, sweating beneath our pads. The tension in the Superdome is thick, the hum of excitement and anticipation practically vibrating the turf below our feet.

We're in overtime. Our line was able to stop the Viking's last drive before they made it too far past the fifty-yard line, but their defense has been just as effective. Monty just called for a long-range field goal as a desperate attempt to end this game.

Blane Kiff, our top kicker, hasn't had the highest accuracy in the league this year, but he hasn't had the worst either. We have faith in him. All our hopes for this game are riding on his shoulders.

"Come on, baby. Come on. End this thing," AJ chants, squeezing my bicep hard enough that I'm starting to lose circulation.

The line moves. The ball is snapped.

Kiff's cleat makes contact, and the ball cuts through the air.

For a heartbeat the entire Superdome is silent. Time stands still, the ball hovering in midair. On the sidelines, the coaches, players, and trainers all lean to the side to get a good angle.

It's true.

It's good. We all simultaneously turn our heads to the officials, who hold their arms straight up in the air.

IT'S GOOD!

The stadium erupts. Cyclone logos flashing, gold towels whipping through the air, a sea of white and gold letting out a roar that jars my bones. We rush the field, a mob of crushing bodies, pads, and helmets clanking against each other. AJ is screaming in my ear, laughing and wailing, *"We did it!!!"*

We're going to the Super Bowl! For the first time in the team's history, the Shreveport Cyclones are headed to the big game. The biggest game.

The biggest stage.

I want to call him. The locker room is a chaotic mix of sweat and celebration, but there's only one person that I want to celebrate this moment with. I keep glancing at my phone to see if Jesse has texted. I know he was watching. He always watches me. I know because I can feel his eyes on me when I'm on the field, or when the cameras pan the sidelines.

AJ spots me checking my phone for the millionth time and smirks. "Go quick while everyone's distracted. I'll run interference." He gestures to a back office, a training room that's still dark.

I duck my head and make a beeline through the chaos, smiling and thumping teammates left and right as I make my way across the room. My hands are shaking as I swipe my phone awake and hit dial.

He picks up on the first ring. "Hey." His raspy voice settles me, and the happiness over the win finally sinks in. There's a lot of noise in the background where he is, too. I forgot what they're working on today. Are they in the studio preparing the new single they plan to debut at the Halftime show?

"Luc?"

I clear my throat. "I'm here. Sorry, it's loud."

"I bet. Congratulations."

I nod, even though he can't see me. I should have video called so I could see his face. Everything feels muted without his green eyes on me.

"So I guess I'll be seeing you at the Super Bowl." I grin so hard my cheeks hurt. "I wasn't sure if you saw. I wanted to call you right away. And I wanted to say I love you. We're so close."

Maybe I'm mistaken, but it sounds like he repeats my last words in an almost sarcastic tone.

"What did you say?"

"I love you, too, Luc. So fucking much."

Something about his tone doesn't sit right. My stomach twists. "Are you alright?"

"I'm good," he says, too fast. "It's just loud back here. Every-one's celebrating your big win."

I swallow the urge to press my gut feeling, and smile. "Tell everyone I'll see them soon. Two weeks, baby."

"Yeah," he says. "I can't wait."

We hang up, and I stare at my blank screen saver for a moment. Am I overthinking, or did something seem off? I can almost hear Shawna's voice in my head, telling me to quit worrying and allow myself to enjoy the good moments. I shove it down and head back into the fray, to celebrate a momentous win with my teammates.

Morning comes early and brutal, sunlight slashing through the curtains and my eyelids. Ugh, my head hurts. Why didn't I pull the blackout curtains when I finally made it home last night?

I blame everything on champagne.

I'm not a drinker. I'll have a light beer on rare occasions, but I don't think I've had even a sip of alcohol since Jesse and I got together in September. I feel a little guilty for getting as tipsy as I did, but those tiny glasses of bubbly snuck up on me.

My phone is buzzing out of control. I didn't set an alarm this morning, since we don't have to be at the field until after noon today, but my automatic bedtime settings prevent me from getting notifications in the middle of the night. If it's after seven, I'm getting all the notifications from our big win yesterday.

Damn, there's a lot of them. I let the notifications load, and roll onto my back, smiling up at the ceiling. Everything is coming together. My team has made it to the Super Bowl, and Jesse will be waiting for me after the game, ready to start a life together. I'd be lying if I said I wasn't a little terrified. There are going to be a lot of people in my business speculating about Jesse's leaked videos, but I'm ready to stop living in fear and finally allow myself to just let go and live.

I'm not sure my phone is ever going to stop buzzing. I talked to all of my family last night and got their congratulations in person, and it's not like I have a ton of friends outside of the team. Are they tagging me a bunch, or what?

I hold my phone up and unlock it, nearly dropping it on my face when I see the first thumbnail.

New Year's Eve. Jesse sprinting offstage, shirtless and glistening with sweat, grabbing me and kissing me like the world was ending. A kiss he teased the crowd with but never confirmed, and hid from everyone but his bandmates and manager, who was nearby.

This picture wasn't taken from the crowd from a lucky angle. It was taken from backstage, close enough that you can see the love and lust radiating off both of us. There's no mistaking what we are to each other.

I'm not mad about the picture. It's beautiful in its own right. Something I'd probably save or maybe even frame, so I could look at it all the time and see our obvious love for each other radiating from a simple photo.

It's the headlines that turn my stomach. I know I should stop, but I can't help but thumb through each and every one of them, wishing more and more that I could bury my head in the sand and disappear.

Cyclone's Defensive Anchor Caught In Steamy Photo with rockstar Jesse Moore

Shreveport's Silent Star Outed as Jesse Moore's Mystery Man

Mr. Colgate Caught On Camera With Lest Is Moore's Frontman

Mystery Man In Viral Videos Outed

NFL Hero Shocks The World With Rocker Sex Scandal

New Year, New Power Couple?

From Sidelines to Stage: Luc Martín's Secret Romance Goes Viral

Private Leaked Footage Goes Viral Again After Mystery Bottom Uncovered

Is Luc Martín's Relationship Proof that the Super Bowl is Staged?

Integrity On The Line: Can Luc Martín Survive Scandal as Cyclones Head to Super Bowl?

Faith, Family, and Football: Did Luc Martín Betray the League's "Good Guy" Ideal?

Conservative Critics Call for Cyclone's Defensive Player Suspension

On and on and on they go, until I'm forced out of bed to hunch over the toilet. Last night's celebration tastes twice as bitter on the way back up.

———————

By the time I make it to the team facilities, there's no question that all my teammates, coaches, and trainers have seen it. I enter our usual post-game film and debrief meeting to wolf whistles and jeers. Even if most of the reactions seem playful and teasing, not disgusted or hateful by any means, I'm still humiliated. Every man in this room, every teammate with whom I'd found mutual respect, has seen me at my base, most vulnerable moments. They've seen parts of me that no one other than Jesse should have seen.

I try to play it cool, laugh it off where I can. I keep my head down and speak even less than usual. Every phone in the room is buzzing and pinging with the trending news blowing up all over sports news, social media, music blogs, and political trash fires everywhere.

Unsurprisingly, the leaked photo and confirmation of my involvement in a major rockstar's sex scandal overshadow our team meeting. I'm excused from the mandatory press interviews that are supposed to take place this afternoon, but the story dwarfs the team's accomplishment. Our rise from the bottom to the biggest championship in American professional sports is diminished to a byline under the news of me bottoming for an international superstar.

I wait until most of the team is gone before braving the swarm of media waiting for me outside. As soon as the doors open, I'm hit by a wall of flashing lights and shouted questions that range from stupid "Can you show us a smile?" to downright intrusive "How long have you been Jesse Moore's gay lover?"

The driver Jesse's label hired to help protect me from the vultures is trapped inside the SUV, cameras and people pressed closely against the vehicle. The poor guy looks as panicked as I feel. There's no clear path to get to the SUV, much less for Graham to get us out.

A firm hand closes on my shoulder.

"Come on, Martín," Coach growls, pulling me back inside. "This way."

I let him steer me away, pulling my cap lower as a member of the janitorial staff leads us through a service door and down a maintenance hallway. The shouts dull to a muffled buzz behind us.

"Thanks Jerry," Coach calls to the janitor, who nods as he holds a door open to the loading dock behind the stadium, where a black sedan idles. "Get in before any of them get wise," he orders, and slides behind the wheel.

A few people snap photos and try to run after the car when we exit through a back gate, but we're gone before most of the mob realizes we've given them the slip. My pulse throbs, too hard and too fast, and no amount of deep breathing will make it settle.

"Hell of a mob out there," Coach mutters finally, his hands steady on the wheel. "You kept it together alright."

I'm a little shocked those are his first words to me. If anything, I'm expecting him to ream me out for embarrassing the team and making a spectacle of myself.

"Doesn't feel that way," I say, my voice hoarse. "Sorry for all the trouble this is causing. I didn't mean–"

"Of course you didn't mean for any of this to happen. It's not your fault the press is no better than a pack of wolves." He glances over. "Listen, right now your best move is to lay low. Take a break for a couple days and let the hype wear down."

"But Coach–"

"You can't tell me that a couple of days is going to get in your way of helping your team bring home a Super Bowl win."

"No, sir."

"Let the PR team mitigate this mess and do what you need to do to get your shit in order."

"Yes, sir."

I wonder if he noticed that I don't put up much fight. The truth is, I'm not comfortable in the locker room with my teammates right now. Not because any of them are being inappropriate, but because I feel exposed. All my nerves are raw, and I am way too aware of the eyes on me.

Coach ends up dropping me off at a hotel. The entrance to my building is jammed with camera crews, vans, tripods, and people milling about waiting to get a glimpse of me. Even if we could get inside, I'd be cooped up in there knowing that I'm trapped inside unless I want to go through all of them. If there's one thing being with Jesse has taught me, it's that money and celebrity come with perks that can make my life a whole lot easier.

"Thanks, Coach."

"Get some rest, Martín. And call me if you need anything."

I wave him off and check in to the hotel, making sure that no visitors are allowed to ring through or come up to my room. When the door clicks shut behind me, silence crashes down, almost as loud as the mob of reporters.

Sitting on the edge of the bed, I pull out my phone and hover over Jesse's name. After turning off all my notifications and news apps, I'd sent Jesse another text–my third of the day, but there's been little response other than a short, "I'll fix this."

I'm not sure if he wants to talk, but I call anyway. Like the incident with Jesse's cloud account getting hacked, it feels like we're allowing too much distance to settle between us when we should be supporting each other.

It rings. And rings. I'm just about to give up when the line picks up.

"Luc?" Jesse's voice is pained, raspy in a way that sounds raw rather than sexy.

"Yeah." I sink back onto the pillows, my hand resting across my forehead. "Sorry it's so late. I should have called earlier, but it's been…" I huff out a breath. There isn't a word for the unexpected bombardment today turned into. "It's been a lot."

"Baby, I am so sorry."

"It's not your fault," I remind him. "It's more than we wanted to deal with, but we'll get through this."

"You don't want to run for the hills yet?"

"I've got my running shoes on and everything," I tell him. "But I'm staying put. My condo is swarmed so I'm lying low at a hotel."

"That's smart. You need to stay safe. These people are like vultures."

"What about you?" I ask. "Are you okay? Staying somewhere safe?"

"I'm trying to fix this," he says. "My PR team is working on it from all angles, but it's taken off even more than we expected. Who knew we'd be the 'it' power couple of the year and it's only January?"

I chuckle humorlessly. There's a quiet stretch where I can hear him breathing. We trade small reassurances that feel as fragile as my tenuous control over my emotions. The affection is there, but there's an awkward silence that spotlights everything we don't say. I want to tell him that I love him, that we'll weather this storm together, that everything will be okay. Of course, I don't know that everything will actually be okay. My life is forever changed. But I'm less afraid than I was before, because I know what we have together is worth it. What we have is worth it. But I've never been good at words. Instead, I just tell him those three little words that mean so much more than words can ever express.

"I love you."

When we finally hang up, I stare at the photo I stupidly saved as my screen saver. The moment felt huge, but really it was such a small, simple gesture. A kiss to ring in the new year, stolen quickly in the shadows. Yet the bomb that's detonated because of it has blown everything apart.

I trace the edge of the screen with my thumb and remember the way Jesse makes me feel, how he's always made me feel, from the first night I met him. Is it naïve to wish to be nothing more than two people in love? Not headlines and mobs of flashing cameras and intrusive questions.

How long will it take before the world quiets again? Or is that gone forever?

THIRTY-THREE
JESSE

I'm not asleep when Blake kicks my door open. I'm not sure I've gotten any real sleep in days. The sound of the door hitting the wall makes me jolt upright, heart in my throat.

"What—" My voice is raw, like I've been screaming even though I haven't. I've wanted to, but there's no point.

Blake stands there with his phone in his hand. His eyes are sharp, worried. "The extra security finally got to Cane Ridge this afternoon," he says, no preamble. "But it was too late."

Ice slides down my spine. "What does that mean?!"

"Everyone's okay," he says, holding his hands up. "But Luc's youngest sister—"

"Talia," I fill in for him.

He nods. "A photographer harassed her on the way to school this morning. She was riding her bike and swerved off the road." His voice softens. "She's thankfully okay. Quite a few scrapes and bruises, and she's shaken up, but there weren't any broken bones or anything like that. Luc is on his way to the hospital, where she's been moved to a private room until security can set the family up somewhere more secure."

I sit there, blinking, as if the words don't want to compute.

"Why didn't Luc call me?"

Blake frowns. "You haven't been answering your phone."

I look at my phone lying next to me in bed and remember. It's been dead since last night. Luc and I both fell asleep with each other on video again, and I haven't had the motivation to get up and find my charger. I haven't had the motivation to do more than lay here and daydream about being back at Luc's family home in Louisiana.

"Jesse?" Blake's voice is a mix of sympathy and concern. "Are you okay? Do we need to call–"

"No," I say. "I'll be fine. But this–what happened to Talia–isn't okay. I can't let anything happen to Luc or his family."

"We're going to protect them the best we can," Cory interjects from behind Blake. "We're pursuing charges against the photographer who ran her off the road, as well as threatened legal action against anyone who continues to harass the Martín family. I suggested Luc stay clear of the area, but he understandably wants to be with his family right now."

The daydreams I've been using to comfort myself fade away like mist. I can no longer picture a future where Luc and I can be together without causing him and his family pain.

"We're supposed to be on a plane to Miami this afternoon. We've got staging and rehearsals to get through. We're beefing up security for the whole band and working with the venue to approve stadium security as well."

I don't hear any of it.

Blake reads something in my face. He tentatively sits on the edge of the bed near my feet. "Jesse…"

I can't look at him. I stare at my hands, at the faint tremor there. "His little sister is in the hospital because of me."

"She's okay."

"Because of me," I repeat. "This isn't just about Luc anymore. It's his whole family. He doesn't deserve this."

Silence stretches. Blake exhales, heavy, but he doesn't contradict me. If they say anything else to me, I don't hear it.

"Cory, can you take me to the airport?"

Cory pauses a moment, and I know he wants to argue, but he takes a deep breath and nods. "Of course."

"We'll charter a jet," Blake says, raising his phone to his ear while he helps me pack a bag.

Minutes later, I'm plugging my phone into a car charger. As soon as it boots up, dozens of notifications buzz and ping simultaneously. The little light at the corner of my phone blinks an angry red.

Twenty-three missed calls and texts from Luc.

Not only am I responsible for his sister being terrorized and injured, but I wasn't here for him when he needed me.

My chest clenches so hard it hurts. I'm in danger of dry heaving, because Lord knows there's nothing in my stomach.

I never thought I'd regret this life. There have been moments that I regretted, sure. Days, weeks, or even months that I have regrets about. Never did I think I'd regret being who I am.

And never once did I ever consider that I'd regret falling in love with Luc Martín. Or rather, that he ever fell in love with me.

I'll always love him, but that's not enough. Not if it's putting a target on the people he loves. I'm terrified that the only right thing to do is to walk away. The only way I can protect him is to push him away from the fire.

I just don't know that I'm strong enough.

I try three times to call Luc, but there's no answer. Oh, God, he probably hates me. I thumb out a single text:

ME: I'm on my way, baby. I'm so sorry.

The apologies are getting tiresome, even for me. How long could our relationship reasonably last when all he gets from me are apologies? There's nothing worth this drama, and his and his family's safety.

I need to do the right thing. Once I check on his sister and apologize to his family, I'll find the strength.

I press the heels of my palms to my eyes and try to believe that hurting him now is better than destroying him later. I'll do anything to keep him safe, even if it means cutting out both our hearts.

Because Luc is better off without me. He has to see that.

It takes longer to sneak me into the hospital than it did to get here. But finally, I'm bursting through the doors of the private room Blake set them up with. My eyes lock on Luc immediately, and the pain I see there nearly brings me to my knees.

Tears well up in my eyes before I can even speak, but I will them back and look at Luc's family. Both of his sisters are in the hospital bed, watching something on a tablet. Talia looks okay, but the knowledge of just how much worse the accident could have been makes me sick. Mr. Martín and Shawna are sitting with Luc on either side of the hospital bed.

Luc stands and runs over to me. His arms wrap around mine and I'm not sure who is comforting who. He leads me out into the hallway.

"I'm so sorry," I whisper hoarsely, repeating it over and over again. "This is all my fault."

"It's not–"

"–It is!" I practically shout. "This would have never happened if we weren't together, and you know it. This is far worse than the kind of publicity you've avoided all these years, Luc. This is insanity, and I should have protected you better."

"Jesse, I was the one who said I didn't want to hide anymore."

"That was before you got a taste of just how fucked up this life could get. I think…" A knot threatens to close my throat before I can get the words out. My head bows. "I think you would have been better off if I'd never learned your name."

"Jesse–"

"I'm serious, Luc. I've brought nothing but chaos into your life since this whole thing started."

"That's bullshit and you know it."

My head snaps up, and I lock eyes with sad, blue eyes that have turned stormy with exhaustion and worry. The dark circles under his eyes and his hair, messy from running his hands through it, don't take away from how heartbreakingly gorgeous he is.

"You never wanted this."

"That doesn't mean what we have isn't worth it. I love you." He says it like it's so simple, like how much we love each other washes everything else away.

"Enough to watch your family get caught in the crossfire? Talia could have been killed, Luc. They don't deserve this. You don't deserve this."

Luc's mouth opens to argue, but no words come out. He knows I'm right. I take a step back from him and head back into the room, where I spend a little while talking with the girls. When Luc doesn't follow me back into the room, Shawna leaves to check on him. Luc's father watches me quietly, concern etched in the lines of his stoic face.

After apologizing a few more times, and promising the girls I'll arrange something better than hospital food for their breakfast, I say goodnight and get up to leave. Just as I reach the door, Mr. Martín grabs my arm to stop me.

He clears his throat. "This wasn't your fault, son."

My heart clenches at his use of son, and tears threaten again."It wouldn't have happened if not for–"

"Shit's gonna happen. Sometimes it'll be your shit. Sometimes it'll be his shit. What matters is how you handle it."

"I'm handling it, sir. I promise. I'll make this right."

I'm handling it the only way I know how. By walking away from the one thing that I want more than anything else in this world. To protect him. To protect his family. And maybe a little to protect myself, because I don't think I could manage a future where Luc grows to resent me because of the chaos loving me will continue to bring him.

Cory leads me down a darkened hallway back towards the maintenance entrance we snuck through earlier. It's quiet enough that I can hear footsteps echoing down the hallway before I can see who they belong to. Luc calls out, trying to keep his voice low, running to catch up to me. He doesn't slow until he's right in front of me.

"What happened today sucks," he says. "I've never been so terrified in my life. And yes, I realize it could have been much worse. But it wasn't. Talia is okay." Emotion chokes his words, betraying his fears for the future. "Don't let this break us, Jesse."

He steps closer, cupping my jaw in his big hand, his thumb rubbing over my lip ring. "I'm scared," he admits. "And I know you are too. But we'll get through this–together."

His lips press against mine, tenderly at first, but the kiss grows deeper and more desperate the longer it goes on. It takes a strength I didn't know I possessed to pull away from him.

"I love you," I whisper, my forehead pressed to his. "Everything will be okay." He nods, but I can tell from the stiffness of his posture that he knows there's more to it. "We need to take a step back," I say, fighting to keep my voice level. "Until things die down, we need to be more careful. At least until after the Super Bowl."

A tear falls and splashes against my shirt. I'm not even sure which one of us it came from.

"We can figure the rest out later. But for now–for the sake of your family, and your teammates, it's better if we play it safe. We can still come out after, if it's what you still want."

"Don't do this, Jesse."

"For once in my life, I'm not making a hairbrained, half thought out decision. This is the smart thing to do, and you know it. We need to play it safe–no sneaking around, no sending each other sexy videos. Nothing they can use to make this worse for your family. And it'll give you time to think about whether this life is something you really want."

"I don't need space." He steps forward, and I take two steps back.

"Play it safe, Luc. For now. We'll reassess after the game." Maybe if I repeat those words enough, he'll understand that I'm trying to do the right thing for him. He can't deny that I'm right, not after what happened to his sister.

At least, that's what I tell myself when I turn away and follow Cory out of the hospital. This time, Luc doesn't try to follow.

The stadium is half-finished chaos. Lighting rigs swinging, pyrotechnics going off randomly, stage crew shouting over each other. It's sticky and hot under the lights, even in February. I'm barely aware of any of it.

We've just run the full halftime set from start to finish. I hit every mark, every note. My muscle memory doing what my heart doesn't want to. I'm determined to see this show through the end. I've brought enough pain and embarrassment to Luc's life, the least I can do is be a professional now. I'd back out of the show entirely if it wouldn't make things worse for everyone involved.

Naz drops down beside me, dangling his legs over the edge of the stage. Like me, he's soaked in sweat, but unlike me he looks…alive. There's a glow beneath his skin I used to have.

"You gonna make it through this?" he asks quietly, without his usual cutting sarcasm.

I wipe a towel across my face and let it hang around my neck. "I have to."

Naz studies me, not convinced. "Jess–"

"Save it, Naz. I just need to get through the next few days, and then…"

"And then what? You ride off into the sunset like the paps will never find you again? What if something else happens? Are you just going to keep pushing him away until he breaks?"

There's been no sign of the press losing interest in our story. In fact, it's gotten worse. To the point where Luc got into some trouble with the paparazzi that was surrounding his family's home.

"I'll do whatever I have to to keep him safe," I say, my voice dead and emotionless. I rub my hands over my arms, as if I could wipe away the humid air that feels like a billion tiny needles against my overstimulated senses.

"Are you okay? I mean, obviously you're not *okay*, but are you hanging in there?"

I know what he means. Blake has checked in with me so many times that my response feels robotic. "I haven't been drinking or using, if that's what you're asking." I don't want to admit that the need to numb myself is stronger than ever.

"Look, I'm just going to say it. I think you're making a mistake."

"Being with me only continues to hurt him." Nevermind that I've been wavering between my resolve to give him the opportunity to realize he's better off without me and wanting to go crawling back and begging him to never stop loving me.

"Not being together is hurting you *both*. You're a fucking idiot if you can't see that."

It wouldn't matter even if I did break my resolve. Luc hasn't tried calling me. He's probably pissed at me for walking away. Or the press coverage is making him think twice.

Good.

I'm not sure how well I'm going to handle being in the same place as him. It's already hard enough not to call him every night just to hear his voice. To take back everything I said because I'm not strong enough to live without him. But I have to be strong enough for him. For his family.

It's for the best, I keep reminding myself. *I'm keeping him safe.*

The possibility of him realizing he's better off without me makes me feel like I'm drowning.

We're called back to our places to run through the show one more time. I push to my feet, shoulders heavy but squared. If nothing else, I can do this. I can give the world a show and keep the man I love out of its crosshairs, even if it costs me.

LeST is
MooRE

THIRTY-FOUR
LUC

"Will you leave those alone," AJ snaps, slapping my hand.

I look down and realize I've been worrying at the healing scabs across my knuckles again, dragging a thumbnail over the rough edges until little spots of red bloom. It's a bad habit I've picked up since busting my knuckles open on a wall a few days ago. I curl my fist shut and lean back in the leather seat of the team plane.

AJ doesn't stop staring. "You're gonna open 'em up again and get blood everywhere," he says, crunching his nose.

"At least I didn't break anything," I mutter, opening and closing my fist.

"Like that reporter's face?" AJ jokes, his voice too loud over the engine hum and soft hiss of the cabin's A/C vents overhead.

I huff a humorless laugh and let my head fall against the head-rest. The truth is, I came close to doing something I never thought I'd do. I'm twenty-seven and I've never been in an actual fistfight. I've certainly never in my life resorted to violence because someone pissed me off. But one more cheap shot about

Jesse, about how he's ruining my career, about those damn videos or how I feel having my family know what kind of debauchery I engage in. Yeah, I lost it.

Monty and AJ pulled me away just in time, and I was able to take my anger out on some drywall instead.

To put it mildly, it hasn't been a good couple of weeks.

When Talia got hurt, I thought my heart was going to stop. Seeing so many missed calls from my dad during weight training and then hearing Shawna's frantic voice repeating, *"She's fine, she's fine, but some asshole with a camera ran her off the road."* That was easily the worst moment of my life. If Jesse's security hadn't stepped in after, gotten them to a private room and locked the place down, I don't know what would've happened.

I haven't talked to Jesse since that night at the hospital. I've spent just about every minute outside of practice and Super Bowl preparations staring at my phone, willing it to ring. I've almost sent him a thousand texts, almost called him to beg him to reconsider, because even two weeks without him is excruciating.

What he said at the hospital made sense. And I can see the logic behind keeping a low profile until things are calmer. But does a low profile have to mean no contact?

I've been trying to respect the space he asked for, even if he only asked for my own sake and I don't want it. If he wants to wait until after the Super Bowl–fine. But I'm walking out of that stadium with him whether he likes it or not.

While I haven't been talking to Jesse, that doesn't mean I haven't been keeping up with him. After about the third day of no calls from him, I called Naz. He told me Jesse thinks he's doing the right thing to keep me safe, but that his worry and sadness have him in a bad place. I'm more than a little worried he's going to keep running from me, but I can't let that happen. I need to find a way to show him that I'm serious.

Mr. Holland, Naz and the other guys, his security detail, and his mom are all on my side, not only keeping an eye on Jesse in case he's spiraling, but helping me plan how to corner him. Because he can't ignore me in person. In a few short hours, we'll be in the same city. In two days, the same stadium.

"So what's the plan?" AJ asks casually, like this isn't the most important thing I've ever done in my life.

"Naz and Mr. Holland are going to keep him busy after the game. I'll need you to cover for me, so I can disappear and get to him before he tries to leave. Cory is going to instruct the security teams to help me get to him.

AJ studies me for a beat, then nods once. Approval, maybe even respect. "Good."

I glance down at my hands again. "I know Jesse thinks he's sparing me from something, but it's not worth losing what we have."

"The press will die down eventually," AJ says, although I'm not sure he believes it. I'm not sure I do, either.

For the first time, I don't care. I don't care what any of them see or think or say. I care about the way I feel when we're together, about the way he looks at me and treats me like I'm the only thing that matters. The last week and a half without him has only made that more apparent, and I'll do what it takes to keep him in my life.

"Doesn't matter," I say firmly. "I'm not letting them take this from me."

AJ smirks faintly. "That's my boy. Too bad we don't have more time. Can you imagine what it would be like to stage one of those flash mobs in the middle of the Super Bowl?" His eyes gleam.

"I'm pretty sure that would get us kicked out of the game."

AJ laughs. "I don't know, man. The whole world saw Jesse's dick and what it gets up to and they still didn't fire him from the Half Time Show. That's how fucking famous he is dude."

I try to ignore the reference about what exactly the whole world saw. "I'm not sure Jesse's fame extends to the rest of us."

He shrugs. "The things we do for love, right? You gotta do what you gotta do. Jesse seems like a grand gestures kind of guy. And with everything that's happened, I think maybe showing him just how little you care about public opinion could be what breaks him."

"Have you been talking to Shawna?" I ask dubiously.

"No. Why? Did she talk about me? What did she say?"

I roll my eyes and ignore him. Shawna is on board the grand public gesture train, too.

"They fly in tomorrow, right? If you're not gonna propose to Jesse, can I propose to Shawna instead? It's really a shame to waste the opportunity."

"It's like you want to get kicked out of the game," I say, laughing.

Then again, I did say to my whole family and AJ that I cared more about getting Jesse back than I did winning the Super Bowl. I even got a *hmph* of approval from my dad.

They'll all be there for Sunday's game. Even dad, who grumbled about my life and job being a circus, is coming. He, Shawna, my sisters, Luc's mom, and a buttload of security will all be there cheering me on and there as moral support while I try to win my man back.

I've got a plan, and I'm ready. Jesse thinks pushing me away protects me. He doesn't know I'm done hiding.

No leak, no headline, no paparazzi is going to ruin this. Not for me. Not for him.

THIRTY-FIVE
JESSE

We're counting down until showtime as the teams exit the field and a crew of men and women dressed head-to-toe in black rush to put the stage together.

I've spent the first half of the game hiding. I don't want to know the score. Don't want to see Luc's number on the field or feel the echo of his cleats on the ground under me. Just the thought that I'm walking the same turf he's walked makes my chest ache.

I sent him a text this morning. A simple, **"good luck today,"** that he didn't answer. I got left on read, and I realized that my plan worked. I gave him the time and space to step back, and he made the right decision. Loving me isn't worth his privacy. It isn't worth his family's safety and peace of mind.

I keep telling myself that I did the right thing. That letting go is the kindest thing I can do. That his protection, and the protection of his family, is worth more than my selfish, obsessive love. If I repeat it enough times, maybe I'll stop feeling like I'm bleeding out.

Our dressing room is a cave of cables and manic energy. The guys are bouncing on their toes, ready to play one of the biggest, but shortest, shows of our lives. It might also be my last show for a while. I need to take some time to disappear, and forcing myself to absorb the world around me while the abrasive walls close in is only going to send me down a dark path.

Naz breaks away from the tech crew and crouches in front of me. "Hey." His eyes search mine. "You ready?"

"Yeah. But I think I need to leave right after this. It's too much."

Being here, in the same place as Luc, hurts too much. I'm worried I'm too weak, that I'll run to him and drop to my knees in front of everyone and beg him to love me enough to make all the chaos and trouble worth it. I let him go but I'm breaking inside, and I can't deal with the aftermath of my own decision.

The band pulls in for our usual pre-show huddle. Normally someone cracks a dumb prayer–*Bless us, rock gods, let our eyeliner stay intact, please make sure Jesse's dick stays inside the confines of his danger pants*–but tonight nobody jokes. They just press in close, arms over shoulders, heads touching mine.

"We're behind you all the way," Naz says, quiet but firm.

Something in my throat breaks, but I nod and let them hold me together for just a moment.

Then it's time.

I walk to my mark where rigging techs wait to strap me into a harness. Cool straps cinch across my chest and hips. I'm about to dangle over a hundred thousand people and a global broadcast, and I feel…empty. Hollow but determined to prove I'm above the rumors and speculation and what the public thinks of me. If the world is going to watch, it won't see me crumble. They already stole my love, they won't get my dignity too.

The stadium lights drop.

Deafening cheers rise up, tidal and alive.

The guys hit the stage first, a thunder of guitars and flashing lights. Naz pounding out the heartbeat on his kit. From above, I watch the field fill with dancers who blossom into color–red, orange, yellow, green, blue, purple–until they're a rippling rainbow flag. A drum line marches in, echoing the beat Naz leads. And then it's my cue.

I breathe once and start to sing a stripped-down version of *You Can't Make Me*. Our messy anti-establishment anthem that will probably get us in a little trouble from the network, but we've cleaned up all our songs with the radio-friendly versions. My voice threads through the dark, raw and alone. Below me, the crowd searches, necks craning, trying to find where my voice is coming from. Until a camera finds me high on a platform, and the audience roars.

I turn, open my arms wide, and let myself fall backwards into the middle of the rainbow, the choreography meant to look like ripples from a stone dropped in water. Gasps echo as the lights cut out completely. In the dark I sprint under the stage, tear off the harness, and pop up at the main riser just as a blinding wash of color explodes across the field.

The show is on.

We burn through the set, sweat and sound and heat. The dancers whirl, the drumline driving a steady pulse, the flag ripples and reforms into pulsing geometric shapes. I lose myself in the set that's full of subtle but meaningful imagery and depictions of a country growing stronger in diversity and love.

Then it's time for the closer.

The crowd knows from the first guitar lick what the song is going to be. It's the fan favorite. Our first hit. The song that made us famous. The song I wrote, once upon a time, about a boy on a beach I never thought I'd see again. The song that very same boy heard and felt close to before he ever knew it was for him. My marrow is in this song.

I step to the mic and try to sing, but my voice shakes. Cracks. I stop for a second, eyes closing against the swell of noise and light. I am raw, hollowed out, missing everything that matters.

I glance back at the guys. Naz meets my gaze and mouths, *You can do this.*

The intro rolls again. The crowd hums the melody, thousands of voices guiding me back until I can find my own. I start to sing, soft at first, then stronger. I walk the long catwalk we built for this moment, the one that earlier belonged to a parade of drag queens in gowns and glitter, now a runway of light and raw emotion.

Halfway down, a single white spotlight locks on me. My voice carries over the stadium, ragged but sure.

Someone yells something from the front rows. I don't catch the words, but then there's a sudden ripple through the audience. A gasp, then a roar that's different from the usual reaction this stripped-down version of *Remember My Name* typically gets.

The hair on the back of my neck lifts.

LeST is MooRE

THIRTY-SIX
LUC

The locker room is buzzing with adrenaline. Coach is pacing, drawing lines on a whiteboard, but I can't hear a word of the halftime strategy talk.

Out there, Jesse is singing and I can't stand to miss it. Even if I can just hear one song.

I slip away without much notice. Anyone who does notice doesn't try to stop me. I duck through the tunnel until the music fills my ears and veins and heart.

A security guard spots me and hustles over. "Are you Luc?"

"Yeah."

He hesitates, then says, "Cory sent me a message from Naz. They're leaving immediately after the last song."

My stomach twists. Shit. He was supposed to stay and talk to me after the game. Naz and Mr. Holland were going to make sure he didn't leave. I was feeling so hopeful after getting a text from him this morning, but I didn't get to respond because we were getting off the team bus at the stadium, and it's been too busy since then to even attempt to check my phone again.

What if he thought I was ignoring him?

Then I hear it. Jesse's voice cracking on the first line of their closing song. Our song. *My* song. The one that changed my life before I even knew his name. It's raw and breaking and beautiful, and it cuts straight through me.

Something AJ said the other day slams into my chest.

A grand gesture.

My heart lurches hard enough to hurt.

I snap my head towards the guard. "I need your help."

He doesn't question it. He just turns and starts running with me, keeping up surprisingly well considering I'm a professional athlete on a mission. He clears a path through dancers and tech crew, jumping over tangles of cable.

When I reach the base of the stage, Cory is there, grinning like he's been waiting for me all night. "Welcome back, Mr. Martín," he says, and offers a hand. I grab it and haul myself up.

The lights are blinding, music vibrating through my ribs. Naz catches sight of me first, eyes going wide, the steady heartbeat he's playing on the drums getting louder like an announcement. Will and Ari both reach out as I pass, giving quick slaps on the shoulder, and nods that say, *go.*

Jesse is out on the catwalk, a lone silhouette under the white spotlight, voice shaking but carrying through the roar. He doesn't see me yet. Not until the crowd goes from pointing and gasping to screaming, a new wave of sound that makes him glance back.

His vivid green eyes find mine.

For a heartbeat he falters, barely a hitch in the chorus, but he doesn't stop singing. Step by step he starts back towards the main stage, towards me. I move to meet him.

The lights blaze, the band behind us pushing the final chords higher. We stop inches apart, center stage, the world roaring around us.

The last note hangs in the air, echoing across the stadium.

Remember my name

(I wish I'd stayed)

Remember my name

(and told you the truth)

I'm shaking, heart hammering against my ribs, but I manage a single word, a desperate breath against the mic between us.

"Jesse."

And then my lips are on his, and he tastes like cinnamon and all the things that are home and happiness and love.

THIRTY-SEVEN
JESSE

My mic falls to the stage, the sound of it hitting the surface jarring me back into my right mind. I pull back, but only far enough to get a breath.

"What are you doing?" I ask as the lights go down, but I'm acutely aware of the cameraman still trained on our faces. We're still being projected onto every screen in the stadium.

"Loving you," Luc says simply, "out loud." His chest is heaving, either from being out of breath or from the adrenaline of what he just did. "I needed to show you how serious I am. I don't care who sees or photographs or talks about me, I can live through all of that. But I can't live without you, Jesse."

"But–"

"I don't care," he says, and kisses me again, pulling me tight across his body. My arms come up to wrap around his neck, and the crowd roars again before we're plunged into darkness. We stay that way until Cory taps us on the shoulders and tells us we have to move because they're breaking the stage down.

Luc takes my hand in his and pulls me into the closest tunnel until we find a quiet space.

"You're fucking crazy," I say, although my tears and the smile trying to take over my face aren't exactly an admonishment. I feel like all the weight of the world has been lifted off my shoulders, or like the sun has finally come out on the coldest, grayest day. Just his hand in mine feels like the whole world has been set right.

"There's not a chance in hell I was going to risk you walking away again without showing you once and for all that I'm not afraid. I want you and whatever comes with that."

Turns out, what comes with that is a suspension and a hefty fine, but both of us still have smiles on our faces when we walk out of the stadium hand-in-hand.

EPILOGUE

The sun is sliding down behind the dunes, smearing the sky in bright orange and pinks. The air smells like salt and smoke from the bonfire. Every so often a wave slaps the sand and retreats with a sigh.

Will and Ari's argument drifts from the porch before they disappear into the house. Luc's dad and my mom are shoulder to shoulder at the grill, shucking oysters and laughing, enjoying each other's company. Down at the waterline, Luc's sisters shriek as a cold wave collapses over their ankles. Shawna, Naz, and Scott are sitting around a picnic table, discussing the merits of hockey romance.

I'm barefoot in the sand with my guitar balanced across my lap, idly picking at a tune while the fire crackles beside me. Luc sits behind me, his back against a log, his long legs stretched on either side of me, one hand resting warm and easy around my shoulder.

I turn my head to glance back at him, and my chest goes tight in the best way. I think about the first time I saw him sitting in this exact spot, almost six years ago exactly.. A stranger at a bonfire, stoic, quiet, brooding strength and a blush that made me hold my breath.

I still don't know how I left that morning without even knowing his name. I built my entire life chasing the ghost of that connection. And somehow, after all the noise, the fear, the cameras, the chaos, we made it here.

I know his name now. And I know without a doubt that he loves me as much as I love him. He was willing to lay it all out on the line, which thankfully didn't end up costing him his career. Since the public's response to Luc's grand gesture was overwhelmingly positive, the NFL Commissioner was more lenient than he admittedly wanted to be, likely not wanting to risk public opinion by punishing Luc too harshly. It helped that his coach and the owner of the Shreveport Cyclones advocated and stood up for him. Luc may never be able to turn down another press interview again, but he seems okay with the consequences.

It's been almost three months of meetings and internal hearings, but we can finally relax and just enjoy each other.

Luc looks down at me with his slow, crooked smile he once tried to keep hidden from the world. He leans in, easy and sure, and kisses me. It's just a soft press of lips, but it's more than that. It's memories and love and family and everything we fought for.

The fire snaps, a wave folds over the shore, and the night exhales around us.

For the first time in forever, it's quiet where it matters. And it's ours.

LeST is MooRE

ACKNOWLEDGMENTS

It needs to be acknowledged that while writing this book, I made a huge life change that required me to pack up and move into a new home. The patience and support I received from my teams and readers helped get me through something that could have been a lot more stressful. I'm grateful for every inch you all gave me, and I hope the wait was worth it for you. Writing this book was a joy, and it was Luc and Jesse's love that helped keep my spirits high during one of the hardest times in my life.

I'm so thankful to get to do this- to be a real life author who gets to sit down at my desk every day and give life to all the voices in my head. And I wouldn't get to do this without you.

Thank you for picking up this book, for giving me a chance, for reading even one word that I put out into the world. Just by holding this book in your hand, you are making an eight year old Becca's biggest dreams come true. And I am just so thankful for you.

I have an amazing support system that I wouldn't be able to accomplish anything without.

My amazing PA Darcy is the absolute best fluffer in the game, and keeps a raging ADHD maniac like me from completely losing the plot. You put up with SO MUCH BULLSHIT from me, and I am eternally in your debt.

The best editor in the world, the Book Witch herself, who understands my voice and leaves the best snarky comments.

This year I added a second proofreader to my process, and it has been such a boost to my confidence- Megan from Feral Fiction Edits is amazing. Thank you for helping me give my manuscripts that last polish!

My street team- My "Ball Handlers", you not only support and encourage me every day, but you're helping me put some good out into the world when things feel so bleak. I can't imagine not having a street team behind me.

My favorite guys- To all of my lovely amazing, genius friends who not only read my books and make sure that I'm doing my best, most authentic work, but allow me into their brains and share highly sensitive, intrusive information with me. Without you, I wouldn't feel comfortable writing in this genre and telling these stories. Your opinions, your support, your insight, and our chats keep me going.

To my family and in-person friends that put up with my incessant chatter about how a character won't behave, or sit back and smile and nod while I work out plot holes and ideas, and are always understanding of my unhinged cycles of hyper-focus- I don't deserve you. Thank you for putting up with my brand of unique.

I love you. I love you all.

LeST is
MOoRE

ABOUT THE AUTHOR

Human rights are not politics.

Don't tell me to keep my mouth shut, or to keep politics out of my books. My characters might be fictional, but their struggles are entirely real and often based off true stories.

The United States is backpedaling, falling back into the wrong side of history. The BIPOC and LGBTQ+ communities are not only experiencing an unprecedented attack on their rights, but they're more at risk than ever after years of finally being able to emerge from society's closet.

When we're being force fed rhetoric that trans people are dangerous, that we shouldn't say gay, or that we shouldn't have autonomy over our own bodies- we need to fight back with our votes. There is no election too big or too small, and big changes start at the local level.

Check your voter registration at vote.gov and make sure you are using your voice to support a future that benefits a beautifully diverse America.

Unfortunately, in the wake of the atrocities happening all around us, **your vote isn't enough**. It's time to rise up, to love loudly and support each other in any way we can.

The powers that be are force feeding harmful rhetoric and trying to overwhelm us with darkness. Don't let them.

LeST is MooRE